First Degree Burns

Other Books by S. L. Kassidy

Please Baby

Scarred Series
Scarred for Life - Book 1
New Cuts, Old Wounds – Book 2
Bandages – Book 3

First Degree Burns

By

S. L. Kassidy

Desert Palm Press

First Degree Burns

By S. L. Kassidy

©2017 S. L. Kassidy

ISBN (trade): 9781942976240
ISBN (epub): 9781942976257
ISBN (pdf): 9781942976264

Desert Palm Press
1961 Main Street, Suite 220
Watsonville, California 95076
www.desertpalmpress.com

Editor: CK King (https://www.facebook.com/RavensEyeEditing)
Cover Design: Jamani Hawkins-El (http://www.maddrandom.com)

Printed in the United States of America
First Edition May 2017

Dedication

This book is dedicated to my family, who support my writing long before I thought it was worth anything, and to my friends, who helped me believe in myself and allowed themselves to be conscripted into betareading stories, whether they wanted to or not. Thank you all.

Chapter One

THE RAYS OF MORNING sunlight flickered through closed blinds into the bedroom of Nicole Cardell causing her emerald eyes to open. The light wasn't bothersome; not even shining by the bed, but Nicole woke up and immediately appreciated the energy. Easing herself out of bed, making sure not to wake her partner, she went to the window. A soft smile graced her face.

It looks gorgeous outside. I hope the weather forecast was right, because today looks like the perfect day for a picnic. Nicole beamed right along with the sun as it cast highlights in her long, auburn hair and made the world shine bright.

Danny Wolfe groaned in her sleep, drawing Nicole's attention from the window. She looked at her girlfriend and noted that the sun gave Danny a bit of a golden halo around her body. Danny's copper toned arm moved around under the covers, searching for her missing lover. Nicole smiled. *She misses me in her sleep.* Moving silently, she went back to sit on the bed. Danny groaned as Nicole's hand settled on Danny's thigh.

"Chem, lie back down." Danny's voice was a mere grumble, and she didn't bother to open her beautiful, grey eyes.

"Sorry, baby, but I'm up and I think I'm going to get ready for Luke and Thomas." Nicole leaned down to kiss her lover's slightly chubby cheek.

Danny's nephews were coming over, as they did almost every Saturday now. Sometimes, they took the boys on short trips, like to the zoo or the children's museum. It was also a chance for Danny to experience things she'd missed out on in her childhood.

"They won't be here for a couple of hours," Danny said.

"I know, but I want to take them on a picnic, so I need to get things ready."

"Picnic?" Danny's forehead wrinkled before she opened one eye. "What's this about a picnic?"

"It's supposed to be really nice today. I want to take the boys on a picnic in the park. I'm sure they'll love it. In fact, I'm sure you'll love it, too." Nicole leaned down and kissed a now smooth forehead.

Danny made a noise, and her eye shut once more. A soft chuckle escaped Nicole, as she eased out of bed again and went downstairs. Most of the food she'd prepared last night, while Danny had occupied herself with her guitar. But she needed to check her list, pack the items, and also make sure there were other things to occupy them beyond food.

By the time she was done, Danny was awake and dressed. Since it was supposed to be warm today, Nicole spared them both the argument of telling Danny to go put on pants. Besides, Danny was in the living room having fun with Haydn, their white German shepherd. There was no reason to bust up a happy morning for everyone with talk Danny didn't want to hear. The doorbell rang, and Haydn high-trotted around Danny as she went to answer it.

"Hey, Dane!" Luke chirped, as soon as the door opened.

Has he gotten taller since last we saw him? Nicole doubted it since they had seen him a week ago, but he was growing like a weed. One day, in a few years, he'd have plenty of girls chasing after him.

"Haydn!" Thomas rushed into the house and hugged the dog. Haydn let out a happy yelp, licking Thomas' face.

Folding her arms down by her stomach, Danny smiled at them and Nicole couldn't fight off a smile of her own. He'd be a little heartthrob, too, when he got older. Thankfully, they'd learn how to deal with it through Luke before Thomas had his go. Thomas had charisma that Nicole was certain shouldn't be in someone so young.

"Nick!" Luke waved to her. He hugged Danny and then ran over to hug Nicole as she stood in the doorway of the living room. Nicole hugged him back before going to help deal with Adam, in case he wanted to chat for a few minutes. Danny didn't do well with Adam and small talk.

Nicole offered him a pleasant smile. "Hello, Adam."

"Hey. I was just telling Dane, I'll be back for the boys at the usual time," Adam said.

The women both nodded, and Adam was gone. Nicole was pleased it seemed to be one of their easier times dealing with Adam. Sometimes, the man lingered with them, asking a million questions and making it seem like he thought they planned to kidnap the boys. Such nervous behavior always set Danny on edge and irked Nicole. They turned their attention to the boys.

"So, who's ready to spend the day at the park?" Nicole inquired with a grin.

"Is Haydn coming, too?" Luke countered. Haydn's whereabouts during trips was always of the utmost importance to both boys.

"Yes, Haydn's coming, too. Nick made a special picnic for us all, and we're going to spend the day at the park." Danny held a hand up like she was delivering an important speech.

The boys cheered, which made Nicole and Danny smile. Nicole gathered the picnic basket, which was more an insulated blue cooler than a basket that she'd bought after her first picnic with Danny. Danny hooked the leash onto Haydn's collar and Luke and Thomas took control of Haydn's leash, making sure the dog did not run off. The weather was gorgeous, especially for early spring, so they decided to walk the few blocks to the park.

"Now, where should we sit?" Nicole scanned the area with her index finger on her chin. There were picnic tables, but Danny had been kind enough to grab the blanket for them to sit on, so they could get the full picnic effect. Besides, most of the picnic areas with tables were taken and crowded. *I guess everyone is taking advantage of the nice weather.*

"How about by those trees?" Danny pointed ahead of them. There were a few trees by the clear pond that'd give them a great view of the field. The air was filled with the smell of freshly cut grass.

Nicole nodded. The nice shady area would still give them a good view of Luke and Thomas when they ran off to play. The couple set up for the picnic while their darling charges ran around the open grass with Haydn. The couple watched them for a moment, just smiling to themselves. Briefly, Nicole reached out and held her lover's hand.

"This was a great idea, Chem," Danny declared, as she laid out the blanket.

Nicole smiled as she helped Danny. "I hope it doesn't rain like it did the last time I planned a picnic."

A light laugh escaped Danny. "Enjoyed that picnic, too. It was my first one. You always treat me to great firsts."

Nicole felt a hot blush in her cheeks from the compliment. "I like it."

Danny flashed her a giant grin. With the blanket in place, Danny moved to go play with her nephews and dog. Grabbing Danny before she got too far, Nicole gave her a little yank.

Danny's forehead wrinkled as she looked down at Nicole. "Uh...yeah?"

"I want you to try something."

"Try something?"

Nodding, Nicole turned and rummaged through the basket until she found what she sought. She held up her bounty. Danny pulled back, scratching her forehead.

"Uh...what is that?" Danny asked.

"This is for your knee, my dear. It should help a little with the pain."

Danny looked at Nicole like she was speaking Greek. Nicole only chuckled. Of course Danny had never considered a knee brace. Nicole was pissed with herself for not thinking of this until now.

Danny nodded. "Okay."

"Let me put it on and then you can go join the other scamps."

Danny nodded again, and Nicole quickly strapped the knee brace in place. Danny stood and shifted a little, testing the knee brace. Giving Danny a thumbs up, Nicole watched as the boys' sapphire eyes lit up with delight. Haydn barked happily when Danny hopped in, rolling around on the green grass.

The sight of Danny playing with her towheaded nephews, and their equally light-haired dog, tickled Nicole. She and Danny had their first picnic on a rainy day in their bedroom. Nicole had expressed her wish that they picnic again, but with a child. Danny naturally volunteered her adored nephews. Nicole had someone different in mind.

Their indoor picnic was the last time that Nicole brought up the idea of them having a child. Danny had confessed that the idea of parenthood scared her. It was a step up from Danny always claiming she never thought about it. Nicole should've expected Danny to be afraid to have children, considering her childhood.

Danny had told her she'd think about it, now. Nicole could only hope time with the boys would change Danny's mind. She was wonderful with children. Every time Nicole saw the crew, it made her long, just a little more, for her own child with her girlfriend.

Of course, she was getting ahead of herself with such a thought. She refused to really consider a child until she was married, and Danny refused to marry her until she "got to a better place." Besides, they had only been dating for a year and a half. They had plenty of time ahead of them, provided Danny didn't ride her bike in front of any more cars and Nicole didn't push an issue so hard that Danny felt the urge to run away.

Shaking that thought aside, Nicole turned her attention back to the crew. The boys had Danny on the ground, tickling her. Haydn circled, not sure whom to help. The high pitched, happy, and infectious sounds brought a smile to Nicole's face, even though she knew those grass stains wouldn't come out.

"Danny deserves a family that can show her how great she is." Nicole sighed into the warm air.

Danny considered her all the family she needed. The nephews were an added bonus they both feared would one day be taken away. After all, the boys' mother hated Danny, hated Nicole for being with Danny, and hated their relationship for being *unnatural*. Adam wasn't the strongest man she had ever met, and she was waiting for the day he caved into his wife's desires to keep the boys away from the evil lesbians. It was like waiting for the apocalypse.

"Danny, you put that boy down right now!" Nicole pointed at them, as her lover limped through the field toward the pond with Thomas over her shoulder. He wiggled like a fish out of water, while Danny threatened to "throw him back."

"Nick said you gotta put me down." Thomas giggled, reaching out as if wanting to fly into Nicole's arms.

"Nick's not the boss of me." Danny grinned, making sure to give her girlfriend a playful wink.

"No, but no treats for you if you don't listen," Nicole replied with a smile of her own.

Danny threw her an adorable, but very much exaggerated pout before lowering Thomas from her shoulder. She placed him in front of Nicole and wagged her finger at him. "You're lucky Nick saved you. Go tell her thank you."

Thomas giggled wildly as he darted toward Nicole to express his thanks. She smiled, but the expression was a little forced after she noticed Danny behind him. Her girlfriend was limping much more than usual. She beckoned Danny with a crooked a finger. Danny pouted, assuming she was in trouble.

"I wasn't really going to do it," Danny said.

Nicole smiled and patted the space by her. "I know you weren't. Sit with me for a moment." She turned to Thomas. "Run and go play Frisbee with your brother and Haydn."

Thomas nodded and picked up the Frisbee from the picnic basket. Danny sat down, and Nicole brought her leg into her lap. Unstrapping the brace, she massaged Danny's knee while Danny offered her a smile.

"What happened? We're here ten minutes and your knee's hurting? Of course, you're not helping it by throwing Thomas over your shoulder."

Danny had the decency to look sheepish, glancing away and blushing for a second. "I figured that was better than throwing Luke over my shoulder."

"Yes, that would have been worse. But, what happened? Roughhousing usually lasts longer."

Danny shrugged. "I think one of them fell on my knee while we were rolling around in the grass. Plus, I need to get used to the brace."

Nicole nodded. "You might want to consider the surgery if you want to keep up with them."

Danny nodded, but she didn't say anything else on the matter. Nicole wasn't sure what Danny's thoughts were on the surgery. The doctor had suggested that he could at least lessen the residual pain from the broken leg Danny received when she was hit by a car, and from when she was beaten by bookies. Danny hadn't shown any interest in surgery.

"I might," Danny muttered, glancing away briefly.

Nicole arched an eyebrow. "What does that mean? Is it something you really want to do?"

Sighing, Danny scratched her head. "Probably should. I'm not a fan of the hospital, but I would like to be able to run around with them and Haydn."

Nicole nodded, but before she could chime in, Danny got up. She went to toss around the Frisbee with the boys and the dog without putting the brace back on. Nicole watched, wanting to make sure Danny wasn't in serious pain. She seemed fine, but didn't move around much to avoid stressing her leg any more than it was already. Nicole brought out juice boxes, knowing they'd be thirsty in a few minutes. She was right on point.

"Empty boxes go in this bag." Nicole showed them the empty plastic bag she'd brought for their garbage.

They only nodded and, as soon as the boxes were empty, they were off again. Nicole joined them for a moment to throw around the plastic disc. She was impressed at how high Haydn jumped for the thing as he stole a toss from the boys every now and then. Danny mostly dropped her catches, so Haydn took the disc from her plenty of times.

"Nick, I'm hungry," Thomas announced, rubbing his little belly, which was covered by a t-shirt with a cartoon alien Nicole wasn't familiar with.

"Well, let's have lunch, buddy," Nicole said with a smile.

"Lunch!" Luke cheered, patting his stomach, too.

The group retreated to the blanket. Nicole passed out more juice and poured Haydn some water in a bowl. The boys got separate halves of a hero sandwich with small bags of potato chips. Danny had a hero sandwich and apple slices.

"No potato salad this time?" Danny asked with a teasing smile.

Nicole shot her lover a slight glare. "You don't need any more potato salad. How do you eat a bowl of potato salad on your own?" Thankfully, Danny hadn't done that recently, but she had done it on more than one occasion.

Danny flashed an impish smile. "Hey, at least I'm not gaining weight."

"Baby, that's not the issue and you know it. It's not healthy to eat a big bowl of potato salad. I don't even want to think about your cholesterol level."

Danny waved her off. "I'm fine."

Nicole couldn't argue. Danny had been to the doctor several times since her accident, had all sorts of examinations, and passed them all, including her cholesterol levels. Danny was healthy, which Nicole always took as a miracle considering her girlfriend's life before they met. Nicole shook that away, not wanting to think about Danny's life back then. Hell, she even wanted to forget some parts of Danny's life that they had shared.

"This sandwich is great!" Luke grinned at Nicole. "Thanks for making such a good picnic."

"You're welcome. I thought this would be nice," Nicole replied, as she leaned down to gently wipe his face of crumbs. *This is nice.*

Giggling, Luke nodded. "It is." He pulled away from the napkin that brushed his cheek.

"Yeah, we never had a picnic before." Thomas beamed. He was still eating his sandwich, but he was almost done.

"Oh, finally did something they haven't done before but I have," Danny playfully cheered, pumping a fist in the air.

"You went on a picnic before?" Luke asked with wide eyes. It wasn't surprising that he was stunned. Usually, when they did something outside with the boys, the pleasure was new for Danny, while the boys had done it at least once.

"Oh, yeah. Nick took me on a picnic before."

The boys turned their attention to Nicole and asked her a ton of questions about the picnic she had taken their aunt on. She smiled and answered what she could, but they were hard to keep up with. She loved their excitement and enthusiasm.

"How come Nick made you a picnic, Dane? Is it because you live together?" Luke innocently inquired.

Danny laughed and looked at Nicole who, only now, realized they had never really explained their relationship to the boys. Hell, she knew Adam would never do it. She wasn't sure if it was her place to explain, but if it came up in the right way, she knew Danny would tell all.

"I just wanted to do something nice for Danny," Nicole replied.

The brothers accepted that with shrugs and turned their attention back to their food. Luke finished first and ran off with Haydn to play fetch with a ball. As soon as Danny was done, she joined him. Thomas, on the other hand, finished and curled up against Nicole to take a nap. She held him close and ran her hand through his downy hair. A soft smile settled on her face.

"I want one of these," Nicole whispered with a light laugh. She held Thomas close and enjoyed listening to him breathe.

She tried to shake the feeling, but it was impossible with the little boy resting on her. She had never felt the tug as much as she did now. She supposed she'd brought it on herself, thinking about kids earlier. She glanced at Danny. *I wonder if she'd want a boy or a girl. Would she want to adopt or have one of us get pregnant? I can't see Danny being pregnant.*

Now, she wasn't ruling out that Danny might want to get pregnant. After all, her love enjoyed describing herself as a housewife, which no one would think if they saw her. Danny might want to go through a pregnancy. Nicole couldn't see it; Danny with a swollen belly escaped her mind's eye.

"I would like that." She smiled.

Chuckling, she pictured a whole "honey, I'm home," afternoon. Of course, it was already something they did, but she tried to add a pregnant Danny to the vision. She attempted to add a baby, too. Then, she tried to shake away the thoughts. They were years away from a child. She was still in school, and Danny did not have a steady income. Although, she imagined Danny would be a great stay-at-home mom.

"I don't need to be thinking about this." She hummed aloud, hoping to take her mind off her current thoughts.

Thankfully, Haydn charged over and she was able to focus her attention on him. Haydn whined for a treat, which she gave him. He slurped up some water and charged back to Danny and Luke. Their laughter filled the air again, competing with a few birds. After fifteen minutes, Thomas awoke with fully charged batteries and joined the fray. Nicole played a little, but mostly watched. She supplied drinks and snacks to them whenever they came back to the blanket. They all picked up the area when it was time to go.

"We got this, Chem. Just cool out," Danny said, as Nicole moved to throw out their trash. Danny took the bag to the nearest trashcan.

Danny carried the folded blanket, while Luke took charge of the empty basket. Thomas had Haydn's leash, and Nicole had Thomas' hand. They walked back to the house to find Adam leaning against his car, which was parked in front of their house, shaded by a tree.

"Dad!" Both boys grinned.

Luke put the basket down, while Thomas passed Haydn's leash to Nicole. The brothers charged Adam, who crouched down to hug them. They laughed and began rattling off about their day in the park. Danny and Nicole watched the scene as Adam led the boys to the car.

"Wait!" Luke turned around and ran back to hug them. He looked up at them with shining eyes. "Thank you for a great picnic." His little brother followed his lead.

"Yeah, thanks." Thomas gave a massive grin.

"We'll do it again sometime soon." Smiling, Nicole rubbed their backs. She thought picnics with Danny and her nephews could easily become her favorite way to spend time outside.

The boys nodded and it seemed like they were gone in the blink of an eye. Thanks to Adam, they saw the boys almost every weekend, now. But he still made sure to get them at six on the dot and barely allowed them a minute to say goodbye. There were only so many times they could blame his wife and those times had passed. Now, it was time to blame his cowardice.

"Let's go cuddle on the couch." Danny grinned, undoubtedly trying to lift Nicole's spirits.

Nicole smiled a bit and shrugged. "That does sound like the perfect way to end the day."

They walked inside, and Danny took a shower while Nicole fixed some snacks. When Danny was done, Nicole went to take a shower and they met on the couch. A movie played on television, but Danny fell asleep with her head in Nicole's lap, worn out. Nicole zoned out, listening to Danny's light breathing and staring at the framed picture sitting on the coffee table.

The photograph was possibly the only baby picture of Danny in existence. She had taken it from her mother, Christine, who had kept a shoebox of keepsakes from Danny's childhood. Nicole couldn't understand how anyone could keep an entire childhood in a shoebox and think that meant something, but she didn't understand Christine at all.

Christine had tried to do the impossible, forsake Danny *and* keep her close. It had worked as well as one might expect. She had thrown her daughter away to please her husband. She still didn't want to admit the ghastly decision, but she was now trying to build something with Danny. *Is it only because she's certain her husband won't leave her now?* Nicole didn't know the whole story, but little by little, Danny was telling her about Christine. Every new bit of information troubled Nicole a little bit more. She didn't understand how Danny managed to survive that household.

"Not that it would ever come up, but I can't see Mommy throwing me away to save her marriage," Nicole muttered. "But, then again, I am Mommy's only child." Christine had three others before Danny.

"She wouldn't throw you away if she had a dozen kids," Danny assured her with a yawn.

Nicole glanced down at Danny. "When did you wake up?"

"As soon as the credits started rolling. Movies are getting so boring now. Why are you thinking about my mother?"

Squinting a bit as she eyed Danny, Nicole couldn't help wondering if her beloved was suddenly psychic. "How'd you know I was thinking of your mother?"

Danny wiggled a bit, popping a couple of joints in her neck. "Because you're trying to figure out how someone could throw away a child to save their marriage. One of the many things my mother has done. So, why are you thinking of her?"

Nicole smiled a bit. "I was admiring your baby picture and she popped into my mind. Have you spoken to her recently?"

A snort escaped Danny, and she stretched as she yawned again. "She's been calling, but I haven't been in the mood to talk to her. It takes a lot of work to wade through the bullshit. I try, but it's so Goddamn hard."

"Well, let's not think about that. We still have a couple of hours before we need to go to bed."

"We should have a light dinner. Want me to heat up that pasta from last night?"

"Yes, please."

Danny walked into the kitchen, and Nicole took the time alone to try to get her mind right. She hated being unable to get babies off of her mind today. But, looking at the baby picture of a red-skinned, curly-haired, almost blond Danny made her think about holding such a child to her chest, singing a lullaby. The way her body melted at the thought, she knew she was a lost cause. Her biological clock was about to explode before she turned thirty.

"I can't jump the gun like this. I have to get married first, and I have to let Danny get settled, whatever that means. So, stop thinking about this," Nicole ordered herself in a low growl.

She shook it off enough to enjoy dinner. Danny ended up playing with Haydn before they both took him for his nighttime walk. Once their little man was tucked away in his crate, they retreated to their bedroom.

Danny was in bed first, mostly because she had fewer bedtime ablutions compared to Nicole. In fact, Nicole was the one that put lotion on Danny every couple of days, because Danny would just let her skin go dry. If Nicole tried to lotion her every day, Danny would complain about being babied. Nicole also had to remind Danny to floss, no matter how much she complained about it.

"Today was great. Had a lot of fun with the boys." Danny smiled, as Nicole lay down next to her.

Nicole wasn't sure where her response to this came from, but she blamed her Goddamn, overactive ovaries. She rolled over onto Danny and gave her a sexy smirk. Danny's arms automatically went around her, as Nicole said the least sexy thing possible.

"How about we practice making one of our own?" Nicole purred, gently grinding against her lover's leg. As soon as the words left her mouth, she felt horrified. She thought Danny might see right through her forehead into her mind and know exactly what had been on her mind all day.

Danny did give her a tilted look and, for a long moment of silence, Nicole was sure her heart would beat right out of her chest. She wasn't sure about Danny's stance on children now, but she knew the suggestion, in the past, hadn't garnered much of a positive reaction. She hoped she hadn't accidentally blurted her way out of making love with Danny.

"Practice does make perfect," Danny replied with a sexy smirk before going in for a kiss.

She smiled against Danny's lips and opened her mouth to receive her lover. Internally, she breathed a sigh of relief and decided that full sentences were done for the rest of the night. She limited her vocabulary to moaning, crying out, and occasionally screaming Danny's name to the heavens.

***

The night was quiet, except for Danny's heavy breathing. Nicole would have to move Danny off of her stomach if she didn't roll over on her own, not because of the breathing, but because she wanted Danny to hold her in her sleep. Of course, she had to fall asleep for that to happen, but her mind wasn't ready to turn off just yet.

She was still stuck on the idea of having a baby with Danny. If that was her heart's desire, she realized she'd have to do something to move their relationship forward. She didn't want to think about it that way, because the last time she pushed Danny, they had almost broken up and Danny had been hit by a car.

It wasn't about shoving anything on Danny, especially not after they had made such great progress. They had gone on dates and trips, getting closer and gaining a better understanding of each other. They had also gained a better understanding of what they wanted from their relationship. It made her confident that one day she and Danny would have a family together.

Yes, these six months had made them stronger, but now they needed more. She needed to do something to remind Danny that she was endgame for her. She had taken to letting Danny come with her on business trips, mixing business and pleasure. Danny understood what that meant, but it had been a while since they had done that.

What's there to do? Nicole stared off into the darkness, as if it had the answers. Unless the occasional passing car and floating headlights were answers, the nighttime had nothing. She really didn't know what to do beyond what they were already doing. She had known Danny for as long as her longest relationship had lasted. She felt like she had done everything with Danny as she had with other lovers, and more. She never imagined marriage or fantasized kids with another lover. Between meeting her family and their vacations, she wasn't sure what was left. *Wait, she hasn't met my whole family, and she hasn't done one of the things that I love to do.*

There was still her father's side of her family. They'd probably receive Danny similarly to how her mother's side had. Her mother's family liked Danny and had, albeit playfully, encouraged her to marry Danny. Of course, there had been a few hiccups, like when her grandfather embarrassed them at Thanksgiving. Benito misunderstood why Danny proclaimed she wouldn't see her family for the holiday. Thankfully, her girlfriend and grandfather worked it out and came out stronger than before. *I should let Danny meet my other cousins and aunts and uncles. It's been a while, anyway. We should go camping.*

Glancing at her lover, Nicole knew Danny would go, even though Danny had, admittedly, never gone camping. Danny had gone skiing with her, even though she was fairly certain she wouldn't be able to do it with her knee and leg. Danny liked to try things, even things she didn't think she could do. Besides, Danny seemed to be of the mind that camping was easier compared to being homeless.

Nicole didn't like to think about Danny being homeless, but she was slowly accepting that part her lover's life. She hated that homelessness probably had been the better choice for Danny, instead of living at her parents' house. She refused to even think of that place as Danny's home. No place that held tortures in the walls, blood in the floorboards, and screams in its memories could be home. The few things she knew and continued learning about her lover helped her accept Danny's vagabond lifestyle, because she could see how much Danny was improving. *Is that her way of moving us forward? Opening a little more each day?* Nicole mused.

Danny groaned and moved a bit. She turned onto her side and reached for Nicole. Unable to stop it, a smile settled on Nicole's face as she moved closer to her beloved, tingling at the feel of their naked skin touching once more. Danny wrapped her up in her arms and held her close without waking up. She put her hand over Danny's, which was over her heart.

"I love you so much," Nicole whispered and brought Danny's hand to her lips. She placed a gentle kiss to those long fingers and closed her eyes.

She dreamed of camping, instead of babies, which cemented things for her. She'd put together a camping trip for them and her family. Danny would meet some of her favorite cousins and hopefully things would go well. If nothing else, she'd be able to share a well-loved tradition with her beloved. Maybe they'd be able to carry on the tradition if Danny enjoyed herself.

Chapter Two

DANE SAT ON THE sofa in the living room, staring at a blank piece of paper. Her pen hovered above the page, never moving. Silence hummed through the air. It was like it invaded her, conquering every part of her, and stalling her until unwanted thoughts edged their way into her brain. She was supposed to be composing a new song, but nothing came to mind. There used to be a time when music dominated her brain, drowning out anything else. Times had changed, though, and now she had something else that stayed on her mind, proving change was often good.

Her brain was stuck on thinking about Nicole, who had been acting strangely since their picnic with Luke and Thomas. Nicole had gotten lost in watching them play, and she'd appeared so peaceful while holding Thomas. Dane could guess what played through Nicole's mind, as it had come up a couple of times. Dane tried not to think about it, even though she'd had a rather nice dream about it not too long ago.

Nicole had stated she didn't want children until after she got married, and she had also claimed that if Dane didn't want children, she was all right with that. Dane imagined Nicole would go along with that, but resent the hell out of her and would inevitably leave or throw Dane out, as it were, since it was Nicole's house. She wouldn't blame Nicole.

Dane still wasn't sure about her opinion on children. She liked the few kids she knew, but she doubted that qualified her to do anything beyond play with them. Yes, Nicole had faith in her, which was probably one of the reasons Nicole allowed that to play through her mind. She was fine with her nephews, because she only had them for a few hours and almost always with Nicole around. Dane also enjoyed playing around with Nicole's young cousins, but she was with them even less than with her nephews and plenty of adults were around.

"I don't think anyone in their right mind would trust me alone with kids," she muttered.

She had no idea what she'd do if Nicole weren't there. She assumed it was all common sense, but that had failed her many times in her life. She was pretty sure her common sense meter was broken and it probably had a lot to do with her own really crappy childhood. She had already displayed remnants of her shitty childhood, lack of common sense, and antisocial behavior to Nicole. She didn't want to do that to a child. A child wouldn't know how to handle or process her mess-ups. She didn't want to risk that. She didn't want to ruin a child as her parents had ruined her. The cycle needed to end.

Despite that thinking, Dane wasn't totally opposed to the idea of having children. She hadn't thought she'd be able to take care of Haydn and she was doing fine with him. She had never yelled at him, despite his mistakes, but that could be because he couldn't talk. Of course, her nephews could talk and she never hollered at them, either. But, they were polite and relatively well behaved. She was sure that came from good parenting, despite their mother being an asshole. *Could I be good at parenting? I mean, if Adam can do it, it can't be too hard, can it?* Somehow, she doubted that logic.

She conceded she had healed some, and she thanked Nicole for that. It felt good to be Dane for the first time in her life without the aid of alcohol and narcotics. *Maybe someday I will want a kid, but I want to be sure I can do it on every level possible. I want to be able to take care of Nick on every level possible. Need to get her to understand that.* She needed Nicole to realize she wasn't ready for more than what they had. She hated that she had no idea if she'd ever be ready. *Hell, I don't even know if I know what ready is.*

She dismissed the thoughts as Nicole came into the living room, easing down next to her. A smile settled on Dane's face, as Nicole moved Dane's legs onto her lap and began massaging her lame leg. Nicole smiled back, and her eyes drifted to Dane's baby picture. Dane could practically see her lover's thoughts.

"What were you doing in the kitchen?" Dane asked to draw Nicole's attention away from the picture. She knew Nicole wasn't cooking for the simple fact that she didn't smell food in the air and Haydn hadn't charged into the kitchen to beg for anything, as he often did. And, who could say no to those begging eyes?

"Just talking to my dad," Nicole replied.

"How is Raymond? Did you tell him the boys still want to know when he's going to take them to another baseball game?"

Raymond, along with Dane and Nicole, had taken Luke and Thomas to their first baseball game, not too long ago. Dane had been bored out of her mind, as she always was with Nicole's favorite sport. Everyone else had an amazing time, which was all Dane cared about. She'd put up with baseball forever if it kept Nicole and the boys happy.

"I told him and he's looking into when we can go again. That's not why I called him, though."

Dane drew her eyebrows in close, feeling her forehead wrinkle. "Then why'd you call him?" She knew it was normal for people to call their parents, even though she never did and wouldn't start any time soon, but Nicole would see her father tomorrow. It seemed like a waste.

"Well, I wanted to run an idea by him. What do you think about camping?"

Dane shrugged. "You know I've never been. As I've said before, I've slept outside on the ground, so it can't be that bad. You want to go camping?"

A soft smile settled on Nicole's lovely face, as she hit a particular sore spot on Dane's knee. Dane winced a bit, but didn't move. Nicole glanced up, checking on her. "It's not just regular camping. I want to do what was once a family tradition. We used to go camping every year at the same place, with my uncle and some of my cousins on my dad's side. I want to do it again, and I want you to be a part of it." Nicole looked up again, gauging her reaction.

Dane ran her hand through her hair, which earned her an admonishing look. Nerves jumped in her forearm and she dropped her hand. "You want my first camping trip to be with your family? Are we sure that's wise?" She squinted as she studied Nicole, searching for any small sign of discomfort. All she got were bright eyes and a smile.

"It'll be fun to camp with a group. It's always great. We do all sorts of fun stuff. I miss it and I want to share it with you. It's special to me."

Those words could cause Dane to walk off a bridge with Nicole, but thankfully it wasn't that serious. She wanted to go camping, if only to see what it was like. She wanted to see what Nicole liked about it, too. She was certain she'd enjoy it since she had come to love the outdoors.

"How long of a trip?" Dane asked.

"Probably three to four days. Nothing too long. It'll be fun, baby," Nicole promised.

"I think so. Your cousins won't mind a greenhorn tagging along?"

"They'll mind in a way that they'll probably tease us a little. Well, tease us a lot, but it'll be fine. They're all very cool. And you'll get to meet the people I hung out with as a child, including my 'little sister.'" Nicole snickered a bit.

Dane knitted her eyebrows together again and felt her brow furrow. "Little sister? I thought you were an only child."

Nicole laughed. "I am. She's really my younger cousin, Lillian. I've spoken to her on the phone a few times while you were around."

"Yeah, but you never called her your little sister." Dane had noticed, a long time ago, that Nicole kept in touch with much of her family, even if it was only through short phone calls every couple of months. She texted with a few of them whenever she got a spare moment, too.

"I know, but we're really close. That's what I usually call her. She's two years younger than I am. She has two older brothers, who used to get on her nerves when she was little, even though they loved to get me involved in crazy stunts and stuff. She didn't like doing things like that. She used to shadow me whenever I was around. One day, she declared us sisters. We were Nikki and Lilly." She smiled.

"Lilly?" Dane echoed, shaking her head a little. She was happy to see Nicole smile, but she couldn't imagine someone grown going by the name of Lilly.

"She goes by Lillian now, but the family calls her Lil. I can't wait for you to meet her. I'm sure you'll adore her like I do."

Dane nodded. "If she's anything like her 'big sister,' then, yeah, think I can manage adoring her." Those words earned her another smile. "I guess I could do this. I wanna see what camping is all about and it'd be nice to meet your family. I mean, your dad is cool."

Honestly, Dane liked both of Nicole's parents for the simple fact that they were great parents to Nicole. It was the icing on the cake that Raymond accepted her and liked her to a degree. He'd have conversations with her and didn't openly sneer at her. Nicole's mother, Kathleen, remained completely in the territory that bordered hatred, but it seemed mostly born out of the idea that Nicole could do better. Dane was sure Kathleen was correct, but she wouldn't walk away if that better person ever showed up.

She even liked Kathleen, despite the fact that she seemed to be prejudiced against homosexuals. She wasn't sure where Kathleen picked up the attitude, since her parents didn't seem to have a problem with Nicole dating a woman. Kathleen, on the other hand, seemed to think Nicole needed to be with someone better than Dane and also a male.

"Yeah, I think he wants to show you how to camp." There was an impish twinkle in Nicole's emerald eyes. Clearly, it meant something to Nicole that her father wanted to do something with her girlfriend.

Dane chuckled. "Okay, but I want you to take care of all hands-on tutorials. We get to share a sleeping bag?" That sounded like all kinds of fun.

Nicole gave her foot a teasing squeeze. "If you want to, but we can't do much. My father will be in a tent nearby, after all. Not to mention my uncle and cousins, too. But, if you find you like camping, we can try it again on our own and then we can do a lot of things."

"Anything that lets me sleep next to you is already great in my mind." Dane smiled. Nicole smiled back and the light in her emerald eyes called to Dane like a shining beacon. "Come here." She opened her arms for Nicole.

Nicole nodded and released Dane's leg. Dane moved over a bit to give Nicole space, and Nicole settled down next to her. She put her arms around Nicole, brushing aside soft auburn hair before she placed a gentle kiss to the side of Nicole's head. Nicole cuddled against her, draping her arm across Dane's stomach and putting a leg over Dane's legs. Of course, she was careful, not wanting to injure Dane. Dane patted Nicole's leg, to let her know it was fine where it was.

"So, why do you think Raymond wants to teach me camping? Maybe he's excited about going out with you," Dane said, caressing Nicole's bicep.

"No, he asked me if you'd ever gone camping, and then he started going down a list of all of the things we could do. They weren't activities for me because he knows I either know how to do those things or don't like them. Plus, he knows I wouldn't hang around him on a family camping trip, anyway."

Dane blinked hard. "You don't hang out with your dad on the camping trips?" She figured Nicole was a daddy's girl, so she thought they'd spend a lot of time together on trips, like they did with sporting events.

"Nope."

"Tell me about these family camping trips."

"What do you want to know?" Nicole began caressing her lover's stomach.

Dane couldn't understand Nicole's fascination with her pudgy paunch, but she was happy Nicole liked her body. She struggled to hold in a light purr, wanting to continue their conversation. "Don't know. Anything you can think of. Everything."

A light laugh escaped Nicole, and her fingertips danced across Dane's stomach. "*Everything* is a lot to cover, baby, but I'll see what I can do. It's a family tradition that started with my father's father. He used to take his kids to the same place: my dad, my uncle, and my two aunts. He went on a couple of trips with us, the grandkids, but he died before we really got to know him. My dad and uncle have stories, though."

Dane smiled upon hearing her girlfriend's loving tone. *How could this woman, who has so much love and respect for family, not have at least one child? She'd be a great mom. How could I keep her from that? How could I keep the world from having someone brought up by Nick?*

"What's your uncle's name?"

"Richard. He's the oldest and then my dad and then my Aunt Susan, and, lastly, my Aunt Stacy. My aunts don't really go camping, anymore. I think they grew out of it. Plus, they always talk about how it's boring to go to the same place every single year, but they never once brought up another place to go camping. Of course, we love it, so we don't know what my aunts are complaining about."

"They all have children?"

"Yes, they do. Uncle Richard has three children. Lillian is his youngest. Richie is his oldest. We all call him Junior. The middle one is Webber. We call him Spider."

Dane nodded. "That's a cool name and nickname."

"He takes it very seriously. He used to climb everything. He collects spiders and has for almost fifteen years. He's got so many spider tattoos it's unbelievable."

Dane's eyes went wide. "He has tattoos?" *That's unexpected. Raymond is cool, but always so professional and straight-laced.*

"He probably has more tattoos than you do." An amused smile appeared on Nicole's face, as if she were teasing Dane. The sparkle in her eye was confirmation.

"I'll believe it when I see it. The brothers are older than you?"

"Yup." Nicole gave her a firm, slightly goofy nod. "I looked up to them. Spider's only a year older than I am, but it seemed like so much more when we were little. Junior is three years older than I am. In my head, that made him practically an adult, but a very cool adult. He was always so amazing. Junior was my hero, and Spider was his sidekick."

Twisting her mouth up to the side, Dane wondered what made this guy so great that Nicole had awe in her voice even now. "What did he do?"

A brilliant smile lit up Nicole's face. "What couldn't Junior do? Sports, exploring, building stuff. The best thing was that he always included me when we were around each other. I wasn't used to that from boys at my school or in my neighborhood. Junior never in his life said I couldn't do something because I was a girl. He got me for being too small a few times, but never for being a girl."

Oh, he does sound like a cool dude. I wonder what that translates to in adulthood. "He sounds like a good guy."

"The best."

"Keep telling me, please." Dane caressed her girlfriend's arm again.

Nicole grinned. "Well, as I said, Junior is great. Of course, I love Lillian. She's wonderful. I used to help her with her homework and we talked on the phone all the time through our teen years."

"Like now?"

Nicole snickered. "We're nowhere near as bad as we used to be. We'd talk on the phone for hours almost every night. Our parents were always complaining, wanting to know how the hell we could still have topics to talk about if we spoke every day, all night long. Now, we're lucky if we talk to each other every couple of weeks."

Dane frowned a little. "Why? What changed?"

Nicole shrugged. "Things change when you grow up. It's a dull, horrible fact of life. You find yourself with less time, job worries, bills to pay, and other relationships to focus on. We catch up when we can now. Actually, one of the reasons I want to go on this camping trip is an excuse to see her. She often says she'll come here, but something always comes up, so it'll be nice to see her."

"What about your other cousins?"

"Well, the only other one that'll go camping with us is Beth."

That was a name that Dane knew. "The photographer?"

"Yes, she's Aunt Susan's oldest. She's got a baby sister who hates camping. I think she hates outside, really. All three of Aunt Stacy's kids hate camping. They only went on the family trip once and complained the whole time they were there. I think they even left early, which we were thankful for because they were killing our vibe."

A small chuckle escaped Dane. "Do your aunts hate camping now?"

"No, like I said, they grew out of it. They claimed they got bored with it. They made the trip about fifteen times, so it's possible that it was too much of something and they grew to hate it. But I think they're really bored with the whole idea."

Fifteen times had to make a lot of things seem boring, Dane figured. "And you're not bored with it?" She watched Nicole carefully.

A smile that showed off Nicole's cheekbones adorned her face, like she was holding in a laugh. "No, because I haven't gotten a chance to share it with you. It's a magical experience. You'll like it."

Dane smiled back. They sat silently for a while, before Nicole reached for the remote. The sound of the television caught the attention of their busybody puppy. Haydn charged in from the den, yapping happily. He hopped up onto the couch and tucked himself against Dane. Both ladies laughed as Haydn settled himself. Dane scratched his neck and he whined lightly while a show played and they laid around for the rest of Sunday.

***

Nicole needed to see her father, but she'd wait until after work. No matter what, she always needed to keep work about work. She was beginning to understand that her need to separate business from personal came from a desire to stay sane. But, she found more and more she was learning to deal with work. She wasn't interrupted and pestered so much, thanks to her parents not wanting her to be overwhelmed while she was worrying about her classes.

She was still a little surprised by how accommodating her parents were about her courses. They had been against her returning to college, pursuing a master's degree in chemistry. In fact, her mother had been insulted by the whole thing and blamed Danny for Nicole doing something rather foolish, in her opinion. But her parents made sure she had enough time and energy to handle her classes. She wondered if they'd be proud of her when she had her degree, which would probably be in another year if everything went according to plan.

She also had to give Danny credit for her evolution at work. Danny, first and foremost, helped her relax at home. It hadn't been a concept she'd fully grasped before Danny came into her life. Being able to go home and put her work down, to be able to forget the day and make new happy memories with a person who made her feel special and loved had been beyond her. It was one of the many things that caused her to fall in love with Danny.

Nicole went about her day as she normally did. She took a morning phone call from Danny, who liked to check on her to make sure she wasn't stressed out. At noon, her friends, Mina James and Clara Ramos, came to pick her up for lunch. At the end of the day, she met up with her father before he left. She was staying late because she had class in an hour.

"Hey, Daddy, I wanted to talk to you about the camping trip," Nicole said, as she entered Raymond's office. Her father paused in the middle of putting papers away in his briefcase to look up at her.

Her father smiled and straightened himself up, resting his palm on his big oak desk. "I thought you'd come by sooner, considering how much you love the annual trip."

Nicole laughed. "I was bouncing in my seat all day. Did you call Uncle Richard?"

"I called Richard and he was all for the idea. The last time he went camping was with us, three years ago. He's been dying to go out again."

Her mouth twitched a bit. "Wow, I didn't think Uncle Richard would fall behind like that. He always seemed to love camping."

"He's been trying to save money. He's got those grandkids to think about. He wants to be able to afford fun things with them when they're old enough to remember fun things. He'll be the one that continues the camping trips with them in a few years, I'll bet."

Nicole nodded and thought about her cousins, Junior and Spider. They were the reasons why her uncle was now a grandfather. Junior had a son and a daughter on the way. Spider recently had a son. *My cousins actually have kids*. It felt like her heart sighed.

"Hey, Daddy..."

"Yeah?"

"What do you think about Uncle Richard being a grandpa?"

"I say he doesn't have a choice in the matter thanks to his sons and their offspring." He laughed.

"Daddy," Nicole said in a stern tone, crossing her arms over her chest. She wasn't really sure what she wanted him to say. Maybe she needed something to make her feel less crazy for having kids on her mind so much lately.

He smiled at her. "I think he's quite happy being a grandfather. I'm sure he'd be happier if Junior was actually married and Spider was still with his young woman."

"You don't even remember her name do you?" Nicole shook her head, trying her best not to appear amused.

He had to laugh again. "I don't. Richard refers to her as 'the crazy one.' As much as he acts like he wishes Spider were with her, he probably wishes Spider had a child with a more stable woman. At least

Spider has custody of Spencer. Now, if only he had saved that poor boy from that name."

Nicole laughed. "It's not a horrible name. Is he coming?"

"Who, Spencer? No, Richard has made it clear. He's not taking any of those kids into the woods until they're at least school age, even if their fathers come with them. I think his boys are in agreement. So, you won't get to see them on the trip."

She pouted. "I want to see them. The only one I've seen in person is Spence and he was a baby."

"Well, you have to work that out with your cousins." He gave her a shrug as condolence.

Sighing through her nose, she rubbed her forehead a little. "Junior and Spider are coming, right?"

"Richard said he's going to call them and Lil to find out when a good time for them would be. I told him you still have school, but you only have a couple of weeks left. He felt that should be good notice for all of them."

She nodded. "I'll call Beth and see if she can make it."

"Good. I need to check my equipment. Your mother might have thrown it out." He laughed.

"That sounds like something Mommy would do. Let me know if you need to go shopping. I'm going to have to take Danny, anyway."

He blinked. "Danny's really going to go?"

"Yeah, she's looking forward to it."

Scratching his chin and irritating his olive skin enough to turn it a slight red, he turned his attention back to his briefcase for a moment, securing the leather case shut. "She doesn't seem like the type. Are you sure she's not going because you asked her?"

"Well, I'm sure that *is* a reason she's going, but she seems very curious about camping."

He nodded. "Okay, remember how serious everyone takes it. You might want to prepare her for that."

"I know, Daddy." She wouldn't let Danny go without preparing her, to make sure she didn't make a fool out of herself. She didn't want Danny to feel uncomfortable or become the butt of a joke that might turn her off camping. "Do you think Mommy will join us?"

Raymond snorted and chuckled while shaking his head. Kate had never gone on a family camping trip as far as Nicole knew. Her mother wasn't the camping type, but Nicole often wished every now and then her mother would do something out of the norm. After all, she might have fun.

"Maybe you should ask her, just in case." Nicole flashed a hopeful smile and batted her eyes at him, wanting to get her father to give in.

In return, he rolled his eyes. "I could get down on my hands and knees and beg her, but she still wouldn't go."

"She'll be lonely without you for three or four days, though." Her parents, though they were somewhat different from each other, still loved each other quite a bit, and she knew they preferred not to be apart for days at a time.

"She'll find something to occupy her time. She always did when we used to go when you were younger."

Nicole nodded, because he was right. *I wonder what Mommy used to do when we left.* She felt like it involved anywhere away from dirt. *What's Mommy going to do when we leave now? It'll probably involve a spa.* Or so she hoped. She didn't want her mother to work the whole time that they were gone off having fun.

"She'll probably go stay with her parents," Raymond said, as if he could read her mind.

"Is that what she used to do?" *I guess that makes sense.* Her mother enjoyed being around her parents.

"Most of the time. If not spending time with her family, she worked. You know how your mom is. She'll be fine for a few days. Now, if we were both gone a week or something, she'd go crazy." He chuckled a bit, but his face looked soft. She wondered if her face softened like that when she talked about Danny.

She tittered, too. "I guess. As long as Mommy has something to do."

"Like I said, she'll be fine." Raymond waved the matter away and picked up his briefcase. "The last person you need to worry about is your mother. She doesn't become a mess, she fixes messes."

Nicole smiled and nodded because he was quite right. Her father grabbed his jacket from a nearby hook and left while she returned to her office. She did some work until Danny called.

"Hey, Chem," Danny greeted her, a smile in her voice.

"Hey, baby. How's your day going?"

"The same as always. I had to scold our little man. He tore pages out of my song pad, but other than that, everything's the same as always."

"He tore the pages out of your song pad? Were you able to save them?" Nicole frowned, picturing their usually well-behaved, white shepherd happily yanking the pages from the simple legal pad that collected Danny's musical musings.

"Oh, yeah. He didn't chew them. He tore them out. Some of them are wet and have small tears, but I can figure out what was there and if I don't, it'll come to me. How are you doing? Is everything fine?"

"Everything's fine. I spoke with my father about the camping trip. He called his brother, and Uncle Richard is ready to go. He'll call his kids to find out when they can go, and I have to call my cousin, Beth, to see if she wants to tag along. We'll probably go once school is over for me."

"That's a good plan. Were you able to get a summer class like you wanted? I don't want you to miss class because of the trip."

Nicole smiled. *She's always thinking of me.* "It's all right. There's plenty of time. I couldn't get a class, because they weren't offered late enough. It's fine. I'll try for the other summer session and if nothing comes of that, there's always the fall semester. I'm doing well."

"I have no doubt that you are. Do you want anything special for dinner? I'm about to take the horrible Haydn out of his crate and maybe do a little shopping."

"I can pick up dinner. You shouldn't have to cook every day. Every now and then, let me treat you to some takeout," Nicole said with a light laugh. She could do more, but Danny seemed to like her housewife status. But, Nicole knew, every now and then, anyone would need a break.

"Oh, treat me?" Danny sounded delighted. It sent a shiver down Nicole's spine. Not too long ago, Danny actually would have felt a bit troubled by the offer. Danny had admitted it used to bother her when Nicole tried to take care of her, but she was gradually accepting it. This was one of the things that made their relationship so much stronger than it had been. All she could do was thank the fact that they spent time together, talked more often, and just opened up.

"So, what kind of takeout should I pick up?"

"Surprise me," Danny chirped.

"So, I should enter the house nude?" Nicole teased.

"That damn sure would surprise me! I'll take more surprises like that, actually."

Nicole tittered. "Yes, well, it won't happen, my love. I'm sorry."

"It's happening right now in my fantasies."

Nicole laughed. "That's the only place it will be happening, Danny. I promise you that."

"What? This could be a good time to role-play or something."

Nicole had to work very hard not to laugh at that. She didn't want to encourage Danny. She enjoyed role-playing, even though it took some getting used to. That was something else they had learned in the last few months. She was certain that exploring their sexual fantasies had helped bring them closer. But, she didn't consider it role-playing to walk in the house naked with food in her hands. Besides, she'd never do something intimate with the chance of her neighbors seeing her.

"I'm hanging up now, baby."

"Love you."

"I love you, too." Nicole disconnected the call. She checked the time and decided to call her cousin Beth. Once upon a time, it never would've occurred to her to call anyone except a client while she was at work, but Danny had changed that, too. Danny had changed so much of her thinking, in a positive way. She could only hope she had done the same. She shook that thought away as her cousin answered the phone. "Hey, Beth, I was wondering if you wanted to revive our old camping tradition..."

S.L. Kassidy

Chapter Three

"SO, THE TRIP IS all set. Everyone I told you about is going to come. We'll meet at my uncle's house. We need to go shopping," Nicole said to Dane, as she flopped down onto the sofa.

Dane bounced a little when Nicole landed next to her. Dane had the end of a rope toy Haydn liked, pulling it slightly as he clamped down with a strong jaw, growling while trying to yank it from her. She felt it was a good way to keep him busy while Nicole had been on the phone for the better part of the afternoon, setting up the trip.

"Shopping? What for?" Dane gave Haydn a good yank, picking him up in the air. He growled a bit, but kept on fighting with her.

"For camping equipment, love. What did you think; we would show up in the woods and sleep on the ground?" Nicole smiled.

Dane chuckled. "No, because that means I wouldn't be able to share a sleeping bag with you, which would be a crime against nature, in my opinion. Do we really need more than that?"

"I would like a tent suitable to protect us from the elements while we try to get some sleep." The green of Nicole's eyes shined like the emeralds they were colored after. She was highly amused by this exchange for some reason.

"Guess a tent would be nice. Didn't think about that." Dane scratched her forehead a bit with her free hand. "You know, I have no idea what we need for camping." She gave the dog another yank. Haydn growled some more and tugged harder.

Nicole leaned over and kissed the side of her head. "I know you don't, which is why you're going to come with me. You should learn, in case you like camping and we start making a thing out of this. You'll know what to get and how to prepare."

Dane nodded. It was good logic. She suspected she'd enjoy camping. She had no problem with sleeping and living outdoors, having done it a few times in her life with relatively no supplies at all. She'd like to continue going on trips with Nicole. Their trips had partially saved their relationship after a rough spot involving Dane's family, if they could be called that.

It was through their trips she had learned to finally allow Nicole to be there for her. It used to annoy her when Nicole tried to do things for her, things she knew shouldn't bother her, but this was her first real relationship. Nicole had warned her there'd be bumps and mistakes, but now she was sure they'd survive those things. They had more to learn about each other, but they'd make it.

"Danny, baby, you listening to me?" Nicole asked, waving a hand in front of Dane's face.

Blinking, Dane shook her head. "No, sorry. What did you say?"

"I wanted to know if you want to go today or some other time?"

Dane thought about it before giving a firm yank to the rope in Haydn's mouth. "Can you get Mina to watch Haydn on such short notice?"

Nicole made a face and reached for her phone. She called Mina, and Dane turned her attention completely back to Haydn. He was growling and shook his head, giving it his all to take the rope from her. She chuckled and pulled a bit again, lifting his front paws off of the floor. More growls escaped him, as he tried to back up and gain some traction. She gave him a little slack, letting him think he was winning. She pulled again and scooped him up in her arms, petting him and praising him as if he had done something worthwhile. He barked, letting go of the rope, and then nuzzled her, rubbing his wet nose against her neck.

"We'll have to go tomorrow. Mina wasn't free today," Nicole said, putting her phone down again.

Dane smiled. "No problem. We get to chill today, and we'll go shopping tomorrow. We can watch a movie or something right now."

There was a nod, and Nicole retrieved the remote for the television. She found something to watch and curled up against Dane. Haydn settled down at the bottom of the couch, wanting to share in the movie with them. Sometimes, Dane wondered if he could actually tell what was going on in a movie. He often sat quietly through them when he settled in and whimpered at sad parts or barked at certain scenes, depending on what was going on.

Dane really didn't pay much attention to what was going on in the movie, especially after she noticed Nicole had fallen asleep against her. Leaning down, she kissed Nicole's forehead and adjusted the redhead to make sure Nicole was comfortable. Nicole didn't stir as Dane moved her across her lap.

She caressed Nicole's shoulder and lost herself within the touch. Nicole's skin was always so soft and relaxing. Her mind wandered, camping at the forefront. *What's it like to camp?* She tried to imagine it as something different than being homeless, but only the setting changed. She'd slept in parks on many different occasions.

Thinking about the trip they'd soon take and the trips that they had already taken, Dane's mind drifted to their relationship once more. She was certain they were stronger than ever, moving to some level she had never known existed until they reached it. She thought on this and considered what she'd have to do to 'be better.'

She had promised Nicole that she would propose when she was better, but now she believed she had no idea what that meant. She believed she had no idea what any of this meant. It caused a nervous flutter in her belly.

I have no freaking clue what I'm doing. Dread bubbled in her belly, weighing her down like hot iron. It felt like her stomach fell into her feet. *But, then again, I haven't had a clue as to what I was doing since I showed up on her doorstep, not that I knew it was her doorstep.*

Taking several deep breaths, Dane kept herself from panicking, but she was now very aware she needed to figure out how she'd be better. She believed their relationship would keep progressing and she needed to keep up or she'd be left behind, then she'd be left by Nicole. She needed to figure out what she'd need to do to get herself in a position where she felt comfortable asking Nicole to spend the rest of her life with her. She supposed she'd have to do some soul searching.

Maybe if I talk to Crow, she can help me figure it out. Of course, as far as she knew, Crow hadn't had a relationship that lasted longer than a year. Dane had definitely passed Crow in the lasting relationship department. *But, that doesn't mean she doesn't know what I should do to be good enough to ask Nicole to marry me. If nothing else, she could recommend a book or something.* Crow working at a bookstore could come in handy.

Beyond that, Dane considered some of the things she was already aware of. She knew eventually she'd have to get comfortable with the idea of having kids. She was already sure Nicole wanted at least one, even if she tried to act like she didn't or she could do without. So, if nothing else, Dane had to work past her issues with her own childhood.

She frowned at that. *I wonder if that means I'll have to talk to my mother.* Just saying the words left a bad taste in her mouth.

The very thought of talking to Christine Wolfe made Dane want to forget everything. Her mother continued to push to try to better their relationship, and calling it a relationship was exaggerating. The woman had gone as far as giving Dane a small trust fund, more than likely trying to bribe forgiveness out of Dane or buy affection from her. *To hell with that bullshit.*

Dane still couldn't bring herself to forgive the woman who silently stood by as she was beaten and abused by her father and two siblings. Even when her mother suggested they start over, she found she couldn't pretend her mother hadn't ignored her for most of her life. Even when her mother showed her something no one else in their family had seen—Christine's father's grave—Dane found she couldn't bond with the woman. She wasn't sure she wanted to.

Did I ever bond with her? Dane scratched her chin in thought. She had called Christine her mother, but only because she had felt like it upset her. When Christine seemed interested in accepting the title, if not the job, Dane stopped using it. Her mother was Christine to her and what she felt for Christine was on the same level she felt for her siblings, including Adam. There was no familial bond, nothing that made her feel connected to them beyond pain and suffering, which wasn't something she wanted to dwell on.

But, the idea of family brought her back to the notion of children with Nicole. A child would connect them, make them a 'real' family. *Am I ready for that? Will I ever be ready for that? If not, I might as well say goodbye to my angel now, and I'm damn sure I'm not ready for that.*

She really didn't want to engage in such heavy thinking, especially when she had already figured out that she'd probably have to give in to the kid thing. Nicole wanted and deserved a child, and Dane would do anything for her beloved. Of course, to get there, she still had to figure out how she could 'be better,' to get to the point of proposing to Nicole. *I do want to propose to you, Angel. Want to spend the rest of my life worshiping you, being worthy of you, but how do I get to that point?* Dane ran her fingers through Nicole's wavy auburn mane.

Right now, she knew she was the best she had ever been in her life, and she still felt unworthy of Nicole. Nicole's father and Nicole's mother's side of the family had accepted her, and she was about to meet Raymond's side. No one had ever given her so much, shared so much with her, and she felt like she never had anything to give back.

The most she could share with Nicole was music, which was her whole world, but didn't feel like enough.

Music could reach inside of a person and draw out emotions, but it couldn't offer physical comfort. Music couldn't hold, hug, or respond. While music had carried her throughout life, it couldn't compare to the amount of family and care Nicole had bestowed upon her.

Dane really wished she at least had a tradition to share with Nicole. She had no traditions, no family, and barely had any real friends, except for Crow. She had nothing to offer. Sighing, she glanced down at Nicole and smiled.

"Well, she knew I didn't have any of that when she got involved with me. Maybe my music was enough, *is* enough. Maybe I'm worrying about nothing," Dane muttered.

"You're talking to yourself, love?" Nicole mumbled, yawning a bit as she stretched out in Dane's lap.

"Just thinking aloud."

"About what?" Nicole shifted her body a bit, making herself comfortable against Dane, who enjoyed the press. She didn't bother to open her eyes for the conversation, but she smiled a bit, as if she was quite happy where she was.

Everything. "The trip."

"It'll be fine. You'll have a good time." Nicole patted her thigh to soothe her.

A small smile settled on Dane's face. "I'm sure I will. Think your family will like me?"

There was another soft pat to her thigh. "They'll adore you, like I do. My uncle will like you just like my dad does."

"Your dad doesn't like me that much." Dane was certain that if the right young man came along, Raymond would do his best to get Nicole to go out with him without any thought to Dane. *Hmm...maybe that's what I mean when I say 'be better.' I need to be like what Raymond and Kathleen would approve of as far as Nicole dating. That's definitely a step up from where I used to be, anyway. But, I don't want to change into something that Nicole doesn't want.*

Nicole chuckled, moving to cuddle into Dane's stomach. "My dad does like you. He can't show it or it might make Mommy show that she likes you, too."

Dane couldn't help the scoff that escaped her mouth. "Now you're being crazy. Your mom doesn't like me."

Emerald eyes opened, and Nicole shot her a delightful little smirk. "You're growing on her. I'm sure she views it as a fungus, but you're growing on her."

Dane laughed, even though she didn't think that was true. Kathleen never expressed anything beyond contempt and irritation, as far as Dane noticed. Kathleen's family, on the other hand, was very friendly with her. She didn't even get a thank you out of Kathleen when she'd sent the her and Raymond flowers thanking them for being wonderful parents to Nicole. But, the gesture had earned her brownie points with Raymond.

"Still sleepy, or do you want to get dressed and we can take Haydn for a walk?" Dane suggested.

"Your nephews aren't coming over today?" Nicole asked, rubbing one eye with the lower part of her thumb.

"No. Adam called at the last minute, saying they had something, or whatever, to go to today." Dane shrugged. She hadn't paid much attention once she realized why he called.

"Something or whatever? What kind of details are those?" Nicole laughed, focusing on her girlfriend.

"I was half-listening after he said the boys wouldn't be coming over. Honestly, I almost hung up on him after that. Don't really care to know why they're not coming over. No matter what, I'm going to suspect their mom doesn't want them around us and somehow talked him into the idea because he's a fucking sheep."

"Baby!" Nicole scolded her for her language, like she didn't curse worse than Dane most of the time. "He's the reason we get to see the boys as it is."

Dane snorted. "You can give him credit for his one good deed while I'm going to keep track of his mess-ups."

Frowning slightly, Nicole shook her head. "You know you'll never be on friendly terms with him if you do that."

Dane drew her eyebrows in a little. "What makes you think I want to be on friendly terms with Adam? Tolerate him, but that's about it, and only because he brings the boys over."

"Oh, I thought you liked Adam. Or at least you wanted to like Adam."

Dane opened her mouth, but closed as she realized she was probably about to lie or say something that made no sense at all. She thought on that, running her hand through her hair. Once upon a time, she had believed she wanted to like Adam. The idea of having a big brother had always appealed to her. When she was on the street, the first person to care for her was Animal, the drummer in a band she played with. He was older than she was and treated her how she imagined an older brother would treat a little sister that he cared about. He died from a drug overdose while she was right next to him, too high to figure out what happened. The loss had opened a hole in her, and she now realized she subconsciously wanted to fill that hole with some other big brother figure. Adam would never be the one to fill that void. For a moment, her heart hurt. *Animal's not replaceable, and I understand that now. He's gone and I should properly mourn him as best I can. No one will ever be him.*

"I did, but not anymore. If we end up friends, cool, but it must be through his effort. Not putting anything out there for him. I don't ever want him to think I forgive him for what he did, unless I actually do get to the point that I forgive him."

Nicole nodded. "And you're not at that point yet, huh?"

Grinding her teeth for a second, Dane shook her head. "Definitely not."

"Do you think you might be able to fake it?" Nicole gave her a hopeful, but awkward looking smile. Her face was tense, and her top teeth showed as her upper lip spread across her face. "I mean, if you end up liking camping, I'd like for us to go with the boys, at least once. I think they'd have fun, but Adam might not let it happen."

Dane grinned. "That's a great idea. I guess I could fake it, if I need to."

Nicole giggled, looking much better. "You're something else, Big Dog. Do you think Adam would let us take the boys camping?"

Blowing out a heavy breath moved Dane's hair a bit. "Probably not. His wife would accuse us of molesting them. Hell, she might even call the cops on us and say we kidnapped the boys or some shit. He might have no problem with them spending eight hours with us, but anything more than that is too much for him because she'll flip."

Nicole nodded, but she frowned slightly again. Of course, that troubled Dane because it bothered Nicole, who wasn't used to being disliked and viewed with suspicion. Dane had dealt with it most of her life, so it wasn't much of a bother for her.

"Why don't we take your little cousins if we can't take the boys? We should hang out with them more. They're cool kids," Dane pointed out. Plus, their mother didn't mind them being around her or Nicole, didn't suspect them of anything horrible.

"Yeah, they're cool kids with busy schedules. Their parents have them signed up for all sorts of things. They let them try out everything that comes to mind, too. But, we could try. I'm sure they'd love it."

"Cool." *It seems like Nick wants to hang out with some kids. God, I am so screwed on this. Gotta get my fucking act together.*

"Let's get up and walk Haydn before he goes on one of the plants and I have to scold him."

A chuckle escaped Dane. "Twice in two days? The poor, spoiled guy will get a complex."

Nicole laughed, as they tore themselves from the sofa. They put on proper clothes and grabbed Haydn's leash. He was up in a flash when he saw the leash and stood stock-still to allow Dane to attach it to his collar. They took him for a walk together, which was rare for them. Dane tended to do most of the walking, because she was the one home almost all day. Whenever Nicole was home during the times for Haydn to get walked, Dane insisted she stay home and relax.

"I like this." Nicole took Dane's hand in her own. Her thumb caressed the back of Dane's hand. "It's nice. I want to do this more often."

"Walk Haydn together?" Dane guessed, as their pup dashed ahead of them, sniffing everything. The sun set above them, bathing the world in orange and red, and giving Nicole's hair extra pop. Dane was tempted to release Haydn's leash, so she could run her free hand through the auburn locks.

"Yes."

"But, you have class," Dane said, as if Nicole didn't know that. Usually, Nicole was too tired or too busy working on homework to do the evening walk with her.

"I know, but I won't always have class. I know you're trying to look out for me, baby, but I want to spend time with you and with Haydn. Simple things like this and like lying on the couch with Haydn watching more of the movie than either of us. These are the things that make life wonderful."

"We'll be here. You take care of that degree first, okay?"

Nicole smiled and kissed Dane on the cheek. Dane smiled as Nicole squeezed her hand. Dane squeezed back and silently vowed to figure out what she needed to do.

***

Nicole had to fight off a laugh as she and Danny walked into the sporting goods store. Those lovely grey eyes went wide, as if Danny had never seen anything like it before. It was possible she hadn't. Danny always made it known she was horrible at sports and, even though she occasionally dressed in basketball shorts, she purchased them at a thrift store. Nicole did most of the clothes shopping, because Danny didn't seem to think she needed new clothes. Unless maybe Haydn ate her shirt, and even then Danny might try to salvage the thing.

"Do you want to look around, or are you going to stick with me?" Nicole asked, as she grabbed a shopping cart.

Danny's brow wrinkled, as she seriously thought on the answer. "Uh...stick with you. Wanna see what you need, and I might be able to help."

Nicole smiled and took Danny's hand to help guide her for the moment. "My father taught me to always make a list of items I need. 'No matter how many times you go camping and you think you'll remember everything you need. There's nothing worse than getting to a site and finding you don't have batteries.'" She wagged her finger and drew her mouth down, mocking a stern face her father made when he gave her this lecture.

Danny chuckled, but probably only because Nicole did the same. She had her checklist on her phone. Danny peered over, wanting to see. Smiling, Nicole tilted the screen in her lover's direction. Danny read it over, face moving slightly every time she got to something she probably didn't think would be on the list.

"This is a lot of stuff for a three or four day trip," Danny said.

Nicole nodded. "You need a lot of supplies if you want to go camping properly, and you don't want to get caught in the woods missing something you suddenly need."

"Yeah, I guess it'd suck to be in the middle of nowhere..."

"Yes, trust me, it does. One year, my father and uncle both forgot flashlights. Another year, I forgot to pack socks. It was horrible. We'll buy what we need. I'll explain it to you, and we'll mess around with the stuff in the backyard for you to be familiar with it, okay?" Nicole smirked to show Danny what she meant by 'mess around.'

The burning intensity that showed up in those smoky eyes let Nicole know her message was heard, loud and clear. She gathered the small items first because they were nearest. She explained the things that weren't obvious, but most of them were self-explanatory, especially since Danny knew what it was like to live outside. Nicole frowned as soon as the thought entered her head.

"Hey, what's up, Angel? They don't have the type of biodegradable toilet paper you like?" Danny asked with a laugh.

Nicole shook her head. "I was thinking about...well, you. I was thinking about you and your time on the street." She should talk about this. They should talk about this. She didn't want to be uncomfortable over it forever. It was a part of Danny. It happened. It was over. It didn't need to be ignored.

Danny shrugged. "It wasn't that bad, Chem, and I wish you'd stop thinking about it. Or worrying about it. I made it out stronger than ever."

"Tell me about it," Nicole said in a breath before she realized what she was saying. Now wasn't the time or the place for it, but it was out there.

Danny was silent for what seemed like eternity, and Nicole was about to take it back, but then Danny opened her mouth. "I really should tell you about it, huh? That way you don't keep wondering about it and thinking the worst. The worst I did to myself, except my leg, you know?"

"The story you told your mother...when she said she was keeping an eye on you and you wanted to prove her wrong..." Nicole hated even thinking about that moment. She wished she hadn't heard Danny, but she'd practically been screaming at Christine at the time. It would've been impossible not to hear her unless she went down the street.

Danny swallowed a little. "Oh, with Animal. Yeah, that was pretty bad." Taking a breath, she ran her hand through her hair. "But, again, I did that to myself. I was getting high with him. I was the one who was too messed up to do anything."

"That wasn't your fault, Danny." Nicole dropped the items she held, so she could take both of her lover's hands. "Baby, that wasn't your fault. Yes, you were high, but he was using, too. How could you know his limit if he didn't and he was the older one? He was supposed to be taking care of you."

Danny frowned. "No, he wasn't. I wasn't his responsibility."

Nicole looked Danny straight in the eye. "Okay, and he wasn't yours. You didn't cause his death. You weren't responsible for him. He should've taken care of himself, just like you needed to take care of yourself. So, it wasn't your fault." She made her tone deliberate. This was something Danny needed to hear.

She could feel Danny's hands trembling, and Danny sniffed. As tears welled up in Danny's eyes, Nicole realized no one had probably ever said that to Danny. Slowly, she pulled Danny to her and hugged her, even though they were in the middle of a relatively busy store. She cradled Danny's head against her shoulder.

"Baby, it wasn't your fault," she whispered.

She felt and heard Danny sob. Her shoulder muffled the sound, but they still earned a few stares. She ignored them, holding Danny close. For a few seconds, Danny shook, obviously crying. Then, she felt and heard Danny take a deep breath, trying to compose herself. It took a few more seconds, but Danny stepped away and Nicole knew it was the end of their discussion for the moment. They continued with the shopping as if everything was normal, but Danny didn't let go of her hand.

"We definitely need sleeping bags," Nicole muttered as they wandered into the aisle. She looked through several of them before picking up one. "Should I choose one for you, too, love?"

"Uh…yeah, I don't know a damn thing about picking a sleeping bag," Danny replied with a lopsided smile. It was forced, unlike her usual expression, not quite reaching her eyes.

Nicole smiled. "Well, you're right about that." She grabbed another sleeping bag and inspected it, causing Danny to raise an eyebrow. "I have to be sure they can zip together." She wiggled her eyebrows.

For a moment, Danny's eyebrows knitted together and then realization dawned on her. Grey eyes opened wide, and Danny pointed at her. "Ohhhh! Yeah, that's definitely a good thing."

Nicole chuckled and then marched off to continue shopping. "Flashlights…flashlights…flashlights," she said to herself, under her breath, wondering where she'd find the flashlights. They were doing well on supplies, and then they walked by the shoe section. "Baby, do you own a pair of boots?" She was fairly certain she knew the answer to that, considering the fact that Danny only owned a pair of beat-up sneakers before Nicole had purchased a new pair for her.

"Boots? Don't think I've ever owned a pair of boots."

"Of course, we've got to get you a pair. You can't go camping without some boots."

"Why? My sneakers lasted through time in the park."

Nicole shook her head and dragged Danny over to the boot section. Her girlfriend had big feet for a woman. Danny blamed it on her height. She wore a size ten in men's, so, yes, big feet.

"Any particular color you want?" Nicole asked, as she began looking through the shelves.

Danny shrugged. "I dunno boots."

"All right. After this, remind me to get you a multi-tool. I have one, but you should have one of your own, just in case."

Danny nodded. She then had to sit through trying on and walking around in several pairs of boots. It was a little funny to see. Danny walked like the boots might crumble on her feet. Nicole knew she would need to buy some gel soles to give Danny real comfort in the boots. Once the boots were chosen, they had to pick up a few more items and most importantly—the tent. After getting the tent, Nicole made sure to pick up individual items, including Danny's multi-tool.

She paid for everything using a debit card from their joint account. They both deposited the same amount of money in every month and, whenever they did something together, they paid for it from that account. It saved on arguments about money.

"So, now what?" Danny asked, once they were in the car and headed back home.

"Well, we have a few hours before we have to go get our little man, so I'll show you how some of the equipment works, like how to set up the tent," Nicole answered with a grin and Danny grinned in reply.

***

Dane had no clue how to put up a tent. The reason for that had nothing to do with the fact that she hadn't paid attention when Nicole put it up, took it down, and put it up again in the backyard. It had to do with the fact that Nicole was straddling her lap and kissing her senseless, on the air mattress, in the tent, in the backyard! How in the world was she supposed to know or remember how to do anything beyond return the affection? So, she held onto Nicole and did her best to give as good as she got, despite how shocked she was. This was a woman who was embarrassed they had been overheard in a hotel room on their first vacation, and now they were possibly going to do the deed in the backyard. Oh, how far they had come.

Focusing on Nicole's lips and tongue, Dane moved her hands from Nicole's hips to pull her shirt out of her pants. Nicole moaned, as Dane's hands slid up her bare belly. Dane purred at the feel of her lover's smooth skin, and thoughts of playing with Nicole's breasts danced through her head. Nicole must've realized where things were going, because she pulled away. She gave Dane a chastising look, and Dane countered with an innocent grin.

"Can you blame me for trying?"

"No, but we're not going to third base in the backyard, even if we are in a tent." Nicole rolled off of Dane and settled against her side.

Dane whined at the loss. "Even if I do that thing you like with my tongue?" She gave Nicole some pretty big puppy eyes. Well, so much for sex in the backyard.

"Especially if you do that! The whole neighborhood would hear us." Nicole chuckled, tucking herself against Dane. "We have to leave to get Haydn soon."

Dane nodded and they were silent for a while before Dane remembered their moment in the sporting goods store. No one had ever told her that what happened to Animal wasn't her fault and it had never occurred to her it wasn't. She had walked around with the blame—and shame—for years. She doubted she'd ever totally believe it wasn't her fault. After all, he was dead and she'd been there, doing nothing, but Nicole at least made sense and tried to help her. Maybe she needed to tell Nicole about that time, not just to ease Nicole's mind, but to help herself. *I am trying to be better. Hope it doesn't lower her opinion of me.*

"My time with Animal…it was weird. I don't remember a lot of it. Between the drinking and the drugs, I'm not even sure how I made it to school every day."

Nicole's eyebrows shot up her forehead, and she stared at Dane with wide eyes. "You went to school every day? Despite all of that, you actually went to school every day?"

"Yeah, it was somewhere to go. There was food."

Nicole nodded and emerald eyes glanced away briefly. "So, you went to school for meals?"

Dane ran her hand through her hair and shook her head a bit. "I didn't qualify for free lunches or anything, but I had a teacher who took care of me as much as I'd allow. Brought me food, asked about me, tried to keep me in a good headspace. Mr. Preston. I didn't let him do too much for me, but he tried. The scorch marks from Lynn and Henry Briarmoor remained years after they burned me. He tried to get me help, a lot, always talking about programs and junk. I didn't want that, though. The drinking and drugs helped me deal. I felt like they kept me sane or balanced or alive. Something like that." She wasn't sure how to explain it and hoped that made some semblance of sense. *How the hell do I write lyrics if this is how I talk?*

"That's not really dealing," Nicole whispered. She put her hand on her lover's hip and pulled them closer together.

Turning her mouth down a bit, Dane shook her head. "I didn't know that at the time. I thought I was dealing. I took showers and stuff at school, in the locker room if I didn't have a girl I could stay with. I joined a music program in the summer, so I could keep going to school when it was over. Mr. Preston made me wanna graduate, so I tried to keep it up when I could. Don't get me wrong. I didn't have all the answers. How could I? Was only fifteen. Sometimes, I starved, was cold, sick. I fucked up a bunch in that year. Got into fights. Woke up in strange places. Didn't know if I was coming or going sometimes. It all runs together sometimes. As bad as it was, I never once thought to go home, though. Never."

Nicole played with Dane's fingers briefly before kissing her cheek. "Because it wasn't home."

Dane turned to look in her emerald green eyes. There was no pity, but that level of compassion and sorrow that she had grown used to from Nicole. She leaned down and offered her lover a sweet kiss.

"No, it wasn't home." *But, this is.*

Chapter Four

NICOLE WAS OUT OF school and had taken three days off from work for their camping trip, giving her a total of five days off because of the weekend. Dane helped her load the car with their camping gear. Haydn would stay with Mina as usual. They dropped him off and then they were off to meet Raymond. Nicole practically bounced in her seat, obviously eager to start this trip right now. As Nicole pulled into the driveway of her parents' house, Dane was left astonished, her eyes wide and her jaw slack.

This was a mansion. Not quite like where Dane's parents lived, but definitely unexpected. Nicole's grandparents lived in a little, middle-class neighborhood like she and Nicole did.

"Your parents got a house like this off their own hard work?"

Nicole laughed. "Yes, not everyone inherits their money like your mother, or marries into that money, like your father."

A chuckle escaped Dane as she rubbed her head, pushing her hair back. "You know, sometimes I feel like I have no clue how the world works. I'm guessing that's because I was high for most of my life. Well, that, and I didn't care how the world worked."

Nicole only shook her head as she parked her car. "Didn't you earn a lot of money when you were leading your band? Isn't that when you were able to stop depending on random women to feed you and offer you a comfortable bed?"

For a moment, Dane could only look at Nicole. She was surprised her girlfriend had brought that up. Nicole was curious about her past, but didn't often bring up what Dane used to do for a warm place to stay. Dane didn't blame her. It wasn't like Dane wanted to think about people Nicole had been with.

"I did earn money, but that was entertainment. I can see how that happens, because it happens. It's hard to picture regular people building up their fortune to buy a mansion, though. Don't think I'd have made it this far unless I eventually signed with a label or something," Dane replied, glancing once more at the large estate.

Dane had never been inside Nicole's parents' house, and she didn't know what to expect. There was no valet, which her own parents tended to have whenever they had a party. And while the house was much smaller than her parents' house, she was quite impressed that a colonial style mansion could be earned through regular, basic hard work. She never got the impression that her father had been a good enough attorney to earn such a thing on his own, but then again, she didn't pay her father any mind.

"Your parents must be awesome at their jobs," Dane said, as they exited the car.

Smiling, Nicole nodded and stood with her head held high and proud as they stood at the door. "They are. They always have been." She rang the bell.

Dane looked, taking in the well-kept lawn and the lovely landscaping across the front yard. There were colorful, beautiful flowers in bloom, lighting up the area. A small statue of what appeared to be the Virgin Mary was nestled between some of the sculpted bushes. Dane couldn't help wondering about that, as she had gotten the impression that Kathleen wasn't a very devout Catholic. Nor was Nicole.

For a moment, Dane tried to imagine little Nicole running around the yard. Raymond probably allowed it, but Kathleen probably worried about her getting hurt or ruining the lawn. This yard had probably heard plenty of fun giggles in its time and held love in every perfect blade of grass.

A person that Dane assumed was the maid answered the door. She was a small, plump woman, probably in her late forties. Her creamy complexion seemed healthy and there were no real stress lines on her face, so Dane assumed that working for Kathleen wasn't like working for the devil. She had black hair that was done in a tight bun, and she was wearing a plain maid's uniform. She smiled at them.

Nicole's face lit up when she saw the woman and hugged her, so she had probably been working for the family for years. Dane had always felt more comfortable around her family's servants than around her family. She doubted Nicole was the same. Nicole looked at her family's servants as people, which was something the Wolfe family ever did, so at least Nicole would treat the woman kindly.

A bright smile danced on Nicole's face as she introduced the two. "Danny, please meet Mrs. Harlow. The only woman who can scold me better than my mother."

"This girl would leave her softball equipment all over the place," Mrs. Harlow complained, reaching out to shake Dane's hand.

Dane smiled. "I'd never believe that. She's the neatest person I've ever met." So neat, in fact, that living with her had turned Dane into a neater person.

Mrs. Harlow laughed. "I'm glad she's cleaned up her act then. She used to be terrible after games. There'd be muddy shoes, soiled uniforms, and equipment all over the place."

Nicole pouted. "I was not that bad." She laughed, which suggested she might've been *that* bad. It was a little hard to imagine.

Mrs. Harlow gave her a teasing smile. "No, you were *worse*. Your father's in the back, still gathering his camping equipment, and your mother's in her study."

Nicole nodded. "Thanks, but I want to give Danny a little tour before I start bothering Daddy."

Mrs. Harlow smiled, and Nicole took Dane by the hand, pulling her into the house. They stepped into the foyer, which was fairly large and held a dark wooden table with pictures on it. Dane wasn't surprised that the first thing she saw were family photos lining the wall, the table that Dane first noticed, and a table that was opposite it. The pictures weren't just immediate family, but there were pictures of all of Kathleen's family as well as pictures of people that Dane didn't know. She assumed those people were Raymond's family.

"I want to show you my bedroom before anything," Nicole said, with an impish glint in her eyes, leaning toward the stairs at the end of the foyer.

"Lead the way, Chem." Dane smiled, earning a chuckle from her beloved.

They made their way up the stairs, which also had pictures and such lining the walls. There were a few paintings and prints, but mostly family photos. For some reason, that warmed Dane and she thought it was wonderful to have a house full of family pictures.

"It's cool your parents have so many pictures hung up."

Nicole smiled. "They're both very family oriented. They have very supportive families."

Dane nodded. "Kinda know what that's like now." She gave Nicole's hand a squeeze. The redhead smiled at her.

The hallway went by in a blur, as Nicole pulled her into a nearby room. The room was as big as the master bedroom in Nicole's house, but this was not the master bedroom of the mansion. This was Nicole's bedroom from when she was a teenager. It was painted an inviting mint green. There were a few posters on the wall: a baseball player Dane didn't know, a softball player Dane didn't know, and what was probably a play Dane didn't know.

Her imagination went wild as she tried to picture Nicole here. Against the wall, by the far corner, was a neat and tidy white desk. She thought of teenage Nicole there, working on school stuff. Her heart fluttered a little, finding the image cute. She thought of teenage Nicole rummaging through the bookcase of five shelves, next to the desk. It was lined with books, as well as a couple of boxes and magazine holders, for researching school things because, surely, her lover had been a bookworm.

The image was disturbed as Dane looked around the rest of the room, and her mind wandered. A white vanity stood by the white canopy bed covered with a mint-green bedspread with outlined white hearts. Dane had to hold in laughter as she looked at this 'princess' bed, which held all sorts of pillows and plush toys. She couldn't imagine her lover, who underneath it all was very much a tomboy, had slept on this bed.

"Your mom bought this bed, didn't she?" Dane guessed.

Nicole smiled. "No, I picked this bed out when I was about ten. It seemed cool then. It's very comfortable, though. I didn't keep the decorative pillows and stuffed animals on the bed when I was younger. I think my mom did that, just to make the place look nice after I left for college. It's pretty much for decoration."

"This is a cozy place. Did you used to have friends over a lot?" Dane asked, flopping down in a nearby chair. It was quite comfortable, despite sitting low and somewhat reclining. It seemed like something to be found in a college dorm. *How many friends sat in this chair and gossiped with teenaged Nicole?*

"I entertained study groups and such," Nicole answered with a coy smile, as she sat down on a white chest at the foot of the bed. She had to slide a couple of plush toys out of the way.

"Oh, did my angel bring boys and girls up to her bedroom and...*study*?" Dane wiggled her eyebrows.

A little giggle escaped Nicole. "We were actually studying. My parents never allowed me to close the door when I had company. I think, early on, my mom worried I was gay, because she'd come in every five seconds if I had a girlfriend over, but practically praised me whenever I had a guy over. Of course, the door still had to stay open."

Twisting her mouth up, Dane looked around the room once more. "Your parents were really involved, huh?"

"Yeah, sometimes it was annoying, but eventually I realized they were worried about me, cared about me, and wanted to make sure I did the right thing. But, every teenager hates to be looked in on when they have company over. In fact, every teenager probably hates that they have parents whenever they have company over. I know I sure did. My mother was so embarrassing." Nicole smiled as she shook her head.

Dane laughed a little, even though she didn't know anything about that. She imagined it was true. It wasn't something she had ever worried about. Even if she had stayed home, she doubted her parents would've checked on her, her mother especially. She opened her mouth, about to share, but decided against it. This was supposed to be a fun time, after all.

"Nice TV and stuff." Dane motioned toward the television stand and DVD player, which was opposite the bed. It was close to the door. There were a couple of stacks of DVDs next to the DVD player.

"Yeah, I had a pretty good life here." Nicole nodded as she looked around and then her eyes settled on Dane. "I still have a pretty good life."

"Mine isn't so bad either," Dane replied with a smile of her own. She looked around the room. "So, wanna tell me something about the girl that lived in this room?"

"What do you want to know?"

"Well, when did she first develop a love of chemistry?" It was something Dane often wondered about, because she had never gotten into science or any school subjects.

"That was a late love that blossomed in high school. When I first stepped into a chemistry lab, it was like the world suddenly made sense to me. I mean, I've always been fascinated that things change, especially when something else is added in or taken away, but it came into focus in my chemistry class. I mean, the way things transform in chemistry and how things are made…I don't even know how to explain it. From that moment on, every elective I took was in chemistry, and I joined the science club. It was hard to attend because I was already on the softball team, the debate team, and my mother talked me into signing up for mock trial, but I did what I could. I enjoyed it and even showed up when I was dead on my feet, because I loved science."

Dane smiled. "Glad you're going after it again."

Nicole got up and went to sit on Dane's lap. The chair groaned a little from the extra weight, but Nicole didn't move. "Because of you and your encouragement. It's all thanks to you."

"Don't give me any credit, Angel. You had to make the decision."

Nicole's eyes shined and she leaned in to kiss Dane. Dane accepted and returned the show of affection. Nicole wrapped her arms around Dane's neck, bringing them closer together. Each touch of Nicole's lips sent warm waves through Dane, and she was certain she'd never tire of such a delightful touch. She sighed as Nicole pulled away from her, ending the wonderful kiss.

"Come on. Let me show you the rest of the house," Nicole said.

Dane pouted. "No more kisses?" She was tempted to suggest some role-playing, but neither of them would dare do that here.

A soft chuckle escaped Nicole. "Not if you don't want to chance getting caught." She laughed again as Dane grimaced. "Yeah, I thought as much. So, let me show you the rest of the house."

Dane gave a short nod and followed Nicole through the rest of the house, minus the master bedroom. There were two guest bedrooms upstairs and two small offices. The living room looked like it came out of a magazine, including shelves full of ribbons and trophies displayed by proud parents of their winning, only child. They went to the den next, which was across the foyer, and they both jumped because Kathleen was in there, which they hadn't expected.

Nicole recovered first. "Hey, Mommy." She gave her mother a smile while Dane's heart finally calmed down. Nicole moved over to the leather armchair Kathleen sat in and hugged her. Kathleen had to put down a notepad to return the embrace.

"Hello, Nikki," Kathleen replied without sparing Dane a glance. She was dressed in what Dane could only assume was a suit that she'd wear to work. She wore a pantsuit with a blush-pink blouse, complete with the jacket, while lounging inside of her own home. It wasn't surprising Kathleen dressed formally in her own house, but it was still weird. *It does explain a little about Nick and what she used to relax in, though.*

"Hi, Kathleen," Dane muttered, giving a weak wave.

As expected, Kathleen ignored Dane as Nicole sat down on a small sofa. Dane sat down next to her and looked around the den. *Or maybe it's a family room.* There was a bookshelf on the back wall. Well, more like the shelf was the back wall and it held more awards for Nicole. On the bottom shelf, there were board games. *Did they play board games as a family? Nick probably smiled a lot if they did. I liked that with the*

Briarmoors. Would Nick want to do that with me and a kid? We've never done it with Luke and Thomas.

Nicole patting her leg and laughing brought Dane out of her thoughts. Her eyes searched Nicole's face for some clue as to what she needed, but all she saw was an amused glint in her lover's beautiful emerald eyes. She smiled softly, knowing she had been busted daydreaming. Truthfully, she had little interest in what Nicole was speaking about with her mother. She actually felt like a trespasser and she knew Kathleen agreed.

"I was telling Mommy we're taking you on your first camping trip," Nicole said, holding her chin up.

Kathleen made a noise and frowned. "Enjoy yourself."

"Mommy never goes camping with us."

Dane could believe that. She couldn't see Kathleen camping, but then again, she couldn't see Kathleen doing a lot of things she was sure Kathleen had done. After all, Kathleen had grown up in a rather modest household. It was hard to tell that when the woman was sitting around the house in a suit that probably was worth more than Dane.

"Too many bugs, too much dirt, and there's no privacy." Kathleen wrinkled her nose.

The comment drew a laugh from Nicole. "There's bug spray, dirt is kind of the point, and you want to do stuff with the people you go with, which is why you go with people. Where's Daddy?"

"Actually, he wanted me to send you to him when you showed up. He swears you'll know where his camping tool box is because the Lord knows he has no clue," Kathleen said.

Nicole blinked and her eyes went wide. "I do know where it is." She turned to Dane. "I'll be right back. I need to go get that thing or we'll be here all day waiting for him to find it."

Nicole rushed off before Dane could respond, leaving her with Kathleen. She suspected that might've been halfway planned. She wasn't sure if Nicole, or Raymond, or both set it up, but it really felt planned. She squirmed a little, feeling like the air in the room got heavy.

Kathleen continued to ignore her, turning her attention back to the notepad she was reviewing when they'd first entered the room. Dane busied herself by scanning the nearby bookshelves. None of the titles seemed familiar, so she focused on the awards, wanting to see what else Nicole was a champ in. There were so many softball things, but also tennis and school stuff.

"So, she talked you into meeting her father's family during their one-time annual camping trip," Kathleen said out of the blue. She didn't take her eyes off her notepad, so it was as if she spoke to the air.

Dane couldn't control her hard blink as she drew her hand through her short hair. "Uh...she didn't talk me into it. I want to go."

Kathleen glanced up and made a curious, but soft noise as she focused back on her notepad. "I never would've thought you'd be the type to go camping, being a city gal and all." She didn't look at Dane at all as she spoke.

Dane opened her mouth, but closed it. She wasn't sure what was going on, if she was in a parallel universe or if she was being pranked somehow. Briefly, she wondered if she had fallen asleep in Nicole's bedroom and this was a dream. *What the hell do I say? What do I tell her? Come on, brain, make words!*

"I want to see if camping is like sleeping in the park," Dane replied, and then mentally slapped herself. *Shit, why the fuck did I say that? I don't want her to know I was homeless or else she'll keep thinking I'm a gold-digger!*

Kathleen arched an eyebrow as she looked up again. "Like sleeping in the park? Why would you want to make such a comparison? After all, once you go camping, then you have to go sleep in the park."

A grimace cut through Dane's face and she glanced away. "Uh...I covered the sleeping in the park already."

Kathleen stared at her now, notepad forgotten and sitting on the armrest. A small frown marred her face and her chocolate eyes studied Dane, almost as if she were about to cross-examine her. Dane did her best not to squirm or gulp. She hoped those words didn't bite her in the ass, even though she was certain it'd be hard for Kathleen to hate her any more than she did.

"You slept in the park? For how long?" Kathleen asked, sounding only curious and maybe with a hint of anger. Dane didn't know what to make of that.

"Uh...I never calculated the days." It was hard to figure out, even now, because of how high she was the first time.

"More than a week?"

Dane shrugged. "Uh...yeah."

Kathleen's gaze narrowed. "More than a month?"

"Yeah."

Now, Kathleen frowned. "More than a year?"

Her hand sailed through her hair. "Probably around that if you add up the days."

"So, you mean to tell me that your parents have all of that money at their disposal and they allowed their own child to sleep on the streets for almost a year?" Kathleen growled.

Dane blinked again, as she realized Kathleen was angry *for* her, not at her. Kathleen was outraged on her behalf. Her brain could hardly comprehend. She was dumbfounded, completely aphonic to the point she was sure Kathleen was questioning her intelligence. She nodded, if only to show she was paying attention.

"Why would they do that?" Tension tugged at Kathleen's face, making her scowl very tight. A vein in her forehead seemed like it was about to poke out, but it wasn't quite there yet.

Dane didn't want to risk opening her mouth and not being able to speak. She took a deep breath and swallowed, hoping to calm herself. *Maybe Nick was right. Maybe she likes me more than I thought.*

"They wanted a different type of kid," Dane managed to answer.

"So? They had you already. It's a parents' job to take care of their child, no matter what they wanted. They should take care of what they have," Kathleen stated before she sucked her teeth. "Every time I think that bastard Russell couldn't be any lower, I find out something new and unholy about him."

Dane's shoulders shook a little as she held in a slightly nervous laugh. "Yeah, tons of skeletons in that closet, probably. It's okay, though. Didn't want their help."

Kathleen shook her head. "That's another failure on their part then. Besides, you shouldn't have to ask for their help. They're your parents. They should've been there for you. That's what parents do. When were you sleeping in the park and why?"

Dane took a deep breath and rubbed her forehead. "I don't really...I don't really want to talk about it. At least not right now. Nicole deserves those details first." She wasn't sure if she'd ever be able to talk about it with anyone beyond Nicole, anyway.

"Does she know what I know?" Kathleen asked.

"Yeah, she knows that much and beyond."

Kathleen frowned and turned her attention back to her notepad. "Be careful while you're out there camping. Raymond's family...they're not as welcoming as mine."

Twisting her mouth a bit, Dane drew her eyebrows in close. "What do you mean?"

"There's a reason I don't go camping and it has nothing to do with bugs, dirt, or privacy."

Kathleen then began to write on her notepad and Dane knew the conversation was over. The world returned to normal where Kathleen pretended she didn't exist and she could breathe easy. Well, she would've been able to breathe easy if only Kathleen hadn't left her curious by simply talking to her.

She wondered if this brief moment of conversation was brought on by her little gift many months ago. She had sent Kathleen and Raymond flowers and thanked them for being good parents after she had to deal with her own mother. Or maybe Kathleen noticed how happy Nicole had been for the past few months and accepted that Dane had helped bring about that emotional state. She wasn't sure, but she was pleased she was wrong to think Kathleen completely hated her.

***

"Hey, Daddy." Nicole greeted her father with a smile as she stepped into the garage, which was more his man cave. He'd had such a thing before they were in style. It was his section of the house that allowed him to be alone and focus on his hobbies. Her mother had the same with a little sunroom in the back of the house where she grew plants and, very rarely, crocheted and knitted.

Her parents had long ago had a wide driveway paved on the side of the house, so that was where the cars went. There was a canopy built over it for days when it rained to prevent them from getting wet while going to the car. Thinking about that, for a moment, Nicole considered how good her parents were at their jobs. They had gotten so much work done on the house over the years. It hadn't really been something that crossed her mind, but now that Danny brought it up, she realized her parents were extraordinary, beyond being great parents.

"Hey, Nikki." Raymond was going through one of his tool cabinets. Her father was into woodworking and building things when he had the time. He enjoyed working with his hands.

"You still looking for your camping kit?" They exchanged a brief embrace, before he went back to searching.

"Yeah." Standing still for a second, he scanned the area. "Where's Danny?"

"I left her with Mommy." She jabbed her thumb behind her.

He chuckled. "You've made us both widowers."

"They'll be fine. They need to learn to get along. I want Danny to see that Mommy doesn't hate her, and I want Mommy to stop acting like she does hate her. I mean, I know Mommy's not a fan or anything, but I feel like if she gets to know Danny, she'll be happy I have Danny in my life."

Snorting, he looked at her with his mouth turned up on one side. "That's a tall order, sweetheart. Besides, I'm sure they both realized you did that on purpose. They might react poorly if you try to shove them together."

She shrugged. "I knew it could end badly, but I wanted to take a chance." It was worth it if things turned out right.

He shook his head. "Danny's first time in the house and you get her killed."

"Well, at least I gave her the tour beforehand. I showed her my room, and I told her about how you guys never let me close the door when I had company. Do you think Mommy thought I was gay when I was younger?"

Raymond was silent for a moment and, she suspected it was to make sure he didn't make an old mistake. When Nicole took a girlfriend to her senior prom, her parents accused her of being a lesbian. They got into a huge fight, because she didn't like the label. She knew she was still attracted to males as well as females. They were surprised when she started yelling back at them, but she couldn't take being called something she was not. They had no idea that she put up with every name in the book at school, and she refused to be subjected to the same thing at home.

"Well, you quit dance so quickly and took to softball like a fish to water."

"Wow, really?" Nicole asked as she drew back a little. She hoped that wasn't the real answer. She couldn't believe her mother was that shallow.

"I think your mom worried when she saw how touchy your softball team was. She doesn't get sports, you know? She doesn't get that you congratulate your teammates in certain ways. She was also concerned with the fact that you were always touching people when you were helping them with their batting stances and stuff. Hey, she was half-right." He gave her a playful smirk.

She laughed. "You guys always taught me to help if I could, and my coaches always encouraged me to help, too. One of the great things about team sports is working together and helping each other." It was a basic concept that she took to her heart, even now, which was one of the reasons why she used to get so rundown at work. She was a team player to a fault.

"Your mother liked that it taught you the importance of teamwork and kept you active, but she worried about your being a tomboy, of course."

Nodding, Nicole scratched her chin. "Did it ever worry you?"

"Honestly, I preferred it when you were a teenager. When you brought a boy home, I had a panic attack. I was so scared that my little girl was growing up and might be doing womanly things. Remember when you brought Grant home and I almost passed out?" He chuckled, even though that was very accurate. He had turned so pale that it looked like someone had tossed white paint in his face. His breathing had been so bad, and he held his chest, scaring her into thinking he was having a heart attack.

"I couldn't understand why you were so worried about Grant. He was so wonderful. He was the perfect gentleman, even when we broke up."

Raymond sighed, shaking his head. "I don't think you'll ever understand unless you have a little girl who decides to grow up."

"Is that a hint, Grandpa?" she teased.

"Grandpa?" The color drained from his face as his eyes went wide, and she laughed. "Don't do things like that to your father, Nikki, unless you want to give me a heart attack." He wagged his finger at her.

Nicole smiled and decided to help her father locate his camping kit. She guessed there were some things she'd never understand unless she was a parent. Hopefully, she'd get the chance, and she hoped her father was ready for it. The look on his face showed he hadn't given much consideration to being a grandfather.

***

Dane noticed Nicole and Raymond outside by a black SUV she didn't recognize. Nicole popped open the trunk of her car and began to move things from the car into the SUV. Dane moved to go help, but paused for a second, looking at Kathleen.

"Just remember, Raymond's family isn't like mine," Kathleen said.

Dane wondered what she meant. "Yeah, I'll keep it in mind. Sure you don't want to come?"

Kathleen's face twitched like something smelled bad. "Positive. This is the time I get to catch up on my own hobbies. You'll learn. Or maybe Raymond's family will help Nikki see what I couldn't."

Dane's forehead wrinkled at that. Just when she thought Kathleen was growing to like her, she seemed to pull back. Dane decided not to think about it and trotted outside as best she could to help pack for the trip. She could only wonder what Raymond's family was like and what Kathleen was trying to tell her.

"Need a hand?" Dane offered, as she stepped outside.

"Well, the sooner we get packed up, the sooner we get out of here," Raymond replied.

Dane fell right into step with them. Once they were done, Kathleen came out to bid them farewell. Thankfully, she and Raymond weren't big on public displays and parted with a simple kiss and hug. She also hugged Nicole, but pretended like Dane didn't exist.

They climbed into the SUV with Raymond behind the wheel. Dane sat in the back, getting comfortable on tan leather seats, with her guitar next to her. She made it a point to take it with her now, not because it broke the ice, but because music was back in her life. She had to play, she had to write, and the feeling struck her at any time. She liked being ready.

"So, Danny, Nikki said this is your first time camping," Raymond said.

"Formally, yeah," Dane answered with a shrug.

He looked at her through the rearview mirror, arching an eyebrow briefly. "You think you're ready for it?"

She shrugged again. "Yeah, I think I can handle it."

She had handled everything life threw her way and with Nicole by her side she had handled even more. But, her stomach flipped, letting her know there were some doubts. As she listened to Nicole and Raymond travel memory lane from the excitement of their family trip, she thought about how she had no family traditions to share with Nicole. Last year, Nicole took her to Thanksgiving with her family and Dane was so out of touch she didn't even know it was Thanksgiving. *How many people don't even have a Thanksgiving tradition to share with their partner?* She doubted there were many and, right now, she felt like the only person on Earth like that. *I'm so pathetic.*

Deciding her head was a dangerous place for the moment, Dane checked in on the father-daughter conversation. If nothing else, she might learn what she was in for. She might also learn about the people that she'd meet on the trip.

"Remember when Junior almost drowned Spider to keep himself from drowning?" Nicole asked with an amused grin on her face. Raymond laughed, so it must've been something funny, but Dane wasn't sure how two people almost drowning was funny. *Guess you had to be there.*

"I remember you were right behind them, and I had to almost snatch you out of your skin to keep you from going out in the river with them. Was it Junior's idea that you guys were going to surf in a river?" Raymond inquired.

"Who else would get me and Spider in a river with rotting tree bark?"

"It's a good thing your mother never came along. God, she'd have had a heart attack the first day. Imagine if she was there when you and Junior decided to climb that cliff."

Nicole snickered. "She would've killed you before having the heart attack, because she would definitely blame you."

"Thank God you didn't get Lil involved in any of that stuff. I always thought Lil would calm you down, but you followed Junior and Web like it was in style, even when she was there," Raymond said.

"Lilly never wanted to do all the fun stuff. We couldn't even get her to touch stuff."

"I love this, 'touch stuff.' It's a good thing you know what poison oak looks like. You hooligans were in the woods grabbing stuff. It explains when Beth came back to camp one day, arms full of mud. 'Oh, I think there's treasure in here.' Then you and the boys got all hyped up, swearing Beth had found pirate gold. Turns out it was nothing more than old pots. I hope you've all grown out of that!"

Nicole laughed again and Dane couldn't help sighing. Again, she wished she had something like this to share with Nicole. She didn't have cousins for Nicole to meet or tell interesting stories about. She could hardly share her stories with Nicole because they were mostly bad. *Oh, God, they're all going to be telling stories and times about their childhoods. What I am going to do when they ask me about mine? I'm screwed!*

Chapter Five

THE RIDE WAS THREE hours and Raymond drove the entire way. He and Nicole spent the first hour reminiscing about past camping trips and how many times she and her cousins had almost killed themselves or almost killed their parents. Dane could hardly believe her ears. She knew Nicole hadn't been a delicate flower as a child, but she hadn't expected her prim and proper girlfriend to be such a wild child.

"Danny, I swear to you, all the stuff you're hearing about happened before we were in double-digits, age-wise. We weren't this crazy when we started to realize you don't live forever," Nicole said, but then Raymond laughed.

Dane wondered if Nicole was understating when their antics had stopped. How did Nicole go from crazy young person to so put together as an adult? It seemed like such a big change, and Dane couldn't understand it. *Do all people change so much from teenagers to adults? Maybe it was just the company she kept?*

"Don't let her fool you, Danny. They continued almost killing themselves well into their teens. One of the last trips we went on we had to leave early after Beth fell out of a tree onto Junior, and they both had concussions. Beth was, what, seventeen when that happened?" Raymond asked Nicole.

"Okay, so maybe we had a few minor problems every now and then as teens." Nicole threw her hands up in defeat.

"They had problems all the way until the trips stopped. Our last one, they all almost got killed by a bear," Raymond said. Dane's eyes went wide at that news, especially since she hadn't been told there might be bears around.

"Daddy!" Nicole playfully swatted at her father, but didn't touch him since he was driving. "Now, you're telling stories. There's not a bear within a hundred miles of our campsite." She turned around to look Dane in the eye and let Dane see that she was telling the absolute truth.

"Thank God for that or one of you little monkeys definitely would've gotten eaten. Of course, you'd have given the bear indigestion, but still," Raymond said.

Dane chuckled as Nicole turned to give her a mock glare. Dane held her hands up in surrender. Before she could get into real trouble, the car pulled into a gravel driveway. Dane couldn't help looking up and down the drive to see that the nearest house was a decent walk away. *Is this, like, the country?*

Dane had been many places in her short life, but all those places involved urban areas where the nearest building was no more than five feet away. She wondered what it was like to live someplace where, looking down the road, she couldn't even tell if the neighbor had lights on. Once upon a time, she would've probably enjoyed that, but now, she felt like it'd bother her. *I'm less antisocial than I used to be, but nowhere near as social as I once was.*

Raymond and Nicole got out of the car and Dane followed and gave the house the once-over. It appeared to be an average, two-story home. There were a couple of cars parked in front of the SUV. There was a large garage with the door closed and Dane wondered if they used it the way she had learned Raymond used his garage, as an additional room in the house. They walked across the large, perfectly cut lawn. The soothing scent of fresh grass crept into her as they walked next to a lovely stone walkway that led from the driveway to the door.

The house was bigger than Nicole's. Dane could only wonder if it was a product of being in the country, or if Nicole's uncle was well off like his brother. There were flowers and bushes lining the raised front porch, a bay window to the side of the door, and another window on the extended right side of the house. Thin, white columns held the roof over the porch, and white railing ran between the columns. Another large window looked out onto the red-colored stones of the porch and stairs. All and all, it was a nice house, but felt imposing.

Nicole took Dane's hand while Raymond opened the door. Dane forgot there were places on Earth where doors were left open, even though she suspected she lived in such a neighborhood, now. Ten years of her life were spent in places where the doors were locked all the time. Even that didn't spare people the horrors of the outside world or hide the horrors of what they were doing from the outside world.

"Hello, hello," Raymond called as they stepped inside to a small foyer.

Dane gave the new area a quick study. There were pictures, which she had come to expect. There was also a mirror above a table, which held a little bowl that had keys in it. Down the hall, she could tell there was a kitchen, and she glanced to the side to make out a dining room. She didn't get to take in much more before finding out there were people home.

"Raymond? How did you get here so quickly? Did you kill people on the highway?" a female voice said lightly from somewhere in the house.

He chuckled a bit. "We slaughtered many to get here before five."

"I told her you would," a male voice replied before the owner of the voice came down the stairs that faced the door. He was a tall, broad man with dark, auburn hair. Dane couldn't help wondering if the Cardells were a family of redheads.

"Hey, Rich, how's it going?" Raymond pulled his older brother to him and they embraced, doing a man-hug complete with a back slap. Dane held in her laugh.

They could've been twins, except for the fact that Richard had a short beard and mustache, sort of like he was trying to be rugged. Richard was thicker than Raymond, and his t-shirt showed off muscled biceps. He had green eyes that were a bit brighter than Nicole's, almost like jade, and they shined as he gazed upon his younger brother. Raymond was the taller of the pair, though.

"It's going the same as always, man. What about you? You think you can handle camping after spending your life in a suit?" Richard laughed as he hit Raymond in the chest with the back of his hand.

"I can handle it as well as you. Where are your nutty kids, so we can get this circus on the road and I can show you up?" Raymond replied.

Richard scoffed and rolled his eyes. "You're living in a fantasy world now, huh? Laura'll call them to come now that you're here. We didn't think you'd be here for another hour. You got here really quickly."

Raymond shrugged. "No traffic, what with my killing people on the road and everything."

"I should've known." Richard smirked and then turned his attention away from his brother to Nicole. He grabbed her into a bear hug, practically engulfing her. They both laughed as he patted her on the back and then released her. For a moment, he gave her a look like the proud uncle he was.

"God, it's been way too long. I feel like the last time I saw you, you were in a cap and gown," Richard said, giving her one more squeeze.

"It's been a while, but not that long. What happened to the long beard?" Nicole asked, reaching out and tugging his short whiskers. He chuckled and continued smiling, making Dane think this was something normal between them.

"I told him it was me or the hermit beard." A woman approached the group with a confident stride, from down the hall, smiling as she grabbed Nicole into a hug.

She was shorter than Nicole and had flowing black hair without a spot of grey, despite her age. While she wasn't thin, she was in very good shape for a middle-aged woman. There were some lines near her eyes, but makeup covered them, for the most part. She was a lovely looking woman.

"Hi, Aunt Laura," Nicole grinned and stepped back from the embrace. She grabbed Dane by the hand. "Uncle Richard, Aunt Laura, I'd like you both to meet my girlfriend, Danny. Danny, my uncle and aunt."

Dane might've lived much of life in an alcohol and drug induced haze, but she had lived even more of it with people sneering at her. While Richard and Laura didn't openly frown at her, she could see it in their eyes. The cheer and joy left almost immediately, as she put her hand out and they got a good look at her. She wasn't sure what it was. She was dressed in her usual manner, but the clothes were relatively new, so it wasn't like she looked like a hobo. She hated to think it was another "h" word that bothered them. After all, Raymond never gave her the impression he had a problem with her being gay. He had a long list of other problems, of course.

But, then again, she should know by now that just because one sibling was all right with homosexuals, it didn't mean all were. After all, Kathleen's sisters never once batted an eye at Dane for being a lesbian, but it was definitely one of the problems Kathleen had with her. So, it was entirely possible for Raymond to be fine with gay people and his brother could have a problem with them.

"Uh...hi." Dane held her hand out, hoping they didn't leave her hanging. While she didn't think that Raymond's family hating her would be the end of her relationship with Nicole, she disliked being a reason why Nicole had issues with her family.

"Hi..." Richard said, almost as if in a daze. He gave her a handshake, and she tried to make it a strong one, remembering that had left an impression on Raymond.

Unfortunately, Richard didn't offer much in the handshake department, clearly trying to avoid touching her. Now, she had to hope this wasn't a race thing. She got enough of that bullshit from her own family. Of course, it was possible he was disgusted and offended by her obvious homosexuality that he didn't want to touch her.

She shook hands with Laura, but it was over as quick as it had been with her husband. Nicole noticed something was off because she grabbed Dane's hand as soon as it was free and held it tightly.

"I've been seeing Danny for a year now. It's been really nice," Nicole said, as if she was warning her uncle and aunt about something. Her eyes were sharp for a moment. "Before that, we were friends and she helped me through a lot."

"Danny's an interesting one," Raymond said, smiling a bit, like he was trying to let them know Dane was all right.

"Aren't they always? Nikki never dates boring," Richard remarked with a smile of his own, but it seemed kind of like an insult. It didn't help that the smile didn't quite reach his eyes.

Dane wondered if she was being judged by the assholes Nicole had undoubtedly brought around them before. Nicole had a track record. So, maybe with some time, she could prove she was nothing like the people Nicole usually dated...like she didn't have a full-time job or a place of her own. Groaning, she mentally shook that train of thought away.

"I'm pretty boring. I stay home most of the time," Dane said. Truthfully, she felt that all of her interesting days were behind her.

"When you hear her play her guitar, you'll see she's far from boring." Nicole puffed up a little.

"You play the guitar?" The news seemed to shock Laura. Again, it was something Dane could only wonder about.

Dane shrugged. "Yeah. I brought it for the trip. I mean, that's what they do on TV, right?"

Nicole laughed, but everyone else looked at her as if they weren't sure it was a joke or not. Richard and Laura even looked a bit disgusted with the remark, frowning a little. Dane guessed she had work ahead of her. But, she hoped the guitar would be a good icebreaker, as usual. If not, she had trivia on her side and a few embarrassing stories that rated PG-13 and wouldn't leave people thinking that she was a lowlife degenerate.

"I need to go finish packing my last bag." Richard used the excuse to go back to whatever he was doing upstairs.

"I was about to start making some travel snacks," Laura said.

"Oh, we can help, Aunt Laura." Nicole volunteered herself and Dane, pointing to them with her free hand. Dane managed to keep in a groan.

Laura didn't respond as she walked toward the kitchen. Nicole seemed to know it was all right to follow. She tugged Dane's hand slightly, as if pulling her to come along.

"You do realize these guys don't like me already," Dane whispered to her lover.

"Give them a few minutes. They're used to me bringing some fairly rotten people on trips. Once they see you're not like anyone else I've ever dated, they'll warm up to you. It'll be fine, just like it was with my mom's family," Nicole tried to assure her.

Dane wasn't inclined to believe that and wished Nicole would take off her rose-colored glasses for a moment. Of course, Nicole wouldn't be Nicole without her rose-colored glasses and way too much faith in the human race, especially those related to her. So, Dane decided to go along with it since she had to anyway. It wasn't like she could go back home or anything. She followed Nicole into the kitchen to see what she could help with. She hoped Nicole wouldn't be hurt if things didn't go the way that she wanted.

"All the real food and everything is packed already. I wanted to have some stuff for you guys to snack on while you're driving there," Laura said, as she pulled out a loaf of bread.

Nicole shook her head. "Aunt Laura, you don't need to make sandwiches. It's not even two hours away. You're going through way too much trouble for us."

"If I don't have the sandwiches, Junior and Spider are going to moan the whole ride about how hungry they are. Richard might do the same since he last ate a couple of hours ago and your father will probably do it, too," Laura replied.

"Are you coming, too?" Dane asked.

There was a beat of silence before Laura seemed to consider Dane worthy of an answer. "No, I'm not coming. I have a little ritual I follow for these trips, even if everyone is an adult." While she wasn't exactly rude, her tone seemed short.

Dane nodded and decided to keep quiet. She moved around the kitchen more than helped with anything. Every now and then, Laura would glare at her, as if she were in the way. Nicole gave her a sad smile, which she shook off. As much as she would like for Nicole's extended family to like her, she wasn't going to bend over backwards for them. She saved that for Kathleen, knowing she would have to deal with Kathleen for life if things went how they should with Nicole. These people she might never see again, or see once a year. She could deal with them.

What hurt was the way Nicole looked. She obviously wanted Laura to like Dane and with every glare Laura tossed her way, Nicole's eyes got sadder. If they didn't leave soon, Nicole might actually break down and cry.

The sound of the front door opening caused Nicole and Laura to turn for a moment, possibly saving them all from a scene. Dane hoped whoever entered would save her from any more of this awkward kitchen dance. She looked to Nicole to see if they'd go out and see who arrived or if they'd go back to helping with the sandwiches. Nicole stepped out into the hallway, so Dane did the same.

"Junior! Spider!" Nicole practically cheered as two large men closed the door behind them.

"Hey, Nikki!" both men replied with giant grins.

Nicole rushed over to the pair and hugged them. They both took a moment to lift her off her feet. They all laughed over it as if it was the funniest thing they could ever do together.

"It's been too long," Nicole said with an almost tearful smile.

"Way too long. Being an adult with a job is awful! Keeps me away from my favorite cousin," one of the men commented. He had dark brown hair that was cut short and brushed back. He had a mustache and a beard, but it looked more like he didn't bother to shave that morning. He was over six feet and dressed in a plain, black t-shirt and cargo shorts.

"Yeah, you're right. Oh, Junior, Spider, let me introduce you to my girlfriend, Danny." Nicole put her hand out for her lover. When Dane stepped next to her, she put her hand around Dane's waist.

The guys, to their credit, were much subtler than their parents. There was a facial tick on the one with the beard, but the other one actually smiled. He was another redhead, but it was lighter than Nicole's. His face was clean, but still rugged. He was taller than the other gentleman, but leaner. He was dressed casually with a short-sleeve, button-down shirt left open to show a white tank top with dark jean shorts. He offered his hand.

"Nice to meet you. Uncle Raymond told me a little about you. I'm Spider," he introduced himself politely and shook her hand.

"Danny," she replied, noting how rough his hand was. She also noted he had almost a full sleeve of various spider tattoos on his left arm, complete with a Spiderman symbol, a spider web, and a black widow. His right arm also had tattoos, but more like a half sleeve that his short-sleeve shirt mostly covered. She could also see some ink peeking out under his tank top. "Nice ink."

He smiled. "Yeah, thanks. I'm a bit obsessed, or so my father and uncle want me to believe."

"Daddy told you about Danny?" Nicole sounded a touch surprised.

"Just in passing. I spoke to him about some business stuff, and he was catching me up with you. So, I know you're back in school now, and I know you got a new girlfriend," Spider replied with a proud smile.

"I hope he said good things," Dane said. Spider gave a slight grimace, so she assumed it wasn't all sunshine and praises from Raymond. She wanted a few good words, not a speech as if she'd won the Nobel Peace Prize.

"It's a pleasure to meet you. I'm Junior," the other one said, jumping in to possibly save his younger brother from embarrassing four people at once. He shook hands with Dane as well.

"Are you sure pleasure's the right word?" Dane smiled to let him know she was joking, but, not really.

Junior only shrugged, but from the way he squeezed her hand in the handshake, she safely assumed *pleasure* wasn't the word that he really wanted to say. He released her hand faster than his younger brother, but not as quickly as his parents had. Dane mentally conceded it was probably going to be a very long trip.

Suddenly, a young woman pushed her way from behind the two men. They barely grunted as she elbowed them in their tapered sides, wanting to get past them. Nicole practically squealed and enveloped the young woman in a hug, picking her up off her feet. They both giggled as they hugged tightly. They stepped back, getting a good look at each other. Dane guessed the young woman was Lillian.

Lillian was another redhead. Her hair almost matched Nicole's perfectly. It flowed over her shoulders with a slight curl to it, not as much as Nicole's but close to it. She had cerulean blue eyes, as if a crayon had colored them in. She was smaller than Nicole by a couple of inches, and thinner. All and all, she was cute.

"It's been way too long, Lil," Nicole sighed, smiling all the way through.

"It has, but we've both been busy with work," Lillian answered with a smile of her own.

"I still wish that wasn't the case. I always miss you so much," Nicole said.

"What? You never miss us?" Spider grinned, earning a light smack from Nicole.

"I always miss you guys, but I miss my little sister in a special way," she replied, and her male cousins seemed to accept that without a problem. Lillian beamed as Nicole turned her full attention back to the younger redhead. "How are things working out for you? I bet Daddy could've given you a much better deal working for his firm."

Lillian shrugged. "I'm sure he would've, but I like living around here. I like being close to family, especially my brothers."

That drew another smile out of Nicole, and she nodded with understanding. Junior chuckled. "Now, if only Nikki felt the same." He hit her with the back of his hand on her bicep.

"I do, which is why I'm still close to home. I can't be physically close to everyone at once," Nicole replied.

"But, you should visit more often," Spider insisted.

"So should you. Speaking of visiting..." Nicole turned her attention to Junior. "When are you going to come back to fix my den door that you so gracefully pulled out of the wall, Mister Muscles?"

"Uh..." Junior glanced away and rubbed the back of his neck. "I had hoped you forgot about that."

Chuckling, she gave him a smile. "It's hard to forget when the door still isn't there." Once more, she turned her attention back to Lillian, taking her cousin by the hand. She pulled Lillian over. "I want you to meet my girlfriend, Danny. Danny, meet my little sister, Lil."

"Nice to meet you." Dane put her hand out.

There was a flash of something in Lillian's eyes that Dane thought she imagined. Lillian shook her hand firmly, more so than her brothers did. She smiled, even though, for a brief moment, it looked more like a smirk. Dane decided to ignore it.

"Nice to meet you, too," Lillian replied.

"So, are we ready to go?" Spider clapped his hands together, grinning.

"Beth isn't here yet," Laura said, as she stepped out to greet her children. She gave all three new arrivals tight hugs.

"She's at her mom's house. We're going to pick her up on the way." Junior jabbed his thumb behind him.

"Well, then, as soon as your dad finishes throwing things in one of his bags, you can be ready to go," Laura stated with a laugh.

Raymond shook his head as he joined the group, making the foyer extremely crowded. "He was always the last one ready and swore he wasn't the one that put us behind schedule."

"Dad is good for that," Junior chuckled.

"You're not much better." Spider swatted his brother on the shoulder.

"I'm still not as bad as him," Junior replied.

"No one will ever be as bad as Richard. We used to have to tell him the wrong time to make sure he showed up on time." Raymond earned laughs from his nephews.

They stood around chitchatting for a while. Dane was silent, with Nicole still holding her hand. She didn't mind. She wasn't sure what to say to Nicole's cousins, anyway. Junior and Spider didn't seem very interested in her, but Lillian glanced in her direction every now and then. After a couple of minutes, Lillian eased her way over to Dane.

"So, Danny, what do you do for a living?" Lillian asked.

"I give guitar lessons. You?" Dane countered, even though she could guess what Lillian did from her brief exchange with Nicole.

"I'm a lawyer. Not as big time as Nicole, but I do all right for myself," Lillian answered with a slight shrug.

"Only because you don't want to move to a bigger city." Nicole bumped her cousin with her hip. Lillian laughed, moving slightly off balance.

"Hey, your mother wanted to be close to her family, I want to be close to mine," Lillian said once more.

"I know, I know, I know," Nicole replied, holding her hands up in surrender.

"So, how did you meet Nikki?" Lillian asked Dane.

Dane glanced at Nicole, wondering what exactly she should tell. Nicole smiled and squeezed her hand, as if encouraging her to tell the truth. She had no problem with them, but as usual she didn't want to embarrass her lover.

"She helped me out when I was down on my luck, and we became friends before we realized we had feelings for each other," Dane vaguely explained. She figured that would keep Lillian from looking at Nicole as if she were crazy. After all, Dane still thought her lover was a little nuts for inviting a homeless person she didn't know to stay with her, even if that homeless person was related to her boyfriend at the time. *Sometimes, I gotta wonder if Chem's rose-colored glasses aren't also beer goggles from some of the things she's done.*

"That sounds like Nikki. She's always been nice." Lillian hit them with a bright smile and a perky bounce.

Dane nodded, but something seemed off to her. She couldn't put her finger on it and dismissed the feeling, as Richard made his way to the group. He held up a bag to show he was ready to go. Laura gave their travel snacks to Lillian and Nicole, and the group marched out. Richard and his offspring piled into an SUV; while Raymond, Nicole, and Dane got back into their vehicle.

"Beth'll ride with us," Raymond called to the other car.

"I hope she's ready," Nicole said.

"She should be. She's usually good with that," Raymond replied.

The drive was barely ten minutes with Raymond leading and Richard following right behind. They pulled up to an average, two-story house. There were no cars out front, and Raymond honked the horn. A woman emerged from the house with a large backpack and a duffle bag. Raymond got out and greeted her with a hug before opening the trunk and tossing in her bags. They both got back into the car.

"Hey, Beth," Nicole smiled, leaning into the back to give her cousin a hug.

"Hey, Nikki! It's been a couple of years, hasn't it?" Beth returned the hug. She sat down and glanced over at Dane. "Hi, I'm Beth," she easily introduced herself, offering her hand.

"Beth, this is my girlfriend Danny, and I think it's been more than two years," Nicole answered while Beth and Dane shook hands.

"Pleasure to meet you, Danny. Nicole's mentioned you in some of our emails and stuff. You play the guitar and you're awesome at music, right?"

Her having information kind of threw Dane off. She knew Nicole spoke with her cousins on occasions, but she never really got the vibe that Nicole spoke about her at any great length. Beth grinned, as if sensing her discomfort.

"Don't worry. She said nothing but good things, and she needed someone to talk to. Not like she could mention you to Junior or Spider," Beth said.

Dane arched an eyebrow and glanced at Nicole. "Why's that?"

"Junior and Spider decided on their own, a long time ago, to be the protector of their female cousins. That means they must hate all our partners until they prove worthy. I don't think they've ever liked one of Nicole's significant others," Beth replied.

"That's not true! They loved Grant," Nicole objected.

"You dated Grant when you were fifteen," Beth countered with a laugh.

"But, they liked him. He was awesome when we went camping."

"They didn't even like him in the beginning. It was only after he proved he was cool on the camping trip that they started to open up with him. Whatever happened with Grant?"

Nicole chuckled. "He was gay is what happened with Grant. Well, not gay. He ended up figuring out that he was attracted to people regardless of sex; he liked personalities, not genders. But, when we were dating, he wanted to step away because he thought he was gay. Turned out to be a good idea, not too long after that, I started to really think about my attraction to women."

"Do you still talk to Grant?"

Nicole shook her head. "No. We tried to keep it up through college, but things got too busy. Last I heard, he was an engineer with two kids and happily married. I hope that's true, and I hope he's loving life."

Beth laughed and nodded. "I hope one day we'll hear the same about you."

Nicole smiled and Dane silently gulped. She really didn't want to think about Nicole having kids right now. The car grew quiet as Raymond drove on. Dane studied the woman sitting across from her, if only to distract her from thoughts of weddings and children. Beth had a youthful face, slightly tanned. Her hair was short and chocolate, with what appeared to be red highlights. There were three faded scars on her cheek.

"How'd you get the marks on your face?" Dane asked before she realized what she was saying. She hoped it wasn't something horrible.

"The genius in the front seat dared me to ride my bike through some bushes when I was younger," Beth said.

Nicole snorted. "Oh, but who was the genius that actually did it for five stinking dollars?"

Beth laughed. "You're older than I am! You're supposed to know better than to dare me to do stuff like that!"

"Says who? At least Junior didn't dare you to do something," Nicole said.

"Yeah, I could've ended up in a thorn bush like you did," Beth remarked.

"I'm still amazed that you made it to adulthood having broken only one bone." Raymond glanced at his daughter.

"Funny, too, how I didn't break my arm doing something with Junior and Spider. You'd think, if I was going to break something, it would've been with at least one of them."

"I thought they'd killed you when you fell off the roof," Beth said, shaking her head.

"Oh, God, I remember Beth's face when she came in to tell what happened to you. I thought she was going to pass out. She couldn't even breathe. We thought she was the one in trouble, until she explained you died falling off the roof," Raymond said.

"I didn't die," Nicole replied.

"She thought you did. You traumatized the poor girl. She was crying so hard, and then she tried to beat up Junior and Spider for daring you to climb up there in the first place. It was a mess." Raymond shook his head.

Beth glanced at Dane. "Your girlfriend was a crazy kid. She was a true tomboy and didn't turn all ladylike until she met Grant."

Dane chuckled.

"That's not true!" Nicole tried to object, glaring at Beth.

"Oh, but it is! Let me tell you how this crazy, daredevil, softball player went from boyish to girly-girl almost overnight," Beth declared. Dane nodded, wanting to hear this.

***

Nicole groaned. She didn't mind the tale, even though she knew Beth was trying to embarrass her. She was happy to see one of her cousins getting along with Danny. She had been scared her cousins would be rude, and outright hostile to Danny. She had brought several lovers out to meet her father's family, just as she had done with her mother's family. The reactions were really the same. Actually, she considered the families themselves similar, so their reactions being similar wasn't much of a surprise. She hoped her father's family would react to Danny in the same manner as her mother's family had done.

She knew Junior and Spider would be the hardest ones to win over. It was as Beth said; they had long ago declared themselves the protectors of their younger cousins. It was rare for them to take to anyone's boyfriend or girlfriend immediately, but they did take to some. She had only experienced that once. She'd like to experience it one last time, even though their approval wouldn't affect her relationship. If her family liked Danny, and vice versa, then maybe she'd have incentive to come around more.

There was also the fact that Nicole really wanted Danny to interact with people more often. Danny needed to see humanity wasn't as horrible as they seemed. Yes, Danny had her friends, but it was just Crow and Terri. Crow was the only one who would drag her out to do things. Danny seemed to like going out once she was out, but it was *getting* her out that was the thing. She was getting better, and Nicole hoped she could encourage that.

"So, Nikki had this huge crush on Grant, and she tried to get his attention by wearing dresses and putting on makeup and stuff. She didn't want to ask her mom for help, so she tried to do the makeup herself. She looked like a clown! I'm talking straight, belongs-in-a-three-ring-circus-juggling-bowling-pins-making-balloon-animals-riding-in-a-tiny-car clown!" Beth was dying of laughter, as she recalled the horrible incident with unfair clarity.

"Hey, Beth, don't tell Danny any more crazy stories about me. She's not going to believe you, anyway," Nicole chimed in. Of course, her first experience with a makeup kit would happen when Beth was visiting. It could've been worse, she supposed, but she wished her humiliation had been a bit more private.

Beth laughed. "I'll save the real crazy stories until after she sees you camping for one day. Then, she will know everything I say is one hundred percent fact," Beth said with a wicked smile.

Nicole sighed because she knew that was the truth, but she didn't mind. She'd love for Danny to see this side of her. Hell, she'd love to let this side of herself out. It had been years since she had been able to let loose like she did when she went camping and was around her cousins. It'd be fun and she was certain Danny would have fun, too.

Chapter Six

THEY MADE IT TO the camping site in the early evening. Nicole inhaled deeply as soon as she opened the door, and Dane laughed because of the happy smile on her face. She must've heard because she turned and gave Dane a cute smirk. Dane only smiled back.

Dane took a moment to admire the scenery. The richness of the trees already let her know that the campgrounds were nothing like a park downtown, even the big ones that were supposed to give the city green spaces. It smelled so different from any park she'd been to. There were no lingering city scents, like popcorn or car exhaust. This was pure earth. The reality of wood, dirt, leaves, and clean air entered her in one breath and dominated her before releasing her, already changing her view of the world.

Glancing up at the sky, Dane noticed the sun was just beginning to duck behind tall treetops. She imagined it'd be a glorious sight when the sky turned orange, as if on fire and dancing above the green. She didn't get much of a chance to think about it or admire the natural wonder around her, though.

"Well, let's get moving while we still have sunlight," Raymond said, as everyone unloaded out of the two SUVs.

Everyone began grabbing their things and marching off a few yards to where they would be staying for the next couple of days. Beth greeted the cousins she hadn't seen earlier and then grabbed her gear. Nicole grabbed a few things and walked off with Beth. Dane was about to follow, after taking hold of her guitar, but she was delayed.

"You brought a guitar?" Junior asked with an arched eyebrow. He looked down on her with something like a tickled smirk and an amused glint in his eyes, mocking her.

"Yeah," Dane answered the obvious and watched as the brothers snickered as if sharing some funny joke. *Asses.* Of course, she had met and dealt with more than her fair share of asses, some even related to her girlfriend. *Guess I'll be ignoring them for this trip. Sorry Nick.*

"You've never been camping before, have you? You only saw it on TV or something, right?" Spider inquired.

"So?" Dane countered, even though she didn't care. Her guitar wouldn't save her now. Well, at least it'd give her something to focus on if the others didn't warm to her either.

"City girl," Junior said as if it was a great insult, shaking his head. Spider frowned before the pair walked off, weighed down by their camping gear.

Dane shrugged it off, even though they clearly had already developed a genuine dislike for her. She wondered if this was what Kathleen had been trying to warn her about. After all, she had used almost the exact phrase that Junior used. Maybe it was a family taunt against outsiders. She wondered if they even knew anything about her to judge her so harshly, so quickly. Even if they did, she didn't think they were being fair. Even if they thought of themselves as protectors, there was no reason to be rude and unjustly judgmental. *But, life has never been fair, so gotta soldier on.*

"Hey, don't mind my brothers," Lillian said, taking Dane from her thoughts. Dane turned to look at her and was surprised by how close she was. "They're like that with all of Nicole's suitors. It's a long list, so it's probably habit by now," Lillian said with a chuckle before walking off.

Dane blinked because that was an odd thing to say. She decided to shrug it off because the family could just be weird. She refused to let their negativity or strangeness ruin her first camping trip. She wanted to like this. She wanted to get into camping, because she wanted to want to do it again with Nicole and possibly her nephews and maybe even Haydn when they could trust he wouldn't lose himself in a hole or get swept down a river. She wanted to have a *thing* that she did with Nicole, something that could become a tradition.

She followed the family to the campsite, seeing them laughing and setting up. She didn't have time to feel out of place, because Nicole called her right over to help. She put her things down and jumped in as best she could. She ignored looks from the family and mumbled comments about her being a city girl from Junior and Spider. She noted Richard practically refused to even look at her, but she refused to let it bother her.

***

The sun was departing, lost behind the trees and the sky was a brilliant play of colors. If Nicole had a moment, she'd grab Danny and pull her off some place for them to watch the sunset, if not tonight then one of the other days they were here. Nicole was pulled from that thought by Junior's voice.

"Nikki, why'd you bring this girl camping? She clearly doesn't know what she's doing," Junior said as they finished with the set up. He snorted and wiped his glistening brow. They had worked up a light sweat in setting up, which she knew her male cousins enjoyed.

"What? She set up our tent all by herself," Nicole replied. Of course, Danny had gotten tons of practice at putting up the tent before the trip. She thought Danny was doing all right, so far.

"So what? My son could put up a tent and he's two." Spider yawned, stretching out his lean, sinewy arms. He didn't even bother to wipe away the shine of his skin.

Nicole rolled her eyes. "You know, if you guys give Danny a chance, you might find out you like her. She's not like anyone I've ever dated before, and I really don't want you to treat her like she is. She's a wonderful person, and I know you'd like her if you give her a shot."

Spider snorted. "Not like anybody you ever dated?" He made a face, sticking his tongue out and looking like a jerk.

"So, we won't have to hear her screaming about there being bugs on her?" Junior inquired.

"She wouldn't scream if there was a bear on her," Nicole replied. She truly believed Danny would try to talk the bear down and if that didn't work, she might try to fight the bear off. Danny wasn't likely to scream, because that'd bring help and, really, the only person Danny accepted help from was Nicole. It took a serious emergency for Danny to request others to assist her.

The brothers twisted their mouths in disbelief. "Let's be serious, Nikki. That girl hasn't been in the woods before. She probably thinks this is a big park," Spider said.

"Uh...cuz, I love you and all, but you do know this *is* a big park, right? Giant national park," Nicole replied, making a whirling motion with her index finger.

Spider got red in the face while Junior hid a snicker by turning his head. Spider glared at his older brother with incensed lime-colored eyes, which only made Junior stop hiding his laughter. In fact, Junior let out a loud, belly laugh to irk Spider more. The noise earned them some glances, but nothing more. Everyone, except for Danny anyway, was used to the brothers.

Nicole shook her head. She needed them to see how great Danny was, because she truly believed they'd love Danny if they took the time to get to know her and accept her. She imagined all the great trips and good times they could have, if only her cousins saw how good Danny was.

"That's not the point. The point is she's probably as clueless as the last two idiots you brought with you," Spider said.

"She's not totally clueless and, unlike those people, she's willing to learn if you give her an opportunity to do so." Nicole scowled. "So, how about, instead of judging her, especially based on evidence from other people, you give her a chance? You never know, you might like her."

"Give her a chance? What? So, she can set fire to the camp like the last asshole you brought around?" Junior huffed, scrunching up his face a bit.

Nicole flinched and stepped back. "Uh…" She was at a loss for words briefly, because that seemed like an attack on her and, despite not liking her past partners, her cousins had never attacked her over it. "You know what, I'll keep her away from you guys. I hope you enjoy the trip." Nicole turned to walk away. She wasn't going to put up with shit from them on Danny's first camping trip. She'd make sure Danny had a good time, so they could do this again with just the two of them.

"Nikki," Junior sighed, reaching out and taking her by the wrist. Even though she halted, he still held her securely, but in a gentle manner, as if that were his apology. "Don't be like this. We want to have a fun trip and it's usually best when it's just us here. You're not the only one who's brought around party poopers. I'm not saying it's your fault or anything."

She turned to face them again and frowned slightly. "No, you're saying you don't like Danny because I brought her and that means she's more than likely an asshole. But, you don't know her and you don't care to know her. That's your right, but I'm not going to let you ruin her first camping experience by being an ass to her."

"We're not going to be asses to her," Junior replied.

"She'll handle that," Spider mumbled, earning a heated glare from Nicole.

"You two may not get this, but I love her. Okay? I fucking love her and I'm not going to let you treat her any way you feel. So, if you're not respectful to her, then keep your distance. Understood?" She narrowed her eyes and scowled at them, wishing her stare alone could hurt them enough for them to understand.

"We got it." The brothers sighed.

From the way they glanced at each other, she wasn't inclined to believe them. She'd jump down their throats, if necessary, if they did anything to Danny. She decided to talk to Danny to make sure she knew she didn't need to take the abuse.

She was tired of Danny putting up with open scorn, ridicule, harsh words, and even worse treatment because of her. *She's not always going to put up with being degraded and she shouldn't have to. But, what if she blames me?* Nicole managed to shake that thought away. Taking a deep breath, she reminded herself she was secure in their relationship. She and Danny were doing well, and she wanted things to go smoothly. She wanted their relationship to last forever.

She just wanted Danny to be happy, and she'd allow Danny to find that path, however she believed was right, as long as it didn't involve excessive drugs or alcohol. As soon as she was done with her tasks, she made her way over to her beloved, who had made herself comfortable on a rock a few feet from everyone else. She seemed to be watching them and purposely staying out of the way, which made Nicole frown. *I hope they haven't ruined this for her already.*

"Baby, don't worry about them, okay? They're being mean-spirited right now. It has nothing to do with you." Nicole rested her hand on Danny's knee. She softly caressed the area.

"But, they're your family," Danny replied. "You like them, so I want to like them, and I want them to like me."

"It's all right. If you've taught me anything it's that sometimes, no matter what you do, people won't acknowledge how good you are. You're perfectly fine and if they can't see that, it's their loss. I want you to have a good time while you're here and if that means I have to steal you away and we do things on our own, then so be it." Nicole moved closer to Danny. She put her free hand on Danny's other knee. She was careful since that was Danny's bad leg.

Danny's smile bordered on perverse, but Nicole decided against scolding her. Danny's day had been rough, so her mind could take a trip to the gutter if it wanted. Of course, whatever she was thinking would stay in her mind until they got home. *I guess if things are really bad, I can at least spend some time at home making it up to her.*

"You won't get more than a kiss out in these woods, Big Dog," Nicole said.

"I'll take what I can get," Danny replied, still smiling. She opened her legs a little, giving Nicole room to step in between them if she wanted to do so. Nicole held off, thinking that might be too much. Danny didn't appear bothered by the decision. "I'll do my best to have a good time, but like I said, I wanted your family to like me. I didn't think I'd be judged as soon as they saw me." She sighed and ran her bronze hand through her hair.

"I didn't think they'd do that either. I was sure they'd like you. I mean, you're not very different from them. They work hard, just like you, enjoy the outdoors, and even like dogs. I still think they will like you once they see you're nothing like the people I used to date. I think that's the real problem anyway." Nicole closed the space between them and put her arms around Danny. She pulled her lover into a warm hug.

"So, it's not really me?"

Nicole shook her head. "Well, I hope it's not. I mean, if it is, then that means they can judge someone two seconds into knowing them and be dead wrong. They're not the people I thought they were if they do that."

Danny was silent, and Nicole decided to enjoy the press of their bodies together. Placing a gentle kiss to Danny's forehead, Nicole pulled away. She looked down at Danny for a moment before Danny nodded toward the rest of the camp, quietly urging Nicole to join her family. She gave Danny one more kiss before leaving, thinking Danny might want to be alone for a moment. Besides, she might need to get enough family time in before she'd have to step away from her cousins. If they really didn't like Danny, well, this was the end. She wouldn't give Danny up because they were jerks.

***

Dane watched as Nicole joined her cousins and they laughed over something. She was glad Nicole was enjoying herself. Now, she needed to figure out a way to enjoy things, without somehow ruining the trip for Nicole. She figured she had to do something that at least wouldn't make the family dislike her even more.

She had her guitar next to her, so she wasted no time picking it up. She was about to play when Lillian suddenly sat down next to her. To say she was surprised by the company didn't begin to cover it, but she made sure not to show it. While Nicole seemed fine with the idea of her avoiding the family, she doubted her girlfriend was all right with her insulting them, even if it was with a simple facial expression. She also doubted it'd endear her to these people if she gave as good as she got.

'*These people*'? Dane echoed in her head. She realized she had already set herself apart from them, mentally, in the same way they seemed to dismiss her as 'the other.' She'd have to stop doing that if she wanted to become an insider. *I never thought of Kathleen's family as these people. Weird.*

"Not going to join the festivities?" Lillian arched an eyebrow and nodded toward her family. There was a strange glint in her eyes that Dane decided to chalk up to a trick of the twilight.

"Eventually," Dane replied. *It's not like I can sit away from camp for the whole three days.*

"What's the problem? I mean I'm sure you know how to camp and everything. It's not like this is your first time out, right? I mean that's one of the main problems with the other people Nikki brought. They never knew what the hell they were doing and always messed stuff up. I doubt she'd ever bring another novice out here, knowing how much everyone hates that. So, you should be fine."

Dane shrugged. "Yeah, I should be fine." Nicole had prepped her for the trip as far as the motions of camping, and she had plenty of experience in living outdoors. Of course, that didn't translate into camping experience, so she was still very much the novice and probably going to make some mistakes. *Great, I can see this is going to be much like the story of my life—it gets worse before it gets better.*

"Yeah, you're nothing like the other people Nikki's brought around. I mean, you don't even look like them. She always showed up with some business-looking asshole, even when she was in college. They were always dressed in these designer clothes, wearing big-name brands, even in the woods. One girl she brought out here had brand new expensive boots, and she got uppity and belligerent when mud got on them, like it was our fault. I mean, come on, duh. It's camping, in the woods, of course there's going to be mud."

No one could accuse Dane of wearing designer clothes. Some of her gear was name brand, but mostly because Nicole bought it and it was better made than the things Dane dug up at secondhand stores. She'd never complain about mud or really anything from nature. *People are the assholes, not nature.* But, what she really wondered was where Lillian was going with this little discussion, if it could even count as a discussion.

"You know, you're probably more Nikki's speed, anyway. I've met some of her other lovers, beyond the ones she's brought on the camping trip. You're nothing like them." Lillian nodded to herself. "I mean, they didn't know Nikki very well. They were always shocked by stuff she did."

"Shocked, huh?" She guessed they were shocked to find out that a prim and proper woman like Nicole would, or could, enjoy camping.

"Oh, yeah. They couldn't do much with Nikki...in bed. You know." Lillian wiggled her eyebrows.

No, I don't know. What the fuck is this girl talking about? Are we supposed to be bonding or something? Dane ran her hand through her hair, trying to figure out what was going on. Whatever it was, she didn't like it.

"I don't really want to hear about Nick in bed with anyone else," Dane replied honestly. If she wanted to know about Nicole's sex life before her, she'd go to the source. She hadn't done that because she damn sure didn't want to know.

Lillian's eyes went wide, as if she were the one surprised. "Oh. I figured you'd have already heard all the stories. I guess Nikki doesn't talk about that stuff, huh? Well, not with you, anyway."

"No," she stated as bluntly as possible. She tensed and squared her shoulders, glancing around. She attempted to mark out an escape route.

"She used to talk to me about stuff like that, when we talked more often, before we both got really busy. She was wild. I figured...well, that she was with you to feed her wild side." Lillian gave Dane a strange, sidelong glance with a bit of a smirk.

Again, Dane wondered what the girl was babbling about. She felt insulted, but she couldn't entirely figure out why. It seemed like Lillian judged her based on her appearance, but she couldn't pin down what exactly Lillian judged her about. There also seemed to be something weird about the way she spoke about Nicole. It wasn't what Dane expected, but then again, she really didn't know what to expect. Something was off, though.

"Nick has a wild side?" Dane couldn't help sounding skeptical. While she imagined Nicole had been quite the tomboy from the way Junior and Spider treated her like one of them, she couldn't see Nicole having an adult wild side. Hell, she couldn't even see Nicole having a teenage wild side, beyond being a tomboy.

"Oh, yeah. Well, she used to. Maybe she grew out of it. She used to tell me some crazy things she did with her boyfriends. Oh, and girlfriends. Crazy things. I guess, I thought that…never mind." Lillian shook her head and waved the whole thing off with one hand.

A frown worked its way onto Dane's face and she couldn't do anything to hide it. The hairs on her body prickled a little each time Lillian open her mouth. Lillian bothered her in some way she couldn't put her finger on yet. *I'm not sure I want to find out, either. This was the woman Nicole considered her little sister.*

"I don't know about feeding her wild side. I guess she just wanted a change," Dane answered with a slight shrug. She was certain one of the reasons Nicole loved her was because she was incredibly different from any lover she'd had in the past.

Lillian looked her up and down. There were hints of a smirk on her face. For a moment, Dane considered Lillian was hitting on her, but she was certain that wasn't it. There was something about Lillian, and now it was creeping into Dane, crawling slowly through her. She was unable to suppress a shudder, feeling invaded.

"You certainly are different. No suit, no pretentious vocabulary, and your nose isn't stuck in the air. Completely different," Lillian said, and Dane wondered if that was supposed to be a compliment.

"Yeah, well, just trying to make Nick happy," Dane replied.

"Well, I'm sure if you're just, you know…" Lillian wiggled her eyebrows again and Dane wanted to punch her in the face. "All that in the sack, then you're probably keeping her really happy."

Dane decided she didn't like Lillian, and she was thankful when Lillian walked away. She wasn't sure what to make of that conversation and she was almost certain she didn't want to know what it was all about. Putting it out of her head, she picked up her guitar, planning to work on her music. She didn't get the chance. Beth wandered over, standing right in the spot Lillian had vacated.

"Hey, I want to know if it's cool with you that I took this picture." Beth held up her camera. She showed the most recent photo to Dane, which happened to be her as she was reaching for her guitar.

"You're good at capturing an image," Dane said. The lighting in the back with the fading sunlight breaking through the trees made it seem like some mystical moment.

Beth chuckled. "I need to be if I want to feed myself."

"You know, you should show it to Nick. She likes hanging your prints up and she might like the picture."

Beth nodded. "All right. I owe her some prints. I haven't sent her a picture in months. You okay?"

Sighing, Dane looked around. "Yeah, I'm good."

Beth nodded toward the others. "Then rejoin the group. We're about to start cooking and hopefully we'll be done before it gets dark. We're going to tell ghost stories once the sun goes down."

Chuckling, Dane nodded. "Now, that sounds like something right out of a TV show."

Beth laughed again. "You're right, but it's something our fathers started when we were younger. They used to scare the crap out of us. Imagine a tent full of kids jumping at every sound in the woods, swearing a ghost bear was going to come eat them."

Dane smiled a bit, picturing a tiny Nicole huddled together with her cousins, flashlights on, unintentionally encouraging each other to be afraid of the dark. The very thought made her feel light inside, and she'd love to experience things like that. Beth tapped her on the shoulder, jabbing her thumb toward everyone else. She walked off, in case Dane didn't get the message.

"I like that one a lot more," Dane decided as she hopped off the rock. She rubbed her knee a bit and strapped her guitar around her shoulder. She was hungry enough to endure whatever the hell they wanted to put her through, and she wanted camping memories with Nicole just like everyone else had. Sure, they might not involve huddling together, thinking they were going to be eaten by a ghost bear, but she'd take anything.

Nicole glided over to her and wrapped her arm around Dane's. "I'm glad you decided to join us. I was about to come kidnap you to eat." She smiled.

"You don't have to do that. I'm pretty interested in food," Dane replied with a grin.

"Good because we're about to make some campfire chili dogs," Raymond declared.

"Chili dogs?" Dane was very interested now. She wondered how they were going to do that. She'd never seen cooking done over a campfire.

"Too rich for your blood?" Spider sneered at her.

Dane chuckled. They acted as if she were pretentious; when she was certain she was the only one among them who knew hunger pains; knew what it was like to go for days without food; and knew what it was like to sleep on the cold ground, because there were no other viable options. Of course, she didn't suffer much considering she starved on days she was high.

"Considering how many chili dogs Danny wolfed down at her first baseball game, I think we might have to feed her last," Raymond said, and winked at her.

"That wasn't a pleasant night, I will tell you that," Nicole added, shaking her head. "She complained about her stomach for the rest of the night."

"Considering they were baseball dogs, I think you got off lightly with her just complaining. Eyes bigger than your stomach that time, eh?" Raymond threw her a teasing smile.

With a half smirk, Dane held her head high. "It was still better than watching baseball."

There were collective gasps. Clearly, the national pastime was the family pastime. Well, that wouldn't make Dane learn to like the sport, or any sport, really, that didn't involve partially clothed ladies. The only reason she watched football now was because Nicole's grandfather pretty much forced her to.

"You don't like baseball?" Junior shook his head and glared at her.

Richard did the same. "That's a damn shame. Not that I expect anything less from someone Nikki brought." He muttered that under his breath, but it seemed clear enough for others to hear since Dane did. She didn't like that statement and was about to say something, but the air was filled before she could open her mouth.

"How can you not like baseball? You might as well say you don't like Nikki while you're at it," Spider declared, throwing his hands up.

"She likes me more than you think since she sits with me through every baseball game I watch." Nicole smiled proudly, like Dane made some great sacrifice for her. She took Dane's hand and gave it a little squeeze.

Dane only smiled and shrugged. The family looked at her oddly, but Raymond smiled. Dane figured that was a good thing. She made sure to stay out of the way as dinner was prepared. It was not as complicated as she thought it might be. Honestly, beyond knowing how to set up the equipment, camping didn't seem that complex. She'd like to do this again, with her nephews and Nicole. It didn't matter how crappy this trip was.

"Don't gorge yourself this time." Nicole wagged her finger at Dane with a grin, as she handed Dane a chili dog.

That got a chuckle out of Dane, who ate several chili dogs. "They're so good," she moaned, patting her stomach. She licked her fingers, making sure to get any stray chili off her hands.

Raymond grinned. "I know how to make chili dogs."

Junior and Spider kept pace with Dane while everyone else appeared quite disgusted with how many franks they put away. Nicole ended up putting an end to the unspoken contest after Dane ate four dogs. That probably was Dane's limit, but she didn't know because she never stopped at four. Of course, it usually didn't end well once she made the decision to stop.

"God, do you have a cast iron stomach?" Beth asked Dane.

"Nah, I just like what I like," Dane answered with a grin.

"That was possibly the most disgusting thing I've ever seen." Lillian shook her head.

"It was rather gross, love," Nicole said with a slight frown.

Dane shrugged, knowing Nicole was probably thinking back to the last time she had a bunch of chili dogs. She had done her best to suffer in silence that time, but Nicole had developed a sixth sense when it came to Dane's wellbeing. Suffering alone wasn't allowed if it could be helped.

"So, who has a ghost story to share?" Nicole inquired as the darkness settled in. Dane couldn't believe they actually did that.

***

Nicole sighed as she and Danny settled into a two-person sleeping bag. They lay on top of an air mattress, even though Danny claimed that didn't count as real camping. Of course, Nicole had laughed at that.

"Trust me, it's still real camping, because we have a tent," Nicole said.

Her lover laughed and gave her a lopsided smile. "Oh, is that what makes it camping?"

"Well, part of it. You've seen other parts of it."

"I can't believe you guys actually tell ghost stories and make s'mores, which are fucking delicious in case you didn't know," Danny said with a chuckle.

"I'm not sure which I find more incredible, the fact that you ate that many s'mores or the fact that you actually scared them with that story. Did you actually ever stay in a haunted house?" Nicole inquired, even though she suspected she knew the answer.

Danny smiled. "I knew someone that did."

"Of course," she laughed.

As her laughter faded, they both made themselves comfortable. Nicole tucked herself against Danny, who put her arms around Nicole. Nicole sighed contently, caressing her lover's hip.

"I can't believe you've never had a real s'more before," Nicole said. It was a little sad to her, like so many things Danny never got a chance to do. Danny had been so cheated.

"I'm glad I had 'em now. I hope Luke and Thomas haven't had them before. I want to see their faces when you make them their first one."

Nicole beamed. Even though her family had been unfriendly, Danny wanted to do this again! That was great because Nicole rather enjoyed camping, at least for a couple of days. It was relaxing and peaceful.

"We can come camping one weekend when they're free if their father allows it," Nicole said. She'd have to start planning right away, and they'd have to be very nice to Adam to butter him up.

"I think it'll be fun, especially telling them ghost stories."

"We probably wouldn't be able to sleep alone like this."

Danny smiled. "I don't think I'd mind. Although, I like this, too." Her hand crept toward the hem of Nicole's shirt.

"You stop that!" Nicole giggled, gently slapping at Danny's wandering hand. "My dad is less than fifteen feet away from us. Do you really want to make that impression? You want my dad to hear you making me scream and beg? You want him to never be able to look me in the eye again and make him want to kill you?"

There was a light laugh. "No, I don't want that. I'll behave. After all, I'm starting to see what you mean by your father liking me. I'm really glad he's warmed to me. He's a nice guy."

"Yeah, I know. My dad's great. He sees you're a good person, too, and he knows you take good care of me. He sees I've been happier with you than any other person I have ever dated. I think, after this trip, he'll probably be even better with you."

"As long as I don't screw up," Danny mumbled.

"Unless you dump me on the trip or purposely injure me, I don't think you'll have much to worry about. Oh, and definitely don't give him the impression we're having sex in the tent."

That got an arched eyebrow from Danny. "What?"

"I brought a college boyfriend up here one time. He was joking around, making sounds like we were having sex, and my dad almost killed him the next morning. We couldn't share a tent for the rest of the trip. In fact, we couldn't even sit next to each other on the ride home. Junior and Spider took him into the woods for a few minutes, and he came back white as a sheet. At first, I was a bit upset, but we broke up a couple of months after the trip, anyway. Actually, I told you about him already."

Danny blinked a few times and her forehead wrinkled. "You told me about him? I don't remember this story then."

"No, not this one, but it's the same guy who thought he could shove his fingers places I didn't want them." She frowned.

Danny frowned and she was quiet for a while. Her hand drifted from Nicole's hip to just behind, calmly stroking the area with her fingertips. In the past, Nicole would've tensed, even with Danny. She had slowly managed to taper the reaction after Danny pointed out the unconscious panic. She trusted Danny and knew there was no way Danny would ever disrespect or violate her in the manner her former boyfriend had.

"I feel like I'd hate all of your former lovers and not because they were lovers or because they had you first. Have you ever dated someone who treated you with the love and respect that you deserve? Did anyone you date notice they had an angel in their lap?" Danny asked quietly.

"My first boyfriend, Grant. He was a sweetheart. I'd had a crush on him since junior high, but we didn't go out until we were fifteen. I brought him on one of these camping trips. He was great. He did all of the crazy things we did. I think he's the only person I've ever brought here that Junior and Spider didn't want to beat up almost immediately, which I think was because he knew a lot about cars and stuff."

"They're into cars?"

"They're mechanics. They own their own garage. Uncle Richard's a tow truck driver, and they grew up around all sorts of cars. They're gear-heads and Grant was a gear-head. It got him an almost instant in with them."

"So, what happened with Grant?"

"The same thing that happened to me, oddly enough. He found himself attracted to a boy and it really confused him. I told him that he needed to figure it out and he agreed, so we broke up. Not too long after that, I found myself attracted to a girl."

Danny nodded. "So, whatever happened to this only nice guy you ever knew?"

Nicole frowned slightly, and she quickly got rid of the expression when she realized what she was doing. Whenever she thought of Grant, she felt a bit of a hole in her. It wasn't as acute now as it had been in the past, but it was still there. Sometimes, on dark days, she wondered what would've become of them if they had remained together. She never spoke the words aloud, but it echoed in her mind occasionally.

"He hurt you?" Danny's voice was quiet, gentle.

"No, he didn't hurt me. I was the one who urged him to figure out what was going on with him. I wanted him to be happy."

"Is he?"

"I used to email him every now and then, but we've fallen out of touch, busy with life and everything. From what I remember, he seemed okay. He's married now with two small children. According to him, he had all of the gay sex he could stand in college." She laughed.

Danny laughed, too. "I do not feel his pain. I'm hoping for a lifetime of gay sex." She held Nicole a little tighter.

"I'll try to oblige, but you'll have to understand, there'll be days when I will have a headache or two."

A smile remained on Danny's lovely copper face. "I'll take that as long as you're lying next to me or letting me bring you aspirin."

Nicole smiled and offered a kiss to Danny's shoulder, the closest body part to her. "Of course."

"So, how many boyfriends have you brought up here for camping anyway?"

"Just those two. I have also brought two girlfriends. One liked camping a bit too much and came up here with guns, thinking we were going to go hunting, too. The other hated everything about this and even complained it was too dirty."

Grey eyes blinked in disbelief. "Too dirty? Didn't she realize there's dirt in the woods?"

"I don't know what she thought it was going to be like. I think she wanted to meet more of my family, thinking they were wealthy beyond belief because of my parents. Of course, she was wrong, which made her so grouchy and uppity. Junior and Spider were unkind to her."

Danny snickered. "Sounds like I could like these guys if only they weren't unkind toward me."

"I think you'll grow on them, but they're probably going to harass you, now that I think about it. They harass everyone I bring up here. Hell, they even harassed Grant. But, I'm pretty sure you'll grow on them."

"Like a fungus?" Danny joked.

Nicole laughed. "Yes, like a fungus. Isn't that how you've grown on me?"

"Think I've grown on you more like a barnacle." Danny hooked her leg around both of Nicole's.

"Yes, well, once upon a time, you weren't so attached to me."

Danny smiled. "Things evolve and change. You've changed me. I know I can depend on you, and I know it's all right to let you take care of me. And don't let that go to your head."

An innocent smile lit up Nicole's face. "I would never do that, Big Dog!"

"I'm so sure."

"I'm glad you're open to that. I'm glad you're here."

"There's no place else that I'd rather be, Angel."

Nicole smiled and leaned up to press a soft kiss to Danny's lips. They sighed and settled for sleep. Though, Nicole's mind wasn't ready to turn off yet. She went back to thinking about Grant, but not in any way that she could recall having done before.

Did Grant's wife make him feel as special and loved as Danny made her feel? She hoped that was the case. He was the only person she'd ever described as a sweetheart before she was with Danny. Danny's words echoed in her mind, *he hurt you*. Maybe he had in a way, and she had spent her entire life dating people that wouldn't remind her of him. *It doesn't matter. I would do it all over again if it brought me to this moment.*

For once, instead of looking back at her love life with regret, she smiled at it. Everything that happened to her with her lovers had brought her to this point. Danny was it for her. She loved Danny more with each day that passed, and she enjoyed the fact that they were growing together, learning together. So, she was going to enjoy this trip, no matter what her cousins did.

"And then we'll do this again, just us and maybe the boys," Nicole whispered, giving Danny another soft kiss. Danny purred and her grip on Nicole tightened.

Chapter Seven

THE FOREST NEVER REALLY went to sleep, Dane noted, but when the sun came up, the place came to life. She groaned from the noise, mostly birds. They seemed to get up before the crack of dawn. She heard Nicole chuckling next to her, as she tried to burrow deeper into the sleeping bag with the hope of going back to sleep.

"You might want to get up and wash for breakfast, baby." Nicole's kiss to her forehead was small incentive.

Dane snorted and tried her best to block out the noise. She really had no problem with getting up early, especially since they went to bed early, but she wanted to lie there for a few minutes. After all, this trip was supposed to be a mini vacation and, as she understood vacations, that meant sleeping in. Nicole must've had a different view, or at least changed her view from their last trip, because she playfully smacked Dane on the butt.

"Come on, get up. You'll want to see us making pancakes for breakfast, if only to tell them they're doing it wrong," Nicole joked.

Dane chuckled and rubbed her eyes. As she sat up, she ran her hand through her hair and focused on Nicole, whose back was facing her. Nicole was already dressed, but the sight was still quite glorious. She had on a fairly tight, black, sleeveless shirt and little shorts that cradled her ass. Dane's hands itched to touch, but she knew that'd be a bad idea with Raymond probably right outside.

Thankfully, Nicole crawled out of the tent and removed the temptation. Of course, before she did that, the little minx turned and winked at her, showing she knew exactly what she was doing. Dane groaned and laughed. *I love that woman*.

"I'd better get up. See how they make these flapjacks and stuff," she muttered.

She also wanted to know about showering, or bathing, in this case. She supposed she'd have Nicole show her. As much as her girlfriend enjoyed the outdoors, she knew Nicole wouldn't stay somewhere for days on end if they couldn't manage to remain relatively clean.

There was a time when Dane wouldn't have cared about that. When she met Nicole, she had reeked enough to choke a fly, she was sure of that. Somehow, she had gotten used to smelling horrible and having an itchy scalp, and the grime on her skin had barely registered to her. But, that wasn't the case anymore. She had skipped a shower one day and was certain of two things. One, Nicole could somehow detect she hadn't showered the moment they woke up. And two, she hated how oily her skin felt being covered in yesterday's dirt. The moment actually made her smile, as she thought about how Nicole had restored her pride and self-respect. No one had ever touched her enough to do that before.

"My angel." Dane sighed, as her heart thumped lighter than usual before going after her lover for camp bath tips.

Once Nicole showed her the basics of hygiene while on a camping trip, Dane went to put on some clothes. She felt somewhat refreshed, but she figured she'd have to get used to camp bathing. While she had spent a part of her life being homeless, and definitely not being able to bathe every day, she had also spent much of that time too high or drunk to care.

"You okay?" Nicole inquired.

Dane nodded. "Fine. Just missing the shower and respecting the people who lived before there was one." Nicole chortled at that.

"Aw, you hear that? The city girl misses the shower," Spider said from a seat by their small grill.

"She's not the only one." Beth scoffed as a smile worked its way onto her face. "I'd kill for some shampoo with that shower. In fact, I'd club one of you to death right now for some shampoo." Her cousins chuckled.

Dane was starting to get a feel for the cousins' humor and thought it was nice. She really wished she could share in it, but she knew Junior and Spider wouldn't allow that. She wasn't too sure where Beth stood, yet, but she got the suspicion Beth might try to get to know her before judging her. She didn't even want to think about Lillian.

"We're only here for a couple of days, so stop whining already, Beth. Go take some pictures or something." Richard shooed her away with both hands.

Dane couldn't tell if he was being playful or if he was serious. Beth seemed to droop a bit, shoulders slumping, and her smile disappeared, so maybe he was serious. She was beginning to think he was probably the strict uncle, which would leave Raymond as the fun uncle. That idea would take some getting used to.

"Uncle Richard, leave Beth alone. She's the only one of us that knows how to survive if we lose everything in a freak accident," Nicole said, giving her cousin a wink. Beth tittered while Richard snorted.

Dane glanced at the pair, wondering what that was about. Nicole waved her off, which was a way to say she'd explain later. Dane shrugged and scanned for who had the pancake batter, if only to see if there was a difference in outside pancakes. Thankfully, Raymond was doing the mixing, so she drifted over.

"You do a lot of cooking?" Dane asked, glancing at the pancake batter. It didn't look any different than something she or Nicole might make at home.

"Not nearly as much as you to hear Nikki tell it," Raymond replied with a small half smile. "I'm one of those guys who handles 'guy' cooking. I man the BBQ grill at home, and I do the cooking when we go camping."

"We've never grilled," Dane realized. *I think we might want to try that this summer. We can have her family over and the boys. Everyone'll like that, especially in that huge backyard.*

"Why do I get the feeling that, if you do, Nicole would be the one at the grill?" He smiled, almost as if he were teasing her. She supposed Nicole had told him about her being a self-proclaimed housewife. She truly believed she was, and there was nothing wrong with that, but she'd like to run the grill if they were to ever have a cookout. She could probably grill well with practice.

Smirking a little, Dane ran her hand through her hair. "Think she'd chase me away if I tried to take over?"

Raymond chuckled. "Probably, but it never hurts to try."

Dane shrugged. "Guess I'll have to talk her into a cookout to see. Maybe for my birthday." She gave Raymond a sidelong glance. "Unless she has other plans." Nicole liked to surprise her for her birthday. Dane had learned that over the past couple of years.

"She hasn't said anything to me about what she might do for your birthday, but you might want to throw out this cookout idea before she does get a notion in her head. I've already figured out that she's borderline obsessed with giving you things you missed in your childhood. Next thing you know you'll be having a party at Rockin' Mouse's Pizza Party Palace."

Dane practically guffawed as that image assaulted her mind; standing ankle deep in a ball pit with her nephews, as some lame, short-circuiting, woodland creature animatronic band played the crappiest rendition of "Happy Birthday" imaginable. While she knew Nicole would never do anything like that, she found it too funny that Raymond would suggest it. They shared a look before he turned his attention back to the pancake batter.

"I won't ask about it," Raymond said in a low, but clear voice.

She knew he referred to her childhood. While she had never spoken to him about it, she was aware he'd figured out things were bad for her. When they first met, he had seen her father throw her down on the ground. Well, they hadn't really met then, since Nicole had fallen to Dane's side and pled with Raymond to leave while she ushered Dane into the house. Then, there was her outburst at Thanksgiving after Benito tried to kick her out of the house because he thought she didn't respect family. No, she didn't respect her family, even though she saw family in a different light now. The Wolfes weren't her family, even if they were blood related.

Being with Nicole allowed Dane to see so many different aspects of what made up a family, and Nicole had given her family. Family was something wonderful, not the nightmare she had put up with at the Wolfe home. Family was fun, warm, secure, and loving. Family was the people who wanted her around and that she wanted to be around. Family wanted her to succeed, rooted for her, and supported her. This lesson alone made her love Nicole all the more, and she doubted her angel was even aware she had provided Dane with the lesson.

"You don't have to ask. Whatever you think happened probably did and worse. Except, no sex stuff, okay?" Dane told him.

"Well, that's something, I guess," he mumbled with a frown. "I never could've thought Russell would be an abusive bastard, but it seems like he always finds a new low to sink to...I'm sorry, Danny. That's not my place to say."

She shrugged. "You're right. Not that it matters. Not bothering with him ever again."

He nodded and, for a moment, she could've sworn that he looked relieved, almost like he wanted to smile. He looked down at the batter. "Ready to make some pancakes?"

"Just plain pancakes?"

"When camping, you have to make do," he laughed.

She nodded and watched the man work. He didn't say much as camping pancakes were pretty much regular pancakes, except they made them over a grill instead of on the stove. They ate a hearty breakfast of somewhat small pancakes, but there were plenty of them.

"They taste all right," Dane said before shoving a forkful in her mouth.

"Don't eat too many of them." Nicole patted her lover's knee.

"Yeah, don't want you to get a tummy ache," Junior said, making a face, a few feet away.

Nicole glared at him. "Don't be mad because she beat you in that chili dog contest last night."

"She didn't beat me!" Junior puffed up with indignation and the other cousins snickered.

"You didn't finish the last one," Nicole said with a taunting smirk on her face. Dane never thought she'd see the day when her girlfriend was defending her ability to gorge herself on junk food.

Beth backed her up. "You definitely didn't."

Junior appeared murderous, and Dane figured it was because his subordinates were making fun of him. Junior seemed like he was supposed to be the leader of their little pack, but right now, Nicole dared to take on the alpha and another joined in. Dane wondered if Junior would be able to handle that.

Junior scoffed. "Whatever. I had sandwiches on the way here, so I was already halfway full. Next time, I doubt the little city gal will be able to touch me in a hot dog eating contest."

That seemed to be the end of it there. Dane had to admit she thought he handled that better because he didn't lose his temper or throw a tantrum of any kind. His cousins seemed to buy that excuse or, in Nicole's case, lose interest in him. They all returned to eating, Dane stuffing her face with a couple more pancakes before Raymond grinned at her and informed her that she was on dish duty.

"Gee, thanks. Was dying to wash the pancake thing," Dane said with a slight grin. Nicole smiled as well, happy that her father was including Dane in things.

"I thought you were," Raymond replied with a smile of his own. His eyes dancing with mirth.

"I'll show you what to do," Lillian said, standing from her seat a couple of feet away.

"I think I can figure out washing on my own," Dane tried to assure her, because she really didn't want any more alone time with Lillian.

"Why don't you catch up with Nick? I mean, you guys haven't seen each other in a while, right? And you haven't really had a chance to sit and talk."

"We can do that later," Lillian replied, flashing a bright smile at Nicole, who smiled back.

Dane held in a groan and figured she was stuck with Lillian for the short time it'd take to clean their cookware. The dishes were in a bucket that was brought along for just this purpose. She grabbed them, the soap, a rag, and headed for a stream not too far from them, where she had been assured earlier it was okay to use the water. Of course, she was less inclined to believe that when they had brought plenty of bottled water. *But, what do I know about proper camping anyway? Not like Nick would let them poison me.*

"So, how are you liking camping with us so far?" Lillian gave her a sidelong glance.

"Fine," Dane replied, doing her best to not grunt out the word. She would've gone into more detail if she trusted Lillian a little more. She wondered what Nicole liked so much about this woman. She seemed weird, but not in a good or interesting way, even when starting what should've seemed like an innocent conversation.

"Still tired? It's an obscene hour to be awake, and I'm sure you had a busy night," Lillian said, lips pursed, but a smile in her eyes.

"Why would you say that?" Dane inquired against her better judgment, as she got started on the dishes.

"Nothing. It's just I know Nikki likes, you know, sex. I figured you two in a small, enclosed area would...well, you know, partake of some adult entertainment."

"You seem rather interested in my sex life with Nick and Nick's sex life in general." *Why the hell does this chick wanna know so much about what we do in bed? Cousins shouldn't act like this, right?* She really wished she knew the answer to that, so she could figure out what Lillian was playing at or if this was as weird as it felt. *I'll have to ask Crow when I get a chance.*

Lillian tilted her head and blushed. "I'm sorry. I haven't offended you, have I? That wasn't my intent. I mean, this is stuff I usually talk about with Nikki, and her lovers tend to be rather boastful. One time, she brought this awful woman with her that kept going on and on about how she'd tie Nikki down and have her way with her. Nikki seemed to like it."

Mentally, Dane called bullshit. Now, either Lillian or the former lover was a liar. She hated to think it might be both. Also, she hated talking to Lillian and Lillian talking in general.

"So, how did you and Nikki meet? At her job? I know she's a really successful lawyer and everything, but I can't see you being a lawyer," Lillian said with a smile, as if that was supposed to soften the blow of her words.

"Not a lawyer, a musician," Dane answered, even though she didn't think that was accurate. It was close enough without having to explain anything.

"So, how'd you meet her? She went to one of your shows or you needed to sue somebody or what?"

Dane shrugged. She couldn't help feeling that Lillian was trolling for information. She wasn't sure what Lillian would do with the information, but she didn't want to find out. Again, she wondered what her angel saw in this woman to consider her a little sister. She'd have to remember to ask.

"You don't talk much, huh?" Lillian asked, and Dane shook her head to answer.

Despite Dane being rather tight-lipped, Lillian stayed with her the entire time she washed the dishes. She asked several what would seem like innocent questions: How long have you and Nicole had been together? What type of dates do you go on? What kind of special things do you do for Nicole? Dane considered Lillian might, in a very awkward and clumsy way, be trying to figure out if she was treating Nicole right. Still, she didn't go into detail in any of her answers and never said more than a sentence for anything she did respond to.

***

Nicole smiled as she watched Danny and Lillian walk off, even though she knew Danny wasn't happy with the company. She hoped Danny would manage to bond with Lillian. She and Lillian had been so close when they were younger and sometimes she wished they had never grown up. But, she liked to think they were still as close as they had been, even if they didn't talk as often. When they did talk, they could still go for hours, unless one of them got called away, so that had to count for something.

"You're looking mighty pleased with yourself," Beth said, stepping over to Nicole.

Nicole smiled more. "Yeah, Lil's being nice to Danny. I'm glad someone's trying." She said that last bit a little louder, so that her other cousins could hear.

"Why should we be nice to someone who isn't going to be here the next time we do this?" Junior inquired.

Nicole bristled. "What does that mean? I told you Danny's it for me, so are you uninviting me from any other family camping trips?"

"Don't twist my words, Nikki. You've been in love with plenty of people before. Just like web-head," Junior replied, jabbing his thumb in his brother's direction.

"Hey!" Spider looked up from a bag of his gear to glare at Junior.

"He's right," Richard chimed, chuckling at his son's indignation. "You fall in love with almost any girl that holds your hand."

"Hey!" Spider huffed once more and glared at his father.

"Look, Spider might not have found his perfect mate, but I have. I already told you. Be as skeptical as you like. I'll be sure to invite you to our wedding in a few years, where I'll also be sure to serve you some good crow with humble pie, okay?" Nicole told her eldest cousin.

Junior scoffed. "We all know no one here is getting married, ever."

"Hello!" Beth protested, now glaring at Junior with a heated gaze. His brother and Nicole did the same.

"Beth, you can't even find a date. You don't stay anywhere long enough to make a friend," Junior said with a chuckle.

Beth laughed, but picked up a handful of dirt and threw it at Junior. "Shut up. I have friends!"

"Junior, how about instead of being a jerk to your cousins and brother, even though I know that's what you were made for, figure out what we're going to do today." Richard had apparently had enough of their childish arguing. He had no problem with them squabbling and things, but he'd rather they not do it around him for a prolonged period of time.

"It's day one. We go fishing. Problem solved," Junior said with a big grin to annoy his father.

The cousins all snickered at Junior being a smartass, which was par for the course. But, they did always go fishing on the first day of their camping trip. They never caught much, but it wasn't really about fishing, which was why Junior went to check the cooler. He needed to make sure everything was packed.

"A morning of fishing and teasing before I move on to taking pictures," Beth hummed with a happy smile.

"How is the photography going?" Nicole inquired. "I worry when you stop sending things."

Beth smiled more and patted Nicole on the shoulder. "You shouldn't worry. When I stop sending things, it usually means I'm busy taking tons of photos. I do owe you prints, though. I haven't really shot anything that I think you'd like. Well, except a couple of shots I took of Danny yesterday."

Nicole snickered. "Now, that does hold my interest. You'll show me them, right?" She could only imagine how breathtaking the pictures would look. She'd have to go out and buy frames and figure out where to put them in the house.

"Of course. I took them for you. She seemed cool with it."

Nicole nodded. "What have you been doing?"

"Mostly landscapes, but they don't have any animals in them, so I didn't think you'd be interested."

Nicole nodded. "I do prefer critters with my grasslands."

Beth chuckled. "I know. I prefer that, too. Unfortunately, the magazines and websites I freelance with keep pushing landscapes right now, without the critters. They're usually trying to promote vacation areas and things like that. Hopefully, eventually, I'll get picked up by one of them. I can get animals in the shots eventually if I just get enough work."

"You should talk to my father. We have clients in the magazine industry."

"I know, believe me, I know. Uncle Ray is always going on about how he could help me. If he's not telling me, he's telling my mother to get her to talk me into taking his help, but I want to do it on my own...until it drives me crazy. But, I could be doing worse, so I'm all right. I mean, I'm living my dream."

Nicole smiled. Beth had always wanted to travel when she was younger and she was doing that, managing to support herself on her freelancing photography. Nicole respected that and respected that Beth chased a dream that everyone else told her wasn't going to work. Her father's side of her family didn't think pursuing a career in anything that vaguely looked like art was a way to make a living. Art was a hobby, not a job, not a career. Beth proved them wrong, but they still worried about her, fearing the photography could dry up at any moment.

Nicole knew it wasn't that they didn't respect art, but that they didn't think it was possible for the sporadic income to support anyone. There were times, too, when Beth lived hand to mouth. When she was first starting out, she had a couple of slips that forced her to move back in with her parents, which had the family swearing it would always happen. Beth never let it get her down, kept on going, and continued living her dream, loving every second of it, even the hard times. Nicole had to admire her determination and tenacity. Of course, there was a little envy in that as well.

She dropped that line of thinking, as she noticed Danny and Lillian returning. Lillian was talking, but Nicole couldn't hear about what. Danny didn't look pleased, face tense and mouth turned down in a slight frown. In fact, those grey eyes begged, "Save me!" Nicole chuckled and decided to go help her beloved.

"Baby, let me help you with those dishes," Nicole said, rushing to her lover's aid.

"Thanks," Danny muttered.

Nicole helped Danny put the dishes back in their container, but before she could say anything to Danny, Lillian came in. Lillian wrapped her arm around Nicole's and pulled her away. Lillian smiled at her and patted her forearm.

"Danny isn't very talkative, huh?" Lillian said.

"No, she needs to get comfortable around you. I'm glad you're trying."

Lillian's face lit up as she gave her cousin a cherubic smile. "Of course, I'm trying! You love her, so I want to like her. She's different from everyone else you've dated. Does she treat you good?"

Nicole had to suppress a grin. "The best."

"That's good."

"What about you? Are you seeing anyone?"

"No, I've mostly been working as usual. I'm trying to keep up with you, after all," Lillian gave her an impish grin.

"I've told you time and time again that you shouldn't be following me. Do what makes you happy." She knew chasing someone else's dream or living in someone's shadow was no way to live.

"You make me happy, cousin."

Nicole chuckled. "That's sweet of you." She leaned her head against Lillian's for a moment. "So, what have you been doing besides work? Are you still clubbing and things like that?"

"I have been. I am trying to meet someone, after all. I don't think the club is the place to do it. How did you meet people?"

"You know you don't want to know how I met people. Everyone I've ever dated has been a disaster. Danny's the best relationship I've had, and I met her by accident. Although, I guess that's how you usually meet people."

A light laugh escaped Lillian and her cerulean eyes sparkled. "This is true."

"Come on. Let's get ready for our fishing expedition. We'll talk about how you might be able to meet someone while we do that." Nicole wanted to talk to Lillian about everything, catch up in her life, and reconnect with her. Lillian agreed with an enthused nod, and they got to work while running their mouths the whole time.

S.L. Kassidy

Chapter Eight

DANE LEARNED THEY WERE going to spend the day fishing. Nicole had tried to help her get ready, but Lillian was with Nicole, so Dane decided to try to do it on her own. She truly didn't want to spend any more time with Lillian than necessary, even though they seemed to be discussing something rather benign, cases they had worked. Surprisingly, Raymond stepped up to show her what to do.

"Have you ever gone fishing before?" Raymond asked.

"Nope." Dane didn't even know what most of the things were that Nicole bought her when they went shopping for fishing gear. She hadn't known what to pack either, so Nicole had to handle it when they were home and, now, Raymond instructed her on what she should carry down to the river.

"Try not to talk too much. You'll scare the fish, city girl," Spider said, apparently listening in.

Raymond smiled. "Don't worry. Webber's face scares the fish."

Junior burst out laughing. "Oh, so true!" He pointed at his brother.

"What? Yours isn't much better. You're the reason none of the bears ever come around," Spider countered, speaking to his brother.

"Don't worry. You both came by your ugly honestly. Haven't you seen your father?" Raymond nodded toward his brother.

"Oh!" Both brothers cried out, while Nicole snickered.

"He got you good, Uncle Richard." Nicole pointed at her uncle with both index fingers.

"He's mad because Mom and Dad actually found him in these woods. You know a Bigfoot abandoned him right outside our camp. We're guessing they couldn't stand the smell of him," Richard shot back.

"Oh, Nikki, Dad said you're the daughter of a baby Sasquatch!" Junior grabbed her around the shoulders and proceeded to give her noogies, which was the strangest thing Dane had ever seen.

She knew Nicole could be playful, but this bordered on childish. It didn't bother Dane. It was always nice to see Nicole let loose. This had to be a glimpse of Nicole as a little girl, playing around with her older cousins, getting a chance to be irresponsible and carefree. *Dammit, now I want these guys to like me again, because I want them to see that Nick is in good hands. They clearly mean so much to her, and she seems to mean a lot to them.*

"I'll show you baby Sasquatch!" Nicole hit him with an elbow in the ribs. He coughed and backed away from his younger cousin.

"She got you!" Spider laughed, patting his brother on the back. He was more smacking Junior, but the older brother didn't seem to mind.

"All right you three. Stop being yourselves and let's get going. None of these screwball antics when we get to the spot, so we can actually catch some food," Richard ordered with a smile. The expression seemed to suggest the screwball antics weren't likely to stop.

The three nodded and everyone set out for the river. The walk was a few minutes long, down a worn dirt path with plenty of trees and birds to see. Over the tweets and calls of the birds, Dane could just make out the sound of the river rushing through this majestic place. *It's nothing like a park.* She liked it. She wanted to see more of the forest.

Dane was about to set herself up next to Nicole, if only to enjoy the trip more, but Junior and Spider quickly flanked her. Nicole glared at them, but they appeared a bit contrite. Dane wondered if she was about to get pranked or something.

"We always stand together when we fish. Is it cool?" Junior inquired, as if he was asking permission.

"Yeah, I mean, if you're going to be around as long as Nikki says, and you're going to do this again, you can stand with her then, but we don't get to see her a lot, anymore," Spider added. It would seem despite all their mean-spirited behavior, they still wanted Nicole's company and would actually put up with Dane for it.

Nicole's expression softened, obviously touched by their desire to be closer. Dane couldn't help thinking maybe they weren't total assholes. They might not like her, but they seemed to honestly love Nicole and really wanted to spend time with her, even if it was just teasing and horsing around. She suspected Nicole felt the same way, even if the brothers treated her horribly.

"No problem. I'll watch you guys," Dane answered. What the hell did she know about fishing anyway? She couldn't even say that she saw it on television, except for in movies.

"Cool. Gotta show Nikki how it's done." Spider chuckled, slapping Nicole on the back rather roughly.

"I do believe the last time we came out here I caught more fish than you did," Nicole argued with a smug look.

Spider made a mocking gesture with his hand as the trio set up along the wide river. This wasn't anything like the stream Dane had washed the dishes in. She could hardly believe what she was looking at along the thin strip of rocky shore that met the water. In some spaces, the soil and grass went right to the river. She had never seen anything like the clear, running waterway, and she was shocked into silence for a long moment. Nicole noticed and took Dane's hand in her own.

"How you doing, love?" Nicole inquired in a low voice.

"This is awesome," she replied in a whisper.

Nicole smiled and kissed Dane's cheek before Junior snatched Nicole over to their fishing spot. Dane was content to sit back and watch, but Beth waved her over. Hoping that Beth wouldn't prove to be as strange as Lillian, Dane went over to see what she wanted.

"Those three are going to zone out in a second, trying to beat each other in catching the most fish, which is stupid in and of itself, as the most any of them have ever caught is two. But, I figure I could walk you through the motions of fishing," Beth said.

Dane nodded. "Okay, that's nice."

Beth smiled at her and eased her through the basics. It seemed simple enough. Raymond even let her practice casting with his rod, as she did not even bother to touch hers beyond carrying it down to the river. Every now and then, she glanced at Nicole to see her standing quietly with her two cousins. They seemed content, softly smiling at each other. Once, she even saw Junior patting Nicole on the shoulder, as if congratulating her.

I don't get it. They clearly love her and like being around her, so why do they keep giving her such a hard time about me? Don't they get that they're upsetting her? Maybe it's some family thing that I don't get. At least she's having a good time with them, finally, just like she wanted. That thought alone put a small smile on Dane's face.

She noticed Lillian sat back on a folding stool, watching the action. "Lillian doesn't fish?" she asked Beth.

"Not since Spider put one down her shirt when she was eight," Beth answered.

Dane's eyes went wide. "He put a fish down her shirt?"

"Put a fish in Nikki's shirt and mine, too. Still alive. Horrible experience." Despite her words, she laughed a bit.

Dane didn't see what was funny about this. "What the hell is wrong with him?"

"He was just a little boy. He acted like a little boy. He never did it again after Nicole put a fish down his pants and then managed to push him into the water. Seems Lil's never gotten over it. I did enjoy Nicole's vengeance and took it as my own, too," Beth replied with another laugh.

"Sounds like Nick played right along with them."

"Oh, yeah. Nikki gave and got with Spider throughout their whole lives. For Junior, it's like having two sidekicks. They did some crazy things when they were younger. You should ask her about those."

Dane nodded; she'd definitely do that. She had seen pictures of Nicole as a child, but those mostly had to do with sporting events. She knew those stories, but now she wanted to know about this roughhousing version of her girlfriend. Seeing her with her cousins, though, made Dane understand even more why Nicole thought family was so important.

At first, Dane had assumed Nicole got her ideas of family from Kathleen's side because that was a very tight-knit group, but Raymond's side seemed to be the same. Nicole was definitely more carefree with these cousins, not having the pressure of being the example for at least two of them. But, she seemed to get along with all of them. She was close to all of them, and they all seemed to enjoy each other. She could see why Nicole thought all families were like this, until of course the Wolfe family shattered the image and put a dent in her lovely rose-colored glasses.

After a while, fishing got boring. "I'm going to go walk. I want to see what's farther up the river." Besides, she should move before her leg stiffened up.

"It all looks sort of the same, but feel free to check it out. It's beautiful."

Dane nodded. Walking around was breathtaking, feeling the mist from the flowing river. She paused to take off her shoes, wanting to feel the grass under her feet. She scanned the trees, looking for wildlife. The animals seemed to be pros at hiding, because the most she saw were birds, soaring through the trees. She saw the occasional small rodent, but nothing bigger than a squirrel caught her eye.

She wasn't sure how long she walked, but she paused several times to make sure her leg wasn't injured. There was a dull throb, but nothing she hadn't ignored before. Nicole had packed her knee brace, which she decided to wear because it helped. She should be fine for a while longer.

She came to some massive rocks that jutted out into the river. Unable to help herself, she gingerly made her way onto the rocks. Stepping up on one of the larger ones, she sat down and looked out into the wide river.

***

"There you are. We thought you got lost, city gal," Junior said, as he and Spider practically swaggered over to her.

Dane arched an eyebrow. "Thought I got lost?"

"You've been gone for a couple of hours. We're about to head back for lunch," Spider said.

"And you're the search party?" Dane was skeptical. Maybe they were out here to drown her in the river.

"We volunteered," Junior told her with a shrug. And now, she was even more skeptical.

"It'll give us a chance to talk to you about Nikki," Spider said. Well, that made sense, to a degree anyway. She hoped they didn't want to talk to her like their sister had been talking to her for the past two days.

"I'm sure Uncle Raymond already gave you the dad talk, but we've got the big brother talk to handle." Junior pointed to himself and then his brother. They stood up tall, squaring their pretty massive shoulders.

"I was unaware that Nick had big brothers," Dane said dryly.

"You're looking at 'em." Junior then made a show of flexing his rather impressive biceps. They were definitely big, she'd give him that, but she wasn't exactly intimidated.

"Okay, so this is where you guys get all threatening and everything?" Dane rolled her eyes. *Whatever.*

"No, this is where we tell you flat out that you're not good enough for Nicole. We haven't met a single person that is good enough for her, especially someone she's brought up here. You've got her enamored like every other asshole she's been with, and she can't see the forest for the trees. But we know what you're all about," Junior said with a stern gaze and an even sterner point.

"Let's say what you said is true, what the hell would you do if I was such an asshole?" Dane scratched her chin. After all, they lived over three hours away from Nicole in another state.

"You think we won't drive down there and whip your ass until you leave her alone? We will," Spider promised her and the look in his eyes told her it wasn't a bluff. She suspected they might've even done it before.

"What makes you think I'd let you two whip my ass?" Dane was bored with this.

"I don't think you can handle both of us. So, here's how it's going to go, whatever the hell spell you're weaving on Nicole stops now. You quit playing with her head and quit lying to her. Eventually, she'll get it and dump you, but you'd better not break her heart." Junior made a fist, perhaps a not so subtle hint.

"You want me to wait for her to break up with me?" Dane asked, running her hand through her hair. She hated that she actually respected the guys for trying to stick up for Nicole. Of course, she disliked them for their prejudice and entire handling of the situation. If they only respected Nicole enough to believe her, they wouldn't have to go through all of this nonsense.

"Yeah, city girl. It's not like you can offer her anything, anyway," Spider said.

Those words hit Dane like a bullet. Even though she knew she was getting flack for past lovers, that statement seemed too accurate for her. *Am I so worthless it's written on my face?* And, if it was, of course Nicole couldn't see it because of those lovely rose-tinted glasses.

"Nicole's one of the best people I've ever known in my life. She deserves to be happy, not played with," Junior said, pointing at her like that made his words all the more powerful.

"Agreed," Dane replied.

"Then do the right thing." There was a hard glint in his eyes that promised consequences if she didn't obey.

They walked off, not bothering to look back at her. She wondered who in the world Nicole had brought for them to meet in the past because they were beyond concerned. Of course, if judging by the one ex Nicole had that Dane did know, her own cousin Tyler, she could understand why the brothers were so worried about Nicole. It didn't matter though. She wasn't any of those people and they'd have to deal with her, because she wasn't going anywhere. She'd love Nicole for the rest of her life. Her eyes shifted to the river and she sighed.

"That might be the case, but it doesn't stop the idea that they're actually right about me having nothing to offer her. Hell, that's why her mom hates me," Dane said to the air. The roar of the rushing river and the shrill cry of some birds were the only responses she got, trying to drown out the loud wail of her own misery.

She and Nicole had spoken about this topic before, and she knew she gave quite a bit to Nicole. But, underneath it all, she guessed the insecurities would exist for a while, until she could prove to herself their relationship was somehow balanced. Emotional and affection-wise, things might've balanced out, but that was the only place. Everywhere else, the weighted scales practically tipped over from what Nicole brought to the table.

While Dane had learned to accept Nicole taking care of her and being there for her, she disliked not being able to pull her own weight. Her job, if it could be called that, paid peanuts in comparison to Nicole's. It'd take her months to save up to take Nicole to the restaurants former lovers could've easily taken Nicole to. She couldn't even pay the bills in the house. Even though Haydn was technically hers, she couldn't even afford his vet bills or sometimes even his toys.

"I'm practically a deadbeat, so probably not that different from the people that Nick used to date. Hell, even Tyler could at least take her out. Of course, he probably made her pick up the check...which is what I do." Dane scowled. *Maybe Nicole's cousins have a point.* She didn't even have family traditions to bring to the table like Nicole did. She had nothing to give Nicole. Nothing at all.

S.L. Kassidy

Chapter Nine

NICOLE HAD BEEN SO happy when Junior and Spider volunteered to go get Danny, so they could all head back to camp. She thought they were showing signs of trying to warm up to Danny after the musician had so graciously allowed them to steal her for their morning of fishing. She thought they were trying to be helpful, so when they returned without Danny, Nicole was left confused.

"What happened?" Nicole asked, tilting her head as she observed her cousins.

"She's coming. She's sitting on those rocks up there, probably awed by the view," Junior answered with a shrug.

Nicole nodded, knowing the exact spot he meant. It was a beautiful area, and she could understand how Danny could get lost in the view. In fact, she'd love to go see the spot with Danny and enjoy the company and the view. It'd be very romantic, but that could wait for another time. It was getting late, and she knew that Danny had to be hungry. She glanced up the path, knowing Danny wasn't too far away.

"Okay, but you guys were supposed to bring her back," Nicole told her cousins.

Spider scoffed, like that hadn't been the understanding. "She's coming."

"Unless she got lost walking straight up the river, which I guess you might have to worry about with that city gal." Junior smirked.

"It is pretty likely," Richard said, encouraging his sons. Nicole scowled at them, ready to bite back, but she didn't get a chance.

Raymond spoke up. "I'll go get her. You all head back and make sure Richard doesn't burn the fish. We don't have enough for his usual mistakes." He chuckled.

Richard snorted. "I think we can finally be assured a meal will be edible with you away from the grill."

"Are you sure, Daddy?" Nicole asked, surprised her father would miss a chance to grill up the fish they'd caught. Uncle Richard, while a man of many talents, wasn't very apt when it came to working the grill.

In fact, she noticed it seemed to be a source of competition between her father and her uncle with her father winning every single time.

"I'm sure. I haven't seen that spot in a while, too," he replied with a soft smile.

Nicole shrugged because she couldn't stop her father. Besides, she noticed her father had taken an active interest in Danny for the trip. It seemed like it was a good step for their relationship that Danny didn't seem to recognize and that her father never mentioned. They might even leave the woods close to being friends, or better still, in-laws. The thought brought a smile to her face and, as she watched her father walk away, her eyes glistened with hope.

***

Over the sound of running water, Dane could hear someone coming and she thought Junior and Spider might've returned for round two. She didn't see why they'd come back, but none of the cousins really made much sense to her, except for Beth anyway. Beth seemed like a nice person, willing to give her a chance. She was surprised to see Raymond walking toward her.

"Did Frick and Frack at least tell you that we're eating before they shot their mouths off and threatened to kill you?" Raymond inquired with a soft smile.

The gesture was a bit of a shock. As he came closer, she could see his expression reached his eyes and made his face seem soft. She wasn't sure what to make of it, the inkling that he held affection for her. She decided to dismiss it, thinking she was reading too much into things. Why should he have affection for her? She was holding his daughter back, after all.

Dane chuckled. "They didn't really threaten to kill me."

"I'm surprised by that. It wouldn't be the first time they made the threat." Emerald eyes scanned the area, and Raymond motioned around them. "We're in the middle of nowhere. They know the place like the back of their hands, and they could probably hide your body for years to come."

"Guess you could do that, too, since you probably know this place better than they do." *Is he about to make the threat or go straight for the kill? I'm being too paranoid. He's been cool.*

Raymond shrugged. "That I do, but I have no intention of killing you. I don't have time. I've got work on Monday, after all."

Dane chuckled again. She wondered what had gotten into Raymond. *Maybe there's something in the air.* Of course, if that were the case, she wondered if it was possible to bottle the air and take some home.

"Besides, how would you explain it to Nick?" Dane asked.

Raymond snickered. "Oh, that's easily explained away with you getting lost up here. It's happened to first-time visitors to this park before. My dad used to threaten to leave us out here when we were younger and getting on his nerves. Scared the crap out of my sisters."

A small, amused smile settled on her face for a moment. "Your sisters aren't big into camping, huh?"

"Nah, they never took to it. They came until they could be trusted at home for a few days on their own, because my mother loves camping, so she was always with us. How about you? How are you liking it so far?"

A hand went through Dane's hair as she looked around, taking in the wonders of the forest. "Camping? It's okay, so far. I'm not totally sure if I could get into fishing, though. Seems pretty boring."

"Ah, you didn't stick around when we caught some fish. That's when everybody gets all excited and everything. Besides, you feel that way about baseball and yet, time and time again, you sit through games because Nikki's watching. I'm sure you'd sit through fishing if Nikki were standing right next to you."

She shrugged because she couldn't argue with the truth. There was also the fact that they planned to bring her nephews along on the next trip. If they liked fishing, it was guaranteed she'd, at the very least, stand with everyone. When they were involved, it wasn't about the activity, but about the time spent together.

"So, you want to tell me what the two knuckleheads said to you when they came up here?" Raymond inquired.

She waved the question off. "They were just looking out for Nick."

He nodded. "Yeah, the two gear-heads are at least good for that. I don't want them to scare you off, though."

Rolling her eyes, she scoffed. "The devil himself couldn't scare me off. Me and Nick have a deep history already. So, I'm in it for the long haul or whatever they say. Besides, she's domesticated me and everything. No use letting some other woman enjoy the fruits of Nick's labor."

He laughed. "It's good that you both feel that way about it."

She arched an eyebrow. "You approve of us?" Even though it came out as a question, it really wasn't. It was more a realization that she hadn't meant to say aloud. It earned her another laugh from the man.

"You seem surprised."

"Uh...I am." She rubbed her forehead. "I thought for sure you'd always hate me." Outside of Nicole, the only time she really got love was back when she was with her band, on stage, being the local Goddess of rock and roll.

Shaking his head, Raymond rested his hand gently on her shoulder. "No, Danny, you've grown on me, definitely. I have to respect you. You stand by Nicole and you treat her right."

Dane ran her hand through her hair again, squinting a little as she took this in. "It doesn't bother you that I'm not nearly as successful as, say, Tyler?"

"Success is measured differently from person to person. Does it bother me that you don't have the same amount of money as Nikki or almost any other person that she's ever dated? A little. A father wants his daughter taken care of, and not taking care of someone else. Honestly, if you were a man, I'd probably consider you a deadbeat and pressure you about getting a real job."

She frowned. "So, because I'm a woman it's okay?" That didn't sit well with her, and she wasn't entirely sure why. She knew that much of the time, it didn't feel okay to her. She felt like she should be the one taking care of Nicole, like he wanted, woman or not.

He shrugged. "I'm just being honest, Danny. I doubt any father wants his daughter supporting someone else. But, I think you do a lot of things a guy wouldn't do. You cook every day, you clean the house, and things like that. I give you credit for that. I also acknowledge it's not easy work, taking care of the house. You encouraged Nikki to chase a dream she can afford to chase. You want her to be happy, just like I do."

"I do. I do want her to be happy, but how can I do that if I can't treat her to trips and stuff like she does with me?" Technically, she could afford it thanks to Christine practically forcing a small trust fund on her, but she thought of that as her mother's money, a handout. It wasn't something she'd earned. In fact, it was more a bribe, and she did her best not to touch that money.

"Have you considered getting a real job?" he asked.

She sighed. "I don't have any real skills. Barely graduated high school and, considering my hand and my leg, I'm not very useful in physical labor."

He leveled her with a deadpan look. "Have you ever actually looked?"

Sighing, Dane put her hand through her hair once more. "I've looked before, on days when I really feel bad about not being able to do stuff for Nick. Even if I got a job, at like a fast food place or something, I'd still be making peanuts. Hell, I might actually make more tutoring than with something like that."

He nodded in agreement. "Then do something with your music. Have you ever worked before in your life?"

"I used to get a lot of gigs, but I had a band then, and I could play."

"You can still play and sing. I've heard you. You seem like you've lost your confidence and maybe it's because you're not how you used to be, but you're not horrible. You sound good, really good, actually. Think about it."

She nodded. "This little pep talk for Nick's sake?"

"If that's what makes you feel better. Now, come on, there's lunch waiting. We get to see my brother burn all of the fish." He laughed, softly patting her on the back.

She could only shrug as they started walking back to the camp. She had no clue what to make of this talk, except that Nicole was right. Raymond actually liked her, maybe even cared about her. *How'd I never notice?*

"You know, if you have these thoughts in your head, you should talk to Nikki. Communication is one of the things that all relationships need to keep going. Communication and honesty," Raymond said.

"Trust me, I know that already. We've talked about stuff, but I think I'm hardheaded," she replied and that got a laugh out of him. He hit her on the back as they walked, not a pat like before, but as if they were comrades. Raymond considered her an insider.

***

Nicole was surprised when Danny and her father were laughing with each other as they returned to camp. She didn't realize how great such a scene was until seeing it for herself. She felt real joy. Anything that happened on the trip was worth it for just this moment. Not only did her father like Danny, and show it, but now Danny was aware of it and comfortable with him. They were making progress. *Now, if only Mommy would come around.*

"So, Rich, you burn the fish yet?" Raymond grinned, wiggling his eyebrows in jest.

"He let me do it, Uncle Raymond," Junior said from the grill.

"Best decision of his life," Raymond replied, earning a serious glare from his brother.

"Oh, Dad, Uncle has jokes on you!" Spider hooted, clearly trying to start something. These were their family dynamics when they were away from the mature females of the family, and Nicole was certain all the women knew that.

"He's mad because he's a baby Sasquatch," Richard said from his seat. He was cleaning his hunting knife, trying to look busy as his excuse for why he didn't have time to cook the fish.

"If I were, and I don't eat your food, what does that say about your cooking?" Raymond smirked.

The cousins all giggled over that. Nicole chuckled while moving closer to Danny and taking her hand. She wanted to let Danny know it was all right to laugh if the urge overcame her. After all, they were probably going to be like this for the rest of the trip. Danny glanced at her and smiled, but nothing more.

"I think food poisoning would be an improvement for you," Richard told his younger brother.

"Only if we're in the will," Spider added.

"I'm cutting you all off. I'm leaving all my earthly goods to Nikki and Beth," Raymond said dramatically, waving his hand in their direction.

"I'm taking the car then," Beth called with a bright grin.

"Why? So you can crash it into a wall?" Junior inquired with an eyebrow up.

Nicole had to hold in a snicker. She felt bad for finding that amusing. *How is it I turn fifteen again when I'm around these guys?* Of course, she wasn't the only one with that problem, but that didn't make it any better.

She whispered to Danny, "Beth can't drive for shit and has crashed two cars. We don't usually bring it up, because she was hurt in the second crash. She was in the hospital for a few days, broke a few bones and things of that nature."

Danny nodded, but Nicole wasn't sure if she totally believed her since Spider and Lillian laughed. Thankfully, Raymond and Richard reined that in with a simple admonishing look to the siblings and a glare at Junior, who was properly chastised. He turned his attention back to the food, while Beth marched over to him. She wasted no time hitting Junior hard, several times, on his broad back.

"Hey, stop hitting me, girl. You want me to mess up lunch?" Junior huffed, moving away from Beth, but doing his best not to leave the grill.

Beth gave him one more whack before sitting down. Nicole decided to encourage Beth's bad behavior and gave her a high five. Lillian joined in, but not to congratulate. She knocked their hands apart.

"You can't give her credit for beating up my big brother," Lillian said with a good-natured smile.

"I can when the big lug deserves it," Nicole replied with a smile of her own. She shot a teasing smirk over to Junior, who stuck his tongue out at her.

"Besides, you always think it's okay for Nikki to beat them up after Junior or Spider does something horrible to you," Beth said.

Lillian didn't have a response for that. She more than likely didn't want to sound childish because, of course, to Lillian it was different. Lillian didn't mind Nicole defending her little sister. Well, sometimes anyway.

"Remember that time you pushed Junior out of the tree when he made Lil cry?" Spider piped in as Nicole took a seat.

"Oh, yeah, she totally tried to kill me!" Junior pointed an accusing finger at her.

"I did not! That was an accident! I thought you'd catch yourself," Nicole defended her actions, throwing her hands up wildly.

"Catch myself from what, plummeting to my death?" Junior inquired incredulously, laughing a bit.

"I didn't try to kill him," Nicole tried to assure Danny, who stood in front of her because Lillian had taken the seat beside her. She couldn't help wondering if Lillian was a little jealous of Danny. It wouldn't surprise her, as Lillian had shown signs of jealousy in the past. She'd have to tell Danny not to take the actions personally.

"Sure you didn't." Danny gave her an amused smile, but also reached out for her hand.

"I didn't! I swear, I thought he was going to catch himself!" Nicole squeezed Danny's hand hard in her excitement. Danny didn't even flinch.

"She was more upset than Junior was, though," Spider said.

"I was unconscious!" Junior objected. "I couldn't possibly be upset while being in a freaking coma!"

There was some snickering from the others. Raymond and Richard let them go. Sometimes, Nicole swore she could see the nostalgia in their eyes and the small smiles gracing their rugged faces. They were probably remembering times from their own childhood camping trips. Something about that touched her and made the family trips seem more special, like generations of their families were connected, even if they all weren't there. She could almost picture her grandfather looking like her father and uncle did, smiling in the past about something silly.

"Hey, didn't you try to drown me for no good reason a few months before that little incident? And let's not forget about how you tore open my bicep while we were sword fighting," Nicole said.

"Sword fighting?" Danny stared at her. There was an interested spark in her grey eyes. Nicole suspected her beloved enjoyed hearing these wild stories about her, liked knowing that some sort of feral lunatic lurked underneath the elegance, if the conditions were right. If Nicole thought about it, she sometimes missed that wild child.

"We made wooden swords from bits of fence that our grandfather had torn down, but some genius used a piece of wood with a nail in it. I won't mention any names. Needless to say, I had a fun trip to the doctor and had a wonderful tetanus shot along with some awesome stitches. It was such a great day." Nicole's voice dripped with sarcasm.

"Reminds me of the time you hit me with your bike." Spider made a face at Nicole. "I had an awesome trip to the hospital with my concussion."

"They were rough kids. We were scared to leave them outside together until they were fifteen," Raymond said, speaking to Danny.

"Yeah, Nikki got really boring at that time. She discovered boys." Spider sighed and shook his head.

"What? By then, Junior thought he was an adult and stopped having time for us." Nicole nodded toward Junior.

Spider turned to his older brother. "She's right. You grew that stupid beard, which you still have for some odd reason, and got your job and all of that crap and you were too good for us for like a year."

"Damn right I was," Junior laughed.

"That was a good year," Beth said, earning laughs from everyone else. Junior rolled his eyes and scoffed.

Raymond nodded. "Injury free."

Junior was done with lunch before he had time to mount a comeback. Danny seemed intent on standing, so Nicole grabbed one of the folding stools for her and they enjoyed some fish, beans, and bread.

"Why didn't you make baked potatoes with this instead?" Spider inquired.

"How about you make baked potatoes when you cook? How about that?" Junior countered in a tone that was very close to 'I know you are, but what am I?'

"You two stop bickering like little girls for a second and eat," Richard grunted. His sons made faces at each other and he glared at both of them. The ladies of the family snickered at the brothers being scolded.

"So, after lunch, are we going on our usual hike?" Beth asked no one in general.

"I don't see why not," Richard answered.

Danny arched an eyebrow at the mention of a hike. Nicole leaned over and patted her knee, the one that was undoubtedly throbbing at the thought of walking on unleveled ground. The knee brace could only do so much, after all. The gesture didn't go unnoticed and, of course, her cousins, being the jerks they were, had to say something.

"Aw, city gal scared of a little walk? Does she want to go by car like your last girlfriend did?" Spider teased.

"Have no problem with walking," Danny replied. She didn't have a problem with walking, but she couldn't do it for a long period of time, and she might not be able to do it over rough terrain for more than a few minutes. Hiking was probably very much out of her ability.

Nicole doubted going uphill and over rocks would be kind to Danny's leg. She wasn't going to say anything. She had to taper her urge to baby Danny, even if she was doing it to protect her. Danny knew her body and she'd hopefully stop when her leg was tired of the hike.

"You'll probably really like the hike. We take a path that allows us to see all sorts of sights in the woods and it ends at the top of a hill that looks down into a valley. It's fresh and green for as far as you can see," Nicole told her lover.

Nicole accepted Danny's nod and hoped she'd know when to stop once the hike began. She hoped Danny didn't push herself beyond her limits to see what was at the end of the trail or, worse, try to prove something. She hated that Junior and Spider were certainly going to use Danny's injuries to make fun of her. They'd claim Danny's inability to hike as another reason why Nicole shouldn't be with her. Of course, she'd ignore them, and she suspected Danny would do the same.

"Everybody, get your packs ready so we can get this hike started," Raymond said once lunch was over.

"Make sure to clean up after yourselves, too," Richard ordered, giving Spider a stern look as he was the most likely to leave his trash sitting out.

"I'll do it," Spider huffed.

"Webber." Richard looked down at the empty plate.

"What? What? What? I got it." Spider grabbed his garbage and made sure to get rid of it.

After disposing of their own garbage, Nicole went over to her things with Danny on her heels. She handed Danny a backpack and picked up her own. Grey eyes stared at the pack as if trying to figure out what it was.

"I packed for us when we were at home. You think you'll be fine with hiking? We hike for a couple of hours," Nicole warned her girlfriend.

Danny shrugged. "I'll give it a shot. The knee brace should help some. If I can't do it, I promise to stop. Don't really have any plans to leave here not being able to walk. Unless, of course, you had other plans." A sexy smirk curled onto her lips.

"Hey! Stop that!" Nicole gave her shoulder a playful hit.

"What? I didn't do anything," Danny replied, now smirking and gazing at her with hooded eyes. Nicole gave her another soft hit.

"Stop it or I'll get my daddy on you," Nicole whispered.

Those words sobered Danny up quickly. Nicole couldn't help laughing at her beloved's expression. She could only imagine the passion whiplash Danny went through at having her amorous thoughts halted by the mention of Raymond.

"I hope I didn't short circuit your brain, baby," Nicole commented, taking Danny's hand to intertwine their fingers.

"No, but I'm definitely not looking at you wrong anymore on this trip," Danny replied, and Nicole laughed a bit.

She put on an exaggerated pout, poking out her bottom lip. "I'll miss those looks, though."

"You'll have to wait for us to get home to see them again. I'm finally on your dad's good side. Kinda like it there, so I don't wanna blow it."

Nicole smiled and bumped Danny with her hip to assure her that everything would be fine. Danny chuckled and wrapped her arm around Nicole's waist. For a moment, Nicole forgot where they were and leaned in close to her lover. She remembered suddenly, made a quick check to see that her family was packing for the hike, and laid a hasty peck to

Danny's waiting lips. They smiled, and Nicole backed away as if she hadn't done anything.

"You two going to keep playing kissy-face or can we go?" Lillian grinned at them.

Nicole waved at her cousin. "Oh, hush you."

Lillian grinned more, and they all gathered together. Everyone had their packs ready and strapped to their backs. Nicole took Danny's hand again, giving it a squeeze. Danny smiled at her.

"You worry too much, Chem. I'll be fine."

Nicole nodded because she trusted Danny. Junior and Spider looked at their joined hands and rolled their eyes. Nicole checked to see what her father and uncle were doing. When she saw they were otherwise occupied, Nicole flipped her cousins off. They made exaggeratedly shocked faces and returned the gesture after making sure their father and uncle were still not paying attention.

"Children, children," Beth playfully scolded them, going as far as wagging her finger at them. "Keep that up and I'll be telling everyone's moms." She smirked like a demon.

"Snitch," Spider hissed.

"You always were a party pooper, Beth. Why is Nikki the only cool girl in the family?" Junior gave her a wicked smile, clearly trying to get a spark out of Beth and his little sister.

"Hey," Lillian huffed. "Why are you and Spider such jerks?"

"Talent." Spider shrugged.

"DNA of awesome," Junior said, as if it was obvious. "It's probably on the Y chromosome, which is why you and your ilk remain lame." Spider snickered and gave his brother a high five.

"Cut it out, you guys. God, it's like being around a group of ten-year-olds, nonstop." Richard shook his head at them.

The bickering stopped, and they started for the hiking trail with Nicole staying close to Danny, continuing to hold her hand. They ended up with all the women in the back, because Lillian and Beth walked slowly anyway.

"I miss this trail." Beth sighed contently, making use of a walking stick as some of the effects of her car accident still remained with her.

"You've probably seen a million better ones," Spider called from a few feet ahead of them.

"Yeah, but there's something about this trail," Beth replied, eyes scanning the place.

Nicole smiled. "This one reminds you of a much more innocent time."

"I wouldn't call it innocent. Junior threw a snake on me once, while we were on this trail," Beth replied.

Junior balked, turning around with wide eyes. "I was showing you! Showing you!"

"He got into a lot of trouble for that," Beth informed Danny with a satisfied smirk.

"That's basically all we did as kids, get into trouble for doing something to each other or following Junior into doing something," Nicole said.

"We eventually learned not to blindly follow him when he and Nikki wandered through some poison ivy. He was taunting us all for being scared, and Nikki was the only one brave enough to follow him," Lillian said.

"I think the word you're looking for is stupid. I was the only one stupid enough to follow him. But, it wasn't all bad. Someone really nice kept me company while I was miserable for the rest of the trip," Nicole said and Lillian grinned.

Beth rolled her eyes, which Nicole ignored. Sometimes, Nicole was sure her relationship with Lillian annoyed Beth, because it seemed kind of cutesy or just plain saccharine. It couldn't be helped, as far as Nicole was concerned, because she loved Lillian and wanted to make sure Lillian knew that.

"I think the poison ivy was the dumbest thing you followed Junior into," Beth said.

"Let's be thankful there are no tar pits around here," Richard replied, shaking his head.

"I would've had to go in after her. No way in hell I could've gone home and told Kate I lost Nikki," Raymond said.

"She probably bit your head off after every trip. She lost her mind whenever it looked like Nikki might get bruised," Richard sneered. Little things like that let Nicole know how her father's family felt about her mother. His tone and expression were subtle, and the rest of the family was like that when they spoke of her mother, too, but Nicole noticed. She couldn't make sense of the attitude. She had never seen her mother do anything to them.

"To this day, Kate still goes pale whenever I start off a story 'so, Nikki was with Junior and Spider,'" Raymond said.

She had followed Junior and Spider into some dangerous and stupid situations throughout their lives. Most of the time, the adage 'God protects fools and babies' held true for them, but every now and then, one of them got injured. When Nicole was injured, Lillian was always by her side, helping her through it. She did the same whenever Lillian needed her, be it physical or emotional pain. It was one of the things that made them so close.

As they walked on and minutes passed, Nicole drifted farther ahead of the three women. She didn't mean to, but it just happened that way. She slowed her steps, waiting for Danny to catch up with her. She took her hand again.

"Hey, Nick, you don't need to wait for me, you know? You can walk with the big boys up there. I'm fine."

"I don't want to leave you behind," Nicole said. Yes, she wanted to enjoy her cousins' company, but she also wanted to be by Danny's side for the camping experience. She had hoped she'd be able to do both at the same time, but since Junior and Spider were being asses, she'd definitely rather be with her beloved.

"You're not leaving me behind. You're just going ahead on a hike. It's fine. I've got company back here."

"You sure?" She considered Danny might be trying to get to know the cousins who weren't acting like morons, which was fine by her.

"Yeah, it's cool."

Nicole gave her lover a long look, and Danny responded to that with a bright grin. That was good enough for Nicole, mostly because it satisfied the crazy little kid inside of her. She leaned in and gave Danny a quick peck on the cheek before powering forward toward her other cousins. As soon as she got to Junior and Spider, the pair glanced back.

"Don't say anything," Nicole ordered with a hard glare. She wanted to enjoy being around them and that would be impossible if they said anything about Danny right now.

"What? We wanted to make sure a bear hadn't grabbed the lazy-bones off the trail," Spider said.

"Your city girl's looking like she's working up a sweat already. She's never going to make it to the top, not that you've ever brought someone that made it to the top, except that scary chick with the guns. What happened to her?" Junior wondered aloud.

"What always happens? Eventually, I got tired of being her doormat," Nicole answered.

"Well, you need to get tired of being her doormat down there. I mean, she can't even hike. How's this a good match for you? You two don't have anything in common," Spider said.

"I told you two Danny is it for me. We have plenty in common, and we balance each other out. So, leave her alone," Nicole stated for what felt like the umpteenth time. She loved these two idiots, but she wouldn't let them disrespect her beloved right in front of her.

Spider snorted and shrugged. "Fine."

"Okay, but, on a serious note, is she okay? I mean, she's sweating a lot for such a short walk," Junior said, glancing behind them again. "She's not about to have a heart attack on the trail, is she?"

Nicole looked back, knowing Danny had worked up a bit of a glow. Her copper tone skin was shining a bit, but it didn't look too bad, yet. She trusted that Danny knew her limit and would stop when she needed. If not, Nicole would step in and guide Danny back to camp while everyone else continued on with the hike. Some alone time wouldn't be too bad.

"She's fine. So, how many animals have you guys spotted yet?" Nicole asked. They always kept count of how many animals they saw while hiking. It was the competitors in them. When they got to the top, they'd see who caught the most sights and that person got extra s'mores when they had dinner. The extra s'mores came from the losers.

Spider let loose another snort. "Don't even bother. There's no way you can catch up."

"What makes you think I wasn't keeping count when I was back there? I'm still in this, so tell me your numbers," Nicole stated with a grin. The brothers scoffed, but they smiled while doing it.

***

"So, Nikki left you, huh?" Lillian asked, striding up to Dane.

Dane gritted her teeth. The small jolts of pain firing through her leg didn't need help from Lillian. She wasn't sure how much longer she'd make it on the hike, but she was probably going to cut that time even shorter, because she didn't want to speak to Lillian. She really wished she could make it to the end of the trail. So far, it was as wonderful as Nicole had promised. So many colors, sounds, and smells to experience, and she wanted all of it. She could only imagine the view at the end. *That's probably all I'll be able to do.*

"Lil, leave Danny alone," Beth barked.

"What? I'm just teasing her a bit. Besides, she should know that's what Nikki does when she gets around my brothers. I've seen her get into arguments with a lot of lovers after she's hung out with my brothers. It's like the world vanishes and they turn into the three musketeers. Her lovers hate that," Lillian replied.

Dane waved it off. "She can hang out with them. She hasn't seen them in a long time."

Beth smiled. "See, Lil? So, let it go."

Lillian shrugged. "I'm not doing anything, Beth. It's great that Danny doesn't mind Nikki hanging with my brothers. She's more mature than most of Nikki's other lovers, huh?"

"Who cares about Nikki's other lovers? They're gone and Danny's here. Danny's trying to get along with everyone." Beth scowled at Lillian.

"I didn't say she wasn't. You're jumping down my throat for no reason. Danny's fine with it, right?" Lillian said.

Dane only shrugged. She'd be fine if Lillian walked somewhere else, maybe off a short ledge. *No, that's not fair. This is Nick's little cousin. You only have to stomach her for a couple more days.* Or so she hoped. There was always the chance that the cousins would have such a good time together that they'd want to hang out a little longer, or Nicole would invite Lillian to the house one day.

"Danny's being polite. So, Danny, how are you enjoying camping so far?" Beth asked, almost as if she were trying to keep Lillian from starting her own conversation.

"It's all right. Think I need to get the hang of it, but it seems like something I could enjoy," Danny answered.

"That's good if you're going to be with Nikki. She loves camping," Lillian chimed in, and Dane wondered where she'd take things now. "I think she broke up with a lot of people because they couldn't cut it on these trips, or trips like this."

"A lot of people?" She rolled her eyes. While she didn't know how many people Nicole dated, she disliked Lillian's implications there were dozens and that Nicole dropped people for ridiculous reasons like not being able to camp.

"What? You don't believe me?" Lillian inquired, sounding almost threatening. Dane dismissed the tone and the simultaneous glare by reminding herself that she only had to suffer the woman for a couple of days.

"I don't think it's important. You know, I think I'm going to take a break. My knee hurts." Dane wanted the excuse out there, so Lillian wouldn't press her. Now, she had to hope Lillian wouldn't stop with her.

"I can wait with you," Beth offered, panting a bit herself. "I used to be better at this, before I had a car accident."

Dane nodded. Lillian looked between them, as if she were trying to figure out if she'd stay. *Please, don't stay! Go spend time with this cousin you claim to love so much that you won't even let me sit next to her!*

"I'll tell them you both paused for a break," Lillian said, as she trotted off.

"Tell them we probably won't make it up," Beth called. Lillian waved back to show that she heard.

"How do you know I won't make it?" Dane asked.

"I've seen the limp all day, Danny. Let's take a seat and then make our way back to camp. We can trade war stories," Beth replied with a kind smile. Dane chuckled and nodded. *I definitely like this one a lot more. Why couldn't this be Nick's 'sister'?*

Chapter Ten

NICOLE WAS SURPRISED WHEN Lillian rushed up and fell into line with her. She glanced behind them to see Danny and Beth taking a break. She assumed Danny's knee bothered her, and she was glad Danny had stopped on her own. It saved her the trouble of coming across as a nag. She was also happy Beth stayed with Danny. *At least Danny won't think all my cousins are horrible.*

"What happened? Beth trying to give the city gal a pep talk?" Junior inquired with a teasing smirk, dragging out the word gal to mock Danny even more. Spider snickered, encouraging his brother. Nicole glared at them, but she didn't get the reaction that she desired.

"No, Danny said something about her knee bothering her and Beth stopped with her. Beth said they probably won't make it to the top," Lillian replied. Everyone frowned when they heard those words.

"That accident really messed her up," Spider grumbled, talking about Beth. He glanced back and shook his head. "It's not fair."

It really wasn't. Beth was the most outdoorsy of all of them. Though the car accident almost ruined her livelihood and her passion in general, Beth was showing the strength they'd all come to expect of her, battling back like the boss she was.

"She probably needs a couple more years to get back into tip-top shape. Remember how bad she was when the accident first happened? She's a million times better now. She'll be all right," Junior gave him a reassuring pat on the shoulder.

"Yeah, she'll be okay. She warned me, when I called her about this, that she probably wouldn't be able to handle the hike. She probably could've handled more. She told me she'd probably be able to make it a little more than halfway, but she's keeping Danny company," Nicole replied. She wished Danny could've done more, because she felt like her lover would have enjoyed the view from the top. It made her think about the surgery Danny didn't seem to want to talk about. She wondered if something like this might make Danny at least consider it, since it was obvious the brace wasn't much help.

"And what's Danny's excuse? I mean, we haven't even been hiking an hour yet. It's not like she was really powering through this," Junior pointed out with a snort.

"She's probably trying to figure out how to hail a cab around here," Spider chuckled and got a laugh out of his older brother.

"Danny's got a bad knee from when she was younger." Nicole frowned. If that wasn't enough explanation, too bad. She wouldn't give them anything beyond that.

"What happened?" Richard asked with a curiously arched eyebrow. Nicole was a bit surprised he was interested. Her uncle hardly glanced at her girlfriends when she brought them on trips. Thankfully, he was rarely rude to her girlfriends, even though she was very aware of his stance on her sexuality.

"That's her story to tell, but she's just not equipped to hike now. One day, hopefully she'll improve. I doubt she'll ever be able to go on long hikes," Nicole replied. *It's a bit sad that she'll never be able to enjoy a long hike. I think Danny would love doing stuff like this.*

"Again, I don't understand what you see in her. You love hiking and you're with someone that doesn't like hiking," Junior said.

"Oh, yeah, says the guy who has never dated a girl that likes hiking," Nicole countered in a deadpan tone. "The mother of your children doesn't like hiking and has allergies, so she'd be miserable out here."

For a long moment, Junior was shut down. His brother jumped in, trying to save him. "It's different."

"How exactly is it different?" She frowned, suspecting what was different. Danny should be a butch lesbian who acted like a man, or a man in general, and should be able to do everything they could and more.

"You know how it's different." Junior stood a little taller now that he had his brother backing him up.

"No, I really don't."

Clearly, they didn't agree. Their faces scrunched up in the same manner, displaying the same confusion. *They're lucky I love them, because whenever they act this thick, it's upsetting.*

"You do, Nikki, so don't act like this. It's just different," Junior said, and Spider gave a small nod.

She made a curious noise, grunting a little. *What makes them think that was a good argument?* Surely, they knew she couldn't accept such a thing. She took a moment and thought to the past to see if there ever was a time when she allowed such a weak argument to pass and came up with nothing. She wasn't sure why they thought it'd work this time.

An auburn eyebrow arched as Nicole countered. "Let me see if I understand this. You're allowed a mate that doesn't like camping in general and probably would never come out here, and I have one who is doing what she can and enjoying it, yet, somehow, I'm the one that's doing it wrong?"

"Nikki, we don't mean like that. It's different because...you know...you don't really have anything in common with Danny. I mean, what does she have to give you?" Junior asked. Spider didn't make a sound this time, but studied Nicole. She figured he was waiting for her to convince him to stop siding with his brother.

"We don't have everything in common, but we share interests. Some interests she just can't do because of physical reasons. Besides, even if Danny hiked the whole way, even beat us there, you'd find some way to have a problem with it." Nicole huffed, folding her arms across her chest for a moment. *Why the hell am I trying to justify my relationship to them?* Even as the question drifted through her mind, she knew why.

Spider decided to chime back in. "Except that didn't happen."

"Why don't you two just stay out of it? Danny hasn't done anything to you, and you've been on her case the whole trip," Raymond stated in a no-nonsense tone. He glanced back to frown at them.

"Uncle Raymond, you can't actually approve of the relationship. You know the kind of people Nikki's attracted to. What does Danny do for Nikki? Nothing, I'll bet," Junior argued.

Nicole scowled, feeling tension in her neck. "You don't even know Danny. She does plenty for me."

"Like what? What could she possibly offer you?" Spider asked.

"Love, affection, respect, comfort, support," Nicole readily answered. "Not everything has to be tangible or measurable."

Richard decided to jump in. "What about kids? You can't have kids with her. You can't have a real family with her."

Nicole frowned at the term 'real family.' While she and Danny hadn't discussed how they might go about having children, she was certain they'd love any child they might have with all their hearts, and they'd be a real family. Besides, it was almost as if her uncle were saying that if they didn't have children then they weren't a real family. They were a family already and always would be.

"We're already a family." Nicole and Danny and Haydn were a very close-knit family, like she had while growing up, and had always wanted.

Richard scoffed. "A real family, kiddo. You deserve that. I'm sure your dad told you."

Nicole frowned at the phrase once more and tensed at the idea that her father might think the same thing. She hadn't seen any signs of it, but he grew up in the same household as her uncle. He might hold similar ideas. She shook that away. Her father had been wonderful with Danny recently, so she doubted he harbored any ideas about them not being a real family or not being able to build a family.

"Daddy likes Danny," Nicole felt the need to point out. Richard looked over at his brother.

Raymond shrugged as his brother and nephews looked at him in disbelief. "She's not the ideal mate that I would've picked for Nicole, but she makes Nikki happy and she's a good person. She's probably the best match for Nikki. Plus, I've heard a song and dance like this. No one knows the ins and outs of a relationship like the two people involved, so it might look weird to us on the outside, but it seems to work."

It wasn't the shining endorsement that Nicole would've liked, but it was better than anything her father would've said a year ago. But, then again, it was approval and, really, that was all she needed. Danny would more than likely keep growing on him, and he'd eventually gush about Danny like she did. *Okay, maybe not gush, but he likes her.*

Richard frowned and squinted at his brother. "You can't be serious, Raymond."

"I'm very serious, so how about we all get off of Nikki's case. She's going to do what she feels is best for her and, right now, she feels Danny is the best thing for her. You all *telling* her what's best for her is only going to heighten her resolve into proving you wrong. Thirty years from now, she'll still be with Danny, and you'll be choking on your crow," Raymond said with a strange smirk on his face. Nicole almost got the feeling he wasn't talking about her and Danny anymore.

"Nikki, all we're saying is you should probably find someone more your speed," Richard said, glancing at his brother.

"I don't even know what that means," Nicole admitted.

"It doesn't even matter. Nicole tried to find someone more her speed in nine different forms and they didn't work out. Maybe stepping outside the box will." Raymond practically glared at his older brother.

Nicole cringed, being reminded of the nine times that she got it wrong. She stayed in those relationships longer than she should have, wanting to make them work. Her family had met most of them and didn't approve, even though they were more her speed. On paper, they had a lot in common, but most of them weren't good people. Danny was a good person with a very good heart, despite all that life had thrown at her. She was very different from everyone else that Nicole had dated. *And that might be part of why we work. I'm not throwing that away.*

"I don't think those nine people were even close to Nikki's speed," Junior argued.

"And neither is Danny," Spider added.

Nicole rolled her eyes. She was curious now, so she had to ask. "Okay, who would be more my speed?"

"You should date guys like Lillian does," Junior replied. Lillian smiled at Nicole, who had to struggle not to roll her eyes again.

Nicole had to bite her tongue to keep from saying something mean, because she didn't want to upset Lillian. Lillian didn't date the best of men, from what she could tell from Lillian's occasional comments about her boyfriends. If the relationships were so great, she liked to think Lillian would be more serious about them, possibly engaged to someone. Instead, Lillian treated her boyfriends like passing fancies, even as she tried to make things sound more serious than they were.

Lillian liked to paint her relationships in glowing terms, but Nicole noted that none of her boyfriends lasted longer than three months. It was rare, indeed, for Lillian to have the same boyfriend in between the times they spoke on the phone.

"What do you mean?" Nicole decided to ask, because she wanted to see what Junior thought of his sister's relationships.

"You know what I mean. Stop acting like you don't get it. She dates guys who are generally normal. They come to the house and know how to shake a guy's hand and not try to lord over anyone. They don't act superior. They engage you in a regular conversation without being condescending and they don't brag about stupid shit that none of us care about."

"Oh, you mean like Danny's been trying to do?" Nicole said. Of course, Danny wasn't a guy, so that was part of the problem.

"It's different," Junior insisted, giving her a frown.

"Because Danny's a woman?" Nicole rolled her eyes. She wished they'd come right out and say it.

"Nikki, you know we don't have a problem with that," Richard objected.

Nicole knew that was an outright lie. The first time she brought a girlfriend to meet them her uncle had almost thrown her out of the house. Well, had almost thrown her out after he somehow managed to not faint at the scandal of it all. Her father managed to stop him. From that moment on, they all pretended they tolerated her sexual preferences, but they didn't accept this part of her. She wondered if they thought it was a phase, like her mother tended to call it. They were inclined to ignore her girlfriends, claiming not to have anything in common with them.

"No, but you'd rather I dated a man. It'd make you more comfortable," Nicole said.

"We're not uncomfortable. We'd rather you dated someone who will treat you like you deserve and do all the things you find fun," Spider replied through gritted teeth.

"You're talking about Danny, but you don't know that because you haven't bothered to say a kind word to her or look at her without hatred in your eyes. You haven't given her a chance at all. You're treating her like she's all my exes rolled up into one, but she's nothing like them. You're being completely unfair to her and, to her credit, she's letting it roll right off her."

Honestly, Nicole respected Danny for her patience with her family. A lesser person would've probably snapped at Junior and Spider already. Thankfully, her uncle had kept his opinion to himself for the most part. Usually, he glared at her and her girlfriend when she brought women around him. He did his best to never acknowledge that she even dated women. She guessed it was because they were 'normal' people and liked to pretend the entire world was 'normal.' They didn't take kindly to someone who came around and tipped the balance.

Nicole's words seemed to knock the steam out of her cousins because they were quiet. She hoped they'd think about how they hadn't given Danny a fair shake. She wouldn't hold her breath on it, though. *Hopefully, Beth is at least being nice to Danny.*

***

Dane sat down on a large rock, unstrapping her knee brace. Placing the brace on the ground, she sighed and massaged her knee. She missed Nicole in that moment, knowing she could work out the pain in minutes. Beth eased down next to her on the rock, leaning against her walking stick.

"How'd you mess up your knee?" Beth asked, glancing down at the body part.

"An accident," Dane answered. The only accident, then, had been trusting her supposed best friend.

Beth nodded a little. "Car accident?"

"Nah, but my leg and knee were busted up pretty bad. What about you? Do you usually make this hike?" She was willing to bet that Beth did more than that. Based on the photos that she had seen, Beth seemed to be very much into nature and adventure.

"Yeah, I used to. I got really jammed up in a car accident a couple of years ago, like I said, and I haven't been the same since. I'm slowly getting back into it. My best friend's a good cheerleader. On days I get depressed over it, he's always in my ear, reminding me of all the great stuff we're going to do once I'm totally healed. He damn sure would've been in my ear, if he were here, to get my ass up this hill."

Dane nodded. "No amount of cheerleading would've gotten me up there." She wished that wasn't the case. Seeing how hyped Nicole was over this whole thing, she knew Nicole would've cheered her the whole time if that were all it took. She would've loved nothing more than to be there every step of the way with her ladylove. Plus, she had come to enjoy walks through nature. Sure, they were in the park close to the house, but she liked the trees, the grass, and the smell of the flowers. Here was even better than the park. There was so much stuff here. She'd like to stop and take it all in and memorize the sights, smells, and sounds. If she possibly could, she'd definitely get into hiking.

"No?" Beth twisted her mouth up for a moment and then shrugged. "Well, there are other things to do beyond hiking. We'll get you into fishing yet, since you didn't flinch at the live bait."

Dane scrunched her face up a little. "Flinch? They're just worms." She had shared space with much more disgusting things, as well as scarier things.

"Oh, believe me. We've seen people flinch, most of them brought here with Nikki. Lil still flinches, too."

"What's with Lil?" Dane inquired.

The way Beth glanced away, Dane knew Beth knew what she was talking about. She wondered if she should've built up to that question, but she understood what Junior and Spider's problem was, so she didn't need to ask. Richard hadn't spoken to her, so she wasn't sure if he had a problem or not. Lillian was the only weird one as far as she was concerned.

"Lil trying to look out for Nikki." Beth didn't sound very convincing.

Dane stared at her with a craned eyebrow. "By telling me about Nick's former lovers?"

Beth frowned slightly. "She's trying to scare you off."

"Is she? It seemed like it was something more than that."

"She doesn't want to share Nikki."

Nodding, Dane stared off at some birds nesting in the distance. "Then why does she say some things that make Nick sound bad?" She never once got the feeling Lillian was looking out for Nicole. No, that was Junior and Spider. It was possible she was trying to scare Dane off, but nope, she wasn't buying that. Something wasn't right about Lillian, and Beth probably knew what it was, which explained why she made up some bullshit.

Beth glanced away again and licked her lips. "Look, Lil is a strange one."

Dane's gaze narrowed and she studied the odd, almost guilty, look on Beth's face. "She doesn't feel the same way about Nick as Nick does about her, huh?" This was what it felt like. Lillian had something against Nicole.

"I wouldn't say that. I don't have a psych degree to totally figure out what goes on with Lil. I'm assuming she loves Nikki, in some way, considering she became a lawyer like Nikki, even though she never really showed an interest in law. But, she's lived her life like that, from what I can tell. She got into softball when she found out Nikki played. Tried to get into tennis, but her parents couldn't afford lessons at the time, and she always did her best in school, just like Nikki."

Dane nodded. Despite her own very questionable upbringing, if it could be called that, she knew that younger siblings followed in the footsteps of older siblings they admired. Even she had tried it, for a very short time, when she was a child. It hadn't worked out well, of course, but she had done it. Still, there was something about Lillian that didn't add up.

"So, she wants to be just like Nicole?" Dane inquired, even though she knew that wasn't the case.

Beth allowed a soft grimace to go through her face. It seemed like she wanted to tell Dane about Lillian, but without betraying her cousin. So, instead of saying things aloud, she telegraphed her facial expressions.

Nodding, Dane looked for a second, spotting some chipmunks. They were cute in real life. "Is she jealous of Nicole?"

"I don't know if I'd call it jealous. I'm not entirely sure. As I said, Lil is strange, and I don't exactly talk to her about stuff like this. Some things Nicole does, Lil doesn't even try, especially whenever Nicole did something with Junior and Spider."

"Does she resent Nicole spending time with her brothers or resent her brothers for spending time with Nicole?"

Beth shrugged. "It's not something I've really thought about. I'm the baby of this group. I only started observing these things when I was in my early teens and, by then, they were all set in whatever ways they had. They seemed pretty normal to me, because I was used to them. Junior, Spider, and Nicole are fairly easy to understand. They're very intelligent, but they're reckless, which makes them upfront about things. They don't backbite."

"Lil does." Dane wondered if Beth was like her cousins, very upfront, or if she was more like Lil. So far, she seemed all right.

"But, I don't know what her game is. I don't know what she's trying to do. I can't understand why she does the things that she does."

"But, you know she does it. Have you ever told Nick or her brothers?"

Beth scoffed. "Tell them what? Lil could be joking for all I know. She's got a sick sense of humor, too."

Dane nodded, even though she didn't believe that for one second. She wondered who else knew Lillian talked about Nicole behind her back, and she wondered what type of things Lillian had said to other people. She doubted she'd get that information from Beth, and she didn't want to badger her, so she decided to shift things.

"Want to go back to camp?" Dane nodded down the path. There was no way in hell she'd make it to the end of the trail, and she didn't want to see Lillian again. It'd be nice to sit around camp for a while without having to put up with Junior and Spider.

"Yeah, might as well. You can show me what you can do with that guitar you brought. Despite the guys ribbing you about it, Nicole promised that you play like a master. I really want to hear that," Beth replied.

Dane shrugged. "I'm decent."

Beth chortled and rose to her feet. "I'm sure."

Dane followed suit, even though her knee still throbbed a bit. She put the knee brace back on. Watching Beth walk away with the stick to help support her, Dane considered getting one of her own. Of course, it'd be a little hard to maintain a badass image with a walking stick, even if it did look like a wizard's staff. *Wait, do I have a badass image? Like to think I do, even though I spend my weekdays folding laundry.*

"So, what do you do for a living, Danny? Something with music?"

"I tutor people on different instruments. On rare occasions, I can get a gig in a club," Dane answered, breathing in the feel of the Earth while she had the chance and wasn't bothered by anyone. The warm air seemed to make the forest wash over her and take her mind off of Nicole's less than friendly relatives.

"Hard to make a living?"

Dane shrugged. "Used to be easier."

"That's promising. I feel like I'm always hustling with my photography. My family all thought I was stupid for pursuing that as a career. My mother still thinks I'm going to starve to death, and my dad swears to the heavens I'll end up moving back home after ending up in debt...again. Is that how your family felt when you went into music?"

"They didn't care one way or another," Dane answered at first, and then she stopped herself. Those people weren't her family. But, the people who were her family, the people who had tried to look out for her throughout her life, even if they were only there for short periods of time, they were different. "You know what, actually, they were pretty supportive. They believed I had talent, and they knew I could go somewhere with it." *They probably thought I could go a lot further than I did, actually. Shit, wish I'd thought about this when I was pissing my life away.* Of course, she doubted she was capable of an epiphany when she was pissing her life away.

Beth nodded. "That's nice. So, when were your gigs easier to get?"

"Back when I had a band to go with my guitar. The band was good and we got paid a pretty penny. You have to make the right contacts and impress the right people. Sometimes, I guess, it just comes down to luck."

"I hope I have the luck. I've made some good contacts. There are a couple of magazines that call about my work or hire me to shoot for them. Plus, there are a couple of places that will pick up my prints, and I tend to sell pretty well."

"Seems like you should be fine. I don't know art, but your pictures are cool."

Beth smiled and Dane felt good to help the artist out, even if it was only with kind, but true, words. They fell silent for a moment, coming into the camp. Dane was happy to flop down onto one of the folding stools because her knee was killing her. *I might have to seriously have that surgery to repair my knee for something like this.*

She hadn't made it a point to think about the surgery. She would have to start thinking, point blank. She had to think about improving for Nicole and their relationship, as well as for herself. She had to think about if she'd ever be ready for kids. She had to think about what it meant for Raymond to actually like her. She had to think about what family really was and what Lillian was trying to do, and she had to think about what all of this meant.

"So, you'll play something for me or what?" Beth inquired.

"If you can get my guitar for me. It's in the tent." Dane jabbed her thumb in the direction of her tent.

Beth nodded and found the guitar with ease. Dane shouldered the instrument, flexed her hand, and began playing. Beth smiled as the soft notes filled the air, competing with birds and buzzing insects. *Maybe I'll get along with her.*

***

Nicole was pleased when they reached their spot and looked down onto the whole forest. It was awe-inspiring, feeling like they were standing atop the world, and she wished she could share the sight with Danny. A gentle breeze carried the scent of the trees and made her feel at peace. She imagined her beloved would pen beautiful music if she could take in the view. *Not that Danny needs a reason to pen beautiful music.* Nicole was starting to believe music poured out of Danny, as she sometimes implied, no muse or inspiration needed.

"It's always awesome to just stand here, huh?" Junior said to her, standing close.

"It is," Nicole replied, hoping he was going somewhere with that and not just making idle chitchat. He disappointed her.

"We really should do this more often. We shouldn't have let it fall to the wayside, even if the dads are busy. I mean, we're not kids anymore, right?"

"No, we're not."

"So, we should all be able to get together once a year and do this again, right?"

Nicole shrugged. "Probably." She could do it, but she wasn't sure if she wanted to. She wouldn't want to bring Danny back around and subject her to her cousins' harsh treatment. She also wouldn't leave

Danny at home for three or four days unless Danny was absolutely fine with it. Of course, even if Danny were fine with it, Nicole would be reluctant. She had no desire to spend days with people who'd bad-mouth the love of her life.

Junior looked down at her, brow furrowing slightly. "You don't think we could?"

"Of course, we could. We've gone on this trip enough with our fathers to be able to do it in our sleep."

"So, why so grim about it?"

A tense frown settled on her face. "You know why. Stop pretending everything's fine. You're not dense."

Junior groaned. "Still on this? What if I promised we, me and Spider, will talk to Danny and try to get to know her?"

"I'll believe it when I see it," she replied, not that she thought it'd make a difference at this point. They had made up their minds, and she had made up her mind. She wasn't going to subject Danny to her relatives anymore after this trip.

"Come on, Nikki."

"What come on? Could you imagine how pissed you'd be if I treated Michelle like you've been treating Danny? You'd never talk to me again."

"It's different."

Nicole snorted, not even bothering to ask why it was different. Her cousins weren't listening to her. It certainly took some of the sparkle away from the trip, but it was saved by the fact that Danny claimed to be enjoying herself, even if Junior and Spider weren't behaving themselves. The next time she came out here, she figured it would be her, Danny, and maybe Danny's nephews or her little cousins, but she couldn't see herself camping with these cousins ever again.

"Nikki, we should definitely do this more often, because then we'd be able to see each other more often," Lillian grinned, stepping up behind Nicole. She put her hand on Nicole's shoulder, earning a glance from Nicole.

"I know, but I'll have to think about it. You know, you could always go camping with your brothers," Nicole countered, even though she knew that'd never happen.

Lillian scoffed. "So I can wake up with worms in my bed again? I think not."

"They were little boys when they did that."

Lillian glanced at Junior and Spider, who were shoving each other. "They're still little boys."

Nicole really wished she could argue that. They had been acting like little boys for the whole trip. She supposed the camping trip brought back childhood memories, because they hadn't acted childish the last time she saw them, which was at her house. She considered that maybe if they spent more time together outside, but not camping, her cousins might act more like the thirty-somethings they were.

"We should leave the guys behind and do something with just the two of us. I don't mind Danny," Lillian said.

"You should come stay at my house for a weekend. We could see a show or something," Nicole replied. It had been a couple of years since she'd seen a show. It would be fun. Danny would probably like it, too.

"That'd be nice. I haven't seen a show in a while, and I'm sure they've got good ones where you live."

Nicole chuckled. "Only the best for the big city."

Next to them, Junior rolled his eyes. He and his brother weren't the type to see a show. Honestly, if Nicole were with them, she'd never think to see a show either, despite her love for the theater. When she got around them, she turned into one of the boys, trying to relive a childhood that was a pleasant memory, but a memory nonetheless.

"I think you'd have fun. Danny might take you around to some of the clubs that she used to play," Nicole continued.

"She plays at clubs?" Lillian inquired with slightly wide, interested eyes.

"Well, not as much as she used to. The clubs she plays now are a little different from the clubs she used to play, but I think you'll like it."

"Maybe I'll take you up on your offer. I have to wait a while after taking these days off from work."

They stood on the plateau for almost a half hour, talking about nothing, really, and gazing at the view. They ate some snacks before starting back with the thought of dinner on their minds. As they came close to the camp, with the sun sinking over the horizon, they heard soft jazz, almost the perfect melody for the end of the day. Nicole knew, immediately, Danny was sitting around, plucking her guitar.

For a second, Nicole's family didn't know how to react. Danny and Beth seemed totally peaceful with Danny on her guitar and Beth preparing cornbread and chili. They were exchanging words with relaxed expressions, but they were too low to hear. It was nice to see they were getting along. Well, it seemed that way anyway. Nicole planned to ask Danny about it when they were alone, along with several other things.

"Hey, everybody, how was the hike?" The sound of Beth's easy question got everyone out of their stupor.

"It was good. You missed the view," Raymond replied.

"I'll see it again, one day soon," Beth said with certainty in her voice.

"That's good to hear and, Danny, I see you found something to keep yourself occupied." Raymond gave Danny a smile.

Danny smiled back. "Ah, well, Beth asked." She ceased playing and flexed her hand. Nicole thought she'd start up again, but Danny seemed to be done now that she had a larger audience. Nicole didn't blame her.

"It was a good request. She plays like she should have a halo over her head and the guitar is a harp," Beth said.

"You should hear her sing."

"If someone gave her a cup, she could panhandle," Spider muttered and Nicole glared at him. He held his hands up in surrender.

"Been there, done that. Doesn't make the money I'd expected," Danny said, as if it were no big deal. Spider's mouth dropped open and he was left speechless.

Nicole couldn't help smiling. She moved and sat down next to Danny, putting herself in a position to drape herself over Danny's broad shoulders. Moving her hands, she pretended to strum Danny's guitar. Grey eyes glanced at her as an amused smile settled onto Danny's face.

"I get it," Danny said, and she began to play again.

"You have to sing, now that Nikki let that cat out of the bag," Beth requested.

Danny laughed. "Maybe later. Unless you're making me sing for my supper."

"Don't tempt me. I am the cook, after all, and you don't wanna be on the cook's bad side," Beth chuckled.

Danny smiled and continued to pluck the strings of the guitar. Nicole settled against her, softly inhaling her smell. Everyone else moved about the camp, focusing on their own things, but eventually they sat down. No one asked Danny to stop playing. Usually music was Danny's last resort for people, but Nicole knew she wasn't using it this time. She was being nice to her newfound friend, Beth.

Nicole also knew her cousins and uncle weren't won over by music, even though Junior and Spider had a garage band once. She hoped they didn't somehow try to use this against Danny, too. Not that she could see how they could.

"You know, I play guitar, too. When did you learn how to play?" Junior asked.

Danny shrugged. "When I was little."

"We used to have a band," Spider said.

"So did I. Did you do concerts?" Danny asked in a tone that was slightly taunting. She knew they hadn't done concerts. Nicole gave her a little pinch as a reprimand. Danny barely glanced at her.

Junior stared at her with his mouth turned up. "You didn't play concerts."

"Oh, yeah. We opened for some big names," Danny replied. Nicole made a mental note to one day ask about those big names. She knew why Danny had never gone big, but she didn't know all the details about her career.

"Then why the hell aren't you in a band now, and why aren't you playing concerts?" Junior practically demanded, almost as if he was offended. He probably thought Danny was lying.

Danny paused and flexed her hands, accidentally cracking her knuckles as she bent each finger. "Life gets in the way sometimes and fate has other plans." She went back to playing.

Spider huffed. "What does that even mean?"

"It was a nice way of saying it's none of your business. You guys are so full of crap, you know." Beth scowled at the brothers. "Dinner's done. Let's eat now, so we can make some more s'mores."

Nicole chuckled and smiled at Beth, who smiled back. She was glad someone came out of this as Danny's friend. Now, if only she could get Danny to warm up to Lillian, she could walk away without feeling like her whole family was against the relationship. But one step at a time.

S.L. Kassidy

Chapter Eleven

A COUPLE OF HOURS after sunset, the group called it a night. They had spent time making s'mores and telling more ghost stories. Danny, once again, managed to scare all of them with her tale; Nicole made a mental note to ask what sort of television her lover used to watch to come up with such wild stories. Danny had even regaled them with a song or two from her guitar. Beth and Raymond praised her music, which brought a smile to Nicole's face. But, there was only so much to do by firelight, so they all went to their tents after that.

"Don't get under those covers," Nicole ordered Danny as she sat on top of their sleeping bag.

"What? Why? I'm all dressed for bed and everything," Danny replied with her face scrunched up. She motioned to her pajamas, which consisted of black boxers and a white tank top.

"Yes, you're all dressed for bed, but I'm going to give your knee and leg a rubdown," Nicole said. She had seen enough, since Danny had worn shorts, as always, to know her lover's knee was swollen. The brace had probably kept it from being worse, but she wasn't confident Danny would be able to do much tomorrow. She needed to do something to help her beloved.

"You don't have to."

Nicole let loose a little scoff. "Baby, I know I don't have to. Though, I'm going to. You need it, and I have everything here to give you a proper massage. You'll love it."

The grin that lit up Danny's face was priceless. "Hell, yeah, I will."

"While I do that, you can tell me about your time with your new best friend."

Danny's face scrunched up a little again. "My new best friend?"

"Yeah, Beth. You're playing your guitar for her and everything. Should I watch out before you move in with her?" Nicole flashed her a teasing smile.

Grey eyes rolled as Danny scoffed. "You planning to move in with her? Because we both know that's the only way I'd move. There's nothing to really tell with Beth. We talked, like regular people. Something I can't really get out of anyone around here, ya know?"

"Yeah, I know. I'm sorry about Junior and Spider. I don't know what to say to them to get them to act right. I really wish they'd get their heads out of their asses, because I think they'd get along great with you."

Danny shrugged and brushed it off with a wave of her hand. "They bring out a part of you I didn't know existed and it's rather cute."

Nicole chuckled. "Oh, yeah?"

Internally, Nicole felt a burst of light she didn't expect. It was exceptionally rare for people to see this side of her, but rarer still for someone to accept it. One of the reasons she kept it locked away was to avoid having significant others gawk at her as if she had lost her mind. Being judged by someone who was supposed to care about her was always troubling, even now.

"Yeah, I think it's really cute. I mean, you really are a tomboy. Thought you just played sports and stuff as a kid, but you're really a little tomboy, playing in the dirt, picking up snakes, and all kinds of crazy things. It's really cute." Danny reached out for Nicole, pulling her to the bed.

Nicole giggled in spite herself, knowing it'd only encourage her lover. "Stop it. I still need to get everything for your knee."

"My knee's fine. But, I guess you can kiss me and make it all better." Danny smirked as she caressed Nicole's bicep.

A smile tugged at Nicole's lips, but she managed to fight it off because she didn't want to encourage Danny's behavior. They didn't need to get wrapped up in each other in a tent with her family around. Besides, Danny's knee was far from all right and definitely needed attention. She refused to be distracted from that.

"I'm not kissing it, or you, right now. Now, let me go, so I can finish getting everything. You know your knee needs a massage, especially since we're more than likely going to go exploring tomorrow."

Danny ran her hand through her hair. "Exploring?"

"Yeah, we like to explore the woods, but we always end up in the same place in the end. We know about this cave, and I bet you'd love it. So, what do you say? You let me go, and I make your knee feel better?"

"Then I get my kiss?"

Nicole chuckled. "Only if you're good, Big Dog."

Danny playfully rolled her eyes, but she released Nicole, who smiled again and gave Danny a kiss on the cheek. Once Nicole located the lotion she needed, she sat on the airbed and put Danny's right leg into her lap. When the massage began, Danny let out a loud, almost obscene, moan. Nicole snickered a little.

Looking up, Nicole gave her love a lopsided grin. "Baby, you keep making those noises and the whole camp is going to think I'm doing something really bad to you."

"Or something really good," Danny replied and moaned again, as Nicole's fingers worked her swollen joint. "God, I didn't know how much it hurt until you started making it feel better."

"Maybe you should've stopped sooner on the trail."

"Don't think so. I probably could've gone farther."

Nicole arched an eyebrow. "What do you mean? With a knee like this you could've gone farther?"

"It's not that messed up."

Nicole couldn't help scoffing at what she felt was a complete and utter misrepresentation of the truth. "Then why are you moaning like that?"

Danny laughed. "You're touching me, duh." Her grey eyes shined as she locked gazes with Nicole.

"You are so bad." Nicole chuckled, swatting at Danny. "Maybe I should stop giving you the rubdown."

"You'd better not." Danny gave her a mock glare.

Nicole couldn't help smiling and leaning in for a quick kiss. "You'd better behave then. So, how did you find the day?" It seemed like an odd question for her to ask, considering they were together the whole day, but they really weren't. After all, she had spent almost all of her time with her cousins.

Nicole wasn't too sure how Danny took in the day, especially with the way her cousins had treated Danny. Outwardly, it seemed like Danny was enjoying herself, but internally, the purposely hurtful approach Junior and Spider had taken toward her might've bothered her much more than she let on. Plus, she wanted to know how things were going between Danny and Beth since they seemed to have taken to each other.

Danny was silent for a moment, reveling in having her knee rubbed. Nicole made sure to do it just the way she knew Danny liked it. Danny gave a little chirp and jumped a bit, which made Nicole smile.

Danny sighed. "It was good. I mean, I think one day I'd like to try fishing. Doubt I'd catch one right away, but it seemed really relaxing."

"I'll definitely teach you. We'll take day-trips." Internally, she beamed. It was great that her cousins' attitude hadn't put her beloved down. She believed they had some great trips in their future.

Danny grinned at the suggestion. "Like that."

"Good, because by the time we go on another camping trip, you'll be ready to catch us dinner."

"Speaking of dinner, cornbread and chili? Never thought those two things went together."

Nicole smiled. "When camping, you learn new things. I'm surprised she didn't make cornbread and beans, though. That's usually her favorite camp meal."

Danny shrugged. "Guess that makes sense." She let loose a moan, as Nicole hit a nerve underneath her knee. She threw her head back and moaned once more.

"Hey, behave." Nicole frowned at her. She gave Danny a gentle pinch as punishment, which didn't seem to register to Danny in the slightest.

"Can't help it," Danny purred. "Feels so good." A relaxed, almost lascivious grin slowly seeped onto her face.

"Well, then I guess I should stop."

"Please don't, angel. Please don't," Danny begged, sounding somewhat serious, but not completely.

Nicole chortled and kissed the inside of Danny's knee. Danny purred again and fell back, keeping herself up on her elbows. There was another chuckle and a kiss to the knee, before Nicole continued on with the massage.

"Do you know, I enjoy doing this as much as you do?" Nicole asked.

"You couldn't possibly."

Nicole chuckled. "That's where you're wrong. As you well know, I enjoy making you feel good, but there's something beyond words in knowing that with a simple kneading from my fingers, you melt."

Nicole gave Danny a little dose of what she meant and watched as Danny seriously melted. Her elbows gave out and she dropped to the mattress, moaning in ways that'd make most people blush. Nicole got her to cease the noise by giving her a real pinch and withholding her touch briefly. Danny whined as she sat up, giving Nicole puppy eyes that promised she'd behave, if only for a while.

"So, come on, tell me more about what you thought of today beyond wanting to know more about fishing," Nicole said.

"Well, I finally believe you that your dad likes me…somewhat. I learned today that a double standard works in my favor."

Nicole arched an eyebrow. "A double standard?"

"Your dad said if I was a guy, he'd kind of consider me a deadbeat, but he accepts that I'm pretty much your housewife, because I'm a woman."

Nicole gasped, utterly scandalized. "He did not say that!"

A small, amused smile tugged at Danny's bronze face. "Well, maybe not those exact words, but he also said he's happy that I make you happy."

"You do." Nicole moved to give Danny a kiss on the lips. Of course, Danny tried to deepen it as she tried to pull away. She gave Danny another swat, and Danny laughed as she pulled back.

"What?" Danny had the nerve to ask with an innocuous smile, as Nicole glared at her.

"You don't seem to realize my dad is less than fifteen feet away from us and there are no walls between us, only a thin tent and another thin tent."

Grey eyes went wide, almost comically so. Danny bit her lip, as Nicole pressed on her knee in a way that would've turned Danny into an oozy puddle at home. The groan she tried to block still escaped, joining the rustling leaves to echo through the night. Danny glowered at her, knowing she was doing it on purpose. Nicole gave her an innocent smile right back.

"You're horrible," Danny whimpered. Her face tensed, as she clearly tried to hold in more sounds, but they needed to get out.

"You think so? I could stop."

"Don't you *freaking* dare."

Nicole chuckled at the mock swear word and the growl in her beloved's voice. She continued the massage, but decided against asking more about Danny's day. That could wait, so Danny could focus on blocking out all the moaning. Not that she seemed to be trying to stop making those noises, even as the massage became less intense. Nicole wondered if they'd be in for a lot of teasing from her cousins in the morning. She hoped her father was already asleep and didn't hear anything going on.

She massaged Danny's knee and leg until it seemed like Danny was about to fall asleep. Wiping off her hands, Nicole turned off the lantern and eased into the sleeping bag, next to Danny. Strong, warm arms wrapped around her immediately.

"Don't you dare go to sleep on me," Nicole softly chided Danny, as she snuggled in close.

"I'd never." Danny gasped, feigning shock, even though she let loose a yawn right after.

"You say that now. In five minutes, you'll be out, thanks to the leg rubdown."

Danny chuckled. "You make it sound like you know me so well."

"Because I do. I want to know about how you liked the day. I also want to know what my knucklehead cousins said to you when they were supposed to come get you for lunch. And what you did with Beth while you were alone."

"You want to know a lot."

Nicole grinned, looking into deep grey eyes. She could get lost in those dark pools and be happy for all eternity, never trying to find her way out. Danny smiled softly at her and reached up to caress her cheek.

"I just want to know you had a good time. Tell me the truth. Don't humor me or sugar coat anything. And, if my moron cousins did anything to upset you, tell me. I will go put a snake in their tent right now," Nicole said with all seriousness.

That got a laugh out of Danny. "You don't need to do that. I've been having a good time. Yeah, your cousins are being jerks, but they're not going to make or break my day. I like seeing you have fun with them. Told you, this side of you is cute." She rubbed Nicole's hip.

"I wish they were better to you."

A tender caress from Danny accompanied a gentle smile. "Don't worry about it, Chem. At least I'm not stressing myself out over trying to get them to like me, and you should enjoy their company. They seem like good guys, in their own idiotic way. They're trying to look out for you. I don't agree with their approach, but I am happy they love you enough to say something."

Nicole smiled and gave her lover a sweet kiss. "You are so incredible, baby."

"Well, not gonna argue..." Danny grinned.

"But, I'm happy you're giving my cousins credit without letting the fact that they're being asses get in the way. I wish I could stop them from being idiots."

"Don't worry about them. It's okay. I don't expect you to have control over them, so it's not your fault they're acting that way."

"Fine, I won't think about them. How about I brag that I was right, and my dad likes you?" Nicole smirked and pinched Danny's side.

Danny giggled and pretended to try to push her hands away. "Cut it out or you'll regret it."

"I doubt it. Now, I believe you have something to tell me about you and Beth, or do I have to start tickling you?"

"Tickling *me*?" Danny gasped and then turned the tables on Nicole, who was very much the ticklish one of the pair.

Nicole squealed in spite herself. Danny was merciless for only a few seconds, pinning Nicole beneath her, as her fingers worked along Nicole's sides. Suddenly, the onslaught ceased and Danny leaned down to kiss Nicole's slightly open mouth. Nicole returned the sweet touch and, all too soon, Danny retreated. Nicole whimpered in disappointment.

"We need to do this alone sometime," Danny said, glancing around the tent, but undoubtedly thinking about outside.

"And why is that?" Nicole wondered aloud, even though she was all too aware of the answer to that question. The humming of her body, more specifically the throbbing of her lower anatomy, answered the question.

"Because making you scream in the middle of the woods is a new fantasy of mine," Danny replied with an impish smile, and Nicole moaned slightly at the words.

Nicole allowed the fantasy to play in her mind for a moment. A picture flashed through her mind of the night sky, sparkling with bright stars; the warm air on her overheated, nude body; with Danny, equally nude, panting above her. The brief snapshot made her whimper. She wanted that almost desperately, but not now.

Nicole reached up and caressed Danny's soft, somewhat chubby cheek. "You are so bad."

"Like me this way?"

"I certainly do. In fact, I love you this way and all the other ways you are. We can do a weekend sometime soon. Maybe in the summer. I'll have to see when work is slow."

"That sounds good."

Nicole grinned, because this proved Danny truly did like camping. *Screw you, Junior and Spider! We do have stuff in common.* Of course, she knew that before the camping trip, but still, she felt like rubbing it in her cousins' faces, not that she would. That was too immature. Besides, she didn't need to prove her relationship to them. They were the asses, after all.

The couple settled in once more, Nicole's head on Danny's shoulder, as peace settled into her very bones. The antics had passed and they managed to fall asleep within minutes. *I hope that, somehow, tomorrow, the guys see how great Danny actually is*. But, even as she was drifting off to unconsciousness, Nicole knew that wish wasn't likely to be granted.

***

In the morning, Dane knew something was wrong and she could only guess it was her fault. Everyone seemed to be glaring at her. Nicole didn't see because she was still in the tent, getting dressed. Before Dane could figure out what she had done worth shunning, Junior and Spider were in her face. They grabbed her by the arms and dragged her into the woods. She wondered if they were planning to kill her. *Have they had time to dig a hole?* From the furious looks on their faces, she was leaning toward *probably*. They walked for a few minutes, so they were probably far away enough where no one would hear Dane scream if they did try to kill her. *Hope they don't think it'll be an easy task.*

"What the fuck is wrong with you?" Junior flung Dane away as if she were useless trash. Dane stumbled a bit, having trouble catching her balance. Thankfully, she didn't fall on her face, as she had a feeling they wouldn't have allowed her to get up.

"According to you guys or others or my own opinion?" Dane arched an eyebrow. She had no clue what the hell they were so hot and bothered about.

"Don't be a fucking smartass!" Spider pointed at her with a harsh, tense expression tugging at his features. "We will fuck you up right here and let you drag your gimp ass back to Nikki, just so she can see how fucking lame you are."

"Clever," Dane deadpanned, knowing he thought he was being oh, so smart with his use of the word lame.

Spider growled and grabbed a fistful of Dane's shirt, shoving her back into a thick tree. "I'll just kick your ass then."

"How about before you do that you tell me what the fuck the problem is. Can I have a fucking clue as to why you're so interested in kicking my ass before breakfast? I just got up. What the hell could I have done to piss you off this much?" Dane inquired calmly, completely and utterly unimpressed with their posturing.

"Don't act so fucking innocent!" Junior barked, getting in her face to growl like an angry mutt. His eyes blazed with fury that put the vermillion of the rising sun to shame.

"Then tell me what the hell happened. Catch me up," she huffed, glaring at them for assuming she understood why they were so pissed.

"You know what happened. In all of the years of camping and meeting Nikki's asshole significant others, we've never actually had someone that fucking did some shit like this right in camp, you fucking bitch." Spider shook Dane by her shirt, knocking her into the tree several times. It wasn't enough to hurt, but it was beginning to wear on her nerves.

"What the hell did I do?" Dane inquired once more. "Unless you're trying to kill time to make some shit up." She wouldn't put it past them now. Before, they were being overprotective, which she could let slide, but now they were doing something beyond that. She wouldn't allow them to tarnish her name or her relationship with bullshit.

Spider snarled at her and slammed her into the tree once more. She turned her attention fully to him, staring him down to let him know that was the last time she'd allow him to manhandle her. His gaze seemed to dare her to try something, but before they could go at it, Junior was back in her face.

"We don't have to make anything up! You fucking brainwashed Nikki and actually managed to get her to have sex with you with her father ten feet away, and with us within a stone's throw of you! How fucking disrespectful can you be? Wanted to show us the power you have over Nikki? Fuck you! We won't stand for that sort of bullshit, especially you disrespecting our cousin like that," Junior roared, jabbing her in the shoulder with his thick index finger.

Dane blinked. She had talked Nicole into having sex last night? *Why the hell wasn't I there when this happened then?*

"Did you two hit your heads or something? Probably together?" Dane felt her brow wrinkling as her eyebrows knitted together.

"Hey, I said stop being a smartass!" Spider snarled, tugging on her shirt, but not knocking her against the tree.

"You think I had sex with Nick with her entire family flanking us? Even if I were that bold, Nick would never in her life do some shit like that. Do you two really think so little of her?" Dane inquired with an arched eyebrow.

"We think she has a habit of trying to appease worthless bastards like you," Junior growled.

Dane felt a small ping in her gut because of those words. No, Junior didn't know he had repeated words she had heard all her life, but they made her anger flare at him. She ripped herself away from Spider and tried to assess the situation in case she needed to fight them off. Even with their size, she doubted she could out run either of them with her bum leg. Honestly, she didn't care. She might never walk out of these woods again, but she would be damned if she'd allow them to act like Nicole was so easily controlled or that she was the real problem.

"You know what, fuck both of you. Even if I did manage to get Nicole to sleep with me with you bozos right in front of us, it's none of your fucking business. And, the overprotective act was cute yesterday, but now it's tiring. You're not protecting Nick, you're being assholes," Dane said.

"Oh, says the asshole!" Junior snorted while Spider seemed a bit shocked, staring down at his empty hands with an open mouth. He either wasn't expecting Dane to break free of his hold or curse them both out. She didn't care which.

"Like I said, fuck you. You two obviously need to deal with your own shit that you don't wanna acknowledge, but is fucking there." Again, she seemed to have stunned Spider, who blinked so hard she thought she heard it.

Junior growled again. "Don't try to pin this shit on us because you're the fucking ass, forcing Nikki to do shit for you, trying to hurt her because you're a bastard."

"What the fuck do you know about me, anyway? You wanna throw shit at me for what her past lovers have done, go right ahead, but don't you ever fucking accuse me of not respecting Nicole. You don't know a Goddamn thing about our relationship. And for the record, what you nosy asses heard last night was Nick rubbing down my knee and me tickling her. Get your fucking minds out of the gutters, disgusting bitches." Dane turned to leave.

"Hey, we're not done." Junior reached out and grabbed her. She pulled her arm back.

"Don't you fucking touch me." Dane snarled and pointed at him. "I'm not taking this shit anymore, from either of you. You keep your fucking comments to yourself and you don't touch me. You think you're looking out for Nicole, but all you're really doing is being bullies and trying to cover for the fact that you're fucking homophobic. Well, I'm not taking it anymore. So, fuck you." She spat at his feet, practically daring him to make a move on her.

"We're not homophobic," Spider managed to say, while Junior was frozen in place. She snorted and turned to leave.

"Keep telling yourselves that, champ," she replied, sticking up her middle finger.

Honestly, she felt like she lucked out when Junior didn't move. While she'd had brawls in her day, she doubted she could've taken the brothers on if they really wanted to fight. Besides, while she didn't think Nicole would mind her cursing the pair out and calling them on their real problem, she'd probably get a little huffy if they all ended up in a fight.

Dane managed to make it back to the campsite on her own, only to be immediately reminded that she was currently the worst human being on the planet as far as the family went. It didn't help her when she noticed Raymond glaring at her. *Oh, great, he thinks I fucked Nick with him right there, too. Fuck this shit.*

Yes, she knew she'd have to deal with this crap eventually, but she didn't feel like doing it now. Too much had already happened. She took a turn and headed toward the river. The river was nice. She could remember yesterday when Raymond liked her and Beth was semicool. Maybe she'd stop feeling like she wanted to hit those two morons with a baseball bat and then go home.

"The crazy thing is, I want to do this again. Of course, without everybody else, though," she sighed as the roaring sound of the river reached her ears. Soon, drops of cool water touched her face and she felt calm, at peace. Separate the feeling from everything else; that's what she enjoyed about the trip. This was what she wanted to do again.

***

Nicole exited the tent thinking breakfast would be ready, even though she didn't smell anything cooking. She was surprised Danny was up before her, but that was far from unheard of. The real shocker was to come out and see her family sort of puttering around the campsite. Danny was nowhere to be seen. Junior and Spider were also missing in action. *If they did anything to Danny.*

"Good morning, everybody," Nicole said, putting on her brightest smile and most chipper tone. She didn't want them to know their expressions alarmed her.

No one moved as they watched her. There was no breakfast going and the mood of the camp seemed dead, despite the warmth of the morning and the beauty of the day. She knew she'd have to ask, as much as the idea of doing so bothered her.

"What's going on? Where's Danny and the guys?" Nicole inquired. She did her best not to sound worried because, clearly, something was wrong.

Her uncle and father sneered, but she wasn't sure why. The look they gave her, though, made her stomach drop. An uneasy, almost sick feeling rolled around her belly, and she wondered if something had happened to Danny. Beth approached her and took her by the arm, pulling her away. They walked out of earshot, and Beth looked at her with an almost stricken expression.

"Beth, what's going on?" Nicole implored. It was too early for a mystery.

"Nikki, what the hell? Don't you know how thin a tent is?" Beth frowned at her.

"Of course, I do. What does that have to do with anything?"

"It has everything to do with *everything*. The whole camp heard you and Danny last night."

Nicole arched an eyebrow. "Heard us what?" *Did they hear us talking? We didn't say anything horrible about anyone. Well, we called Junior and Spider asses, but they are, and it's definitely not the first time I've said it. I don't see why Daddy would be upset over that.*

Beth tilted her head and regarded her strangely for a moment, narrowing her gaze on Nicole as if studying her. "What did you and Danny do last night?"

"Beyond sleep? We stayed up a little and talked. I wanted to know how she was enjoying the trip."

"Anything else?"

Nicole's brow furrowed as she searched her mind. "I gave her a massage for her leg."

Beth nodded and turned her mouth up a little. "Did this massage involve a lot of moaning?"

What a weird question. "Yeah, why?"

Beth glanced away for a moment. It was hard to tell with the shade from the trees, but she appeared to be blushing. "Uh...we thought that maybe you were...well, having sex with Danny last night, and it made everyone awkward."

"Having sex with Danny? With my father right next to us!" Nicole shrieked in horror. She wouldn't even be able to get in the mood with her father right there. Danny would never seriously try something like that with her father right there.

"Well...yeah."

"What the fuck, Beth? I'd never do that!" Nicole threw her hands in the air and waved them frantically. "I'd never even think about sex with my father that close! So, now, everyone thinks Danny and I did it in the middle of the Goddamn camp?" Nicole was near hysterical. *Daddy thinks he heard me having sex!* The very idea made her lightheaded.

Nicole could only guess that she'd wobbled, because Beth gathered her in her arms and held her up. "Nikki, get a hold of yourself. It's okay. We made a mistake. We shouldn't have been listening."

"That's not going to make my father unhear what he thought he heard last night!"

"But, he didn't hear what he thought he heard. You can explain that."

"Do you honestly think I want to explain to my father that he didn't hear me having sex with my girlfriend?" Nicole rubbed her forehead, running her hand along a vein popping up in her head. *Oh, God, I feel like I'm going to faint.*

Beth patted her in the back. "You might not want to, but you'll have to. Unless you want to leave your dad thinking Danny's the dirty lesbian that managed to do what even your most asshole of a boyfriend couldn't do."

Nicole sighed and put her hand over her face. *This trip keeps getting worse and worse. First, they treat Danny like dirt and now they're going to demonize her for something she didn't even do. Why didn't we just go camping by ourselves?*

"Fine. Fuck it." Nicole huffed, standing up straight. She took a deep breath before turning to go back to camp. She practically stormed into the area, only to find her father gone. "Where'd Daddy go?" She bordered on screaming and had to seriously stop herself from stomping her foot.

Junior and Spider were back and looking oddly red. Danny was still missing. Nicole stormed over to them.

"Where the hell is Danny?" She glared at them, accusing them off all sorts of hideous things with her eyes.

"We don't know," Spider answered, eyes on the ground and a frown on his lips. He looked a bit troubled, but she didn't allow that to faze her.

"Oh, you don't?" She scoffed through her teeth. "So, it's a fucking coincidence that you were gone while she was, and she's still gone after everyone suddenly thinks she and I committed an act of insanity?"

"Look, we don't know where she is. We're trying to look out for you." Junior had the nerve to glare at her.

"You say that like I should fucking thank you. You're not looking out for me! You're being impossible! God, I wanted to come out here and have a good time with you guys and with Danny, and you're making it virtually impossible to even enjoy being around you. I wanted to share something special and wonderful with you guys, for you to see how great this woman is that I love and how happy she makes me, and you're refusing to see that," Nicole screamed. She was so frustrated that she didn't know what to do. Part of her wanted to strangle them, another part wanted to pace, another part wanted to rip her hair out, and still another part wanted to tear off in every direction.

Her uncle had the gall to chime in. "You should've known better than to bring that girl around here, Nikki. It's not like any of us would approve anyway."

She growled, even though she knew her uncle spoke the truth. It wasn't something she wanted to accept. She had hoped they'd finally see how everything worked for her and be happy for her. Maybe she was a fool to think so and her stupid optimism hurt Danny, once again.

Sighing, Nicole's shoulders slumped. "You're right, Uncle Richard. You're right. I was stupid to bring her around, thinking you'd all enjoy her company. I was stupid to think you'd see her for who she is and see how well she fits with me and how happy she makes me. It was stupid of me to think my family would support me in something so important to me as getting along with the woman I love. I just keep being stupid and hoping."

She turned and fled into her tent, not wanting to even look at them anymore. She decided to start packing up. When Danny got back, she'd suggest they leave. She'd talk to her father later...as soon as she figured out how to broach the subject. Thinking about her father and how his opinion of her had to drop caused her to tear up, her throat tightened, and before she knew it, she was sobbing. Sobbing because of that, sobbing because her family couldn't open up, sobbing because something that was supposed to be beautiful had turned so ugly, so quickly, and sobbing because no matter what she did, she always hurt Danny in the end.

***

Dane retreated to the rocks by the river. Watching the river helped calm her down, but she was still upset. Part of her wished she had never come on this stupid trip, even though she had enjoyed yesterday. It felt like yesterday had been swept down the cold, unforgiving river of gossip.

"I had a feeling you'd end up here," she heard Raymond say, but she didn't turn to see him.

"Gonna push me in?" Dane wouldn't blame him. She imagined she'd be able to swim across if he did, provided she didn't hit her knee on anything on the way over. *Yeah, and maybe I could run home, too.*

"The thought has crossed my mind, but I've learned all too well from Thanksgiving that jumping to conclusions about you can be painful for you and painful to hear. I've calmed down enough to talk about this. So, what really happened last night?"

"Oh, so you don't believe I've managed to brainwash Nick to get her to debase herself and you, by getting her to do unspeakable things with you in earshot?" Dane snorted, still looking out onto the water. Below her, she could see some fish, going to and fro, with the current and against the current.

"I think I'm giving you a chance to prove me wrong, so stop acting like a petulant child about it." He rapped her on the hip with a surprisingly heavy hand.

She hissed and almost turned to glare at him, but she noticed he was partially smiling. He wasn't hitting her like her father would hit her, or striking her for doing something wrong. He was being almost playful with her, even though he believed this was a serious matter. He just didn't seem to want to believe it was what he thought it was.

"What you heard was Nick massaging my sore leg, nothing more."

"So, all that moaning?"

"Was me being an indulged moron. She rubs some stuff on my leg that feels really good and relaxes my leg. So I respond, but sometimes I exaggerate just to be silly."

Raymond nodded, but he was quiet for a while. "How does your leg feel? They'll be doing a lot of walking today."

Dane snorted and shook her head. "I doubt I'll be welcomed on those walks and, honestly, I don't want to put up with it anymore. Tired of being judged all the time. The only person to never judge me is Nick and..."

Raymond sighed and turned, looking out into the river. "Don't let them run you off. Danny, I know you're honest and honorable. I haven't seen you do anything to hurt Nikki or lead her into doing something stupid, which is why I believe you when you say what we heard was a massage. I can't see you pushing Nicole into doing something I know she wouldn't do."

Dane had trouble processing his words and his understanding. It did not make any sense. *He believes me? He thinks I'm honest and honorable? Since when?*

"Don't...don't understand." Her words seemed to be drowned out by the sound of the river as she shook her head and ran her hand through her hair.

"Danny, don't get me wrong, you have faults and there are things about you that bother me, but you're not a bad person. You're not someone who'd pressure Nikki into doing things she wouldn't usually do, not things like this anyway. You make her a stronger person, Danny."

"Then why were you glaring at me earlier?"

"Well, until I had your word, all I had was what it sounded like, and you now know what it sounded like. After giving it some thought and allowing myself to calm down, I was at least able to get past the anger to come have this talk with you. So, pick yourself up, walk back into that camp with your head held high, and make it through this last full day. By this time tomorrow, we'll be heading back home and everything can go back to normal."

Dane looked at him, and Raymond gave her a half smile. She felt herself mirroring the expression. She had never realized, until now, how much she wanted this man's approval. She wanted him to know and accept that she was good for his daughter, good enough for his daughter.

"Come on. Sometimes, people on the outside think they know better, but they're as biased as the people on the inside," Raymond said, holding his hand out for her.

Hesitating for only a moment, she took his hand and he helped her down. "Thank you so much."

"No thanks necessary. You're a good egg," he laughed.

"A good egg? Good enough to marry your daughter?"

"No, I still think you're jumping the gun there. I told you, you have flaws, Danny. I think you need to fix those before you're daughter-in-law material. But, I have faith that you'll work on those. No one Nicole has been with before would've asked me that question. They assume and, even though they smile in my face, I know they wouldn't respect my response if they did ask. These are things that set you apart and, even though I don't think this needs to be said, I notice the things that set you apart."

Dane could only nod, not sure what to say. Thank you seemed odd and woefully understated. He smiled at her, as if assuring the nod was fine. She figured it wouldn't hurt to smile back. She wanted to ask him about his family bias, if only to find out if she'd nailed it or not, but decided it was unimportant. They returned to the campsite to find breakfast done, but everything was somber and still. Nicole was nowhere to be seen.

Glancing at the tent, Dane could see her silhouette. Raymond patted her on the shoulder, and she took that as the signal to get going. She entered the tent to find Nicole a mess of tears, curled up on their air mattress. She wasted no time gathering Nicole in her arms and holding her close.

"Oh, God, Danny!" Nicole threw her arms around Dane and held her tightly.

"It's okay, Chem. It's okay," Dane whispered, caressing the small of Nicole's back. *What the hell did these yo-yos tell my angel?*

"My dad..." She hiccupped.

"Don't worry about him. We spoke. He doesn't believe it."

"He doesn't?" she whimpered, looking up at Dane with red-rimmed eyes.

"He does not, angel. He spoke to me. I mean, we had a really good talk. He asked me what happened, and I told him the truth. It's okay."

"I can't believe...I can't believe...I mean, this is my family. Why are they doing this to us?"

Dane would like to know the answer to that question, too. But now wasn't the time to think about that. She needed to comfort and assure Nicole that everything would be fine.

"They're worried about you." Dane kissed the top of her head.

"Strange way of showing it."

"Well, that's family for you," Dane forced out a laugh. *Maybe that's family*. She didn't think that Kathleen's family would act this way. Of course, she didn't think any of them would be caught dead camping either. *They do think they're helping.* For some reason, her mind chose that moment to flash to a family that wasn't hers, but that she'd had a chance to pretend was, and how they'd returned her. *They probably thought they were helping, too.* She shook that away, since now wasn't the time to get lost in her own trauma.

Nicole was quiet for a while. "Do you want to go home? I think Daddy would drive us back."

"He probably would, but I think he wants us to stick it out. He told me it's just one more day. Maybe prove that we're made of sterner stuff than they are, show them we're in this thing together for the long haul. So, if you're really upset over things, you don't need to associate with anyone today. You can show me around. I'd like that."

"I'd like that, too..." Despite the words, Nicole didn't move. Dane didn't make any attempt to move either. She held Nicole and caressed her back. Eventually, they'd get up.

Chapter Twelve

NICOLE WASN'T SURPRISED WHEN she woke up for a second time, even though she didn't recall falling asleep again. A dull thump beat through her skull, tingling all the way down her spine. But, the minor headache was already being soothed away. She felt Danny's tender fingers still on her back, softly caressing her, rubbing gentle circles in the middle of her back. She was tucked against Danny, as if trying to burrow into her, which wasn't uncommon when she had rough days. She inhaled, enjoying Danny's scent, calming herself and easing the tension in her head.

"How you doing, Angel?" Danny asked, keeping her voice low.

"Better." Feeling Danny's warmth all around was always something that made her feel better, no matter the circumstances. *One of the many reasons I love her, and I will stand by her no matter what the hell my stupid cousins think. She is the one for me.*

"That's good. So, what do you want to do?"

"Well, first, I want to eat something." Her stomach was cramped up. She supposed it was only partially due to hunger.

Danny's hand wandered down to Nicole's stomach and sweetly caressed the area. "I thought you might. I have granola and water. Unless, of course, you're ready to go out and show me what you guys explore."

Nicole smiled, but she didn't make any attempt to move away from her beloved. "Give me the granola and water, and then we'll go out and see the woods. We have an awesome place. It's so beautiful and you won't believe your eyes."

"I can't wait."

Nicole chuckled and Danny kept holding her, even as she stretched out to reach the promised food. She handed Nicole the granola bar and bottle of water. Nicole sat up to eat the snack and Danny followed her, stayed close to her, and kept her calm with caresses. Nicole ate silently, and Danny seemed more than content to hold her in her time of need.

"Thank you for being there for me," Nicole whispered.

"Always here for you, Chem. I love you," Danny reminded her with a bright grin.

"I love you, too." She leaned in for a kiss, but Danny paused her and wiped the sides of her mouth. She giggled.

"You got granola crumbs there."

"Come here, you!" Nicole gave Danny a passionate kiss, which was deeply returned. When they pulled away, she smiled. She felt like she could take on the world with Danny at her side. "Time to face the family."

"Are you sure? We could stay in here all day. Doubt they'd bother us."

"You're probably right, but I don't want them to think I'm ashamed of you or of us. They're not going to scare us off, even if I needed some time to cry it out. We're here and they need to accept that, dammit."

Danny smiled as she nodded in agreement. Nicole smiled as well and gave her a light kiss. Danny returned the sweet show of affection and took her hand. They stood and exited the tent. The air was warm and the scent of the woods comforted Nicole. She gave Danny's hand a squeeze to show her appreciation.

Surprisingly enough, Nicole's family was all still at camp. Nicole wasn't sure what to make of that since usually they'd be off roaming the forest by now. She noticed they weren't glaring at her and were sitting idly around the camp. Her father was with Beth, looking at pictures on her camera, acting as if everything were normal. Her uncle and his offspring all seemed to be hanging their heads in shame. Lillian was the one who trotted up to her.

"I'm sorry we were all acting weird earlier," Lillian said quickly, eyeing the dirt briefly before glancing up at Nicole.

Nicole smiled at her younger cousin. "It's fine, Lil. I'm okay now."

"That's good because we were talking about taking a walk to the cave today. You know, hanging out and having fun together."

Nicole glanced over at Lillian's brothers. "I think I'll show Danny around the woods. There are plenty of other places to see." She wouldn't subject Danny to those idiots any further if it could be helped.

"Nikki." Junior took a step toward her.

"Don't 'Nikki' me," Nicole huffed, halting him with a glare. While she didn't know the exact details of her cousins' confrontation with Danny that morning, she knew something had happened that caused her father to go after Danny, and she was certain it involved these two idiots.

"Nicole, seriously, we're sorry. We'll mind our own business from now on, and we won't say anything to Danny less than a kind word. So, come on. We always go the cave on the second day," Junior said, but she wasn't really feeling up to family traditions right now.

"So? I really don't want to be around people who think so little of me and try to chase off someone very dear to me," Nicole replied bluntly. She felt a little tingle in her stomach from saying that because it wasn't like her. Usually, she was gung-ho for whatever her cousins wanted to do, but they had reached their limit.

"Okay, look, we're going to go to the cave and then you could show up if you're ready?" Junior proposed with a somewhat pleading look in his eyes, looking like a big puppy.

"Yeah, we'll be there all day, you know. So, you can just come when you want," Spider chimed in with an awkward, but hopeful smile on his face.

They were practically begging, but Nicole wasn't moved. She felt a squeeze to her hand and glanced at Danny. Danny gave her a small smile, which she took as encouraging her response. She smiled back.

"I want to be with Danny for a while," Nicole said. She wanted to give her girlfriend a chance to enjoy the day without having to deal with extra, unnecessary drama, which was how the trip should have been in the first place. "Come on, Danny. We should check our packs and make sure we have enough stuff for a day of walking around in the woods."

"Sure," Danny answered, following Nicole back into their tent for their backpacks.

Nicole checked the bags and gathered some things they would need. Occasionally, she glanced at Danny and smiled for no reason other than being happy that Danny was there. Danny smiled back, and Nicole felt a small flutter in her chest. They were ready to leave before her cousins were. She marched away from camp without saying anything to anyone, except for her father. Danny followed, doing the same.

"You two have a good time," Raymond called.

"Danny, do you want to borrow my walking stick?" Beth offered before they were too far away.

"Should be fine as long as we don't go up a steep hill," Danny replied. She had her knee brace on. "Thanks, though." She gave Beth a small wave.

Nicole smiled at the offer, but she didn't bring it up until they were out of sight of the camp. "I guess Beth does like you, huh?"

"Seems that way. Did she think we were having sex last night, too?"

"She did."

A tiny frown marred Danny's bronze face briefly. "Did you set the record straight?"

"I like to think I did. I'm pretty sure she believed the truth, but who knows. I can't believe they thought we were having sex, especially that loudly."

Danny blushed slightly. "Sorry about that."

Nicole shook her head. "There's no need to be sorry. You weren't eavesdropping and jumping to conclusions. Are you sure my dad believed you when you told him the truth? I want to be able to look him in the eye."

A soft chuckle escaped Danny. "Chem, I think your dad knows you've had sex before."

"Yeah, but he's never thought he heard it. Does he think I had sex last night?"

"Nope. I told you; I explained and he believed me. Your dad's okay, Nick, which is why he told us bye and acted totally normal. He's completely cool, and he's probably the one who spoke to your cousins to get them to cool down. Your father doesn't think any less of you, Nick." Danny wrapped her arm around Nicole's waist and the contact was more assuring than the words.

Nicole breathed a sigh of relief. "I know it might seem ridiculous to you, but..."

Danny arched an eyebrow and shook her head. "Ridiculous that you want your father and your family to respect you? Nothing ridiculous about that. I know what it's like to want, but you know what it's like to *have*. You haven't lost that."

"Thank you for understanding, baby."

"Don't see how someone wouldn't be able to understand that one, Chem."

Nicole smiled and decided to take a chance. She wanted to dig into Danny's mind for a moment while she had the chance, since Danny was so relaxed. "I hate to break the mood, but do you ever wonder what it feels like?"

A brown hand went through Danny's dark locks. "I imagine most people that have it don't even think about it. I don't really think about it anymore. I had something similar to it, I assume, when I was with the Briarmoors, and I know what it's like to lose something like it. I mean,

Henry was kinda like a dad to me and he seemed to respect me, as much as you can respect a little kid. But, now, I don't think about it or what it feels like. I have your respect and apparently your dad's, which is weird, and some of your family. That's enough."

Nicole smiled. "Okay." She wished things were different, but as long as Danny was content, then she was fine with it.

Taking a deep breath, Danny looked ahead of them. "So, what are we going to see first?"

"I'm going to show you what we used to call the Witch Tree. It's a really spooky looking tree. It's big and crooked, and the branches look bare even when there are leaves on them. When we were little, we were all certain a witch had planted it and that's why it looks like something out of a horror movie. We used to climb it, always saying that the witch would curse the last one to the top."

A small smile lit up Danny's face, as they strolled through new areas of the woods. "Cute."

"You've climbed trees before, right?" She had to check, because her beloved missed out on a lot of little things as a child, thanks to having drawn the short straw on caring parents.

"Yeah. Sometimes, Lynn would take me to the park when I was little, and I'd climb trees there. I wasn't totally deprived," Danny chuckled.

That's good to know. "Just checking to make sure. Tell me stuff about your childhood, please," Nicole said. "Normal, good things."

Danny scratched her forehead for a second and then ran her hand through her hair. "Hmm...well, Lynn sometimes made me hot chocolate on cold or rainy days. I always thought that was cool and that's one of the reasons I love sharing hot chocolate with you. It makes me think about those times and it feels nice. For a long time, I always tried to avoid thinking about them, because I didn't think living in the past was good, but lately, with you, I've been able to think about the good times and just feel good about it, not hurt or thrown away or anything like that."

Nicole gave her lover's hand a squeeze. "That's good, baby. That's really good."

"I wish I had traditions with them like you have with your family, something I could share with you, even though they're not around. I mean, this camping thing is wonderful. Wish I had something like this and I could share it with you."

"It's all right. As time goes on, we'll start our own traditions, and they'll be just as special. Maybe even more so than this, and we'll be able to enjoy them together. We're both in this together and we're in it forever, so we'll get there."

Danny nodded in agreement, but she still frowned a bit. "Still feel bad about not being able to share family stuff with you like you have with me. I mean, I have Crow and all, but she's not really family."

Nicole gave Danny a playful swat and they both chuckled lightly. "I like Crow, and I'm sure she thinks of you as more than a friend."

"Probably. Though I have a lot of catching up to do with her, emotionally. I mean, it's only been a year since I've accepted her as a real friend, but in her mind we've been really good friends for years, and she's always been there for me, while I have only started really thinking about her. I know I'll get there with her eventually, but I feel...upset...it's taken me this long to recognize her and her worth. She doesn't seem to hold it against me, but I hold it against myself."

Nicole gave her hand a soft squeeze. "You will get there, baby. You're open to so many things now, and you're doing your best. Your insight in regards to yourself is always impressive, Danny."

Danny shrugged. "I live in my head a lot when you're not around, and I get a chance to examine myself. That's where my music lives, after all."

Nicole smiled, but she didn't respond, as they came to the spot that she wanted to show Danny. The Witch Tree was thick and twisted with dark, deformed branches they couldn't really see thanks to the leaves. The leaves somehow curled and seemed as awkward and wicked as the rest of the plant. There were deep grooves and raised ridges cutting vertically along the trunk of the Tree with cracks crisscrossing those lines. As a slight breeze blew, it seriously sounded as if the Tree let out a low growl, warning them away. Danny didn't heed the noise and walked around the massive, winding trunk, having to hop over some of the bent roots that poked up from the ground.

"We always said if you broke a stick off, the Tree would bleed." Nicole wiggled her fingers to mimic oozing blood. She stood almost a whole foot away from the Tree, finding it creepy even now as an adult.

"Why would you do that? Wouldn't it piss off the witch?" Danny asked with an amused half smile.

Nicole let loose a light, airy chuckle. "Oh, yeah, and we were sure she'd come get us in our sleep, steal us away back to the Tree, and then eat us alive. Spider almost wet himself one day when he accidentally snapped a branch to break his fall. He had nightmares for months. We all ran right after he did that, so we didn't get a chance to see if the Tree really bled."

Danny laughed. "So, you never broke a branch?"

"Oh, yeah. When I was about nine or ten. Again, trying to break a fall. I grabbed a branch and it broke off. But, we didn't stick around to see if it bled. We ran like hell back to camp, and I jumped at every little noise from the forest for the rest of the trip. I slept in my parents' bed for a long time. My mother kept screaming at my dad, thinking he'd done something to me on the trip to scare the life out of me." Nicole giggled.

"Your mom blamed your dad every time something happened, didn't she?"

"Most of the time, yeah. If I got hurt playing sports, it was his fault. Whenever I did something whacky with Junior and Spider, it was his fault. She always swore he was going to traumatize me, or I'd end up in a coma. I got him in trouble a lot, but we still did so much together. I mean, my mom got mad, but she never tried to stop us from doing anything. She'd give us a lecture before we went out, but she never tried to stop us. I think part of it was that my dad was my best friend for a while, and my mother understood that. Yes, we worried the hell out of her, but she knew we were enjoying each other's company."

"Do you wish you had siblings?" Danny leaned against the Witch Tree.

Nicole winced and reached out for Danny, but pulled back. *I'm just being silly.* "Yes and no. I mean, I wonder what it would be like sometimes, but there were times when I was happy I was the only one around for my parents to focus on. So, there you go. After I got on some teams and made friends, I never really thought about having a sibling."

Danny was quiet for a moment, seeming to study Nicole. "Do you think you sometimes feel guilty for being their only child?"

Nicole blinked, stunned by the strange question. "Why would I feel guilty?"

"Don't know. I wonder, sometimes, if that's why you followed in their footsteps and things like that. I know you were pressured, which definitely adds to it, but sometimes I think there's more."

Nicole shook her head. "I never thought about it, but thanks to you, I will." Playfully, she stuck her tongue out at her lover. *Maybe that is why I followed in their footsteps.*

The move earned a chuckle from Danny. "Sorry."

"Why don't you try climbing the Tree?" Nicole nodded toward the sinister flora. *She's already touched it, so it won't matter.*

Grey eyes rolled, and Danny scoffed loudly. "And risk being cursed by a witch? No thank you!"

Nicole laughed. "Coward. Want to head to the next spot?"

"Will there be more witches?" Danny asked with a teasing grin.

"No, no more witches."

"Surprising, since we're in the woods and all. I thought you'd show me a gingerbread house next or a tower covered in thorn bushes or something like that." Danny scoffed.

Nicole unleashed a mock glare. "You keep that up, and I'll be sure to find something like that and maybe even leave you there."

Danny smiled and returned to Nicole's side. They strolled off, hand in hand, twigs crushing under their feet. Nicole led Danny to another obvious climbing site. There were rocks that went about fifteen feet in the air at their highest, but some were lower than a foot. It looked like a mini-mountain in the middle of the forest. Nicole led Danny onto the lower rocks and pointed to the opposite side.

"Is that a watering hole?" Danny inquired. There was water right behind rocks that was about the size of the average hotel pool. The water was crystal clear, and if they wandered close enough, Danny would've been able to see the rocks sitting at the bottom of it.

"Something like that. We always called it a pond. The water's deep enough for a short jump, but none of us were ever crazy enough to jump from the top, which I assume is a good thing. We most assuredly would've broken our ankles, at the least, if we did," Nicole answered.

"Still safer than swimming in the river, huh?"

"Oh, definitely. The river might look calm, but it can sweep you away quickly. One day we can go canoeing again, though. Maybe not on this river, but there are many others. That was fun," Nicole said. They had gone on a canoe ride on their first vacation together. Sure, it had been on a calm lake, but she was certain Danny would enjoy a trip down a river.

"Sounds fun."

They sat there quietly for a while, looking down into the pond. It looked like Danny was seeing more than the water, but Nicole didn't want to ask, because she didn't want to disturb her lover. Danny put her arm around Nicole and leaned into her. The action brought a smile to Nicole's face. They shared a light snack and drank some bottled water.

Eventually, they ended up sitting at the edge, allowing their feet to get wet.

"You know, Henry taught me how to swim." Danny sloshed water around with one foot.

Nicole glanced at her. "Henry Briarmoor?"

"Yup. I had forgotten until now. Always wondered why I knew how. I can't remember for the life of me where or when he taught me, but I feel it in my bones. Maybe I did have more of a childhood than I ever gave myself credit for."

"I hope so." But, Nicole didn't think a full childhood could be slipped into eight years, especially when Danny hadn't been with those people every single day. Still, she was thankful Danny at least had time with the Briarmoors.

"This is peaceful." There were sounds of their feet in the cold water, leaves rustling, and the birds busying themselves around them.

Nicole nodded. "Well, now it is. It's not like this when a group of small children are around." A wicked smile curled onto Nicole's face. "We could come back here later, just the two of us. We could have a nice picnic and maybe go swimming."

"That seems nice."

"Swimming without suits."

Grey eyes went wide. "Was wondering why you had that smile on your face. It sounds like something I wouldn't mind trying."

"Good. We'll try it eventually. Of course, we'll have to do it in the summer or we'll get frostbite on places that don't need frostbite." She snickered at her own remark.

"Have you done this before, or have I corrupted you?" Danny inquired, poking her in the side. "Have I corrupted you like your whole family seems to think I have? Brainwashed you?"

Nicole chuckled. "Not hardly." She moved in closer, tucking herself under Danny's arm.

"But, have you ever done that?"

"No, I haven't. I'd never do anything like that with anyone beyond you. Danny, you know my sex life was very vanilla before you showed up."

Danny laughed. "By a lot of standards, it's still very vanilla."

"Even your standards?" Nicole suspected it was, but Danny would never admit it.

"Nope. It's perfect for me."

Nicole smiled to let Danny know that was the right answer. She suspected her sex life would always be vanilla by most standards, but it worked for her. She planned to be a little more adventurous, because she trusted Danny and she wanted to keep Danny interested. Danny leaned over and kissed her cheek.

"You're perfect for me."

Nicole sighed, feeling happiness swell in her breast. "You are too sweet. Come on, I've got one more place to show you and then, if you want, I'll show you this cave my cousins have been going on about," Nicole offered. Truly, she didn't want to subject Danny to the group again, but the cave was a nice place. She might be able to show Danny and avoid her cousins at the same time, or at the very least ignore them.

"Sounds good."

"I want you to be sure. We don't have to go there. It can wait for another trip."

"I told you, I'm not letting them run us off. If this place is special to you, I want to see. I can ignore them if I need to. They don't control me."

Nicole beamed and sat up straighter. "You're my hero, you know?"

Danny laughed. "You need to pick better heroes, Angel. After all, you're mine."

Feeling her forehead wrinkle, Nicole pursed her lips for a moment. "And why is that?"

"Because no matter what, you see good in people. Even though you run into a lot of bad people, you still see good. The glass isn't half-empty with you and you've been teaching me how to see that since we've met."

Nicole nodded. "And you've been teaching me to stand up for myself, little by little, since we met. I think I'm a slower learner than you are, but bear with me and I'll get there."

"Even if you stay this way for the rest of your life, I'll still love you."

"I'll always love you as well."

The couple let the moment last a little longer before they rose to their feet. Using a cloth Nicole brought with her, they dried their feet and continued on their way. The next place wasn't as natural as the other places and probably the least safe, but it had been a huge source of entertainment when she was younger.

They arrived at a broken-down cabin surrounded by a pile of junk. Overgrown bushes and vines had taken over the place, even creeping through a busted window. It was almost like something out of a post-apocalyptic movie, and it wouldn't be surprising if zombies suddenly appeared. Looking at it now, she realized how crazy they had been as children, playing around the cabin, never mind in the cabin itself.

"So, how many tetanus shots did you guys have to get after roughhousing in this thing?" Danny tilted her head to take in the whole messy scene.

"None, thankfully. I'm happy our dads never found this place. This was our fort, but God, I don't remember it looking like this, but I'm sure it did. We used to run all through this place, playing tag and hide-n-go-seek and everything else under the sun, never thinking about how someone could get hurt or even if someone lived here."

"Judging by the beer cans and bottles, someone at least comes by here to drink." Danny pointed at the litter scattered in the junk piles.

"We got really lucky. We never got hurt here, and we never ran into whoever it is that leaves all the garbage behind."

Danny nodded. "You sure did."

Nicole took a deep breath. "My mother would've had a heart attack if she knew I played somewhere like this."

Danny chuckled and Nicole wondered for a moment if she'd have a child as wild as herself. She almost said something, but decided not to bring it up. She didn't want to put that in the air, in case Danny had given children actual thought. No way would this help her case of wanting kids.

"Come on. Show me your cave now. I promise not to bash your cousins in the head with a rock, as long as they don't say anything to you that upsets you," Danny said.

Nicole snickered, even though she knew Danny was quite serious. She was confident her cousins wouldn't say anything that upset her, unless, of course, they started attacking Danny again. But, if that happened, they'd leave before Danny had to resort to violence. "All right, follow me, Big Dog."

Chapter Thirteen

THE CAVE WAS AS advertised—a cave. It was the first cave Dane had seen in real life. The arched stone entrance was tall enough for her to walk in without banging her head on the rocks. Light from outside reached a few yards inside, showing some graffiti on the cave walls. In the distance, she thought she heard the echo of cave dwelling creatures scurrying around in the darker parts of the cavern. There was a smell to it that she couldn't place. It was different from the rest of the forest, somewhat musky and a little unpleasant. But, she'd endure it to see the rest of what Nicole desired to show her.

Nicole's cousins were inside, not really doing anything from what she could tell. They were all seated on rocks by the left wall with cans in their hands and a cooler at their feet. They had been talking until Nicole and Dane entered. Dane tried not to assume the cousins were talking about them, but that had been her experience when rooms suddenly got quiet when she walked in.

"Hey, guys," Nicole said low voice, not seeming too thrilled to be there.

"Hey, Nikki, Danny. We didn't think you guys were going to show," Beth said, smiling. "Nice to see we were wrong. We're just messing around, reminiscing and playing 'I'm bringing to the picnic.'"

"I'm bringing to the picnic?" Dane had never heard of such a game. For some reason, it didn't sound like something that should be played with family.

"It's a memory game. You basically have to name items in alphabetical order. Each person names an item they're 'bringing to the picnic,' and then you have to name all of the previous items," Nicole explained. Dane made a face and shrugged.

"You start with A, so let's say we were playing and I was first," Beth said. "I would go, 'I'm bringing to the picnic an amputated limb.' The person after me has to do B and also repeat my response. The person after that would have to do C and repeat the A and B items."

"Oh, okay. Sounds like a weird drinking game," Dane replied.

Nicole laughed. "Oh, we've made it that before, too."

"I don't think we've made it to F while drinking. Well, really drinking," Beth said, tipping what Dane now guessed was a beer can in her hand.

"I don't think we go in alphabetical order when we're really drinking," Spider commented with an awkward smile. It was like he was testing the waters, wanting to see if Nicole would respond. She didn't even look at him.

"I'm going to show Danny the rest of the cave," Nicole said, eyes remaining on Beth.

Dane guessed Beth was the only cousin not in the doghouse. She disliked the fact that she was actually happy Nicole was still upset with Lillian.

"Come on, baby." Nicole took Dane by the hand and led her away.

The inside of the cave wasn't all that big, unless they were able to shrink down to the size of dogs. It was mostly rocks and darkness. Somewhere, she could hear water dripping, but she didn't see the source. The smell got stronger as they moved to the back of the cave, and she could hear moving animals a little more clearly. She assumed the animals were in the areas they couldn't reach.

"This was basically another playhouse when we were kids. When we were smaller, we could get into other areas. We crawled into a lot of holes and things around here. In fact, Spider got stuck in one of the cracks and we panicked. It took us over an hour to free him. Junior was crying that his dad was going to kill him if Spider died, and Spider and I thought he'd be stuck there forever. Beth was trying to figure out how we'd have family gatherings in the cave to make sure Spider wasn't left out. We were crazy. We loved playing in here." Nicole took a deep breath and let out a sigh.

Despite all the crap Nicole's cousins put Dane through, it was nice hearing Nicole talk about them. There was this amazing closeness among them all, and Dane hoped it somehow survived this trip. While she refused to accept responsibility for things falling apart, she wanted those morons to realize what they were losing before they actually lost it.

"You guys were like feral children in the woods, huh?" Dane said, reaching out to touch the cave wall. The rocks were solid and surprisingly warm. Feeling around, she could make out holes and cracks, but couldn't see how a child could fit in any of them. Of course, wild children like Nicole and her cousins probably found the larger cracks to play around in.

Nicole chuckled. "Yeah, we were wild when we were little. Once we hit our teens, I think we smartened up a little. But, then became dumber in other ways."

"Ah, everyone gets dumber in that way." Dane bumped Nicole with her hip.

Nicole smiled again. "I like to think I've finally smartened up in that regard."

Dane only smiled back, and they enjoyed another quiet moment. They started back toward the cousins once they were done with exploring. They were all still sitting where they were before. When they noticed the couple, Junior and Spider climbed to their feet. They approached, slouched over, maybe humble. Dane could only wonder what they wanted now.

"Uh...Danny, can we have a word with you outside?" Junior inquired, pointing to the front of the cave.

Dane arched an eyebrow. "A word with me?"

"You don't have to if you don't want to," Nicole said.

"Look, we just want to talk this time. Really talk," Junior tried to assure her.

Dane thought about it. The pair appeared contrite, suddenly, probably feeling the sting of Nicole shunning them. She thought about how highly Nicole spoke of them and how happy Nicole had been with them yesterday. So, maybe they finally realized the relationship was crumbling and hoped to save it. She'd do her part if that were the case.

"It's okay, Nick. I'll talk to them."

The brothers breathed a sigh of relief and motioned to the outside of the cave again. Dane nodded, showing she'd follow them. They understood and marched in front of her. Dane glanced behind, before she was completely out, and flashed Nicole a reassuring smile. *Do you see how much I love you, Chem? I will suffer these asses, possibly forgive them, for you. If I'd do all of that, why do I still feel like I'm not good enough?* Nicole gave her a shaky smile in return.

Dane followed the brothers a few yards away from the cave. She guessed they didn't want anyone to hear their conversation. Now, it could mean they were going to apologize and didn't want the ladies to think they were weak, or they were going to suddenly change back to the way they were that morning and they didn't want Nicole to hear. She honestly felt like it could go either way with them.

"So, what's up?" Dane asked, wanting to cut to the chase as soon as possible, especially if they were going to continue to act the way they had.

"Look, first off, you were right to curse us out this morning. We were way out of line. It wasn't any of our business," Junior replied.

"Oh, really? Why is it suddenly none of your business? This morning it seemed like it was the only business you had," she stated.

"That was this morning," Spider said.

"Ah, I see, so you guys had complete and total changes of heart since this morning without any outside interference at all?" Rolling her eyes, Dane scoffed.

Junior frowned. "Uncle Raymond talked to us. He explained it was a misunderstanding and, even if it wasn't, we really didn't have any right to tell you when or where you could be intimate with your girlfriend. Technically, that does sound right. I mean, I wouldn't like it if someone was telling me when and where I could be with my girlfriend. That wasn't our place."

Dane frowned, feeling like he should've known that before his uncle said anything. He was an adult, after all, and in a relationship. Not to mention, she had screamed some of the same things at him that morning and they should've sunk into his brick head, but obviously he needed to hear it from a source he respected.

"And?" She glared at them.

"Look, we fucked up. We know. Can we move on now?" Spider kicked a rock.

"No, we can't move on, because that was one of the weakest apologies I've ever heard and, believe it or not, I have heard some seriously weak shit in my life. So, let's try this again," she huffed.

"We shouldn't have been in between your relationship with Nicole. She's a grown woman and can make her own decisions. We're sorry about that," Spider said.

"Besides, Uncle Raymond actually vouched for you. He's never done that before, even when he tries his best to like Nicole's lovers. He said you're a good egg, and he pointed out you've done one thing that none of Nikki's other lovers would've done," Junior added.

She was curious. "And what's that?"

"None of her lovers would've put up with us. Usually, the guys she brings try to be our friends. Honestly, they tend to start out pretty cool. They talk business and sports, but then we see how they treat Nikki when they think they're alone. If we got hostile with a boyfriend, they got hostile right back and right away. They let it be known we weren't going to tell them how to treat their woman. We barked on them about how we're not going to let them treat our cousin any old way, but they were always immediately in our faces when we got in theirs. They didn't put up with it like you did," Junior explained.

"And the women?" Dane challenged them, folding her arms across her chest. She was willing to bet her good leg they never treated the women like they did the guys. They probably ignored the women, especially if the women didn't come on the camping trip.

Junior frowned and glanced at Spider, who suddenly found the sky very interesting. Dane thought that was an interesting reaction from Spider. After a few seconds, Junior seemed to realize he was on his own.

"It's no secret that we'd rather Nikki be with a guy. We don't usually say anything to the women Nikki brings around. Even the crazy bitch with the guns was a prima donna. Yes, the women she brought on the camping trips were annoying, and we pointed out that they were scared or pissed over the dumbest things, but we knew they weren't going to be around long."

"Because eventually Nick will find a man?" Dane shook her head. So, they were of the 'eventually every woman gets set straight by the right man' school of assholes.

"She will." Junior folded his arms across his chest, as if that made his statement a fact.

An amused chuckle escaped Dane. "If you say so. That's not the way she tells it."

Junior shrugged. "We'll see, but until then, we promise to give you a shot. You do seem like an okay person. You haven't bossed Nikki around at all, from what we can tell, you haven't said anything demeaning to her, and you explored with us. You can't hike or fish for shit, but that's something that you can learn."

Dane chuckled again, deciding not to contradict him. She could learn to fish and she planned to, but she'd never learn to hike. *But, I might see a doctor and see what I can do after getting some surgery.* Junior walked off, going back into the cave after saying his piece. Spider remained.

"Yeah?" Dane inquired.

"I'm not homophobic."

She resisted the urge to scoff. "Oh, no?"

"No, I'm not. I know my brother and my father are. They're not bashers or anything like that, but whenever Nicole is with a woman, it bothers them. I'm not bothered by it. I'm bothered that she's always with someone who doesn't treat her properly, and she folds for them because she's got this damn personality that likes to please people. It's shit to watch, especially when you see how strong she is. But I guess she likes to make people feel good, too, so she folds for bastards all the time."

"That she does, but where are you going with this? You don't have to convince me that you're not homophobic. I don't have to deal with you, and you don't have to deal with me. Though, you have to deal with Nick. I'm not saying she thinks you're homophobic, but I bet it comes across that you have a problem with her being with women."

"Well..." He put his hands in his pockets and rocked back on his heels for a second, dirt shifting under his feet.

"Well, what?" She was still willing to bet he was somewhat bothered by Nicole's sexuality, even if he didn't know it. But, she thought there was some hope for him since being called homophobic seemed to bother him.

Spider shrugged. "I'm with my brother on this one, except for one thing."

"What's that?"

"Nicole has never talked about a relationship being endgame. She's got a passion for you that I've never seen before. She'd never stick up for a lover or anything like she did for you. Usually, by the time we meet someone, they've already worn Nicole down somewhat, to the point where she doesn't bother defending them, but she's all about you. Just for that, I think I'm okay with you, even though you're not the dream guy we all hoped Nikki would eventually meet. Make sure you take good care of her, okay?"

"I plan to do my best."

Spider smiled. "Good. She deserves it."

"No, she deserves more, but she's settling for me."

He chortled, like he thought she was joking, but she felt they both knew the truth. He stuck his hand out and they shook on it. He held her hand tightly, not trying to crush her hand or hurt her, but seeming to convey he was ready to accept her now. She offered him a slight smile.

"Come on. Let's go in there, so you can see how to play this stupid game. It's really fun with real alcohol, but it's tolerable with beer," Spider said with a small smile of his own. She chuckled and followed him back inside.

Chapter Fourteen

NICOLE FROWNED AS SHE watched Danny leave with Junior and Spider. Even though she recognized her cousins looked penitent, she didn't trust them to not snap at Danny as they made some sorry attempt at apologizing. She also didn't trust them to properly apologize at all. There was always a chance they would continue blaming Danny for things that weren't her fault. The very thought made her stomach twist.

God, what if they say something and it's the straw that breaks the camel's back with Danny? I know she wouldn't leave me based on the behavior of my cousins, but I truly don't want her to be upset once more on this trip. I just wanted her to see if she enjoyed camping and have her get along with my family. Was that too much to ask? Was it?

Beth patted Nicole on the shoulder, as if trying to assure her everything would be all right. Nicole sighed. Settling her body on a rock seat did nothing to settle the butterflies that had taken up residency in her gut. She squirmed for a moment, trying to get comfortable on the solid stone.

"Don't worry. They're not going to say anything stupid. They feel bad about what happened." Beth's words still didn't help relax those damned butterflies.

"They should feel bad. They're the ones that basically spread the rumor," Lillian said.

For some reason, Beth glared at Lillian, but Nicole wasn't sure why. Beth usually didn't interact too much with Lillian. Maybe she thought Lillian wasn't making anything better.

"Did they? They told you guys what they thought Danny and I were doing?" Nicole would chew those idiots out and then never speak to them again when they got back if that was the case. It was one thing to think poorly of her, but it was another thing to make the others think the same.

"Not really," Beth replied.

"They were the ones that basically shouted it to the mountains," Lillian said, waving her hand toward the cave entrance.

"Nikki, they only said what we were all thinking. We had even alluded to it before those morons blurted it out. You know they don't have a filter," Beth countered.

The frown continued to mar Nicole's features. "That's not much better, and it's not a good excuse."

"Don't think too much on it. They sat here all morning looking like you kicked their puppy. They're really sorry they made you so upset. Hell, I'm sorry we made you so upset. We shouldn't have been in your business like that, but we definitely should've talked to you about it if we were going to be in your business. It wasn't right of us to judge you like that."

"Thanks," Nicole muttered, even though she felt like Beth had the least to apologize for.

"Although, you do know we worry about you," Beth added, trying to justify them a little.

"I know." Nicole knew it was also in their nature to defend each other, even when they were in the wrong, so it didn't surprise her that Beth tried, somewhat, to defend Junior and Spider.

Truthfully, Nicole felt they had reason to worry. They had watched her go from one bad situation to another as far as relationships went. She wanted them to see she had finally gotten it right with Danny, but they could only see the past. Therefore, they could only see the bad. If that was how it was always going to be, then there'd be a problem, and she really hoped they could avoid having a problem.

"They're going to tease you about it," Lillian said.

Scoffing, Beth rolled her eyes. "They're going to tease you point blank."

Nicole shrugged because she knew that was the case. She didn't mind the teasing, as long as they apologized and treated Danny better. That would put things almost back to normal. She'd prefer things that way, even though she wasn't sure if she was ready to forgive the brothers for all that they had done.

"So, where'd you and Danny go this morning?" Beth moved to sit a little closer to Nicole, as if testing the waters.

"I showed her the Witch Tree, and she might've gotten cursed by touching it."

Beth gasped and her eyes went as wide as dinner plates. "You did not let her touch the Witch Tree!"

"What? I was going to stop her, but it was too late. Besides, she's not a chicken like you guys. She won't care that she touched the Witch Tree. Plus, if touching it gets you cursed, I need my baby to be cursed with me." Nicole grinned.

Beth chuckled. "I guess that would make sense. You wouldn't want to chance the witch's curse separating you from her."

Nicole smiled. "Exactly."

"What did she think of the Tree? It used to scare the crap out of me. I couldn't believe you guys used to climb it." Lillian shook her head. "I always thought you were half-brave and half-crazy."

Nicole laughed. "I remember you were practically in tears, begging me to come down. You promised me all your cookies."

"And yet, somehow, you ended up giving Lil all your cookies. Odd how that happened," Beth said, rubbing her chin with her thumb. Lillian glared at her.

"I had to do something after scaring her to death. She was crying, after all," Nicole argued.

Beth rolled her eyes and scoffed. "Of course, I don't see why, considering that was far from the scariest thing you've done."

Sometimes, when Beth got like this, like she was upset with the way Nicole favored Lillian, Nicole wondered if Beth was a little jealous. She never really dwelled on it, but it popped into her mind, because she couldn't understand why Beth seemed angered for no reason.

Scowling, Lillian glared at Beth. "She got cursed by a witch. What's scarier than that?"

Before they could say anything, Junior wandered back in. He didn't look happy, but he didn't look miserable either. Something about him seemed defeated. He didn't even sit down. He stood a few feet from them.

"What happened, Junior?" Lillian asked.

"Nothing happened. We said we'd give Danny a chance, and we shouldn't have jumped to conclusions," Junior replied, waving her off. He turned his attention to Nicole. "We should've minded our own business."

"Yeah, you should've," Nicole stated with a strong nod and a frown.

"Well, sorry about that. Now, can we stop being all serious and have some fun? This is our last real day in the woods. It's not like tomorrow is going to be full of anything beyond packing and more packing followed by driving and more driving." He huffed, but he was grinning.

"Where's your brother and Danny?" Nicole asked, glancing at the entrance of the cave. She hoped they hadn't set Danny up in some way.

"Huh?" Junior arched an eyebrow and then glanced behind him. "Oh, I thought they were coming. Maybe they found some common ground or something." He shrugged.

Nicole was a tad worried, and she was tempted to go check on them, but she knew she had to resist that urge. She couldn't baby Danny, as the musician put it. But, then again, she also worried about the pair coming to blows. Of course, if she hadn't come to blows with Junior, it wasn't likely she would with Spider, because Junior was the more volatile brother.

"How was the mood when you left them alone?" Nicole hoped he'd tell her the truth.

"Uh...they didn't look like they were about to duel at ten paces if that's what you're worried about, and I'm pretty sure Spider left his shiv at home," Junior replied with an amused half smile.

Beth snickered. "I dunno. Danny's a pretty big girl. She might be able to take Spider if it comes to blows." She balled up her hands into fists and took a few mock shots at the air. They had to laugh because she looked so silly doing that.

"Who might be able to take Spider if it comes to blows? I think I got Danny beat in that department," Spider said, as he and Danny walked into the cavern.

Danny let loose a loud scoff. "What? I could take you with one hand behind my back." Of course, that was probably the way that she had to fight now considering her left hand.

"Really? You don't look that tough." Spider blatantly assessed her.

Grey eyes rolled, but Danny smiled a bit. "Looks can be deceiving. I've never considered myself a fighter, but I can hold my own when necessary." Spider looked at her, inclining his head, almost as if he considered taking her up on that.

"No, no, no. No fighting, playful or otherwise," Nicole said, because he might actually start something. If they were getting along, it would be a game, but Danny could still get hurt or it could turn serious. They didn't need any more drama now that things were good.

Spider gave her a boyish smile and innocent glance. "What? It could be fun! We could bond."

Nicole scoffed. "No fighting."

"Spoilsport." Spider gave her a teasing smile.

"So, Danny, Nikki was telling us how she took you to the Witch Tree and she got you cursed," Beth said.

"Got me cursed?" Danny's brow wrinkled and she squinted at Beth. "I didn't climb it."

"You don't have to climb it to get cursed. You just have to touch it," Junior said.

"Touch it?" Danny turned an accusing mock glare on Nicole and pointed at her. "You said I had to climb it to get cursed."

Shrugging, Nicole laughed while trying her best to look innocent. "Climb it, touch it, almost the same thing."

"What? So, you just let me get cursed?" Danny asked with her mouth gaped open and her eyebrows curled up. She fell to Nicole's side. "How could you let me get cursed?"

"I should be cursed alone? I used to climb that tree all the time as a kid, so I've been cursed for years. I want us to be on even ground, baby. You want me to be cursed on my own?" Nicole pouted and playfully bumped Danny with her hip.

Danny grinned and put her arm around Nicole's shoulders. "Never that, Nick." She absently caressed Nicole's arm as soon as her hand was near the limb.

"So, what else did you see? She get you cursed with anything else?" Beth inquired with a chuckle.

"Dunno. Nick, did I get cursed from touching anything else?" Danny asked.

"Did she take you to the bottomless abyss?" Spider inquired.

Wide, grey eyes turned to Nicole. "There's a bottomless abyss?"

"It's not a real bottomless pit, but it looked that way when we were all under five feet tall. Junior, didn't you climb down there one day?" Nicole turned to him.

"Yeah, Spider bet me twenty bucks that I wouldn't do it, and then you bet me ten that something would eat me. Honestly, I thought the rope would break more than anything else," Junior answered with a shrug and a grin.

"I did, too, which is why I ran back for an adult when you started down." Beth grinned.

"Did the rope break?" Danny asked.

"Nah, I made it. Things got iffy when I couldn't climb back up, but I proved it wasn't bottomless and there weren't any monsters down there. A lot of bugs and rodents and garbage and things like that, but nothing I couldn't handle. Thank God the dads were there to pull me up, though."

Danny shook her head. "You guys were some crazy kids."

Nicole chuckled, happy for some odd reason that Danny thought that. Danny glanced at her and gave her a squeeze along with a small smile. She patted Danny's hand, but didn't do anything beyond that.

"Not all of us were crazy," Beth said. She nodded toward Danny. "What did you do as a kid? You haven't been camping before."

Danny shrugged. "I didn't do much as a kid."

"C'mon. You've heard all about our grand and failed schemes as kids. Now, Nikki has been telling us you're cool and all of this, so you had to do something fun," Spider insisted.

Danny scratched her head. "Not really. I had a lot of music lessons. I play six different instruments. That takes up a lot of time."

Nicole wondered if, once upon a time, that were true. Maybe when Danny practically lived with the Briarmoors she was a kid that did schoolwork and played her music. Nicole hoped that was the case, even if it didn't last long. Just so that Danny had a brief stint in her history where things were normal and wholesome. *I wish she'd share more about them, but I understand it's painful for her to even think about them.*

"So, how'd you get those scars on your leg and your hand? I would've thought those were wild child scars," Junior said, nodding toward Danny's leg.

"Those were from something much less fun than a crazy childhood." Danny glanced down at her legs. Those scars were clearly not from being a crazy kid, because there were too many and they didn't fade into her flesh like aged cuts did. "Now, you guys were going to show me how to play this game, even though you don't have anything stronger than beer."

"We'll improvise. While we might not get as drunk, it'll still make the game less boring than being completely sober," Spider said.

The others laughed, but they appeared to agree. The beer they had was very weak, and they didn't seem to be interested in finishing more than one, so none of them were in danger of getting the least bit drunk. They discovered being sober at least made for coherent answers. Danny got the hang of the game quickly and hung in there with them. It seemed like a fun time for everyone involved. Nicole thought there might be hope after all.

***

The day was drawing to a close and everyone was ready to head back to camp for their last campfire dinner. Dane could only wonder what was next after her cornbread and chili; she'd never get the combination. She'd had a good time playing 'I'm bringing to the picnic.' She decided she'd introduce the game to Crow and Terri. Crow would probably think she was crazy, but Terri would enjoy the goofiness of it.

They also played the drinking game 'Never have I ever.' Dane had to tell a few lies once the game deteriorated into nothing more than sex talk. She was slowly gaining their respect, so she didn't want to set herself back by leaving them believing she had once been a whore. They seemed to believe the things she'd normally label as tame would be risqué, so she didn't want to shock their sensibilities.

On the walk back, Dane found herself a victim of more misfortune. *Maybe it's just not my day, even if things have calmed down with Junior and Spider.* She considered Lillian walking with her to be a fate worse than death at this point. It didn't help that the others were all talking among themselves, getting ahead of her and Lillian.

Briefly, Dane tried to increase her pace, but that didn't work. She'd been walking all day, only stopping for a few hours in the cave. Her leg was in no shape to try to run or even power walk, especially through the woods. She had to grin and bear Lillian's strangeness. *Maybe I'll even get some insight into her if I don't write her off immediately.*

"So, you let Nikki get you cursed by the Witch Tree, huh? She can be tricky like that sometimes. Every now and then she used to play tricks on me when we were younger, too," Lillian said.

Dane didn't respond to that because it didn't sound right. Nicole wasn't the type to trick, and she hadn't once mentioned doing such a thing. She had talked about loving Lillian like a little sister and gushed over all the wonderful things the pair had done together. Besides, everyone had mentioned times when Nicole stuck up for Lillian or had given Lillian something to try to make her feel better. Why would she trick someone she seemed to revel in defending and spoiling?

"But, I guess that's what kids and teenagers do. So, what else did you guys do in the woods? She show you any of her make-out spots?" Lillian inquired with a taunting smile.

"Make-out spots?" Dane felt her forehead crease. *Yeah, I don't think she's going to say anything to make her seem less strange for this walk.*

"Yeah, we all had them for when we brought boyfriends and stuff camping. Our dads let us bring people all the time. Nikki brought the most people, so she had to have make-out spots."

"Okay…" In her mind, Dane called bullshit on part of the statement. She wasn't Nicole's first or anything, and she assumed most normal teenagers made out with boyfriends or girlfriends whenever they got the chance, but she also knew Nicole didn't bring a bunch of people on this traditional camping trip. *Where the hell is Lillian going with this shit? Is she drunk?* It didn't seem possible. Even with the drinking game, none of them had more than two whole beers.

Lillian leaned closer and her eyes twinkled, but it seemed nearly devilish. "You know, Nikki's actually done *it* in the woods before." Her voice was low with mischief, but not in a playful manner.

Dane almost burst out laughing. She couldn't imagine Nicole doing much in the woods beyond kissing, even if she was an adventurous teenager. Nicole had been timid about tying her up with silk scarves and it had taken them most of their sexual relationship to even change positions. Nicole didn't tell her much about her past sexual experiences and, honestly, she didn't want to hear about them, but sex in public with a chance of being caught definitely wasn't something her lover would try. Well, not without a lot of coaxing and trust. *Something to keep in mind.*

"Nick's done what in the woods?" Dane decided to tease, wanting to see how far Lillian would go, and if she would finally give up the game that she was playing. Even if it was true, Dane doubted Nicole would ever tell someone, even Lillian. She also doubted Nicole would do something like that on a family trip.

"You know what. She's had sex in the woods. You know she's wild. Is that what you two did? Sneaked off for a little quickie in the woods?"

"No." That was said as bluntly as possible. And even if they did, she'd never tell anyone, especially Lillian. She wanted Lillian to get it in her head that she was not going to talk about her sex life with Nicole, especially if it seemed likely to degrade Nicole.

Lillian gave her a sidelong glance. "Really? I'd have guessed that she'd want you to tear her clothes off considering all of the moaning you did last night."

Dane scowled. "That was a massage."

"Oh, of course it was," Lillian said with such clear sarcasm.

Dane wanted to punch her in the face. Her hand twitched, but she held off. She took a deep breath to keep herself under control.

"Come on, be serious. Do you think any of us believe that story? That's what Uncle Raymond wants to believe, but he knows, like we all do. Nikki does stuff like this all the time, but Uncle Raymond can kind of delude himself into thinking Nikki's an angel."

Dane snarled. "Nick *is* an angel." *She's my Goddamn angel!*

Lillian scoffed and rolled her cerulean eyes, eyes that seemed to hold something that was clawing its way to the surface with every passing second. "You can't be that naïve. I mean, look at you. You have to know she's with you to satisfy some hood fantasy that she has. Do you really think a lawyer like her is going to stay with you? She's always played sweet and innocent, but she's not. Hell, I know she does all kinds of crazy stuff."

"Like what?" Dane inquired, doing her best to keep from growling. She did want to hear what went through Lillian's mind in regards to a woman who thought of her as a sister. *What the hell do I tell Nicole about this bitch after all of this? This is going to fucking break her heart.*

Lillian shrugged, cool as cucumber, like she wasn't bashing Nicole. "You name it, she's probably done it. She used to smoke with one of her boyfriends. I mean, like weed and stuff. She did ecstasy with one of her boyfriends and always got drunk with him. She let one of her girlfriends spank her. Hell, she let another one of her girlfriends treat her like a pet sometimes. She even let one of her boyfriend's fuck her in the ass all the time. She's into crazy shit."

Dane felt a shot go through her. That she knew was an out and out lie. She could still barely touch Nicole's ass without Nicole flinching and needing to take a moment to calm down. *What the hell is making this woman say this shit? Is she jealous of Nick or a sneaky asshole trying to hurt Nick by making me suspicious? Trying to scare me off by making it seem like my angel is a whore? What the fuck?*

"She let someone fuck her in the ass?" Dane asked, disliking the taste of the words as they left her mouth. But, she needed to know where the hell this was going and maybe even where it came from. *Who the fuck is this bitch?*

"Yeah, she did." Lillian nodded and then shrugged again. "One of her boyfriends from a few years back. He came around a couple of times. At first, he was talking about how much he wanted to pound her ass. I thought it was weird he was saying that when she had already expressed an interest in it, so I figured they'd have done it already. She was probably being a tease, but he was too stupid to figure out she wanted to do it. I had to tell that idiot that she was waiting for him to make a move."

It literally felt like someone slammed on the brakes in Dane's head, and she wouldn't have been surprised if her brain splattered completely against the front of her skull. "Wait, wait, wait, you told her boyfriend she wanted him to fuck her in the ass?" she inquired, feeling her blood run so hot that she was surprised it hadn't evaporated through her skin and surrounded her in a mist of crimson fury.

"Well, she did, but he was too much of a coward to make a move. She's such a damn tease all the time and he needed to get that. She was playing with him, but she really wanted it and I had to tell that idiot, because he couldn't read the signals right. I'm surprised he knew what hole to fuck in the first place." Lillian had the nerve to chuckle, but the words started to sound like nothing more than buzzing in Dane's mind.

Lillian had told Nicole's boyfriend that Nicole wanted anal sex and, if it was the same guy Dane thought it was, he had actually believed her. He had believed her and eventually crossed the line with Nicole, violated her after she had told him no so many times. It was a trauma Nicole still carried with her, a violation that still made her tense if Dane as much as caressed her ass, and this woman was the reason for it.

"She always dates—"

Dane let out a guttural yell that she hardly even noticed and hopped on Lillian with a passion that would make her music pale in comparison. Lillian was on the hard ground, staring wide-eyed at Dane, who wasted no time punching her with her right hand. Dane didn't even think she should protect the one good hand that she had left. No, instead, she'd gladly break every bone in that whole arm if it meant she could make Lillian hurt a fraction of what Nicole had to feel when her boyfriend stuck a finger inside of her without her consent.

Lillian made a noise, which might've been a scream, but Dane wasn't sure. It all sounded like garbled white noise to her ears. Even the crunch of her knuckles smashing against Lillian's face mixed in with the jumble. Every few hits, she used the hand that held Lillian down to slam her into the ground, silently praying there was a rock under her, if only to hurt her even more. She was vaguely aware of Lillian trying to shove her off. It wasn't going to happen.

"You stupid fucking bitch." Dane snarled, straddling Lillian to make sure she couldn't get up. She had Lillian's arms pinned to her side with her knees, and fully intended to beat her until her whole skull caved in.

Dane wasn't sure how long she had Lillian pinned, but it wasn't enough time in her opinion. Grunting, she was tackled off the bitch and coughed as she felt a sting from a quick fist in her ribs as soon as her back smashed into the earth. Growling, she sucked up the pain and tried to pick herself up, but found it impossible. Junior and Spider held her down.

"Danny, what the hell is going on?" Nicole shrieked. She sounded so far away, but Dane couldn't see where she was with the two giant cousins looming over her.

"You think you can beat up on our sister?" Junior barked, and Dane felt that sting in her ribs again. He was the one on her now, with Spider standing by, as if ready to run if she managed to get away.

Dane didn't try to answer, again attempting to pick herself back up to make it to Lillian. How dare that bitch smile in Nicole's face when in private all she did was try to tear Nicole down? How dare she play the victim! Her body blazed with indignation as she tried to shove the big ox off her, but he wouldn't budge beyond rapidly hitting her in the same space in her side every few seconds. In the back of her mind, she thought he didn't want Nicole to see him hitting her and that was why he did it so quickly, but she didn't care about that. She wanted to get back to Lillian but had to concede she probably wouldn't be able to touch Lillian again, as another sting raced through her. The best she could do was look around this behemoth, trying to see what damage she had inflicted.

Lillian sat up, blood pouring down her nose and lip. Bruises were already forming, and her eye was thankfully swelling, but it wasn't enough. The traitorous, deceitful bitch had the nerve to turn to Nicole, sobbing on her. Dane felt her blood ignite again.

"Get off her!" Dane hollered, only to get punched in the mouth for saying anything. Spitting to the side, she tasted the familiar flavor of blood. It hurt so much more than his punches to her side or even being tackled, but she didn't care. It only burned her hotter, wanting to turn Lillian into nothing more than a smear in the dirt.

"Hey, hey, hey!" Beth came over to Junior. "Stop hitting her. You shouldn't be hitting a woman."

"She hit my little sister, so she'll get hit," Junior replied with a growl.

Beth growled right back. "You know how Lil gets," she hissed in his ear. Clearly that wasn't meant for everyone to hear, but Dane heard it all too clearly. She narrowed her gaze on Beth, noting how upset she looked with Junior.

Junior grunted and glared down at Dane before turning to Beth. "Go with Nikki to camp and get Lil some first aid. Make sure her nose isn't broken."

"How about you and Spider go? I'll stay here with Danny and make sure she's all right." Beth didn't even bother to look back at Lillian.

Junior snarled and tensed, but then he looked at Beth. "You make sure you hang back for a while. If I see her before my sister's cleaned up, I might have to put some knuckles on her face, so she can see what it's like," he warned them.

"Don't think it'll be so easy next time," Dane replied. She might not be able to take him, but she damn sure would get some licks in before he overpowered her next time, especially for protecting his bitch of a sister. *Overprotective of Nick my ass. Fucking scumbag.*

Junior growled and punched her in the face one last time, to send a message. She coughed as he got off her. He and Spider walked over to Lillian, who was still clutching Nicole like a life preserver in rough waters and sobbing on her shoulder.

Dane sat up, hissing all the way. Everything hurt, but more than that, everything boiled and raged. She watched as the three cuddled Lillian, trying to comfort a monster as far as she was concerned. They helped her to her feet, and Nicole looked in Dane's direction. She looked like she was about to walk over, but Lillian had both arms wrapped around her, clearly not about to let her go. Lillian pressed herself against Nicole and appeared to whisper something to her, but Dane couldn't hear it.

"We'll talk about this later, Danny," Nicole called to her. "I'm going to help Lil to camp and bandage her up. I want to make sure she's all right."

Dane was very close to responding, "Fuck, Lil," but suspected that wouldn't help matters. She had no doubt Nicole had missed the fact that Junior had punched her several times, too focused on her little sister. Dane wasn't bitter over that, but extremely pissed Nicole was being played. Lillian dared to toy with that wonderful, big heart. She hated that it seemed like the cousins were in on it. *I thought these assholes were looking out for her and it turns out, nope, they're fucking her around in a different way. Fucking bastards.*

Dane didn't try to get up until Nicole was almost out of sight. She didn't want to chance Nicole seeing her all messed up. This was going to be huge shit storm, after all. Nicole didn't need it right now.

Beth stood next to Dane, but she doubted Beth could be much of assistance in lifting. Not that Beth seemed to be offering. As soon as she was on her feet, Dane wrapped an arm around her middle. Her ribs hurt like hell. *That fucking gorilla is real heavy handed for such quick hits to hurt so Goddamn much.* She began walking, even though she didn't know the way back. Beth followed along.

"You guys know, don't you?" Dane said, after some silence.

"Know what?" Her voice was low, so yeah, she knew.

"Don't act so fucking innocent. You know Lil talks about Nicole behind her back. You know Lil actually fucking hates Nick, and you don't say shit about it."

Beth frowned. "I wouldn't say Lil hates her."

"Oh, no?" For her, it only made sense that Lillian hated Nicole. Why else would she encourage someone to do something to Nicole that she knew Nicole wouldn't want? They honestly got lucky he only put a finger there. He could've pushed even further, thinking it was a game, or Nicole really was teasing and he was owed. Lillian didn't know what type of man he was. She could've easily gotten her cousin into serious trouble and maybe she didn't even care.

"I'm not sure what Lil feels for Nikki, but it's clear Nikki loves her with all of her heart. Nikki treats her better than her brothers, for God's sake."

"So, why the hell hasn't anyone ever told Nick what the hell Lil does? You're making her look like an idiot." *What the fuck is wrong with these people? They're all so fucking holier than thou, but they're fucking assholes.*

"We don't think Nikki looks like an idiot. It's fucking amazing that she's able to love Lil like she does. That she's able to look past the envy and desire and love her is beyond incredible. Not just love her, but like her, too. So, what good would it do to tell Nikki about what Lil does? Have you seen how she lights up when Lil is around? Do you want to be the one that kills that joy? None of us do," Beth whispered the last sentence.

"I might have to." Dane could understand why the cousins hadn't said anything. She didn't agree with it, but she could understand it. Well, she could try to understand it, anyway. Unfortunately, she didn't have the luxury of silence, especially not now.

"Do you think she'll break up with you?"

"No." The thought hadn't even crossed her mind. Nicole wouldn't be happy, because she didn't know the whole story, and then she would feel even worse when she did, but she wouldn't blame Dane.

Beth's eyes were wide. "You're really *that* secure in your relationship?"

"She'll give me the chance to explain. Now, what she believes and doesn't believe is up in the air. I'm not sure she'll advocate my use of violence in any way. Not even sure what happened there. Just..." Dane growled and made a fist. *I wish I could still be beating the shit out of her.*

"What did she say? I've learned to tune her out over the years. I mean, I've heard her talk to some of Nicole's suitors in the past, but no one has ever hit her before."

"It's nothing I want to talk about with anyone other than Nick."

"You know she's in camp playing up being the victim. Are you sure Nikki won't break up with you?"

"We'll find out." Now, she couldn't help wondering what would happen if Nicole did break up with her. *Will Nicole and Raymond even give me a ride back to their state? Will I be allowed in the car? Would they call the police? How manipulative was Lillian?*

***

The camp was empty when Nicole and her cousins arrived. They weren't surprised. Their fathers liked to fish when they went off exploring. Nicole was relieved, actually. She knew her uncle would probably want to beat Danny's brains in if he saw Lillian's face.

"Get me the first aid kit," Nicole said, as she motioned for Lillian to sit down on one of the folding stools.

"Nikki, you'd better start packing your bitch's stuff and put that bitch on a bus, because the second she comes into camp, she needs to leave," Junior stated while Spider moved to get the first aid kit.

"Lil, what happened?" Nicole asked in a gentle tone. *What did you say that set Danny off? I've never seen Danny like that before.*

Lillian sniffled and wiped away tears. "I don't know. I was trying to talk to her, being nice to her like you asked. I was telling her about some of the stuff you've done in the woods and she got all pissed and started punching me."

"That doesn't sound like Danny at all." Nicole shook her head slightly, feeling her face tense and scrunch up. *Danny would never react that way from a simple conversation.*

"Oh, it's not like it would be the first fucking time that one your lovers turned out to be an asshole!" Junior huffed.

Nicole frowned. "Danny is not an asshole." *There's more here than Lil's telling us.*

"She fucking hit my sister, Nikki! Several times from the looks of things. Look at her fucking face, Nikki. Your beloved fucking Danny did that." Junior's voice was a bellow, as he pointed to his bloody sister.

Nicole sighed, but she couldn't argue that. Danny had hit Lillian several times, extremely hard from the looks of things. She had never seen Danny raise her hand in anger. Sure, Danny had talked about it, but it was when she was younger and on several drugs, as well as drunk. Something was wrong, very wrong, and Nicole couldn't figure out what. She knew that Lillian wasn't giving her the full story, making her think Lillian had done something to provoke Danny. *But, what the hell could Lillian say to make Danny react like that? Danny didn't even seem to hear me calling her before Junior got her off Lillian.*

"Is it possible that Danny misunderstood something you were saying to her?" Nicole asked Lillian as she began working on her cousin's face, which was swelling rapidly. Her left eye would probably be shut completely in less than a half hour.

"Don't make fucking excuses for her, Nicole." Junior glared at her and threw his hands up.

"I'm not making excuses. In the two years I've known Danny, I've never seen her do anything remotely like this, so I'm trying to figure out why." Nicole thundered right back. She was careful of Lillian's face.

"Yes, you are. Fix Lil's face. I'm packing this bitch's shit," Junior said.

"Don't touch any of Danny's things," Nicole ordered before focusing completely on Lillian. She noted Spider was unusually quiet through it all. Glancing at him, he appeared more frustrated than angry. Something was going on, but she didn't have time to really contemplate it.

"Is it broken?" Lillian whimpered about her nose, as Nicole tended to her.

"No, it's fine. Hold still," Nicole stated.

"It's not fine. It feels broken. It hurts." Lillian sniffled, and tears rolled down her cheeks.

Nicole didn't doubt that it hurt quite a bit, but she didn't comment on it. Everything seemed to be going as expected, as she tended to Lillian's face. Suddenly, she heard the sound of wood splintering against a tree, and she turned to see Junior holding the remains of Danny's guitar. He locked eyes with her and chucked the shattered instrument on the ground.

"The bitch is next if you don't pack her shit," Junior threatened before disappearing into the woods.

Nicole focused on the guitar in the dirt and thought of how brokenhearted Danny was going to be when she saw it. *Shit, this was supposed to be a simple, fun family camping trip. How did things come to this? Now, it's never going to be the same.* Tears burned her eyes, but she held them at bay as she finished up with Lillian.

Chapter Fifteen

DANE COUGHED AGAIN AND paused, leaning against a solid tree. The bark was rough against her body, even with her shirt. She needed to catch her breath again, but it hurt so damned much to breathe at all. The tree scratched her with each shallow inhale and exhale.

Beth watched her with concerned eyes, but Dane didn't bother to acknowledge her. Honestly, she wished Beth would get lost, even if it meant she'd end up wandering the woods like Hansel and Gretel's long-lost sister. Hissing, she felt around her ribs, needing to make sure they weren't broken. *Those muscles aren't just for show. He got me good.*

"You need help?" Beth inquired with her head tilted to the side as if studying Dane.

"You and your walking stick going to help?" Dane snapped. She knew she was upset with Beth, but not particularly angry like she was with Junior, or livid like she was with Lillian.

"Probably not. Junior's pretty heavy-handed. Did he break anything?"

"Nah. Come on, let's get going." Dane began walking again. Breathing hurt, and it didn't help that her knee throbbed and burned thanks to being slammed on the hard ground. She feared she might not make it back to camp.

Dane followed Beth, wondering if they had taken long enough for Nicole and Raymond to decide to drive off without her, leaving her to the mercy of Lillian's male kin. She could imagine how much Junior would love to finish what he started, but she couldn't figure out why. He knew what his sister did. *Does he condone it? Does he engage in it, too?* He seemed to love Nicole when she was around, enjoying her company and everything, but Nicole also thought Lillian loved her, and Lillian put up a hell of a front. *Maybe Junior and Spider are like their sister. If they are, what poison are they putting in my angel's head right now?* This thought took her back to Nicole and Raymond deserting her in the middle of the woods.

In truth, Dane knew Nicole wouldn't leave. She didn't have it in her. She wasn't too sure what Raymond would do. Her first instinct told her that he'd commend Junior for hitting her if he saw what she had done to Lillian's face, but she hadn't been very accurate in guessing what he'd do in a lot of situations. Shaking it off, she'd play it out as it happened. It wouldn't remain a mystery for long, even though it seemed like the walk back to camp took an eternity, and then some.

"You bitch!" Richard roared as soon as Dane came into view. Next thing she knew, he had his hands wrapped around her throat and she couldn't breath, no matter how much she tried. In an instant, her lungs burned and her chest throbbed in agony as pain shot through her ribs.

"Whoa, whoa, whoa! Rich, that's a woman!" Raymond shot over in a flash and ripped his brother's rough hands away. He stood in front of Dane and put his hands behind him, keeping a hold of her. She understood this was protective, but it didn't make any sense. Surely, he knew what she had done by now, and she had no doubt it had been spun to make her sound like the devil incarnate, so he shouldn't be trying to save her.

"She hit my daughter then she needs to get her ass beat, woman or not!" Richard's eyes blazed with pure, unabashed hatred. "I'm sure you'd be the same way if she fucking hit Nikki, which she probably does because she's clearly a fucking animal." He glared at her, letting her know he wanted to be the one to put the animal down.

"I'd never hit Nicole!" Dane tried to jump over Raymond. She wouldn't have touched his stupid daughter if she weren't such a cow. "You don't know me to say shit like that. I'd never, ever hit Nicole because she's not awful and rotten on the inside like your fucking daughter is."

"Danny, stay still." Raymond held her back.

"I would never..." Dane whispered, her chest heaving as she panted wildly. Her stomach twisted and a lump got stuck in her throat. *I'm not a monster. I'm not an animal.*

He glanced back at her. "I know."

Raymond's belief in her made her belly flip, and she truly didn't know what to do with such faith. She almost considered telling him that she might be lying, if only to go into more familiar territory of being loathed. After she got hit by a car and knocked unconscious for some hours, she had awoken thinking she had hit Nicole. Of course, Nicole assured her that hadn't been the case, but in moments of doubt she feared that might not be true. Nicole might've been trying to protect her from the truth, somehow feeling she might've deserved such treatment for emotionally hurting Dane. There were days when Dane conceded she'd never know the truth, but in her heart, she was certain she'd sooner throw herself in front of another car than harm Nicole or allow someone else to harm Nicole.

"Ray, you'd better move. I will go through you to get to this bitch," Richard said, pointing a threatening finger at Dane. A vein in his neck bulged and, briefly, Dane imagined it bursting from the rage spiking his blood pressure.

"Calm down. I'm not letting you touch Danny. If you want to go through me, feel free, but I'm not going down easy. This isn't like when we were kids. So, what's it going to be?" Raymond squared his shoulders and stared his older brother down.

Richard fumed for a moment, staring through Raymond and right at Dane. She returned the favor, almost wanting him to step over for daring to suggest to Raymond that she'd hit Nicole. Spider came up behind his father and put his hand on his shoulder. Richard turned to look at him.

"Dad, I think there's more to this than just Danny coming out of nowhere hitting Lil," Spider said in a low voice. He glanced at Dane and something in his eyes very nearly seemed to understand her. She hated to think what the hell he had heard Lillian say for him to dare try to be sympathetic with her.

"There is. There's a lot you don't know," Beth said to her uncle, moving to stand by Richard.

She patted Richard on the chest, but that didn't seem to calm him much. He continued to sneer at Dane, as if she were some wild beast he wanted the pleasure of taking down. Beth shook her head, but Spider held his father firmly.

"She's right, Dad. There's so much you don't know," Spider said in an oddly gentle tone.

"This doesn't change a Goddamn thing. She hit my fucking daughter, and I'm going to fucking hurt this dyke bitch. Fucking unnatural whore," Richard said, spitting in Dane's direction. Well, it was a bit unsettling to see she was right about the homophobia. It made her wonder if he might talk about Nicole behind her back and maybe he was where Lillian learned it was all right to do.

"You say that now, Dad, but I think you'll change your mind. Just hear me out. Hear me and Beth out and find out a little bit more about what's going on. Come on, we'll go talk a bit." Spider gently pulled his father away, going toward the edge of the camp. Beth followed them, while Raymond turned to look at her.

Raymond examined her face. "Junior hit you?"

Dane shrugged. "He popped me one to the cheek." She didn't think he needed to know anything more than that. She didn't want his sympathy any more than she wanted anyone else's.

His gaze narrowed. "And why did he do that?"

"You've seen why, I'm sure."

"And why did you do that?" he pressed a bit, leaning over, almost looming over her.

Dane shrugged again. "Long story that probably won't make any sense to you. You probably won't believe me either."

He gave her a deadpan expression. "Try me."

Dane ran a hand through her hair, feeling like there was no getting out of this. She wasn't sure why she didn't want to tell him. It wasn't like she thought he'd side with his brother and want to kill her when he heard the tale. It wasn't like she cared about letting him know what type of person Lillian really was. She hated to think it was her street-thinking kicking in and she didn't want to be a snitch. Shaking that away, she opened her mouth and hoped she did the right thing.

"Lillian told me something she once said that led to a lot of pain for Nick and she didn't seem too remorseful about it. In fact, she seemed proud of it, and I couldn't stand the thought of someone being proud they hurt Nick, especially someone Nick loves so much. I was hitting her before I realized it and would probably still be hitting her if Junior hadn't tackled me off her. Messed up, huh?" A hollow laugh escaped her.

His brow furrowed as he took in her words. "You hit Nikki's cousin defending Nikki's honor?"

There was another shrug. "Something like that."

He let loose a long sigh. "Look, I know there's a lot more to this story, and I expect you to tell it if you want my support. I'm trying to give you the benefit of the doubt, because I know my family can be...difficult." He glanced over in the direction of his brother.

"I appreciate that, and I promise, I'll tell you what I can. But, right now, I really want to sit down." Her leg and ribs needed a breather. She really wished she had some ice, if only to numb her throbbing face.

Walking further into camp, she felt a joy that was probably unholy just from the sight of one of those stupid folding stools. As she went to sit down, she forgot all about it as a pile of wood by a tree caught her attention. It sat as if nothing more than a pile of trash, splinters and strings in the dirt and grass. Swallowing a lump in her throat, she moved closer and saw it was exactly what she thought it—her guitar.

"My...my..." Dane sniffed as she bent down and picked up the neck of her guitar. It was cracked, but the body of the instrument was ruined. The back had a hole in it, undoubtedly from where it had impacted the tree. It was separated from the neck, dangling by a couple of strings that hadn't pulled away. She cradled it to her like an old friend.

"Junior..." Nicole said, easing over, approaching with caution. Her head was bowed a bit, bent in guilt, like this was entirely her fault.

"I figured," Dane grumbled, running her hand through her hair. She shouldn't feel as upset about this as she did, but there was still sentiment in the damned thing. There was a reason why she still walked around with the damned thing, after all. "Fuck," she muttered, leaving her hand in her hair.

Something bubbled into her throat and she did her best to swallow it down, but it remained lodged there, threatening to choke her. Gritting her teeth, she tried to let go of the stupid guitar, but found she couldn't. It was part of her, a rotten, broken part, like so many other pieces that composed who she was. She wondered if she sat there forever if somehow miraculously everything would get better.

"Come on, sweetie. Everything's packed. We're leaving," Nicole said as gently and as calmly as possible.

Dane nodded, but kept looking at her guitar, clutching it to her chest. Nicole walked off, backing away with her head down, and Dane noted Nicole didn't use the words, "we're going home." *I may have fucked up, but I think I'd do that shit again. That bitch could've gotten Nick raped. Fuck her.* She knew that was an extreme, but it was a possibility because the guy shoved his finger in her after she had repeatedly told him no. Dane wouldn't apologize for what she did— ever. Someone needed to stand up to Lillian, especially if she had been doing stupid, spiteful things like that all of her life.

What other things has that rotten bitch said that got Nicole hurt? Nicole would have no idea why. What else had the cousins allowed to slide because they didn't want to crush Nicole, not knowing they'd aided in crushing her anyway? Who else had said things, done things to Nicole like Lillian had done? *How could they hurt such a precious angel? Bastards.*

"Come on, baby," Nicole softly urged, wrapping her arm around Dane's shoulder. She eased by Dane, going to open the car door for her. Dane blinked, like she didn't understand the world around her anymore.

Dane found herself clutching the busted guitar even tighter, making sure it didn't get left behind. She wasn't sure why, but it seemed like the thing to do. She turned to go to the car and found herself face-to-face with Junior. His family and Beth were a few feet away, while Raymond and Nicole waited in the car. She stared him down for a few seconds with her head held high, even if her cheek felt like it weighed a ton.

"Hope you feel good about yourself. This guitar is the only thing my mother ever gave me. The only time that she showed me she saw me. And you don't get that because you come from a family that's so fucking perfect your sister talks about a cousin who adores her behind her back and gets that cousin assaulted. You hit me. You hurt me, so you could say you protected Lillian, but remember your actions also show that she can tell the next asshole that comes along that your precious cousin Nikki likes being fucked in the ass. She encourages people to do shitty things to Nick, and she talks about Nick like she's a fucking whore, probably getting off on having people think Nick is a whore. But, I guess that's okay because she's your sister and Nicole's only a damned dyke anyway, right?"

Junior flinched and glanced back. For a moment, she saw regret in his eyes, regret because he knew it was true. They all knew what Lillian did and no one had ever said a word to Nicole. She spat at his feet.

"Fuck her for saying all that shit, but fuck you more for never telling Nicole when you claim you want to protect her. Fuck you even harder if you do that shit yourself, because Nicole fucking loves you and you're nothing but a bastard." Dane turned and walked away.

She didn't wait to hear what he had to say, even though he didn't seem to have anything to say. Dane doubted he or his brother talked about Nicole considering they hadn't talked to her like Lillian did, but still, she believed that something had led Lillian to believe her behavior was all right. She blamed him, along with the rest of his family. So, *fuck them*.

Dane hopped in the back of the SUV. Raymond was behind the wheel, and Nicole rode shotgun. Dane sat her guitar next to her as if it were a small child. She almost buckled it in, but caught herself. She had the urge to put it in its case and bury it in the backyard, if she still had a backyard.

"You okay?" Nicole asked, turning to look at Dane. "Danny, what happened to your face?"

She rolled her eyes, unable to deal with denial right now. "You know what happened to my face."

Nicole swallowed so hard it seemed to echo through the car. "I'm sorry Junior hit you. When?"

"After he tackled me."

Nicole frowned, shaking her head. She massaged her temple, as if trying to arrange her thoughts. Dane wondered what was going through her mind, but she had a feeling she was going to get a piece of it any moment.

"He shouldn't have done that, even if you did hit Lillian. And why did you hit Lil? What's wrong with you?" She was partially yelling, partially crying with her hands flying, and that vein in her forehead making itself known.

"I hit *Lil*, because I don't like the things she says about you," Dane stated through gritted teeth. Just mentioning that bitch's name made her want to hit Lillian again, especially if Nicole was going to defend her.

The reply actually gave Nicole pause, almost as if she had suspicions. She dispelled that with a shake of her head. "What things? Danny, she's probably just playing around. I mean, we're cousins. You see we joke on each other all the time. I'm sure she was only kidding." Her voice was quieter now, but determined to make sense of the whole matter, as best she could, without accepting that Lillian was at fault. But, the unshed tears in her eyes told another story. Dane's heart hurt for her love.

Glancing at her guitar, Dane felt fresh indignation flare in her. Her stomach twisted and her neck tensed, hearing her lover defend that harpy. She couldn't believe those people actually allowed Nicole to believe Lillian cared for her at all. They had allowed Nicole to make a fool out of herself. She wouldn't do the same or give them another opportunity to do so.

"She wasn't joking when she asked me if we had a quickie in the woods. She wasn't joking when she said you do that sort of thing all the time with your other lovers. She wasn't joking when she implied you had slept with a long list of people. She wasn't joking when she told me she encouraged your fucking boyfriend to fuck you in the ass because you like that sort of thing," Dane hissed through gritted teeth. She might never be able to open her mouth again.

"Danny," Nicole gasped and flinched. Her emerald eyes were wide and aghast. She turned around and curled into a ball as if trying to disappear into the seat. "Lil would never…" she whispered, sounding so small that her girlfriend almost felt bad for saying it. Almost.

"Yeah, Lil would," Dane growled. "So, there you have it. She said that, and I sort of snapped."

"Danny, getting jealous is no reason—" Raymond tried to jump in, but didn't get far.

Danny cut him off with a loud laugh. "Jealous? Can't say don't make me laugh, because you already did that. I'm not jealous. Half the shit she said was clearly shit and the other half were lies. You two fucking defend her all you want, and think what you will, but if I had the chance, I'd do it again. And you know why, Nick."

The ride back was uncomfortably quiet. No one said a word and no one moved. Raymond didn't even turn on the radio. Nicole stared out of the window, still curled up with the occasional tear rolling down her cheek. Dane looked at her guitar, a tear in her eye that refused to fall down her bruised cheek. Hours passed in oppressive, bone-crushing silence.

Nicole didn't even spare her a glance as they pulled up to Raymond's house. Nicole dashed inside, either running to her mother for comfort or going to her room, since it had a door to keep Dane out. Dane couldn't chase her, not with her ribs and leg feeling like they were under siege by a thousand thorns. Raymond got out as if he was going to go after Nicole, but he paused and gave Dane a look. She shrugged and then he was gone, following his daughter.

"Hope he can talk some sense into her. Of course, there's always the chance he didn't believe me either," Dane grumbled, as she pretty much slid out of her seat. She winced as her feet touched the ground. "Hope Kathleen won't mind me borrowing some painkillers." *What a time to be fucking sober.*

She reached for her broken guitar for reasons beyond her and dragged it behind her, reminding her of a dog with its tail between its legs. *Maybe because I'm in the Goddamn doghouse.* Limping, she entered the mansion and wondered where the hell they might keep the painkillers. Scratching her head, she didn't get a chance to figure it out as the lady of the house approached her.

"Danny, what the hell is going on? Nicole ran by me like her butt was on fire, and Raymond was right behind her without a word of explanation! I swore she was crying!" Kathleen shouted and then she gasped. "What happened to your face? Have you been fighting?"

Dane waved the question off. "Long story. Got any Advil or something like that?"

"Come, let me look at you." Kathleen waved her closer. Dane didn't have the brainpower to object or wonder what the hell was going on. She hoped there were painkillers in her future if she complied.

***

Nicole wasn't sure why she ran to her room, but it seemed like the best plan for the moment. She didn't want to see anyone, didn't want anyone to see her, especially Danny. Right now, she felt ready to throw up, but she wasn't sure why. It could've been because she didn't believe Danny, but worse, it could be because she did believe Danny.

Whatever the case, it had her head pounding. She massaged her temples and tried her best to stop crying, but the tears continued to flow. Lying down on her bed didn't help, as her brain felt bombarded by everything that had happened. Beyond what Danny had said, she kept thinking about the fact that her actions had gotten Danny hurt.

"Why does every time I try to do something with her end with her being hurt by someone? What the hell does she stick around for? I keep fucking up with her when all I want is for her to be happy. Surely, her life would be better without me, and I know she has to have realized that," Nicole sobbed, wiping away her tears.

She couldn't help feeling like a hypocrite, along with the guilt. After all, she had once tried to show Danny that her family wasn't so bad and she should give them a chance, only to discover her own family was far from perfect and didn't deserve much of a chance. *Maybe all families suck. Hadn't Mina told me that before?*

"Nikki," Raymond called, while lightly rapping on Nicole's door. It wasn't necessary since the door was open. She hoped he hadn't heard her talking to herself.

"I don't want to talk about it right now, Daddy. I don't want to talk about anything." Nicole sniffled and made herself comfortable against the side of her bed.

"Because you're mad at Danny, or because you're mad at Lil?" Raymond asked, walking in the room anyway. He sat down next to her.

Glancing away, she took a deep breath, knowing the answer, but not wanting to admit it. "Do you think Lil said those things?"

"Do you think she did?" he countered.

Nicole rubbed her head and wiped her nose with the back of her hand. "One time…one time…once, when we were teenagers…" She couldn't get it out. She shook her head and the hid her face in her knees. She felt so very young and upset. *I'm such a fool.*

He arched an eyebrow. "You heard Lil talking about you?"

"She laughed it off, calling it a joke, and saying she was trying to keep a boy away from me, because he wasn't good enough for me. I didn't like what she was saying, but I bought her answer. I know she gets really clingy and almost possessive when people, other than her brothers, show an interest in me. I thought that's all it was."

He gave her head a gentle pat. "Now, you think it was more than that?

She swallowed hard. "I…I'm scared it is. What else has she told, and who has she told it to? What kind of things has she made up about me? I mean, the things she told Danny are horrible enough, but what did she say to whoever actually listened to her? God, that thing…" Nicole began bawling uncontrollably as she was hit with what felt like a million emotions at once.

Racing to her feet, Nicole was stunned she made it to the bathroom in time to throw up in the toilet. *Lillian had encouraged that asshole. Encouraged him to…*She couldn't even finish the thought. No, she didn't blame Lillian for what he had done and how he had violated her, as that was his decision. *But Lillian planted the idea, told him to do it, told him I wanted it.* And while she had told Danny he had put his finger in without her permission, she hadn't told Danny about the argument that followed, the names he had called her, and what he had done after their breakup. It had all been beyond terrible.

Who else has Lillian encouraged to try to get me to do things I'd never want to do? Her mind raced over any and every horrible experience she'd had with a lover that Lillian had met; hell, even with friends that Lillian had met. Her stomach bubbled and more bile spewed from her mouth. Coughing, she spat into the toilet before flushing. She noticed her dad in the doorway as she moved to rinse her mouth out.

"What's wrong?" Raymond asked with concern in his emerald eyes. He raised a hand, like he wanted to touch her, but seemed frightened that she might break.

Nicole shook her head. *How could I tell Daddy that I had a boyfriend who stuck his finger in my ass after I told the jerk on multiple occasions I wasn't into that sort of thing? How can I tell Daddy that the damn jerk didn't even care how much it hurt, or how scared I was that he'd try it again or anyone might try it? I couldn't believe Lillian actually encouraged that.* While brushing her teeth, she had to hold her tears at bay, but her eyes burned right along with her heart and soul.

"I thought Lillian liked me, Daddy. She was my little sister. Why would she do this?" Nicole sniffled. *Why would she purposely hurt me like this? I was so good to her.*

Raymond shook his head and walked over to her. He embraced her like he used to do when she was a little girl. It was an all-encompassing hug, holding her together at the seams and keeping all the evil in the world at bay. She turned and hid in his chest, clutching his shirt. He rubbed her back.

"Why?" Nicole bawled.

"I don't know why, Nicole. I wish I could tell you. You've been sweet and kind to Lillian her whole life. Sometimes, people are just mean."

"But, she's my cousin."

"Yeah, but still, sometimes people are just mean."

"Do you think Junior and Spider do the same thing? Do they hang out with me and smile in my face and then talk about me behind my back?"

Raymond sighed. "I don't know. I'd like to think they don't. God, you always have such a good time with them, and it really looks like they love you as much as you love them. I've never...I've never heard them talking about you."

"Yeah, well, I've only heard Lillian do it once, but now I can only wonder how many times she's actually done it. How many times did she tell someone I was a whore and then come and smile in my face, hook her arm around me, and pretend to be my sidekick? How many times?"

Raymond didn't have any answers to that. He only hugged her tighter. She appreciated that more than answers for the moment. She held onto him with a desperate affection, toothbrush hanging from her lips.

S.L. Kassidy

Chapter Sixteen

"SO, WHO DID YOU end up fighting, Junior or Spider?" Kathleen asked from her space on the cushy leather sofa. She had personally bandaged Dane, which was quite weird. They hadn't spoken as she did so, but she had managed to get Dane to let go of her guitar. Kathleen then led her into the den, sat her down next to her guitar, and requested the housekeeper fetch them some tea.

"Lillian," Dane answered in a mumble while doing her best to not think about why Kathleen was being so nice to her. One of the things that aided in that was sitting down on the comfortable couch, definitely a Godsend. *Something is wrong with me to be taking so much pleasure in the simple action of sitting on my ass.*

A shadow crossed Kathleen's face briefly and then she nodded. "What did she say?"

Dane leaned over a bit, studying her. "How do you know she said anything?"

Kathleen's face went tight as a frown pulled its way onto her mouth. "I know her. She's a bitch. I heard her talking about Nikki a couple of times. I threatened her that if I heard her talking about my daughter again, I'd rip out her tongue."

"You never told Nicole?" The very idea stunned Dane, because she was certain that Kathleen, the extremely overprotective mother that she was, would've done something to at least keep Nicole away from that bitch.

Kathleen shook her head. "I don't expect you to understand, Danny. You don't have a daughter, and I can only assume you don't know what it's like to be someone's child, considering what came out at Thanksgiving, but no one wants to tell their child things that will hurt them. Besides, since I didn't hear anything, I thought she'd stopped. I'd have seriously hurt her if I heard anything and she knew that, so like I said, I thought she'd stopped."

"No," Dane scowled. *I can't believe even Kathleen got fooled.* "She was more careful. But, not careful enough."

"So, you cut your knuckles on her?"

Dane nodded and looked at her bandaged hand. Her knuckles had been split, but she hadn't realized it at the time. The cuts burned with satisfaction. She hadn't even flinched when Kathleen cleaned them.

"What did she say?" Kathleen asked, mouth still tense and frowning.

"You don't want to know. It's not so much what she said, but what her words led to. She got Nicole hurt and it could've been worse. Maybe she didn't know, maybe she did, but her words were more than words." Dane shook her head. Part of her wanted to tell Kathleen, if only because she knew Kathleen would make that little bitch pay even more. But, that information would hurt Kathleen and Nicole too much.

Kathleen nodded and did something surprising by moving to sit next to Dane. She put her arm around her and patted her leg with the other one. And then, she leaned over and gave Dane a soft kiss on her forehead.

Dane gasped and became so stiff that she thought she might shatter in a soft wind. Her heart beat heavy in her chest, and she feared it might do what Junior couldn't—break her ribs. Tears burned the corners of her eyes, but they dared not fall. It was the strangest thing she had ever felt.

"Thank you so much for sticking up for Nicole. If Lillian did that with you, I'm sure she did it with other significant others. You're the only one to do something about it, to say something about it. So, thank you from the bottom of my heart," Kathleen said.

"Uh…"

Kathleen sighed. "I know, it's disturbing."

"Yeah, it is."

"Would you like me to move?"

Dane knew she should say yes, but the feeling wasn't disturbing. The situation itself was strange, but having Kathleen show her appreciation at least led her to believe she had done the right thing. She felt validated. And so, for a long moment, Kathleen held her, and she allowed it.

"So, who ended up defending Lillian and hit you back?" Kathleen inquired, moving away from Dane. The moment was gone, Dane assumed.

"Junior. Damn thing is, he knows Lillian talks about Nicole. They all know. I don't think they all talk about her like Lillian, but they damn sure know that bitch does this crap. They don't tell Nicole, because they don't want to hurt her feelings."

Kathleen scowled. "He hit you, even though he knows Lillian is a bitch?"

Dane shrugged. "I guess he has to defend his sister, no matter what. Is it right for them to not tell Nicole? Beth said they don't want to take away the joy that Nicole shows when Lillian is around. Does that make sense?"

"Unfortunately, it does make sense. They're all close. They don't want to hurt each other, but I don't see why Junior would do this to you if he knows that Lillian talks about her. I didn't know they were aware of it. This doesn't make any sense, unless he wants to keep up appearances or something."

Dane ran her hand through her hair. "I don't know if they know exactly what she says, and they probably don't know the consequences of what she says. I only know about one consequence, but that was more than enough for me to pound her face in."

"Was it...was it really bad?" Kathleen's voice cracked at the end of the question, and her breathing sped up for a few seconds.

"I promise you that you don't want to know, but if you think you do, you can ask your husband. I sort of screamed it in the car when Nicole was defending Lillian. She wasn't physically hurt." *Or so I hope. If she was, and I find out, I'm hunting that bastard down next and beating him in the face with a pipe before letting him know first-hand how she felt.*

Breathing a sigh of relief, Kathleen nodded. "Okay, that's good."

"So, I think I figured out what you meant by his family not being as accepting as yours. They hated me the second they saw me, because I hadn't been camping before. Well, among other things. They kept calling me city girl, like it was an insult. Weird."

"No, they're surprisingly judgmental."

"They don't like you because you can't camp?"

Kathleen chuckled and shook her head. "No, that's not why they don't like me. They are of the belief that I changed Raymond. He was laidback to the point that, when I met him in school, junior year, his major was physical education, and he didn't plan on being a gym teacher."

Dane arched an eyebrow. "Then why was he in school?"

"Apparently, he went to college just to go to college. I think his mother talked him into it, as his father would've been more than happy if Raymond drove a tow truck like he did. Richard followed that same course, and I'm sure Raymond planned to do the same thing. His mother wanted a child to go to college and, since Richard didn't go, she forced Raymond to go."

Dane squinted in thought. "But, didn't she have other kids? He didn't have to be the one."

"Yes, he did. She didn't plan on any of her girls going to college. They were expected to finish high school, get some type of office work until they met the right man, and then get married."

"Wait, what?" *Is it 1950 and no one told me?*

"Yes, so Raymond had to be the one to go to college."

"And when he met you, he decided on law school?"

Kathleen nodded. "That's the short of it. One day he returned home with a purpose. Life wasn't all a game, and his family didn't know how to handle it. They accused me of changing him, for the worse in their opinion."

She put him on the path to become one of the best lawyers in the city and they hate her for that? His family's fucked up. "I can believe that."

The bonding was interrupted, when Mrs. Harlow entered with the tea. Kathleen smiled her thanks to the other woman, and Mrs. Harlow took her leave. Kathleen moved farther over as she reached for her tea. Dane had to test her right hand to make sure she could hold a cup. There was no way she'd ever pick anything up with her left hand. Her knuckles stung, but that was all, so she picked up the cup and had a taste.

"How is it?" Kathleen asked.

"It's good. Thanks."

"Be sure to try some of the cookies with it." Kathleen nodded to a small plate of cookies.

Dane nodded as she reached for one.

***

Nicole stopped dead in her tracks as she was walking into the den. Her father, who was by her side, did the same. They stared into the scene, watching Kathleen and Dane calmly sip tea, sitting next to each other, not killing each other, or even belittling each other.

"Let's join them," Raymond said, and Nicole could only nod.

The pair stood there for a few more seconds before stepping into the room. It was surprising there was no tension in the area. For a second, she and her father didn't know where to sit and just looked around. They ended up in the two armchairs, usually reserved for her parents. Once seated, Nicole got a look at Danny.

"Oh, my God, Danny. You should put ice on your cheek," Nicole said. It was swollen and bruised a deep maroon.

Danny waved her off. "It's fine."

Nicole nodded and looked down. Guilt gnawed at her stomach for not having taken care of her beloved's wounds. By Danny's side, she noticed the guitar. She gasped, realizing Danny couldn't let it go.

"Danny, I am so sorry about your guitar. I'll make Junior buy you a new one," Nicole said, even though she knew that wouldn't help.

Danny waved that off, too. "Don't worry about it. He can't replace this one."

"How so? It's just a guitar," Raymond said.

"My mother bought this guitar for me almost twenty years ago. Might be the only thing she's ever bought me in my life. He can't replace this guitar," Danny stated in a deadpan tone.

Raymond colored a bit, obviously embarrassed. "Oh."

"It's okay. Maybe it was time to get rid of the damned thing. Don't know why I've been holding on to it in the first place." Danny frowned briefly before focusing on Nicole. "Are you okay?"

"I should be asking you that. You're the one trying to be a knight in shining jean shorts," Nicole replied with an awkward smile. She wanted things to be okay between them, and she wasn't sure how to begin making up for everything that had happened.

Danny leaned over and took Nicole's hand. "Here to protect you as best I can, Angel. Sorry I ended up hitting her, and I'm sorry she's your cousin. But, if I hear anyone, relative or not, saying stuff like that about you and encouraging people to do bad things to you, I'm going to hit them, because they don't have the right to do that. They don't have the right to cause you that kind of pain and suffering. She's lucky I only had my hands. If I could've uprooted a tree to beat her ass, I would have."

"Did she...do you know...I mean, do you have an idea of how many people she said these things to or what she's said?" Nicole tried to calm her breathing and get her stomach to stop fluttering. She supposed it was good she wasn't hyperventilating or throwing up, but she felt like she might at any moment.

"No, but, from what I can guess, she's probably told every boyfriend and girlfriend of yours that she's ever met that you're into really kinky things and that you've had a lot of sexual partners. I don't know what she might have said to other people."

Nicole nodded and sniffled. "Do you think...do you think people believed her?"

"The people that matter don't believe her. I didn't believe her. I know your parents don't, and your other cousins still respect you."

"Not Junior and Spider..." Nicole sniffled again, and a tear slid down her face. *Why should I care? They're asses, them and their damned sister.*

"I don't think you should write them off just yet, even if Junior is an ass. They probably have to chew on this for a while, but I think they'll come around," Danny said.

"Did he hurt you anywhere else?" Nicole suddenly asked, managing to hold back any more tears. She wasn't even sure when Junior had hit Danny, but she recalled his anger and imagined he hadn't stopped at hitting her once.

Again, her lover waved it off. "I'm a little sore, but I'll live. Give it some time, Nick. I don't think your cousins are going to give up on you, especially based on my actions."

"I might just give up on them. I asked Junior and Spider to give you a chance so many times, and they didn't. And then Junior hits you after knowing about Lillian. She's the bad guy, not you. Or at least to me, but I might be seeing it wrong. Either way, I don't like what he did," Nicole huffed.

"You're upset right now, Nikki. These are your cousins," Kathleen reminded her.

Nicole scowled. "I know who they are." *Assholes who pretended to care about me, like way too many other people in my life.*

"Give it a few days to settle, Nick, before you write them off. It might not be so bad," Danny said.

Nicole couldn't help thinking Danny knew something she didn't. She decided to just trust Danny on it. She moved to be closer to her beloved. She took Danny's hand and held it tightly. *Hold onto me like this, Danny. Hold onto me.*

"You know, you two can stay here tonight, since we're back a day early," Raymond said with a bit of a smile.

"It's no problem." Kathleen nodded to show her approval.

"Thanks for the offer," Nicole said, while Danny pressed into her hand with her thumb. "But, I think we will pick up Haydn and go back home. We'll be fine."

"You sure?" Raymond asked.

"Yes, Daddy. I'm sure. Thank you again for the offer."

Her parents nodded. Danny finished her tea and they stood up to leave. Nicole noted her mother even hugged Danny farewell. The sight of Danny grabbing her busted guitar overshadowed that observation. While Danny might believe she needed to let the guitar go, clearly she wasn't ready to do that yet. *I need to think of some way to help her. To thank her for looking out for me and for being there for me. I have to be better for her.*

Chapter Seventeen

NICOLE HAD NEVER BEEN so happy to be home. It was like being wrapped in a warm blanket on a cold, snowy day. Haydn seemed to agree, running into the house as soon as they opened the door. He sniffled everything he could reach and ended up at the couch. He rubbed his face all over the cushions before settling down in the middle of the sofa. She smiled a bit from the sight, but that disappeared as she turned her attention to her lover.

Nicole watched Danny go into her music room, putting down her broken guitar. She placed it down with near reverence, as if it were a holy relic. Nicole wondered if Danny wasn't ready to let go of her mother yet and that was why she was acting that way with the guitar, but she wasn't ready to ask. Instead, she hugged Danny from behind and placed a kiss to her shoulder. Part of her feared her affection would be rejected. Surely, by now, Danny had figured out she was better off without Nicole.

"Baby, I really appreciate you defending me, even if I didn't show it in the beginning," Nicole whispered.

"I didn't think you'd take it well in the beginning. You looked at her as a sister."

Nicole sighed. "I did, but I know you very well, and I know what she was describing wasn't you."

"Thank you for believing me and for believing in me."

Nicole had to swallow a lump in her throat. Since she was pressed against Danny, she was conscious of her breathing, making sure to keep it steady. She considered Danny might not be leaving her, so she needed to stand strong and not give her anxiety away. She needed to make it through this apology and conversation without breaking down.

"I really didn't want to, because she was like my sister, and I love her so much, but she didn't make any sense when she was trying to tell me why you hit her. I knew there was something wrong with her story. She made it seem like you punched her for no reason. You're not like that. It takes a lot to make you hit someone."

Danny reached up and ran her finger along Nicole's knuckle. "Then thank you for having faith in me, too."

Nicole smiled into Danny's shoulder blade. "I love you. I love you so much, and I keep messing up. I wish I'd helped you when fucking Junior was hitting on you."

"You were busy helping Lillian, and you didn't know he was hitting me."

"Which only makes me feel worse, considering I now know the type of person she is. You're always there for me, and I should be there for you. You should be first, always." She clutched onto Danny a little tighter.

Danny chuckled and patted her hand. "Chem, you're here for me. Who the hell knows where I might be if it wasn't for you, probably a park bench or something, and that's if I'm lucky. I'd be drifting through life without you. Just drifting on the breeze. You take care of me, my love."

"And you take care of me."

"So, why does it always seem out of balance?" Danny seemed to wonder aloud. Grey eyes blinked, and her whole body tensed. "Shit, I said that out loud, didn't I?"

Nicole smiled softly and caressed her beloved's shoulders. "Yes, you did. Can we go sit down and talk about this?"

Danny sighed. "Sure, but can we also order food? I'm starving."

"Of course, baby."

While Danny went to the couch, Nicole ordered Jamaican takeout, a surprising favorite of her lover's. She knew it wouldn't make up for Danny's injuries, but it'd bring her some comfort. She joined Danny on the sofa. Danny had Haydn in her lap, but released him back to the living room as soon as Nicole sat down.

Before she could say anything, Danny moved closer to her, touching their legs together. It lit hope in her heart, and she became more certain of herself and their relationship. She managed a small smile, which Danny returned.

"I'll go first, okay?" Nicole wanted to get this out before she lost her nerve. Danny only nodded. Nicole took a deep breath. "I feel like...well, sometimes I feel like you love me more. You're always there for me emotionally, no matter what happens, even if I screw up, and I seem to screw up a lot. You always have my back...and I feel like I don't do that with you."

Danny's brow furrowed cutely. "Chem, it's not a love contest."

"I know, I know, but I feel like I don't do enough for you, and when I do try to do things for you, they always end up wrong. I mean, look at this whole trip. I wanted you to have a good time and take away this amazing experience that we could share over and over again, but that didn't work. You were treated poorly by nearly everyone there, and you endured it for me. I should've done more for you. I should've stopped Junior from hitting you, and I should've stopped him from breaking your guitar. Instead, I trusted he wouldn't be an asshole. I trusted he'd only grabbed you off Lil, and I trusted that once I told him to leave your things alone, he would. I had too much faith in him, like I always have with people when you're involved. I always trust that people will treat you right."

Danny smiled and leaned down, pressing her forehead against Nicole's. "Angel, don't you understand that's one of the things I love about you? I love that you have faith and trust and kindness inside of you. That warmth in you brought me here and held me tightly enough to get my life somewhat on track. I'm not blaming you for what Junior did. He's responsible for his actions, not you. You stood up for me when he and Spider were being jerks and that's good enough for me. You stood up for me."

Tears filled Nicole's eyes. "But, I didn't protect you."

Danny caressed her cheek, brushed back her hair behind her ear, and gave her a soft, quick kiss. "You did. Before I hit Lillian, Junior and Spider apologized to me and, hell, Spider accepted us. So, whatever you said to them, it was enough. What more do you want to do? Punch Junior for me?" She chuckled a bit.

Nicole smiled slightly. "It might've worked. I used to do it all the time when I was little."

"Then you probably got him for me when you were little. Chem, it's fine. I don't expect you to hit anyone, any more than you really expect me to hit someone."

"But, you would if push came to shove."

Danny nodded. "But, it'd be a really last resort. The only reason I hit Lillian was because she seemed so proud to have told your boyfriend that you wanted to have anal sex, and he took her at her word rather than listening to you. He hurt you, and she'd goaded him into doing it. All the while, she was probably smiling in your face, knowing what idea she'd planted in his head, knowing she'd caused you some amount of trouble. That burned me up. She didn't realize what her words had done...could've done worse."

Nicole gulped because that incident could've been much worse. She hated thinking about it, and images flooded her on how different that moment could've gone, how much worse it could've been. He could've pinned her down and forced her. She wouldn't have been able to stop him, as he was much larger and stronger than she was. The thought made her shiver, as she recalled how he accused her of lying and playing coy. She moved closer to Danny, wrapping her arms around her.

"You're okay, Chem. It's okay," Danny whispered, returning the embrace.

"Danny, he…" She wanted to tell her beloved everything that happened, hoping that, somehow, Danny would magically be able to make it all go away.

"I don't need the details until you're ready. You told me what I needed to know, and I can fill in the rest. That's why Lillian has a black eye now. I won't let her, or anybody else, hurt you and, if they somehow get past me the first time, I'll put them on their ass the second time."

Nicole couldn't help laughing at the sentiment and then she curled even closer to Danny. "Thank you for sticking up for me."

"Thank you for doing the same. Chem, never think you're giving less emotionally. You're the person who made me feel again. You brought music back to my world. What you've given me, it can't even be measured. If it wasn't for you, I'd have no self-respect, no home, no anything, and I wouldn't even care. So, again, never think you're giving less."

Nicole nodded. While she knew that to be true, there were times when it didn't feel like enough. There were times when she felt like all she could give Danny was material, but it was good to know Danny didn't feel that way.

"It's hard sometimes," she admitted in a low voice.

"I know it is. Believe me, I know. " Danny took a deep breath. "I wish I could do more for you, Nick. I feel bad making peanuts for an income. Can't even take you to a nice restaurant without months of saving. I don't have any skills to get a decent job, so I'm stuck."

Nicole reached up and caressed Danny's cheek. "Baby, I don't need you to take me out to a nice restaurant. I like when you cook for me. You're the only person I've ever dated who has done that for me. You show me more love and care than anyone I've ever dated. You have no idea how valued and loved you make me feel. If you want a job, please, by all means, get one, but don't think I hold it against you that you don't work full time. Besides, if it really bothers you, there's always that trust fund Christine gave you."

Danny made a face, which Nicole expected. When she had first discovered the trust fund, Danny insisted they share it and Danny decided she'd use the money on Nicole and Haydn. That lasted all of a week. Now, it was like pulling teeth to get Danny to even think about the trust fund because Danny thought it was a bribe, and she felt like, by spending the money, she was giving in to the bribe.

Of course, Nicole couldn't figure out why Danny thought she was giving in to the bribe, considering Danny still barely gave her mother the time of day. It continued to be incredibly rare for Danny to take calls from Christine and, when she did, they barely spoke for two minutes. In fact, Danny barely spoke at all. Danny still seemed very confused about what she wanted, or didn't want, from Christine.

"Danny, I feel like this is going to be an issue until you either accept that money isn't going to break us apart or you get a job that fulfills you. Maybe you're bored with housekeeping, and maybe you miss your music in a way that you can't even figure out."

Danny shrugged and ran her hand through her hair. "Dunno. I mean, tutoring...is..."

"Fun, but not what you really want to do. You have music inside of you, Danny, and you need to get it out beyond what you're doing now. I think that's why you always feel so restless, and why you feel like you're not enough. You need to do something more with your music and there's nothing wrong with that."

Grey eyes glanced down, but Danny nodded. "Should I try to get more gigs or something then?"

"Only you can answer that question. Just think about it, okay?"

Danny nodded once more. They remained cuddled up and quiet for a few minutes. Nicole took Danny's bandaged hand and traced her lover's fingers. She hoped they'd heal perfectly, as Danny did need to let her music out, somehow, and Nicole doubted having two less than fully functioning hands would help.

"My mom actually bandaged you up. She approved of what you did?" Nicole guessed, fingertips gliding over Danny's bandages.

"She did."

Nicole sighed. "They don't like her much either, you know?"

"She was telling me."

"She doesn't think I know. She wanted me to get along with them, because they're my family and I have cousins my age. She knows we have fun, but I could tell when she was around them. I knew the adults didn't like her much from when I was really little. I couldn't understand it. I still don't understand it. I mean, I know my mother can be difficult to get along with, but I've never even seen them try to get along with her to find out that she's difficult. Did she tell you why?"

"Just that they think she changed your father, for the worse in their opinions. But, that's history there. You'll have to ask her."

Nicole nodded, even though she knew her mother would never tell her. "She's overprotective of me and likes to keep me in the dark about things."

Danny could only agree with that. "She wants to keep you safe. She doesn't like seeing you hurt."

A giggle escaped before Nicole could stop it. "Oh, my God, you two really bonded, huh?"

Danny put a hand through her hair, but a small smile played on her lips. Nicole moved closer, putting her legs over Danny's. They shared a soft, brief kiss. They were okay, yet again. *I hope we don't have to keep going through shit like this. I don't think my nerves can take it.*

They went back to being silent. After their food arrived, they turned on the television and found a movie. Nicole poured Haydn some food to keep him from bothering them, and they relaxed for the rest of the day. Soon, Danny started nodding off, and Nicole felt the same way.

"Baby, c'mon, let's go take a quick shower and go to bed," Nicole said in a gentle tone, giving her lover a soft caress to keep her awake enough to make it upstairs.

Danny only nodded, and they climbed the stairs to their bedroom. Haydn followed. They didn't typically let him sleep in the bedroom, but after such a trying and tiring ordeal, it was fine. They took a quick shower together and collapsed into bed with Haydn already sleeping at the foot.

***

Dane awoke in the middle of the night and was tempted to get up, feeling an urge to check on her guitar. *It's still broken. There's no reason to check on it. It's broken, like your relationship with the person who gave it to you. Why the hell do you care, anyway? You don't care about Christine.*

She hated to think her trouble with the guitar was that she still did care about Christine. After going through all that trouble with Nicole's family, she felt like she should care even less, not more. There were people out there who didn't deserve the love, attention, and affection that someone might offer them. Lillian didn't deserve it. Christine didn't deserve it.

The guitar should've been thrown out years ago. She shouldn't have dragged it around like a physical hope that, one day, all would be well. She had burdened herself with that hope, burdened herself with a desire that Christine didn't even deserve. Her mind traveled back to earlier in the day, when Kathleen had showed her kindness and affection, when Kathleen thanked her for her actions.

Dane sighed and ran her hands through her hair. "I want a mother." This was why she couldn't let the guitar go, let Christine go. The small child in her still desired a mother. Honestly, she wanted parents. She wished she'd had someone who took her on camping trips, taught her how to fish, made her keep her door open as a teenager, and wanted to be part of her life. The way Raymond had spoken to her, patted her on the back, and was polite to her, why couldn't she have a father like that?

"Hard to believe I didn't really like the guy when I met him, and I know he didn't like me. Time does change things," she murmured. Well, sometimes it changed things. Her own father had only gotten worse with time, even after she'd helped save his life after his stroke.

Sighing, she ran her hand through her hair. This issue seemed to plague her more often than it ever had, and she really wished she could settle it. The Wolfes weren't her family. Blood meant nothing. She had come to that conclusion on the trip. But, still she wanted something that resembled a family.

Yes, she had Nicole and Haydn. They were immediate family, and she'd build on that, but she wanted more. She wanted people she could call up and talk to about things, someone with more experience than herself and Crow, her current go-to fountain of wisdom. There was Terri, who, on occasion, gave decent relationship advice. She suspected she might be able to go to Raymond and Kathleen, but she wouldn't be able to talk to them about Nicole.

She frowned briefly before Nicole moved against her, disturbing her thoughts. Nicole remained asleep, but snuggled closer to her. Dane smiled and wondered why at her happiest, she was still unsatisfied with some aspects of her life. She had more than she had ever had emotionally, but it still felt like a huge section of her was missing.

Doesn't make any sense. I don't make any sense. Dane sighed, but she continued to smile. She wondered if Nicole was right. Maybe she felt unfulfilled without true music in her life. Teaching and writing wasn't enough for her. "But, that's not going to give me this family thing I seem to be longing for."

Although once upon a time, her band was her family. They offered her things the Wolfes never gave her, praised her for her ability, and, unfortunately, encouraged her worse habits. Still, they never belittled her or hurt her, not counting Bryan anyway. So, maybe there was a connection. They made her feel like she was a part of something and that she could count on them if the chips were down. Of course, that was sort of an illusion, as she really couldn't count on anyone when the chips were down, until Nicole anyway. But, it had felt like something, something worthwhile.

"Or maybe it's two in the morning and I'm tired out of my mind. Might need another painkiller," Dane mumbled. Nicole had placed a pill by her side of the bed and a glass of water. She downed both, settled back into her pillow, and was asleep soon after.

***

It wasn't a surprise that they slept in. Thankfully, it was Sunday. Haydn seemed to sense things were rough on them because, even though he was awake, he wasn't whining for anything. He had made it his business to climb higher on the bed at some point during the night, ending up on Nicole's legs, which Nicole would've scolded him for any other day. Instead, she rubbed under his chin and glanced over at Danny, who was still asleep.

"Maybe we should get Danny breakfast in bed," Nicole whispered. She thought it'd be a very sweet gesture and thanks for the camping trip from hell that her beloved had endured for her.

"You don't have time," Danny grumbled, yawning slightly.

Nicole smiled softly and then leaned down to give Danny's forehead a kiss. "Sure, I do. You need to stay here while I go make breakfast."

Danny chuckled, they both knew that wasn't likely. They stayed in bed for a moment, cuddling and enjoying the stillness of their home. They tenderly caressed each other, but didn't do anything beyond that.

Before they could get up and start the day, Nicole's cell phone rang. She wondered who could be calling, but it was past ten, so most of her world was up already. Seeing the number, she was tempted to not answer, but Beth hadn't done anything wrong.

"Hey, Beth, what's up?" Nicole said into the phone. Danny arched an eyebrow, but Nicole couldn't offer anything yet to change her expression.

"Hey, I was calling to see how you guys are one day later, especially Danny. How's her face looking?"

Nicole glanced at Danny and winced when she saw her cheek. The maroon bruise stood out on her bronze cheek. Danny seemed to know what she was looking at, reaching up to touch the bruise. Danny grimaced and Nicole gently pulled her hand away to keep Danny from messing with the injury.

"Like she got punched. She'll be all right, though," Nicole answered. As soon as she was done speaking with Beth, she'd go get Danny some ice and try to convince her to have breakfast in bed.

"How are her ribs? Nothing was broken, right?" Beth asked.

Nicole's eyes narrowed on Danny. "I don't know. I'll ask her." She covered the phone. "Why didn't you tell me he hit you in the ribs, too?" she demanded in a low hiss.

"My ribs are fine," Danny replied, waving her off.

Nicole frowned. "You should've told me."

"They're fine."

"Did he hit you anywhere else?" Her eyes trailed over Danny's body.

"No. It's okay."

Nicole snorted, but she didn't have the time to be upset with Danny for omitting information. She turned her attention back to her phone. "She says her ribs are fine."

"That's good. Uh…Nikki…I want to talk to you about something that might hurt your feelings, but I want you to understand why Danny did what she did. I don't want you to be angry with her or do anything rash."

Nicole smiled softly. "I'm not going to break up with Danny, Beth."

There was a sigh of relief. "Good to know, because Danny was standing up for you, Nikki."

"I know she was."

"But, do you know she's the only one?" Beth inquired in a low tone. Shame dripped from her voice.

"Excuse me?"

Beth let loose a long breath. "We knew. We knew about Lillian for a while, Nikki. We knew she talked about you behind your back. Not the adults, but you know...*us*. We knew."

"Why?" Nicole choked out. Her throat felt like it was going to collapse in on itself.

"Why did she do it or why didn't we stop her or why didn't we tell you?"

"All of them. I thought you were my family, my friends, and you let her say these horrible things about me. Did you join in, too? Tell everyone I was a whore? Tell everyone I was into kinky, disgusting, and depraved sex acts?" Nicole practically screamed. Haydn backed up a bit before moving and nuzzling her.

"No, we never did that! We never talked about you. Never. We would never do that. We love you, Nikki, and that's actually why we didn't say anything. Lillian was...God, Lillian was your little sister, Nikki. You love her so deeply, entirely. We couldn't hurt you like that, couldn't tell you this person you love, was doing this awful thing to you. You'd have been crushed."

"But, I wouldn't look like an ass to everyone for my whole life." Nicole was close to bawling, but she refused to spill any more tears over this. Lillian didn't deserve her tears. Hell, she wasn't sure if this family deserved her tears.

"You don't. Lillian's the ass and always has been. We tried to get her to stop when she was younger, but she never listened. We did our best to shield you from it. It wasn't the right thing to do, I know, but it was all we could think of at the time. We didn't want you to get hurt. We didn't want this to happen."

It hurt to breathe. "How many people...what type of things...what?" Nicole wasn't even sure what she wanted to say. Her mind was reeling once more. *If they were all aware, how many people has Lillian spoken to about me as if I was some vile, loathsome harlot or worse?*

"She's told a lot of different people a lot of things, over time, Nikki. Almost everyone you've ever met with her has heard some of her bullshit. Hell, I remember when we were little and in a park one time, when you played softball with some girls. She was talking to them after the game, telling them you were really a boy and that's why you could hit so far."

Nicole felt her throat tighten again and there were tears burning her eyes like acid. "Oh, God. That's why they called me a freak and a cheater. I thought they were sore losers. I wanted to..." She shook it off because it didn't matter now.

Danny pulled her into a warm embrace, and she rested her head against Danny's shoulder. She wished she could crawl into her lover and never leave. Danny would protect her from all of this madness.

"I know. I was little, but I knew. I'm so sorry about all of this, Nikki. I wish I could go back and do things differently, but I can't. I can promise you that I did my best to clean up anything that she said, if I could, but, over the years, she said so much and I didn't hear all of it."

This explained why Beth didn't like being around Lillian. "It's okay, Beth. You're not the one who was saying that stuff. It was all her. I wonder why. Why the hell has she been doing this? I loved her. I would've done anything for her. Why has she been trying to tear me down?"

"I don't know, Nikki. But, I want to assure you that none of us do that to you. Lillian is the only one. We all love you and the adults didn't know, so Uncle Richard didn't know that Lillian does stuff like this, and he thought Danny started wailing on her for no reason."

"Does he now?"

"Spider and Junior said they'd tell him. Expect a call from them, especially Junior. If he doesn't apologize, I promised to take a pipe to his beloved car."

Nicole snickered, even though she really wanted to cry. "You're a good cousin."

"Because I completely and totally love you, Nikki. You're a wonderful person and so is Danny. Lillian is the one who was wrong. Danny said Lillian did something that got you hurt. Things shouldn't have gotten to that. We should've said something. I should've said something."

"Better late than never."

"I wish I felt that way. Is Danny around? I need to say a couple of words to her."

"She's right here." Nicole handed over the phone. "Beth wants to talk to you."

"Hey," Danny said. She made a few uh-huh noises. "Yeah, no problem. Don't thank me. Later." She ended the call.

"What did she say?"

"She thanked me for decking Lillian."

"Of course." Nicole shook her head.

Danny only shrugged. Nicole didn't want to admit it, but she felt a little better knowing Beth had thanked Danny. Sighing, she cuddled in close to her lover.

"How could I never notice? I mean, all this time I thought...well, you know what I thought. I mean, dammit, she said she became a lawyer to be like me. She started playing softball to be like me, to be closer to me. She even went to my college. I used to help her with everything, from schoolwork to guy problems to everything in between."

Danny rubbed the small of Nicole's back. "Maybe she's trying to show she's better than you and she never quite makes it, so she lashes out. Some people are bitter cows. She could be jealous of you, envious, wants to take over your life. Maybe she wishes she was loved as much as you, or something like that. Who the hell knows? It's not your problem, though, Nick. She's worse off now that you're not in her life, not the other way around."

Nicole smiled and gave Danny a kiss. "You're sweet and you're also right, but it's going to take a while to accept that. I mean, for my whole life she was my little sister. Why would she hurt me like this? And I'm really scared to think of what she said to people and who believed her. I mean, what if you had believed her?"

"But, I didn't because I stop and talk to you, Nick, and I love you. So, her making it sound like you had a ton of lovers, I knew were lies. Her telling me that you're kinky, lie."

"Well, we have different definitions of kink."

Danny laughed. "To you, using scarves is kinky. That's not kinky, Chem. Trust me."

"I'm scared to find out what you think is kinky."

"Don't want kinky, so it doesn't really matter. I'm happy with you, and I'm happy with doing whatever you want in bed. I already told you there's little that squeaks me, as long as I'm not calling you and you're not calling me..."

"I remember, Danny, I remember," Nicole interrupted with a blush staining her cheeks.

"Eventually, I would've cursed her out, once I figured out what the hell she was doing, but when she said she encouraged your boyfriend to try to have your ass was when I figured out she's actually dangerous. She might not have meant it that way, but she got you hurt and it could've been worse."

Nicole swallowed. "I know. I've thought about that since you said it."

Danny held her tighter. "It's okay. It's done and over with, but like I said, I'd have kept hitting her if Junior hadn't tackled me. I'd still be hitting her, actually."

"Thank you."

"No thanks necessary, my love. And, if you ever want to tell me the whole thing, you know I'm here to listen."

Nicole nodded. "Thank you for that, too."

The phone going off again interrupted their cuddle session. Nicole sighed when she looked at the screen. She wasn't surprised that Spider was calling her since Beth said to expect it, but she wasn't ready for it. Still, she answered.

"Yes, Webber," Nicole said.

"Nikki, don't be that way. It's me and Junior. We're on speaker," Spider replied.

"Hey, Nikki." Junior's voice was barely a mumble.

"We're calling to find out if there's any way possible for us to apologize. Not just for yesterday, but for everything, you know? I mean, we're supposed to be tight and we...well, we let her talk about you and hid it from you," Spider said.

"Right now, I don't think there is any way for you to make it up to me. I mean, not only did you let Lillian say horrible things—"

"We tried to stop her, but she'd always break down crying whenever we did. She always accused us of loving you more than we did her and that we wished you were our sister, and somehow she always turned it into something about us, so we never got around to talking about what she was doing. The best we could do..."

"Make sure I didn't find out, yes, Beth already explained that. The thing that makes it worse is that, Junior, you knew and you attacked Danny anyway. You hit a girl, first of all, and you hit her for defending me."

He huffed as if she was wrong to point this out. "She hit my sister! What was I supposed to do?"

"Maybe stop your damn sister from spreading rumors about me. How about that? Do you know what she told Danny? Do you?" Nicole screeched into the phone. She didn't even give them a chance to argue. "She basically implied that I was a whore. She told one of my old boyfriends that it was fine to fuck me in the ass and on her advice, he tried it, even though I told him no. Do you know what that's like? Do you? I don't think you do." Her face felt hot, and she could feel a vein rise in both her forehead and her neck. Danny added a little more pressure to the calm rubbing of her back.

Spider growled. "Nikki, that fucking clown...did he...did he?"

"He didn't," she admitted in a low tone.

She heard them gulp. "Are you sure he tried because of her?" Junior practically whispered.

"I had told him no plenty of times before, but now that I think about it, he was a lot more insistent after we came back from visiting you guys. He said I was a tease and then one day...he decided to go for it..." And she was back to clinging to Danny. She never wanted to talk, or think, about that ever again.

"I'll fucking kill him," Junior growled.

Nicole scowled. "Don't act like you give a damn now."

"Of course, I give a damn! You're like my little sister."

"But, I wasn't worth defending to your real little sister, was I?" she countered bitterly.

"We didn't know it was going to get this out of control. We didn't know you'd get hurt over it. Besides, I didn't know that's why Danny was hitting her," Junior shouted.

"Honestly, Junior, I don't care right now. If you want to apologize to Danny, I will put her on the line. Personally, I'm not ready to talk to you, or Spider, right now, but you especially. Not only did you hurt Danny physically, but you hurt her emotionally by breaking something of hers that she can't get back. You really don't know the damage you've caused."

"Nikki, I'm sorry," he insisted.

"I don't want the apology. Danny, do you want to talk to Junior?" Nicole asked, and Danny shook her head. "I think we should stop here, and I'll talk to you guys later when I'm in a better mood and when you've worked out what it is you did wrong."

"Nikki, I still like Danny. She's a good match for you," Spider said in a rush.

"And, you need to know that we never talked about you behind your back, not now, not ever," Junior said.

"We love you, Nikki. We do," Spider said.

"I know. I love you guys, too. I'm just not sure I can trust you anymore." That acknowledgment broke her heart. She disconnected the call and held onto Danny tighter. Danny kissed the top of her head and, somehow, that made things a little better.

Chapter Eighteen

GOING TO WORK THE next day was a struggle for Nicole. She thought about calling in sick. She knew her parents wouldn't call her on it, but they might stop by to check on her and she didn't want that. Besides, life went on. She'd pull through, even if she had been betrayed by the people she thought were closest to her. It hurt, but it'd go away eventually, she liked to believe. If not go away, she'd learn how to deal with it. She looked at her lover as an example of how to pick herself up. Danny had been betrayed by almost her whole family and her best friend, who had helped cripple her, yet still she pressed on. Nicole could do the same.

So, she went into work and went through the motions. While her heart wasn't in it, she was able to get some things done. She could only hope she hadn't made any glaring errors. She wasn't surprised when Mina came in at lunchtime. She didn't even put up a fight. She walked off with a shocked looking Mina and Clara, going to their little lunch spot. She needed the distraction and the normalcy.

They made themselves comfortable in a sienna brown booth away from the few other patrons. A pleasant waiter, who offered them a bright smile, took their drink and food orders. Nicole smiled back until he was gone and then she sighed. She leaned her elbow on the table, despite it being bad manners, while her friends watched her.

"How's Danny's face looking?" Mina inquired. She had seen the couple briefly when they came to pick up Haydn. She had recognized they weren't in the mood to talk about what happened, but Nicole knew that wouldn't last.

"What happened to Danny's face?" Clara asked with slightly bent eyebrows.

"My cousin, Junior, punched her a few times after she punched my cousin Lillian for talking about me," Nicole explained.

Mina's brow furrowed, and she pursed her lips briefly. "Lillian? Isn't that the one who you always called to check on in college and you practically walked her through law school?"

"The very same one. As it turns out, she's been talking about me since she was born, telling lies and spreading rumors about me. Apparently, she said the ugliest things you could say about someone, about me, to everyone that she possibly could. I only found out because Danny said something. My cousins all knew and kept silent to protect me. They're so full of shit." Nicole scowled, glaring down at the cream-colored table.

"Wow. Sounds like you learned way too much on a family trip that was supposed to be fun," Clara said, shaking her head.

"I'm happy it finally came to light, and I am pleased to find out that Danny will defend me, even when everyone else is letting it go. I don't know what I'm going to do about my cousins, though." Nicole rubbed her forehead, wishing she could fight off the headache she'd had since yesterday.

"Hey, don't worry about it, Nicole. If they're not there for you, you're better off without them. At least you don't have to look for knives in your back or fists in Danny's face," Mina said.

Nicole chuckled. "You're right. I do wish things had gone differently. I wish my family was different."

Mina scoffed and rolled her eyes. "You and the rest of the world. There's a reason family's given to you without your permission. If you could pick the bastards, you'd pick other bastards."

"I guess you're right about that." Nicole paused as the waiter returned with their drinks. "But, on a good note, Danny found out she liked camping. She got along great with my dad. They did a little bonding, so it wasn't a total loss."

Mina motioned to her from across the table. "There you go then. And, Danny stuck with you through a terrible time. No other lover would've done that for you in the past." Mina knew almost all of Nicole's awful significant others.

"You're right."

"Then points for Danny." Clara held up her glass and they toasted to that.

"Do you want to talk about the things your cousin was saying about you?" Mina inquired, patting Nicole's hand.

"No, it's pretty bad stuff. I don't even know all of it. I know what she said to Danny and my cousin Beth told me some things. I wonder why she's been doing it, but I don't think I'll ever know. Cheer me up. Tell me about what you two have been up to this weekend," Nicole requested with a smile.

Clara told them about her son and showed them pictures on her phone. They had gone to an amusement park and, from what they could see in the photos, he'd had a great time. From the smile on Clara's face it was easy to tell she had a great time as well. Nicole felt her heart settle as she looked on friendly, smiling faces.

Mina talked about how she was seriously looking into puppies, after having Haydn for a couple of days. She was probably going to get Haydn's breed.

"How are you going to watch a puppy? Huh? Do you or Shawn have time for that on weekdays? Because we all know you don't have the time for it any other time." Clara asked.

"I'll ask Danny if she'll puppy sit for you during the day, if you want me to." Nicole imagined Danny would enjoy being around another dog, and wouldn't mind helping Mina.

Mina shook her head and waved the proposal off. "Nah, I think I know Danny well enough to ask her on my own. But, that's a great solution. If she says she will, we'll probably get one over the summer. You know Shawn was planning to tell you Haydn ran away, so he could keep him. He wants a dog more than I do, and I think he'll be more than willing to adjust his schedule to get one."

Chuckling, Clara shook her head. "You need to have a kid and move on with your life."

"All in due time. I have my entire life mapped out and child is scheduled in there soon," Mina replied.

They laughed, even though they knew Mina was serious. Nicole admired that Mina set goals for herself. She'd always achieved them, ever since Nicole knew her anyway. The thing Nicole truly admired was that the goals Mina set were to please herself, and her spouse if he was included, and no one else.

Lunch was rather light after that, and Nicole felt better when she returned to work. She found she could focus a little more and put more of herself into her tasks. At the end of the day, there was a knock at her door. She wasn't surprised it was her father. She waved him in and he closed the door behind him.

"How are you feeling today?" Raymond placed a gentle hand on her shoulder.

"I'm feeling better. Beth called to apologize for never telling me. Spider and Junior called, but I wasn't up to really talking to them."

"That's okay. Richard called me today. He said the boys explained everything to him after he started talking about how he was going to press charges on Danny and he was encouraging Lillian to go to the cops."

Nicole gasped. It hadn't even crossed her mind that Danny had actually assaulted Lillian. "Are they going to do that?"

"Not unless they want Junior in jail on the same charges, which Lillian might considering what they've been saying about how she truly feels about you. I never realized how, for lack of a better term, evil Lillian actually is."

Nodding, Nicole twisted her mouth up a little. "Is it just toward me?"

"From what your cousins have been telling me, and what I learned from calling around, yes, just you. Richard tried to talk to Lillian to find out why, but she claimed she hasn't been doing anything and everyone else is lying. Spider said he thinks Lillian was jealous of you. Maybe he's right. Do you really need the reasons?"

Sighing, she shook her head. "No, as long as no one else has been doing it."

"I don't think anyone else has, unless they're all covering for each other, which I sincerely doubt... You're a wonderful person, Nicole. I'm proud to be your father."

Nicole smiled a little and sat up a little taller. "Is Uncle Richard all right now?"

Raymond smiled some. "Honestly, I don't think so. He doesn't know how to feel. He apologized for implying Danny would hit you. That was way out of line. How's Danny doing?"

"She'd better be sitting on that couch when I get home, and taking it easy."

He laughed. "You know your mom wanted to take her out for dinner."

"Mommy is that happy she hit Lillian?" She was surprised her mother would be so openly pleased with Danny for using violence. She knew Kathleen was very happy Danny stood up for her, but it was shocking for her to condone the method.

He chuckled a bit. "I'm as surprised as you are for her to be totally fine that Danny punched someone in the face, but it's not just that. She finally sees that Danny puts you first to the point where she's willing to be hated by your family just to stand up for you. Danny's something special. I hope you both work through everything and stay your course."

Nicole felt something inside of her blossom, and it caused a small smile to settle on her face. She knew her father approved, but hearing him say it was something totally different. She wondered if Danny would feel the same if she heard those words or even if Danny had heard them already. After all, her father had spoken to Danny quite a bit during the trip.

"We're fine, Daddy. I'm happy Mommy finally accepts her."

"I think Danny won your mom over a while ago when she sent us flowers and thanked us for being good parents to you. I don't know what happened that made her do that, but it was touching."

Nicole arched an eyebrow. "She sent you flowers?"

"Yeah. It was a few months ago. Not too long after her birthday, actually."

Nicole nodded, having a feeling the flowers had to do with Danny's interactions with her own mother. Nicole could only wonder what Danny would do with Christine. She couldn't see the relationship improving, but maybe something would change Danny's attitude.

"Tell Danny I hope she feels better."

"I will, Daddy."

"And your mother is serious about dinner, so tell Danny to get ready. I think your mom wants to try to start over."

Nicole nodded. "Then maybe we should have dinner again, at my house. Danny and I will cook." She was certain Danny would enjoy that, and she was sure she would, too.

"I'll run it by her and let you know."

Nicole nodded. "No problem. And, I love you, Daddy."

"I love you, too, Nikki." He gave her a big hug and she hugged him back. "I am so proud of you, Nikki. I wish I had taken more time to show that instead of pressuring you to do other things. I love you so much," he whispered and kissed the top of her head.

"I know you do, Daddy, and I know you're proud of me. Thank you for the support."

"I'm always in your corner. I want you to succeed in everything you do, and I always want you to give your best. You're an amazing person," he stated as he released her. They shared a warm smile before he left.

For a moment, tears stung her eyes, but she managed to keep them at bay. Despite it all, she still had a great group of people around her: a wonderful girlfriend, excellent parents, great friends, and cousins she might be on speaking terms with sometime soon. Even if she never got on speaking terms again with her cousins, she did have loving and supportive family members on her mother's side of her family. Life wasn't over.

"Fuck Lillian," she said aloud with feeling. She held her head high as she packed her things and headed out. Lillian didn't control her life, and Lillian was the one with the problem. She consciously decided not to think about it anymore. She had more important things to worry about, like Danny better be on the couch relaxing or there'd be hell to pay.

***

Dane sat on the sofa, not moving as she had been ordered that morning. Her ribs felt better. She hadn't taken any painkillers. Instead, she spent the day staring at her guitar, and she had come to a decision. The guitar would go out with the trash in a couple of days. It was time to move forward. She couldn't become whole again by holding on to pain and confusion.

Another decision she had come to after the fate of the guitar was that she'd move forward with Christine. While she wasn't going to throw the relationship away like she would do with the guitar, she couldn't acknowledge the woman as her mother. She'd take her call the next time she rang, and she'd let Christine know. Maybe then she'd be able to build something with the woman, if Christine still wanted to. This seemed like the healthy decision to make, but she'd discuss it with Nicole to hear another opinion on the matter.

She also had a call to make. So, she picked up the phone and dialed a number that she was extremely stunned to recall. She would've thought that the years of drug use had robbed her of the only number worth remembering. She was glad to be proven wrong.

"Hello?" a voice she didn't recognize greeted her. The voice was too young.

"Sorry. Got the wrong number," Dane said, and she ended the call. "Guess I did smoke that away." It was a little disappointing, but now she'd have to grab the bull by the horns and hope she didn't get gored in the process. "Well, it'll be a nice surprise to do with Nick then."

She knew Nicole wouldn't ask any questions, at least not until things were over with, and she could live with that. She wanted to get this done as soon as possible, so when Nicole walked through the door, she proposed they take a ride. Nicole studied her for a moment.

"Let me take a shower first, okay?" she replied.

Dane nodded. "No problem. I'll be down here waiting, not doing anything, like I've not been doing all day."

"You putting it like that makes me think you have been doing things all day," Nicole said, giving her the once-over.

"I promise. The most I did was walk Haydn."

Nicole gave her a smile, and she was happy she made Nicole smile. She hoped she was doing the right thing. For all of her mental pep talk about moving forward, she felt like she was taking one huge step back, and maybe it was, but she needed to be sure. She had been saying she didn't have family for too long. It was time to be sure of that.

"Haydn, hope I've been wrong all this time." Dane sighed, rubbing the dog's head. He yelped, and it actually sounded encouraging.

When Nicole returned, she was dressed in a t-shirt. One of Dane's t-shirts. Dane was sure she fractured her jaw from how quickly it dropped.

"Chem, you do remember I said I wanted to go out, right?" Dane eyes were glued to her lover's legs. *I want them wrapped around me.*

"Yes, so stop drooling. You never told me if it was formal or informal, so I'd know how to dress. Your clothes, of course, don't help."

"Casual. I'm dressed casually." Dane motioned to herself.

Nicole gave her a skeptical look. It was getting more and more difficult to tell with her, though. Her vests, which had been formal wear, had worked their way into everyday wear. She only wore pants when forced, so it was impossible to tell what the event called for by looking at her shorts.

"It looks like you brushed your hair," Nicole said. Dane only did that for special occasions.

Dane's hand went through her neat and shiny hair. "Oh, well, yeah. Um...it's casual, but not overboard."

Nicole nodded and trotted off upstairs. Dane's eyes tracked her the whole time and she had to sit down. Haydn rested his head in her lap, and she rubbed the dog's ears.

"Haydn, your other mom is trying to kill me. Did you see how she was not dressed?" Dane looked at the dog. "I guess it's best you didn't see. She's your mom, after all. Wouldn't want to scar you, buddy."

Haydn made a whining noise. Dane only laughed. She decided to go crate him, and she turned on the radio for him. They had learned hearing voices and music kept him calm. Nicole thought the music thing made sense, because he was home most of the time with Dane and that was all she focused on. By the time she was done, Nicole waited for her by the door.

"So, where are we headed?" Nicole asked. She was dressed casually, for her, which seemed more business casual than anything else.

"It's a surprise, woman. Let's go," Dane playfully ordered.

"It must be some surprise for you to brush your hair."

"You'll see."

They piled into the car, and Dane gave Nicole directions. As they began driving and the scenery got familiar, Nicole glanced at Dane with an arched eyebrow. She knew Nicole was questioning her sanity, probably wondering if Junior had knocked her brain loose.

"We're not going to your parents' house, are we? I mean, it's fine if you want to see Christine, but I could do without seeing her husband."

"We're not going there. Don't worry." Dane smiled. "But, speaking of Christine. Do you think it would be a good idea for me to try to start over with her? Not as my mother, but you know, as a person?"

"I think it's up to you and her. I mean, if she's going to bring more pain and suffering in your life, or if you don't think her presence is going to enrich your life in some way, I don't think you should bother."

Dane nodded. "Not a fan of pain and suffering, so I'll make that clear to her. Don't think I really want anything from her, but it's time to let go of all this toxic poison that she helped put in me. I can't grow as a person if I let myself be wrapped in the past."

A small smile appeared on Nicole's face. "It sounds like you know what you want to do. I'm here for you, no matter what."

Dane nodded again and smiled. They drove by her parents' house and she didn't bother to glance at the place. A little farther down, she told Nicole to pull over. Nicole's face scrunched up, but she did as Dane told her. Dane stared at the house that they were in front of and her body began shaking.

"Danny...is this...is this..." Nicole couldn't even get the question out.

Dane could only nod as she swallowed down a huge lump in her throat. She put her hand out and Nicole immediately took it. This helped steady her nerves and ease her mind. They marched to the porch of the large house, which seemed to loom, casting a shadow over them. Dane was the one that knocked. She did it without hesitation, which shocked her. When the door opened, she feared she'd faint, and her eyes immediately fell to the floor.

"Can I help you?" a familiar woman said in a friendly voice.

She managed to force herself to glance up. "Yeah, hi, you probably don't—"

"Oh my God, Dane!" Lynn Briarmoor, a short, blonde-going-slightly-grey woman, threw her arms around Dane, taking her into a tight hug. "Henry, get out here! Dane is on our front porch. Actually, you, come in, please." She waved the couple in with a great deal of enthusiasm.

Dane held to Nicole a little tighter, because she was stunned by the reception. She didn't expect them to remember her. She definitely didn't expect Lynn to recognize her. They were barely in the door before Henry joined them. He wrapped Dane in a hug before she realized what was happening.

"Look at you. I can't believe you grew up this tall," Henry said, shamelessly hitting her in the chest with the back of his hand. He was heavier than she remembered, and he was only a little taller than she was now. When she was a child, he had seemed like a lanky giant.

"It's good to see you alive. God, I've worried so much about you." Lynn wiped away tears from the corners of her eyes, which had lines around them that Dane didn't recall. In fact, her mouth also had some lines around it, age lines.

"You worried about me?" Dane echoed the words like she didn't know what they meant. She could hardly believe they thought about her at all.

"Of course, I worried. You were my little girl." Bright, teal eyes went wide suddenly. "Oh, God, I need to add two more places to the table. You'll stay for dinner, won't you? Of course, I mean, I understand you might have somewhere to be, but we'd love to have you for dinner. Will you? Stay for dinner, I mean," Lynn rambled, placing her hand on Dane's arm before turning to look into the house and then turning back.

Dane blinked, a little lost herself, and then she turned to Nicole. "Wanna stay a bit?"

"Of course," Nicole answered. Her eyes sparkled with delight and a sprinkle of surprise in her gaze.

"Okay, so we can stay. Oh, Nicole Cardell, Henry and Lynn Briarmoor," Dane introduced everyone. "Nicole is my partner." She held Nicole's hand a little tighter.

"Pleasure to meet you," Henry said, leaning in to shake her hand. Dane couldn't let go of Nicole, so he had to shake her left. He didn't seem to mind, if his smile meant anything.

"Please, make yourselves at home," Lynn said, also shaking Nicole's hand. "Henry, please, sit them down. I'll be right back. I need to check on dinner, and I'll bring something to drink." Lynn was gone before Dane or Nicole could object.

"Please." Henry took a deep breath as he motioned to the living room, which was to the left of the foyer.

"Are you sure?" Dane asked. She noticed they seemed about as nervous as she was, but she wasn't sure what to make of it. *Are they upset I'm here and trying to hide it, or are they happy to see me?*

"Dane, if you knew. If only you knew. Come on. You can see how we redecorated for the millionth time," he said with a little chuckle and walked off, expecting them to follow.

The living room was completely different from what Dane remembered. There was a new sectional sofa, black and leather. The room was a new color, warm peach that invited friendliness. The television was much larger, almost taking up the whole wall. There were tons of pictures, Henry and Lynn, plus two small people Dane didn't know.

"You have kids…" Dane didn't mean for her voice to sound so disappointed, but she hadn't expected that, even though it made sense. She was not theirs.

"Oh, yeah. You'll meet them in a little while. They're upstairs finishing up their homework." Henry pointed to the ceiling.

"Um…how…how old are they?" Dane asked, but she was scared to find out.

"Allison is twelve and Ben is eight," Henry answered. Well, while math had never been her best subject, it was a little comforting to know she hadn't been immediately forgotten about and replaced with a real child.

"They're going to love you," Lynn said, entering with a tray that held lemonade. She sat down next to her husband, but was close enough for Dane to smell her perfume, vanilla and lilacs. It was the same comforting scent from when she was a child. She was amazed by that little detail. It felt like she could smell happiness and love.

"Why? They don't know me."

"We've told them all about you. And, they've seen pictures. It's a bit sad the pictures stop at eight, but it's better than nothing," Henry replied.

"But…but…but…why? Why would you keep pictures of me? Why would you tell your kids about me?" Dane scratched her forehead, which was creased.

Lynn stared at her, squinting like she was confused. "What do you mean why? You were our little girl. A big part of our lives and a huge influence in us having children."

"But, you gave me back," Dane said with a sting in her eyes. "You gave me back," her voice cracked. Even to her own ears, she sounded small and young. It took all of her willpower not to curl into Nicole and try to disappear.

"No, no, no," Lynn said, almost as if she were shushing Dane. Leaning over, she patted Dane's knee. "Is that what you've been thinking all these years? You think we gave you back?"

"You did." Dane sniffled. She was going to cry and she couldn't stop it. "You took me back home and you never came back and they never let me come over again. You returned me..."

"No, Dane, we didn't return you. You weren't some book. You were a child, *our* child practically. We had you over here since you were six months old, but we couldn't stop what those people were doing to you," Henry said, pointing behind them, in the direction of her parents' house.

"What do you mean?" Nicole thankfully asked, because Dane's mouth wasn't working anymore. It took all of Dane's willpower not to burst into tears.

"Dane had to go back to her parents every now and then for whatever reasons, so whatever we did for her here was almost always undone by those people. As she got older, it was becoming more obvious she was so very troubled. She was acting out in school, not doing her work, screaming at us that we weren't her parents, even bullying kids in school," Lynn replied.

Nicole looked at Dane with disbelief. Dane could hardly believe it either. *I did all of that?*

Dane scowled. "No wonder you gave me back." *I'd have returned me, too.*

"Stop saying that. We didn't give you back," Henry stated with a growl, pointing at her with a shaking hand.

"We tried to get you help. We went to Christine and we told her you really needed help. You needed therapy to work through everything because you weren't talking to us anymore, and we told her that she really needed to get that pig she called a husband to stop hitting you because that wasn't helping," Lynn explained.

Nicole gasped and eyes went wide. "Wait, you knew about the abuse?" Dane's jaw was pretty much on the floor.

"It was an open secret around here, but we couldn't do anything about it because of their connections. We called the police, teachers reported them, but it all led to nothing. Russell always claimed Dane was clumsy or she got hurt playing with our dogs. Unfortunately, Dane never contradicted him, saying she fell most of the time, which we understand." Lynn looked directly at Dane. "We know you were trying to avoid getting hurt even more, so we never pressed you, especially since it was clear nothing was going to come of it."

"But...why didn't I see you anymore?" Dane asked, her voice smaller than before and her vision clouded by tears.

"Well, Christine didn't appreciate the fact that we were telling her what to do with her child, and she said as much. Never mind the fact that we'd had you almost five days a week, ever since you were six months old and she came over here with some BS story about having an emergency appointment and the nanny having the day off." Henry rolled his eyes.

"I had a nanny?" Dane doubted it.

"She was more than likely lying. She never came back. We had to go down there after we ran out of bottles. Making matters worse, she didn't explain anything beyond her emergency appointment, assumed we knew how to take care of a baby, which we didn't. Thank God for my mother or we might've killed you that first time," Lynn said with a sorrowful smile.

"So, why didn't you ever come by or try to get me again since you knew they were so awful?" Dane swallowed a lump in her throat and felt even more abandoned than before. They knew how horrible everything was, but they left her there anyway. She wished they had left her on the street.

Henry sighed and ran his hand through his short brown hair. "A little while after we took you over there to tell Christine that you needed help, real help, they'd stopped bringing you by, and you wandered over to our house in the middle of the night. You were so drunk." He frowned, disgusted at the memories.

"You were eight, but already drinking. You were crying so badly, begging to come back home. You promised you'd be good, and I tried to tell you it wasn't your fault." Lynn had to wipe away tears.

"We called the police, but when they showed up, Russell was with them. We were accused of kidnapping you, and he told them that we were probably the ones that gave you alcohol to make it easier to take you. He didn't press charges, but he promised he would if it happened again. He also threatened to tell the police we were the ones abusing you," Henry finished, scowling and shaking his head.

"Oh, my God." Dane felt like she'd faint. Nicole wrapped her arms around her, holding her together.

"You wandered over a few more times, but we..." Lynn sniffled. "We took you back to your parents. I hate to admit it, but, Dane, you needed them. If they were real parents, they would've gotten through to you. Unfortunately, they're not real parents."

"No, they're not," Dane whispered. *All this time...all this time, I thought they abandoned me, but they had tried to help and fucking Russell ruined my Goddamn life even more. I hate him. I fucking hate him. I am sorry I helped save his life.*

"Dane, I know we have no right to ask, and you might not believe that you've always had a special place in our hearts, but we'd love to be part of your life in some way," Lynn said.

It felt like a rock the size of her head was stuck in Dane's throat. Her mouth trembled and she did her best to swallow. She had to wipe her eyes and her nose with the back of her hand.

"I'm sorry," Dane croaked, hiding her face in her hands. She couldn't believe she was bawling so badly.

"It's...it's okay," Lynn said, obviously trying to hold in her own sobs.

"Danny, I think you need to explain," Nicole whispered to her, causing her to look up. Lynn and Henry looked devastated. Lynn clutched Henry's shirt for dear life, and he held her as if to protect her from all the world's evil.

"Wha..." Dane was confused by their expressions before she realized they took her words the wrong way. "Of course, I want you guys in my life! You were the closest thing I ever had to parents. I wish I'd come here sooner. So much wasted time, so much wasting away. Well, no more."

Lynn and Henry seemed speechless, but they got up and rushed Dane. They engulfed her, and all she could do was return the embrace. Out of the corner of her eye, she noticed Nicole smiling. Henry and Lynn backed away after a few seconds and smiled at her through tears.

"Oh, God, I have to make sure dinner didn't burn." Lynn quickly escaped back into the kitchen. She was probably more concerned with cleaning her face.

"You two can go freshen up in the bathroom. Dane, do you remember where it is?" Henry asked, wiping his face with his hand.

Dane could only nod. She led Nicole to the main bathroom in the massive house. Dane washed her face, while Nicole remained close. As soon as she was looking more like herself, she embraced Nicole.

"They didn't throw me away," she whispered.

"No, they didn't. They wanted to help you. They want to be a part of your life."

"God, it's so overwhelming. I think I need to sit down."

"You can sit at the dinner table."

"Oh, God. Dinner and they have kids. Oh, God." Dane was certain she was about to faint. She stumbled a bit.

Nicole held her steady. "Whoa, hold on there, Big Dog. It'll be fine. They're good people. They took in a six-month-old baby, without question, and then basically raised her for eight years only to have her stolen away when they tried to get her help. It'll be fine."

"What if the kids hate me?"

"They won't. Now, come on. Let's go have dinner with your family."

"My..." She wobbled again.

Nicole chuckled a bit, but held onto her lover. Dane had to take several deep breaths before she could even leave the bathroom. With Nicole still holding her tightly, she led them to the dining room where the Briarmoors were standing and waiting for them. Dane felt those damn tears again.

"Dane, please meet Allison," Henry said, motioning to the short, teenaged female across the table.

"Hi," Allison waved weakly. She was a cute little thing with cropped blonde hair and green eyes somewhat hidden by thin spectacles. She glanced down and fiddled with her fingers, seeming shy.

"And, this is Benjamin. We call him Ben," Lynn said, pointing to the young man next to Allison. He was almost as tall as his sister. He had curly brown hair that fell in his eyes. He smiled brightly.

"I've seen pictures of you when you were my age. You got really tall!" Ben said.

Dane chuckled. "Uh...yeah, I guess I did. Um...I'm Dane and this is my partner, Nicole Cardell."

"Hi." Nicole waved at the kids.

"Hi," the children replied. Ben grinned while he greeted her.

"Let's eat," Henry said.

Everyone sat down and they had a quiet dinner. Dane wondered if they were all overwhelmed. She wished she could think of something to say, but every now and then, Henry or Lynn smiled at her and she felt like things were all right. When the meal was all over, while the kids cleared the table, Henry and Lynn walked Dane and Nicole to the door. They had to get back to Haydn.

"Please, come back as soon as you can." Lynn took hold of Dane's hand for a moment and squeezed it tight.

"And call us, for anything," Henry insisted. "Do you still have our number?"

"Uh…no, you can give it to Nick. I don't have a cell phone," Dane replied.

Henry rattled off the numbers, and Nicole stored them in her phone. Dane found out she had dialed the correct number earlier. Allison probably had answered the phone, and Dane hadn't thought to ask for Lynn or Henry. Everyone got a hug before the couple went on their way.

"That was nice. What brought that on?" Nicole asked.

"I've decided to move forward, and sometimes moving forward involves going back. Glad I did. I can't believe they missed me and worried about me. Crazy."

"Not crazy, baby. Love." Nicole smiled.

"Yeah, love."

This was moving forward. Accepting the love in her life and doing her best to show those who cared that she also cared. She'd try to fill whatever it was inside of her with that love. She hoped that'd be what she needed, because she needed to move forward with Nicole. They had to go on.

The End.

About S. L Kassidy

What is there to know about me? Not much. I was bred, born, and raised in New York and I have no desire to live anywhere else. One day, I would like to travel to a few places, but for now I am content where I am.

I started out writing poetry in junior high and continued to do so for ten years. I wrote short stories, usually fantasy and romance stories, for my own entertainment throughout high school and college. Back then, I wrote strictly for me and those stories remain locked in the back of my closet in little notebooks, written in my almost unreadable, tiny handwriting. In between writing those stories and poetry, I managed to get a college degree in history.

After graduating college, I had a semester off before graduate school and I didn't really have anything to do with my time. So, I took a chance and wrote a fanfic and dared to upload it to the Internet. I was surprised that other people enjoyed my work and I've been posting ever since. I had quite a bit of fun with fan fiction and eventually decided to try my hand in original fiction. I suppose it was sort of like coming back around to what I had been doing in high school and college, except this time the stories were for whoever wanted to read them. I uploaded my first original story a few years ago and haven't looked back. I plan to continue writing as long as I continue getting ideas for stories and it continues to be fun.

Contact Information
E-mail: slkassidy@gmail.com
Facebook: SL Kassidy

Other Books by S. L. Kassidy

Please Baby
ISBN: 9781311485137

 Jayce Newton's life is going downhill after she rescues her little niece from an awful situation. She plans to hold onto her niece and gain custody of her, but there are some factors against her. Her girlfriend doesn't want the baby around. Her mother wants to take the baby from her, and her brother has disappeared. Things only seem to get worse when Gus Tucker comes into her life.

 Gus Tucker's life isn't going much better. She recently divorced her wife and moved into a new home. She's looking forward to a new start and spending time with her sister. Before she can do that, though, she ends up causing trouble for Jayce Newton, getting her fired from her job and kicked out of her home. She tries to make it up to Jayce by taking her in during her time of need. Now, it's just a struggle to see if they're able to coexist in the same house with a baby between them.

Desert Palm Press

Scarred Series

Scarred for Life
ISBN: 9781310171352

 Dane Wolfe is a loner. Forsaken by her family and betrayed by people close to her, she has lost all faith in people and spends her days wandering the streets with no direction or meaning. She drifts through life, existing and nothing more. Nicole Cardell is a successful attorney. She has too much faith in people and is being taken advantage of by her boyfriend, Tyler, Dane's cousin. She's tired of his selfish ways and tosses him out. The bad relationship leaves her questioning her judgment. Circumstances bring Dane and Nicole together and a friendship brings them closer. They're able to heal each other and bring balance to each other's lives. Their peace is shattered when family causes trouble and tears them apart. Will they find their path back to each other and to the love that was slowly growing?

New Cuts, Old Wounds
ISBN: 9781310217289

In this sequel to *Scarred for Life*, Nicole Cardell and Dane Wolfe have been together for a year. They are doing their best to move forward with their relationship and open up to each other. It's time to meet family members. Dane's nervous about meeting Nicole's family, but she's even more nervous about Nicole meeting her family. Nicole is eager for both. Nicole thinks Dane should bond with her family while Dane thinks she needs to get as far away from them as possible. The Wolfe family seems to agree with Dane, but keep inviting her to things and Nicole keeps accepting the invites. Will family make or break Dane and Nicole?

Bandages
ISBN: 9781942976103

Nicole and Dane return in the third installment of the *Scarred* series. Life is good. The musician gave the lawyer a ring, a not-engagement ring, a promise; this is forever. But, they both still had some growing and healing to work through.

Healing is strange. There are those days when the bandage falls off on its own and you think you're good to go. Days when laughter comes easy and you forget the past. And there are days when the past doesn't want to be forgotten; you still need a stitch or a cast to hold yourself together. There are even relapses when the poisonous past needs release.

Share their journey through eighteen short stories of play, passion, and a deepening partnership. You'll enjoy the journey as much as where it leads.

Note to Readers:

Thank you for reading a book from Desert Palm Press. We have made every effort to edit this book. However, typos do slip in. If you find an error in the text, please email lee@desertpalmpress.com so the issue can be corrected.

We appreciate you as a reader and want to ensure you enjoy the reading process. We would like you to consider posting a review on your preferred media sites such as Amazon, Smashwords, Bella Books, Goodreads, Tumblr, Twitter, Facebook, and/or your blog or website.

For more information on upcoming releases, author interviews, contest, giveaways and more, please sign up for our newsletter and visit us as at Desert Palm Press: www.desertpalmpress.com and "Like" us on Facebook: https://www.facebook.com/DesertPalmPress/?fref=ts.

Bright blessing.

Printed in Great Britain
by Amazon